THE CRANBURY
TROUBLEMAKER

MAUREEN LANG

Check out the latest from Maureen Lang at maureenlang.com

The Cranbury Troublemaker, Book Four in the Cranbury Chronicles Series

Published by Maureen Lang

591 Press

PO Box 23

Belvidere, IL 61008 USA

Other books in the **Cranbury Chronicles:**

The Cranbury Papermaker, Book One

The Cranbury Toymaker, Book Two

The Cranbury Picturemaker, Book Three

The Cranbury Troublemaker, Book Four

ISBN ebook: 978-1-943210-20-6

ISBN print: 978-1-943210-23-7

591 Press logo image courtesy of the Early Office Museum (officemuseum.com).

❦ Created with Vellum

People usually arrive at their beliefs not on the basis of proof but on the basis of what they find attractive.

— BLAISE PASCAL

PROLOGUE

Cranbury, Pennsylvania, 1903

*M*eli Atherton whistled and the hawk turned, mid-flight, with an answering call. Only the heavily gloved portion of her hand and arm protruded from the hooded cape she wore against the cold. She smiled when the kestrel dove toward her. His wings flapped as he adjusted his height and speed, slowing to land his talons on her upturned forearm that served as a perch. His delicate wings, now folding, nonetheless rippled Meli's hood. She withdrew a sliver of dried chicken from the small leather pouch strung at her waist, and offered it to him.

She cooed her approval. At ten years old Meli was as proud of Jax as any falconer could be when they tamed such a wild creature —without hurting its nature. She'd tried training Hootie, the old owl her mother had rescued years before Meli was born. But Hootie was a pet, accustomed to being pampered and fed. He hadn't taken to falconry—owlconry, should she have called her failed attempt?—no matter how patient Meli had tried to be.

But Jax! He'd been born for training, a task so easily accomplished after Hootie that Meli's doubts about her inherited falconry skills quickly disappeared.

Were all falconers partial to the first bird they trained? Mother had trained Meli, and now Meli was training birds on her own.

Then she thrust out her arm again, inviting Jax to take wing once more. Off he soared, upward, higher, confidently announcing his arrival among the familiar hills and trees.

A shot fired somewhere in the near distance.

Meli's gaze was already upward, but Jax had suddenly disappeared. In a bare moment, she heard the soft but sickening thump.

Meli could not fly, but she could run. She dashed to the sound, to the direction Jax had surely fallen. Tears followed her instant panic, tears cooled as the wind stole their heat. Where was he? All Meli saw were dead leaves, leftover from a long winter.

Hers weren't the only footfalls breaking the forest's sudden silence. Someone else was rushing to the site of the fallen bird. But she took no time to look; she must find Jax, save him.

There he was. His speckled wings blended with their surroundings, camouflaged as God intended. Meli fell to her knees a few feet away, sliding into the spot beside him.

"Jax," she cried, "what happened?"

Then the other set of footsteps came upon her, ones she'd ignored a moment ago. She felt the presence behind her, but Meli ignored it again. She bent over her bird, caressed his flawless wing, searching for damage. Gently picking him up, she saw them —a few gaping holes made by whatever it was that had ceased his flight. They must have been pellets, small but strong enough to penetrate his chest, lodge inside.

Ending his flight, and his life.

"Jax," she cried again, then buried her face in the lifeless creature and sobbed.

She did not know how long she cried before another thought took shape, rage shooting through her shock. Only a shotgun could do this kind of damage, and shotguns alone do not end lives. Someone had aimed and pulled the trigger.

She raised her gaze in a heated search, hatred already forming before she saw the figure jump as if her eyes had touched him.

He took off at a run.

Meli placed the bird back on the bed of leaves and took to the chase.

She ran and ran, her breath already short from crying. Her hood fell back and the cloak opened but stayed fastened at her throat. She had no idea where he would lead her; she raced through the forest, past her neighbor's cornfield, beyond the paddock where two cows were kept. Down to the patch of green that nobody harvested, with hedges and greenery serving no purpose but to draw an eye to pastoral beauty. She'd forgotten the name of this rich family with land used to decorate and not be worked; she only knew her father talked about the richest man this side of Williamsport, the man who spent his money like it grew from a yearly crop, ready to replace faster than they could spend it, one season after another.

The runner wasn't much bigger than Meli, but he was faster. She never lost sight of him, but couldn't close the gap between them. When he came to the grand house, the one she'd passed plenty of times on her way to Williamsport's market, he disappeared.

DANE WARDMAN SLAMMED the back door behind him. In one quick instant his hunting shotgun landed in the laundry bin. He covered it in case she chased him right through the door. Still breathing hard, he crept to the window and drew aside the edge of the curtain.

At first he didn't see her. She was out there, he was sure of it. She was smaller than he was, but being a girl that didn't mean she still couldn't be older. All that way, she'd just kept chasing him, never giving up the way a kid might've. Whoever she was, she sure could run. He'd had to ignore the stitch in his side to stay ahead of her steps.

Then he saw her. She was at the corner of the yard, no longer running. She looked one way, then the other. Finally, she turned around and walked away.

Dane slid to the floor, wondering if he'd ever catch his breath again. Maybe he shouldn't even try. He'd run like a coward, hadn't he, after what he did?

He scrubbed at his own face, wishing this day had never happened.

CHAPTER 1

Ten years later.

Cranbury, Pennsylvania

Tending the last empty table of the afternoon, Meli Atherton gathered the soiled dishes to her tray and carried it back to the kitchen. Madame Donadieu, the owner and proprietor of Cranbury's tea room, stood over the stove top where the last of today's soup waited to be transferred to smaller bowls. One bowl for Madame's dinner later, and one for Meli to take home to her father.

Madame had been providing dinner for Dad almost six years now, ever since Meli had been working for Madame. The tastiness of the meals outweighed the potential dent to Dad's pride over accepting charitable leftovers. Mama used to say what filled a man's stomach could decide his mood, and Dad turned extra cheerful when Meli came home with a satchel. Surely Madame's culinary skills were at least as good as Mama's had been, though Meli didn't remember her mother's cooking. As much as she tried to recall details, mostly what Meli remembered was Mama's training with the birds.

"Another day finished already," said Meli as she slipped the dishes into the soaking side of the double sink. She would wash them herself this evening, since Irene hadn't come in at all today.

Meli swirled baking soda into the other sink as she pumped water into it, looking up as she did. Madame Donadieu had been so quiet today, rarely leaving the kitchen even to visit with her favorite customers.

Just as Meli was about to ask whether or not Madame was feeling well or just tired after another busy day, Madame took the only seat in the room. It had been placed near the door, for Madame to enjoy the fresh air and sunshine without deserting her ovens. She looked too tired to climb the stairs to her apartment above.

"I'm proud of you, *cherie*," she said.

"Me?" Meli added water heated from the stove to the sink. "Thank you. But is there any particular reason for mentioning that today?" It had taken quite some time for Madame's gentle tutelage to soften Meli's wild edges. Farm life had provided her plenty of strength to balance and carry the biggest trays to and from the kitchen, but her isolated childhood still thwarted Meli's courage to enact most of the social niceties Madame tried to instill. Meli had an affinity for animals both wild and domesticated, but before working for Madame she'd learned little about mixing with the two-legged variety of creation.

"Because you were gracious to your least favorite guests, when I myself could not greet them."

Ah, so she had noticed, after all. Meli still struggled to squash her deep-rooted dislike for each and every member of the Wardman family. It was unfortunate that the two Mrs. Wardmans—the elder, and now the new one married to the oldest son—had come this afternoon, when Madame was too busy and too tired to be the hostess. Meli had seated them herself, at their best table by the window, then given them her most frequent attention. They had even thanked her, probably never guessing the existence of this thing Meli had carried around with her for so many years, this something-next-to-hatred she could neither forget nor pray away, no matter how fond Madame seemed to be of them.

Madame knew of Meli's battle, but only a hint. She knew Meli did not like a single one of the Wardman family. Not Mr. Eliot Wardman, who, though he was seldom seen in Cranbury, couldn't be bothered to greet anyone down that beaky nose of his. Not Mrs. Helen Wardman, a frequent shopper at Leta Perkins-Phipps dress shop and the Casterton Stationery, always stopping in to Madame's tea shop for refreshment. Nor could Meli spare a kind thought to the eldest Wardman, Lance, or his new wife from Williamsport, Susanna. Not that they weren't perfect for one another: a matched set, in a way, with their flawless forms and faces. And though this elder brother had inherited their father's beaky nose, he had his father's pride as well, judging by his stingy smiles. Around the Wardmans, Meli was invisible without even trying.

It was that younger son, Dane Wardman, who had fed her milder dislike for the rest of his family. If Dane Wardman had never been born—something Meli had wished more than once— then the Wardmans would be just like any other group of customers. She might even have tried finding out why Madame actually liked them.

"You are important to me," Meli said, ignoring the ready reminder of why it had been hard to be civil to the two Wardmans. "So your business is important to me. Because of that, I can pretend all of your customers are welcome."

And ignore, as well, the other thing she carried with her. For as long as she could remember, every Atherton carried it, this expectation—or was it fear?—that even the small-town folk of Cranbury would shun them. Letting Meli anonymously serve tea or lunch was one thing; welcoming either her or her father into their community was another thing altogether.

Madame raised one of her spotted, wrinkled hands. "Come here, *cherie*." When Meli looked down at the dishes waiting for her, Madame added, "Leave them, just for a moment."

Meli wiped her hands on a nearby towel, then went to Madame's side. Meli had known Madame only a half-dozen years, ever since Madame had arrived at the very edge of Cranbury to open her tea shop. She'd hired Meli back then to wash dishes, even though they'd only met once—out in the forest when Madame was searching for fresh mushrooms for one of her recipes while Meli searched for orphaned animals to rescue. Meli, like her father, had been a recluse. Her father only mingled with others when he went to market to sell his fruits, vegetables and grain from their small farm. Meli, before Madame's arrival, almost never mingled. She'd learned to read and write at home, never having gone to school despite her love of books. She'd earned one friend, the girl next door, but Cari had died years ago of influenza. She'd been Meli's only tie to company outside of Dad, her books—and her animals.

Their reclusive life had never seemed odd, not even when Cari used to tell her about school and church and people in town and a summertime festival they called the Dash.

Madame reached out to Meli, who knelt at her side. Meli welcomed the chance to talk to Madame about something other than the needs of the tea shop. They'd shared countless moments like this during the years she'd worked there, and couldn't recall a single time she hadn't learned something she'd been thankful to know.

"You've blossomed well, but I don't think you know it." She patted the top of Meli's hand and let out a little laugh. "If you were to cast those sky blue eyes of yours any man's way, he would not be able to help himself. Yet you've taken none of my advice to use your charms, not even your eyes which you keep downcast. It is fine that you are quick to serve others in the dining room without drawing attention, but if you don't attract any gaze at all, how will you be noticed? You're getting older now. For some time, you've been old enough to start thinking of a family."

Heat rushed to Meli's cheeks. It wasn't the first time Madame had spoken on such a topic, but Meli never knew what to say. She was still a recluse, even if she did serve Madame's delicious teas and chicken in mushroom sauce and cakes that people came from Williamsport just to sample. Meli took orders and made only an occasional delivery—Irene usually did that between washing dishes. Customers probably didn't even know her name, and might shun her if they did, the way her father feared.

There was another obvious obstacle to the future Madame wanted for Meli. "I'm not very likely to meet a young man here, Madame. If we ever do serve a man, he's usually been dragged along by a wife or a daughter as old as I am."

Madame was already nodding. "Yes, it's true. So I will ask this again, why will you not come to services on Sundays? It's more than just Cranbury folk, you know. Farming families come from all around and as far away as Williamsport. Pastor Taylor is a good teacher. You're more likely to meet someone at church than here."

"Oh, I couldn't leave my dad alone to worship on a Sunday. We have our sabbath right at home, same as we always have."

"He's a good man, from what you've told me, and raised you to be a God-fearing young woman. But he isn't doing the best for you by letting you hide away."

Meli knew it was true. If it hadn't been for Madame she'd probably have spent the last six years talking to no one but Dad and her birds and forest orphans.

"You might ask him to consider something," Madame went on, eyeing Meli closely, "about mixing with others. How do you suppose he would answer this question: Do we serve a selfish God?"

Meli considered how she herself would answer the unexpected question. The obvious answer was no, of course not. A glance out any window claimed God to have given generously both beauty and bounty. More clearly than that, the Messiah called Himself a servant and surrendered His life to prove it.

She thought of what her father might say. "He could say God called Himself jealous, but that's different from being selfish. He'd have to say the cross proves the opposite of selfishness."

Madame smiled, obviously pleased by the answer. "So we do not live our faith only for blessings since God set an example to bless others. But how can you be a blessing if you never allow yourself to be with anyone else?"

"It isn't that we hold anything against others," she defended, forgetting, for the moment, her feelings so obviously against the Wardman family. "Besides, the vegetables and crops keep others from hunger. You could say that's blessing others."

The older woman shook her head, lips tsking. "That is business. I'm talking of blessing others, for nothing in exchange."

Meli frowned. "Dad always says we wouldn't be welcomed in town. How do we bless those who don't want any such thing from . . . us?"

"He's told you stories that aren't true, at least not anymore."

Meli should agree, at least the tales about how Grandmother was accused of being a witch. It had been over a hundred years since the last of the witch trials ended. Why was Grandmother to blame just because her neighbors' crop had failed, while the Atherton land had flourished? What Meli did know was that people still whispered. Having taken up what Grandmother, then Mother, had modeled by curing hurt animals and taming wild birds most people were afraid of didn't open a pathway to popularity.

Meli squeezed Madame's hand. "I don't think the town is missing us."

"You haven't given anyone a chance! You do not talk unless it is to ask what someone wants from the menu, and you do not speak outside the tea room."

"No one wants a chance to know me."

Now it was Madame who squeezed Meli's hand. "Because they think you don't like them. You scurry away without a glance. Do you know, you have something in common with the Wardmans?"

Meli pulled away, surprised and offended all at once.

"They speak to almost no one, too," said Madame. "Unless it's to Mrs. Phipps at her dress shop or Mrs. Prestwich at Casterton's, simply to place one order or another."

"But I—" She'd been about to say she didn't speak to others because she was afraid she wouldn't be spoken to in return. Surely the Wardmans didn't speak to anyone because they thought themselves better. But how could Meli know, really, why the Wardmans didn't speak to anyone? Dad told her often enough that people were more apt to be suspicious than welcoming, yet even he didn't assign motives to the activities of others. He'd always said people likely had their own reasons for what they did.

Madame smiled gently. "This is what I ask of you, Melisande Atherton." Meli always smiled when Madame used her full name, because she pronounced it the way Meli imagined her mother might have. But Madame always followed Meli's full name with an order. "I would like you to try talking to the townspeople. Say hello; smile! And this Sunday, I would like you to sit next to me in church. Yes?" Then her gaze shifted over Meli's shoulder. "But first, *cherie*, finish the dishes. I would help but I fear I would only slow you down."

Meli helped Madame to her feet, who then walked slowly to the stairs behind the kitchen. The tea room didn't serve dinner, only breakfast and lunch, but Madame always retired after the last of her guests left. Rising at four in the morning cut even Meli's evenings short. The tea room was on the outermost edge of Cranbury, built only six years ago nearest the road to Williamsport.

Like so many businesses in Cranbury, it offered generous living quarters above.

Madame had lived in Williamsport for decades, having been brought from France as a bride to one of the timber magnates on one of his family's "culture tours" through Europe. Upon his death Madame had set about having the tea room built, then surprising everyone by not only overseeing the construction but running it once it was finished.

Meli had heard from Irene that Madame's friends and family—all that was left was a daughter now—had been dismayed that the wealthy widow had turned herself into a businesswoman. At her age! And a cook, no less! But the place had never known a slow day since its doors opened, and anyone who worked with Madame knew she enjoyed her work and her customers. Meli had long ago guessed the Wardman family mustn't have shunned her the way other Williamsporters surely had, since they visited the tearoom so often.

Meli finished the dishes then placed clean bowls and spoons, spatulas and measuring utensils out for Madame's use in the morning. Her hot rolls, cakes and puddings were the most popular items on the menu, and her bread made any sandwich a delight. Her chicken recipes were another favorite, and even little girls would eat her vegetables, the way Madame sauced and dressed them. But all of the recipes needed an early start, so Meli did what she could to help before she even arrived each day.

Finally, Meli checked to be sure everything in the dining room was in order and the front door was closed and locked. The sun still hung in the western half of the sky, and she saw through the wide, multi-paned window that more than a few people still traversed the sidewalks. There was plenty of opportunity for a friendly hello if she went home by way of Cranbury's main street.

Meli lowered the window shade, then returned to the kitchen to make her way out the back. She never saw a soul, keeping to the familiar pines all the way home.

PHILADELPHIA, Pennsylvania

Dane Wardman gingerly touched the swollen spot between his right eye and cheekbone, examining the bruise in the mirror. Last night's crowd had been especially rowdy. Checker, the man Dane had hired to put in "check" any guests that might need ousting, had been in the process of throwing out a drunk when Dane's face had gotten in the way. He'd never seen the punch coming, having trusted Checker's usually firm grip. Lesson learned: even Hercules' strength could be loosened by flailing limbs.

"Somebody's arrived out front to see ya now, boss," called Checker, his Irish brogue as lilting as ever.

Dane had left the bathroom door open, back here in his private quarters. But Checker—six and a half feet tall, limbs as wide as a rhino's, chest as massive as a bull's—often entered Dane's living space without announcement or even a knock. He was the only one on Dane's staff to presume such boldness, even though most of his staff was older than Dane, and Checker the oldest. Besides, it was hard to reprove someone—even an Irishman not long off the boat—who had saved Dane's barroom from disaster more than once.

"Who?"

"It's Thursday, isn't it now?"

Dane grimaced. Time for the weekly visit from Squire Ridley —Squire being his given name, not a title here in Philadelphia, thanks to a Cockney father who'd always wanted one of his family to be addressed in such a way. Some small part of Dane appreciated that, though he doubted his own father had chosen Dane's name because he'd wished they were from Denmark. He was American, through and through, eighth generation born on this soil.

Lately, Squire had set his cap on Dane's place, still named the *Peacock* from its prior owner. Dane hadn't agreed to sell his beneath-the-streets pub. Since he'd taken ownership some three years ago, the place had turned from rust to gold. Even election-time rumblings of prohibition didn't slow traffic into the place—although Dane conceded it might be those efforts that kept people coming. Better to consume all the legal liquor they could before society turned the screws on the tap.

He knew that was partly why Squire was so interested. This location—the main door down stairs from the street—could easily be turned into a private club. It was part of the allure, or so Dane had spread around. A place worth looking for was a place worth frequenting. Put another "checker" at the door as a lookout for raids, as Dane did when he hosted especially high-stakes, late night, gambling parties, the place could go on without interruption if liquor really did become outlawed someday. Dane wasn't a praying man, but if he was he would pray liquor licenses would never be revoked. Men were simple beasts, after all, and had to find a way to tame that beast. Tamping it down with alcohol fit the bill for a wider clientele than an occasional game of chance.

The parlor portion of Dane's quarters was large and generously furnished. Two sofas, three overstuffed chairs, a dining table to one side, a card table to the other. Checker was already pouring drinks at the small bar built along one wall.

"Squire!" Dane greeted the man, holding out a friendly hand. "Nice of you to stop by at this ungodly hour."

"Well, well, look at you." The older man whistled as he stared at Dane's red and enlarged cheek. Perhaps he was glad to make fun of someone else's skin, with his own as coarse as untreated leather. "Rough night?"

"Bad timing. Was standing in the wrong spot."

Squire hooted as he accepted the drink from Checker. Dane's man knew better than to offer one to Dane at this hour. Dane drank, of course, but was a host more apt to give his visitors what they wanted without consuming the stuff himself.

"Then that ought to make my offer all the more enticing. Get yourself out of this business, boy, before you lose your pretty face."

"Better that than my hide," he quipped.

Squire hooted again. "What? You're not accusing me of skinning you with my offer? Near as I can tell, what I'm willing to pay is half again what the place is worth. Pretty generous, if you ask me."

The truth was, Dane *had* been thinking of selling. He'd enjoyed taking the place to its success; he'd found fun and challenge in drawing customers who used to look elsewhere for a good time.

He wouldn't have guessed success could lead to boredom, but here it was. The same thing every night. He needed a change—but not in occupation.

Lately, though, the rowdiness had taken a more political turn, a subject Dane liked to avoid. After all, he couldn't be on everyone's side, so he chose no side at all for fear of alienating half his customers.

Dane didn't care that the only respectable people who entered the *Peacock* were the teetotalers who barged in every so often to smash up the place in protest of the demon rum. Dane had little respect for them; the relish in their eyes as their mallets smashed his bottles convinced him they liked shattering glass as much as they hated what was inside those bottles.

But he'd fallen into a routine, and he was far too young for routine. The same patrons, the same troublemakers—those women who hated him and his ilk—the same . . . well, everything. The times he spent with Ethel were the only hours he really enjoyed anymore.

What he needed was a place off the beaten path but worth the trip, where he could allow men to drink and gamble and have their fun—in a spot that wasn't so conveniently located for either the political organizers or the temperance workers. Home came to mind, between Williamsport and Cranbury. If ever a place could be called off the beaten path, that was Cranbury.

Besides, Dane needed a place where Ethel could spread her wings, where he could be with her more than just on the occasional day he slipped away from business. He wanted to be closer to her, morning, noon, and night.

Still, life here in the city was comfortable. He was prosperous; the city was certainly convenient. Squire would have to come up with more than he was probably willing to spend for Dane to go to all the trouble of moving.

"Double that so-called generous offer," he challenged, knowing the idea was outrageous, "and I'll think about it."

"Done."

If Dane had been holding a glass, it likely would have fallen from his grip. As it was, the bottle Checker had been replacing on the shelf clanked against the mirror behind it, as if he was as surprised as Dane.

"All I said was that I'd think about it," Dane said slowly, only beginning to comprehend the amount of money the other man had just offered. He'd never in his life wanted for material goods; his father had invested heavily in lumber and transportation, both by water and rail, and Dane had been given a generous allowance until his twenty-second birthday. Lance, his older brother, ran the family business interests now and had once written to Dane to come to him if he wanted a job or even needed money. Wouldn't it be something to go back home with *that* kind of a pot, having not taken a cent from either his father or brother for the last two years?

"You do that thinking, son," said Squire jovially. "But I have a feeling we might actually strike a bargain this time."

Perhaps so, Dane conceded. But for Squire it would be anything but a bargain.

CHAPTER 2

*T*he sun wasn't even a promise on the horizon as Meli approached the tea room at four-thirty in the morning. Because the path Meli had cut through the woods was already rough with late spring growth, she barely looked up when she cleared the last of the forest at the back entrance of the tea room. Skirting Madame's herb and vegetable garden, she noticed the beans should probably be harvested soon. She must remember to bring them in before opening the dining room later this morning.

Madame would have been mixing and baking for a half hour before Meli's expected arrival. Besides setting out the now-dry dishes that would adorn each of the tables in the dining room, Meli would iron the laundered napkins, shine away any dried water spots from the cutlery, and then help Madame with some of her cooking and baking. Meli especially enjoyed icing the cakes with flourish, a talent Madame had taught her. Irene wouldn't come until the tea room opened at nine o'clock.

Nearing the back door, Meli noticed the lack of light coming from one of the two windows that faced the yard. That was odd; not a single lamp shone anywhere, either upstairs or down. Surely

Madame wasn't still abed. She had never once been asleep at this hour.

Meli tried the door; she herself had locked it the afternoon before, and it still held secure. She'd placed the key where she always did, in the little hidden compartment behind a strategically loose brick. She pried it from its spot and in a moment Meli was inside. The kitchen was dark, just as she'd left it yesterday.

"Madame?"

Only silence met her call. Confused, Meli inserted the wand on the needle valve to turn on the bright gas light that hung over-head. Obviously nothing was amiss with the lighting, so that couldn't explain where Madame could be.

So Meli retraced her steps outside, wondering if she'd missed Madame's presence. Perhaps she was in front of the tea room, updating the chalk sign advertising today's specials.

She was not there, and the front entry was as secure as it had been the afternoon before.

Meli looked up and down the street, as far as she could see in the pre-dawn hour. Other than the call of a few early birds and one still active owl, she saw and heard nothing.

Meli went back around to the kitchen, going inside to the stairway. A thin hall led to Madame's private residence, beside a small storage room. Meli called again. Still no answer.

She remembered how Madame had been uncommonly tired the day before; perhaps she wasn't feeling up to facing the day just yet. Meli took the stairs, neither fast nor slow, intent on asking Madame what she should do. Could Meli do the cooking by herself? She might make the breads and cakes, she'd been well instructed on those. But the mushroom sauce for the chickens and the strawberry meringue were far more challenging, even if Meli did know where Madame kept the recipes. Perhaps Madame might be well enough to sit in the kitchen, and offer Meli step-by-step instruction.

The second floor was as undisturbed as the first. Madame's

parlor was sparsely but tastefully decorated: a padded settee, side tables beside two Louis XV cushioned chairs, and matching dining table all sat in their places.

Meli called out again. She crossed the parlor, seeing one of the two bedroom doors slightly ajar.

"Madame? Are you feeling all right this morning? It's Meli. Can I help you in some way?"

Nothing but silence, a silence so deep she thought Madame surely wasn't there. But where could she be?

At the bedroom door, she said, a little louder, "Madame? Madame, may I come in?"

Still no answer.

Meli pushed the door a bit wider and peeked around the edge; her eyes were accustomed to the shadows, the only light coming from lingering stars and moon. She'd never seen Madame's sleeping quarters, and her gaze slowly searched the room. A dresser, upon which rested a hand mirror and matching brush and comb set; little bottles of various shapes and sizes, all glass; a small leather box, probably for jewelry although Madame never wore any for fear of losing something inopportunely into a mixing bowl. Beyond the dresser was a tufted chaise longue, with a robe draped across its back. And there, in the farthest corner near the second floor fireplace, was the bed.

Upon the bed was Madame.

"Madame?" She was whispering now, her voice as uncertain as she felt inside. Meli had no right to be here, invading Madame's most private quarters. And yet . . .

"Madame, are you sleeping?"

Meli stepped cautiously closer, quietly then, to listen for any response, even as subtle as breathing. She stepped even nearer, trembling hand outstretched as if to shake the older woman awake. But she pulled back, unwilling—unable—to touch her. She was far, far too still to be merely sleeping.

Meli turned on her heel and ran for Doc Lancaster.

～

DANE CLUTCHED the satchel that contained all of his personal possessions. Even though he'd invested in the look of the *Peacock*, he'd never considered any of its contents to be his. Every stick of furniture, every picture on the wall, belonged to the place, not to him. And he'd sold it all, lock, stock and barrel, to Squire Ridley for more than twice as much as Dane had paid for any of it. Quite a return for only three years! He was pretty sure no bank would have approved a loan if Squire hadn't handed over cash.

He'd been so generous that Checker, who'd informed Squire he didn't come with the deal, had openly wondered about that generosity. Maybe, Checker had said, there was some kind of treasure buried under the concrete in the cellar that only Squire knew about. Like in the Bible story, when the man digging up a landlord's field came across a treasure. He'd reburied it then sold all he had to buy the land, presumably for a fair price only if the treasure remained hidden. Was that what Squire had done to Dane?

Other than the remarkable fact that Checker knew a Bible story, let alone one as obscure as that, Dane didn't care. Whatever treasure Squire saw in the place, it was his now. More likely the man only wanted a place with a convenient backroom for illicit gambling.

Checker's bag was even smaller than Dane's, little more than what looked like an army rucksack. Or maybe it was the same size, only looked smaller on his friend's gargantuan backside.

"So I should probably call you something other than Checker now," said Dane as they walked down the street, away from the *Peacock* for the last time. "But after three years of knowing you, I guess I don't know your name. Or maybe I forgot it."

"Nah. I never did tell you, simply introduced meself as your next checker. I came straight from another job opportunity, one I lost because of me name—or maybe me accent. Laughed outright, they did. Said no Irishman was good enough to grace their pub."

Dane grinned. "Their loss, my gain. So what is it?"

"Finian Finnegan, if you must know. The Third, of all things. Yes, three of us at one point there was, God rest me dear grand da's soul." He eyed Dane with one raised brow, the same look he'd given unruly patrons who may have considered trying to cross him. "Which is why I invited you to be callin' me Checker. Never quite liked the sound of an F, and can live without hearing it if you want to stick with the name you know."

"Probably better if I do," Dane admitted. "You look like a Checker to me. Besides, I plan to open another establishment and you'll have the same job. Unless you want to . . . oh, I don't know, maybe join the circus?"

"Funny, aren't you now?" he said, but didn't laugh. "I supposed you'd follow such a plan. In Williamsport, then?"

"I don't think so," he said. "Williamsport has its share of pubs already, what with all of the lumbermen needing their fun. Nope. My plan is to find a fresh spot, where my kind of entertainment is less common and therefore needed. Even if they don't know it yet."

"But you said we're to buy two tickets to Williamsport. Where is this fresh place you speak of?"

"Cranbury," he said. "It's no less than my duty to rescue the little spot from its misery. They need a friendly face to propose something new—a little music, some fine whiskey, a game or two to spend the last bit of a day's energy on something enjoyable. Yes, that's exactly what they need. Cranbury folks and all the farmers around there with nothing to do but watch crops grow are in dire need of fun."

"Back home, the farmers I knew were happy enough. What makes the farmers around this place—this Cranbury you call it— so miserable?"

"Why, life! All those people do is work. They don't know what they've been missing in their sheltered, dull little lives. The high point of their week is church! Imagine that?"

"There's satisfaction in work. And, I daresay, church, for those who like it."

Dane meant to laugh but even to his ears what came out sounded more like a scoff. "Look, Checker, you know as well as I do that men are the basest kind of creature. You have an advantage, I suppose, because of your size. If you wanted to you could crush nearly every other living being and don't need to prove it. But the rest of us mortals can't stave off the wildness so easily, and so we need something more than work. I thought you understood that, working in my place for three years."

Checker was quite a bit older than Dane, but the difference was more than age. Checker's experiences both here and back in Ireland had somehow left Dane feeling less wise, or at least less generous. He knew they hadn't arrived in the city possessing equal resources. Dane had comfortably invested what he came with and made good on it. Checker, on the other hand, might not be wearing the same ill-fitting leather jacket he'd worn the day Dane had hired him—the one he wore now had been created just for him, upon Dane's insistence—but Dane had the feeling Checker gave away more of his salary than he saved. Hadn't Dane seen with his own eyes when Checker give his old jacket to a blind beggar one cold day?

Since Checker seemed to be considering Dane's words, he thought the man probably agreed. It was obvious, after all: men needed a way to handle the energy they carried around with them. Young or old, married or free, it didn't seem to matter. Men were men.

To Dane's surprise, Checker shook his head. "You offer music and whiskey and never threw out the women coming in to arrange their transactions. But *you* never spent that wildness you speak of in such ways. You barely gamble, you don't even drink, except to sample the quality of the liquor from the salesmen peddling the stuff."

Dane grinned. "I have a job that combines entertainment with work. If every man had a job as enjoyable as mine, they wouldn't need to drink, either. Farmers and those who live in dreary little towns aren't so lucky. Cranbury needs me, only those who live there might not know it yet."

Checker glanced at the clock that hung from the bank at the nearest corner. "Say, we'll be more than a bit early if we go to the station already. Did you have something else in mind?" Then he added, lifting a knowing brow as an idea must have struck him, "Will ya' say goodbye to her, then? At least until you're settled and can send for her?"

Dane nodded, not the least bit embarrassed that he'd been figured out so quickly. "I will, indeed."

Then he led the way to the largest estate Dane had frequented during all the time he'd spent in Philadelphia. Ethel awaited him.

CHAPTER 3

It rained the day Cranbury held a memorial service for Madame, which only Cranbury folk attended. A picture, taken by Cranbury's own photographer, Mr. Phipps, stood in the place of a coffin. The portrait of a smiling Madame in front of her tea house had been taken the day her shop opened. She looked young and lovely despite the black, lusterless crape she'd worn even well past the mourning period for her husband. There was no coffin to bury in Cranbury; Madame's body had been sent back to Williamsport for burial in a family plot. Rumor had it the service Madame's daughter planned was open only to family.

Flowers had been moved from the church after the service to the tea shop's doorway in tribute to Madame's memory. Now, two days later and the first Sunday since Madame's death, Meli had stopped by to remove any wilted bouquets.

At the sound of church bells signaling the call to Sunday service, Meli discarded the withered flowers in the tea shop's refuse wagon. Task completed, instead of heading back home through the forest, Meli turned in the direction of the church. Others had already passed while she'd worked, and she'd ignored them. But now was the moment she must face, the reason she'd come to town today. She might not be considered a family friend by Madame's daughter, but Meli knew one thing: Madame had been Meli's closest—and only—friend.

She swallowed hard, cringing past the pain from the lump in her throat. An accusing thought crossed her mind. Had it taken Madame's death to get Meli to go to this service today? She only knew she must honor Madame's last wishes and sit in on the service to which Madame had invited her.

She could do this. She *would* do this. Despite such intentions, Meli's footsteps faltered.

Taking a moment, she smoothed the skirt she wore; it was plain and black just like the other two she'd inherited from her mother. Madame had said they would do if she took them in for a closer fit, a more fashionable look than the days of bustles. She'd insisted Meli purchase new shirtwaists as the ones her mother had left behind had been so out of fashion. Madame, a devotee of both food and fashion, had said Meli would be a poor reflection on the tea room if she didn't present herself properly. Meli hadn't minded; she'd been grateful to soak in every bit of culture Madame had brought with her, first to Williamsport, and then to Cranbury. So instead of her mother's old flounces and puffs, Meli wore pleats and arm-hugging sleeves despite never possessing a hint of fashion sense before.

The arched, stained glass windows along both sides of the oblong sanctuary allowed only the dimmest light from the dull sky above. Meli wasn't late, but most of the pews were already filled. She stepped to a corner, hoping not to be noticed as she looked around, wondering where Madame would have sat. It had been Madame's wish for Meli to sit beside her, and so she wanted to answer that hope to the nearest degree.

Meli recognized most of the people lining the rows, even from the back. Toward the front sat Mr. and Mrs. Prestwich from the papery, along with the oldest of their children. The rest of their brood were probably in the basement with one of the Mrs. Levicks, the one folks talked about because of the toys she and her husband sold. She took care of everybody's kids on Sunday, not just her own two, and that made her a saint in some eyes. Her Mr. Levick sat with the rest of the Levicks. They took up an entire row, all those married couples.

She swallowed hard. Meli had asked her father to come along but, as expected, he'd refused. Even if he had agreed to come, she doubted it would have made a difference in the way she felt right now. She might believe in the same God they all came to worship, she even read the same Bible most of them carried in with them. But she was an outsider. Church was for families. Her and Dad were more like half a family, but even so, she was at an age where she should have a husband if she was going to slide easily onto any one of the pews in front of her.

Still, she would do what she'd come to do. For Madame. She didn't have to come back after today.

Meli told herself she would ask the next person who came in if they knew where Madame used to sit, but that person turned out to be Mrs. Wardman. Although her unfriendly husband wasn't at her side, her oldest son and his wife were. Just one of her sons. Thankfully the other one didn't live around there anymore, but Meli doubted such an evil man could walk into any church without it tumbling down on top of everyone out of sheer shock.

Meli slid into an empty pew at the back and sat.

Soon the chords of an organ filled the room, and Meli nearly jumped. She hadn't noticed anyone sitting at the instrument when she'd come inside, and couldn't see it now that she'd taken a seat. But it was loud and clear, a few chords for an introduction soon joined by voices. She wished she'd chosen to sit closer then, because even though it was an organ and not a piano, she loved the sounds it made. She couldn't read a note of music, but could mimic any tune she heard.

She looked around when she realized everyone else had joined in. Meli loved singing! But how did everyone know the words? They all seemed to be holding similar books, not Bibles, but something like the one tucked into a little holder attached to the back of the pew in front of her. She drew it out, reading the word *Hymnal*, but the song was unfamiliar to her. How did they know which one to sing? She listened to the words, but they were changing so regularly she couldn't catch a single phrase that might give her an idea of the title.

"This will help," came the whisper from a woman slipping into the pew beside her. In a moment another hymnal, identical to the one Meli had been flipping through, was traded for hers. This one was opened to a song called *O for a Thousand Tongues to Sing*, and by now they were already repeating the tune and so she was easily able to sing along.

As another verse started, Meli glanced up at her helper. She wasn't sure who the young lady was; Meli was certain the woman had been to the tea shop but too rarely for Meli to have learned her name, if only from a companion mentioning it. She was well dressed, in a flowing skirt and loose jacket embroidered with tiny leaves all along the lapel. Her hair was swept up in a thick bun, but it shone like burnt gold. And she sang well, so well that when Meli lifted her own voice she couldn't help but think God might be pleased by the sound of their blending tones. Meli hadn't heard such a pleasant sound since she'd sung with her mother. She did sing with Dad on Sundays, but his ability to carry a tune came and went.

When the song ended, another began and Meli watched as others seemed to know what page was next. The lady beside Meli tilted her book so she could see hers, and it took only a moment for her to know which of the two songs was being sung.

After listening to the first verse to know the tune, Meli joined in.

I must tell Jesus

> All of my troubles,
> He is a kind, compassionate friend.
> If I but ask Him, He will deliver,
> Make of my troubles
> Quickly an end.

The words brought unexpected tears to Meli's eyes, as if heaven itself was telling her something. Ever since the other day when she'd found Madame, Meli had longed to cry. She'd told Dad about what had happened, but he, as ever, was quiet and never asked how she felt. She had attended the funeral in this very church, but other than a nod to Irene who stayed glued to her parents, Meli stuck to the shadows and hadn't said a word to anyone.

She would miss her friend, and longed to tell someone just how much. She would even miss Irene, because they wouldn't be working together anymore. It was anyone's guess what would happen to the tea room, but Meli had the distinct feeling whatever was in store, there would be no place for Meli there.

And so, instead of singing the last verse, Meli closed the book, bowed her head, allowed more tears to flow, and did as the song said. She told Jesus all of her troubles.

DANE LET his nose lead him downstairs, hoping breakfast was being served. Or lunch, considering the late hour. He and Checker, still accustomed to their nocturnal schedule, had spent most of the night at cards. Why change their habits, when they would soon be at it again?

Clearing the last stair, Dane bypassed the parlor and the sitting room across from it. The two rooms were differentiated only by usage, since one was for family and the other for receiving guests. The tall front door between the two rooms had been left ajar, as were the wide French doors leading to the terrace in back, where he headed. He enjoyed the morning breeze crossing through the house—especially since upon that breeze was the scent of bacon. Surely he hadn't missed breakfast, after all.

To his surprise, only his father and Checker were at the table, and neither were talking. As usual, his father was hidden behind a newspaper, his glasses in place. Checker's gaze was cast toward the rolling hills in the distance. The trees were in full bloom, both plain and flowering, and if Dane hadn't been so enamored by the bacon he might have enjoyed the scent of his mother's gardenias on the breeze as well.

"Good-morning!" he greeted them, looking for the source of the bacon. To his disappointment, although the table had been set —for six—only juice and scones had been set out.

Father might have grumbled a response, Dane wasn't sure.

"I heard a church bell ringing earlier," Checker said in lieu of a greeting. "I suppose it came from down there—through the trees?"

"Cranbury," Dane said. "The town I told you about."

"Ah, yes. Church. The highlight of the week."

"Exactly."

"Has your family welcomed your plans to join the town attached to that little church?" Checker asked.

In the two days since they had arrived, Dane had tried limiting conversations with family to pleasantries, even with his more cordial mother. Father had inspired Dane's boundary shortly after his return. While the two of them waited for others to join them at the dinner table that first evening, Father had taken the opportunity to speak privately. He'd pressed Dane about what could be taking so long for him to find a wife and a respectable job. *Look at Lance, practically in charge of the family businesses and married now. About to become a father as well! When was Dane going to do something worthwhile?*

Apparently, this was to be a second chance at meaningful discussion, since his father held aside the newspaper and looked over his spectacles inquiringly. Dane almost wished the rest of the family was here; his mother, at least, tried to soften Father's rough edges—even if she harbored disappointment in Dane, too.

"I thought I'd open a place around here, Father," he said, looking more at the newspaper than at his father. The headlines hailed the winner of the Preakness Stakes, won the day before by a horse called Layminster. Momentarily distracted, Dane wondered how much money Squire Ridley had either won or lost on that, the first of three major horse races this month. Or maybe he was being more frugal with his money these days, ever since forking over so much of it to Dane.

"A place?" his father asked. "What kind of place?"

"A place for fun. For people to eat, to drink, to relax. To give folks more to look forward to than . . ." He'd been about to say church, but thought the better of it. Although his father often skipped Sunday morning services, as he must have today, Dane hadn't forgotten that while he'd lived under this roof, Father had made sure both boys attended with Mother every Sunday. Probably so she wouldn't have to go alone. Dane had half expected to be tossed out of his bed that morning, and had been pleasantly surprised to awaken near noon. "I intend to give people something to look forward to besides going home."

Father looked instantly bored, straightening his newspaper again. "Talk to your brother. See if he wants to invest in it, and maybe it'll work out."

"No, Father," said Dane—without letting his second thoughts stop him.

Father peered around the edge this time, not bothering to shift the newspaper aside. "No? What do you mean? How do you plan to open a place? Isn't that why you came home, looking for the money?"

"No," he repeated. "I have the money. All I need is a place."

"Well, you talk to your brother about that, then. He's always got his nose to the wind, sniffing out good ideas. Your mother will be home any minute now, and Lance and Susanna will be coming, too. You can talk about it while we eat."

He snapped the newspaper, as if to crisp its height. Nonetheless, he added in a pleasant tone, "I'm sure your mother will be pleased."

Dane's stomach was loudly protesting its emptiness by the time he heard the clip of Mother's heels echo through the house, followed by the inevitable footsteps behind her. Lance and his wife lived in Williamsport now, in a house he'd bought along Millionaire's Row. Dane hadn't seen either one of them since his return; he hadn't made any more effort to visit them than they had to welcome him back.

All three men stood when the group approached. Mother went to Father and received his customarily polite kiss upon her cheek while Susanna came to Dane with a stiff hug of welcome, even as she eyed Checker curiously. Lance was looking at Checker, too. Although all the Wardmans were tall, Lance had about a half-inch on Dane but still had to look up to view Checker's face. Dane hadn't realized having Lance look up at Checker would be so satisfying.

When Susanna stepped to one of the empty places at the table, Lance held out his hand to Dane. He smiled, but his eyes had grown serious the way they used to when measuring something.

"Welcome home, little brother," Lance said, his hand firmly enveloping Dane's before extending the same gesture toward Checker.

"This is Mr. Finnian," Dane said, "but he goes by Checker to one and all, so don't worry about formalities."

Lance's smile was considerably more charming than the one he'd aimed Dane's way. Dane was struck anew that although his brother had inherited their father's unfortunate nose, somehow it looked better on him. Everything about Lance jutted—the end of his nose, the line of his chin, the draw of his jaw and brows. Even his cheekbones were defined, providing the appropriate backdrop to the nose. In comparison, Father's cheeks were soft, his eyes somewhat rounded, accentuated by the round frame of his eyewear. He still had all of his hair, the one thing Dane himself had inherited from him, providing curls to complete the rest of Father's facial roundness. Dane kept his hair cropped shorter to keep his own curls under control.

"Mr. Checker," said Lance.

"No, just Checker, if ya please," he corrected, his brogue heavier than ever. "I hardly mind settin' aside the formalities, as your brother said."

Lance looked back to Dane and pounded his shoulder in what was probably meant as an imitation of affection. His parents, and maybe even Susanna, might believe it genuine. "About time you came for a visit."

"Sounds like it might be more than a visit," said Father, setting his newspaper on the edge of the table and retaking his own seat. "Come on, have a seat. Let's get on with this meal. I'm starving."

As if they had only been waiting for such a phrase, a maid and butler appeared, stopping at a wheeled side cart only long enough to remove the covers from heated chafing dishes. Dane knew Mr. Winslow, the butler, but didn't know the young maid serving with him. She was the first new servant he'd noticed since his return, and she surprised him. Neither Father nor Mother seemed to like change, especially in a staff that must be trusted polishing their silver or returning jewelry to vaults. He knew they used an employment agency in Williamsport, but when Dane lived among them they rarely called in replacement staff.

"You're new," he said to the girl, who had kept her eyes carefully lowered. She now looked at him with surprise, a pretty smile on her face.

"Yes, sir," she said quietly, still holding the platter of bacon for him to sample. "On Sundays, for Nora's day off. That is, Miss Robinson's day off."

"And your name?"

"Irene, sir. Irene Robinson. Nora's sister."

That explained why she'd been hired. Father's trust usually extended more easily to family members who had already proven themselves.

Irene moved on to Lance, who was looking at Dane with clear suspicion. Dane deserved that, he supposed, since he'd once been responsible for the dismissal of another pretty young maid. But that wasn't entirely his fault; it wasn't as if he'd gone to her room. She'd come to his. What was he supposed to have done? He'd been only seventeen at the time, and even though she was the servant and he the son—albeit second—she'd been the one with the experience. She'd known exactly how to make sure he didn't send her away.

"So, Dane," said Lance, and his voice was a little like Father's. Gruff, as if fully aware of his need to pull Dane's thoughts back to the present. "What did Father mean when he said this might be more than a visit?"

"I'm planning to investigate the area, possibly open a gathering place around here."

"In Williamsport?"

"I was thinking closer to Cranbury. Less competition."

"What kind of gathering place?" Now he really did sound like Father. And why not? Lance had been mimicking the man his whole life.

"A place for food and entertainment. A place for people to enjoy themselves."

"So, a restaurant, then?" his mother asked. "What a lovely idea to keep you busy. Oh! Eliot, what about the tea room? It'll need a buyer now that Madame has . . . well, passed on."

"The tea room?" Dane asked, courteous rather than interested. It sounded the exact opposite of what he was looking for.

"Yes, it's a lovely place." Mother beamed as if fully on board with Dane's plans. "Not very large, but you could add on, I suppose. The important elements are all there: a dining room and ample kitchen. I saw the kitchen, you know. Madame was a great friend of mine from when she lived in Williamsport—well, not a bosom friend, especially since she became so eccentric by leaving behind her friends in Williamsport. But she was a wonderful woman. Unfortunately, her daughter turned her back when her mother went from society matron to working woman." She sighed. "In any case, I'm sure Madame Donadieu's daughter inherited the place, but what in the world will she want with it? Poor Claudette was so embarrassed when her mother ordered it built, mortified when she ended up running the place. Oh, and you'll need a good cook. After location, that's probably the most important part."

Dane had nearly forgotten how animated his mother could become whenever she hopped aboard an idea. He'd have to put an end to her participation sooner than later, because he was fairly certain she'd jump off this particular train as soon as she heard the details. But before he could speak Lance claimed everyone's attention.

"I spoke to Stanford recently," he said, then glanced directly at Dane. "That's Claudette's husband, so he's the new owner. It's true, he does want to get rid of it."

"Any interested buyers?"

"None that I know of. It's Cranbury, after all, not Williamsport." Then he looked from Dane to Checker, as if considering something. Then he looked back at Dane. "Will it be a restaurant? Or a pub?"

"If you're asking whether or not I'll serve alcohol, the answer is yes."

"Alcohol!" Mother's fork dropped with a clang upon her plate. Well, he'd wanted her to know sooner than later, hadn't he?

Father glared at Mother before Dane could say another word. "What do you think he's been doing in Philly the past three years? Selling phosphates and soda?"

While it was true Mother had never once visited him during

the years he'd lived in Philly, Dane had thought Father would have at least complained to her about the details of Dane's business. Dane had expected the drinking and provision of a back room for illegal gambling to have warranted more than one of Father's rants.

Mother picked up her fork again, while her frown made the hint of wrinkles around her mouth that much deeper. "Well, I suppose it didn't matter in Philly. But it does here." She aimed her gaze at Dane. "I won't have it. Some of my dearest friends are members of the Temperance League."

"Well, at least *you're* not a member . . ." Dane murmured. "Or Father, I'm sure of that." Even though Mother didn't seem to be listening, the disapproval on Lance's face said he'd heard every word.

"You'd need a license, even if you do sell meals with the alcohol. That's expensive, and they can be picky about granting them."

Did his brother think he was completely ignorant? "I had one in Philly. If I can pass muster there, I figure I can be approved anywhere. The fee is the same five hundred dollars as anywhere else in the state."

"And you have that much?"

Dane narrowed his eyes, not bothering to respond.

"Well, Philly isn't Cranbury. The license commissioner in this county won't have the same low standards as a big city. You won't find commissioners too busy to do a thorough job, or agreeable to a payoff."

Dane pushed away his plate, the contents of which were only half-consumed. "Thank you all for another round of approval and encouragement for my new endeavor. I knew I could count on my family."

With that, he stood and left the table. He didn't care if Checker followed, although part of him knew leaving behind a meal would be a lot harder for him than it had been for Dane.

CHAPTER 4

On Monday afternoon, Meli approached the back door of the empty tea shop. Although she'd kept an eye on the place from the privacy of the forest, she hadn't been inside since the awful morning she'd found Madame. Meli was curious about what would become of the place. She'd seen two men circling the shop yesterday afternoon—which might have been suspicious, especially since one of them was humongous and could easily have barged in. But it had been broad daylight and they never went inside. Other than that, the tea room had been ignored. Madame's daughter must own the place now, yet there hadn't been any sign of her.

Meli had come to see about the food that had no doubt rotted during more than a week of neglect. After finding the hidden key she let herself inside. The scent of overripe vegetables greeted her first. Picking up the refuse pail kept near the door, she scooped the offending items inside. Leftover bread and croissants, stored under a loose towel to convert to croutons, were already molding in the humidity of the last few days. Those, too, were added to the bin.

As she worked, Meli hummed the tune she'd learned at church

the day before. She'd been taught many hymns by her parents, but all combined the sum wouldn't have totaled even a quarter of those contained in the hymnals used by the church. She smiled to remember the kindness of the young Mrs. Taylor, the pastor's wife, who had sat beside her. She'd been so friendly to Meli, starting by pointing to a little sign hung above the organ that listed a number matching the hymns being sung from the books. After the service, though Meli had planned to hurry off, Mrs. Taylor had introduced herself and told Meli she was welcome to visit any time—on Sunday, or any other day of the week. She and her husband lived in a little house behind the church and their door was always open.

Meli's smile faded as she removed milk from the icebox. The ice must have long since melted, leaving everything inside nearly room temperature. She wasn't sure which smelled worse, the cream or the milk. If this icebox was to be used again, it would need time to air. Even though all of the dishes Madame had prepared before her death were spoiled, Meli mourned getting rid of it. She herself knew some of the recipes, but no one could make such concoctions as easily or as expertly as Madame.

Meli sighed. She took a cylinder of Bon Ami from under the sink, sprinkling the powder liberally before scrubbing. Afterward, she stopped the drain to create a mixture to clean other surfaces. The sparkle from her mother's ring caught her eye. Meli nearly always wore it, ever since the day they had buried her mother. She supposed she should have left it at home considering she would have her hands in vinegar, sodas, and other products. So she slipped it off, setting it on the countertop next to the icebox. At least there it would be free of vinegar, and the little diamond chip wouldn't scrape the walls of the icebox while she worked. She would save emptying the water tray beneath the icebox for last; the panel hiding the tray always stuck in place and sometimes it took a few minutes to wiggle and tap free.

The door between the dining room and kitchen was on a

hinge that swung both ways, but it was louvered to allow noise—
and scents—to pass between. Madame had wanted the aroma of
her breads and cakes and sauces to easily reach her patrons,
enticing them to desire something they might not have thought of
without a subtle suggestion.

Just now, it allowed the sound of the front door opening.

For a moment, Meli was tempted to run out the back. After all,
she no longer worked here and did not have permission to enter.
No one in town would vouch for her if she were caught trespassing, even if she did have evidence of the favor she was doing.

Meli wrung out the rag she'd been using and dried her hands.
She couldn't very well hide the recent evidence of her work with
Bon Ami and vinegar hanging in the air.

Voices came as easily to her ear as the better scents Madame
used to send the other direction.

"This is ridiculous, Claudette," came a man's impatient voice.
"Sell the place and have done with it. He's interested. He has the
money. He's a Wardman!"

A non-committal "Hmmmph," was the only return.

At mention of the name, Meli froze.

"Why hesitate?" His frustration was building, Meli could tell
that without even seeing the man's face. "The sooner you get rid
of this albatross, the better."

Meli should make herself known; she was practically eaves-
dropping. If they were the owners—and Meli didn't doubt that,
knowing Madame's daughter was named Claudette—then they
would likely thank her for tending to details they must have
forgotten and few others would care to do. They might even pay
her! She didn't yet miss the salary Madame had given her, even
though she hadn't been given her last week's payment—something she wasn't likely to see now. Meli knew she could go back to
depending on Dad for everything, but there was something satisfying about earning her own wages.

"Look, he'll be coming down that street any minute."

Claudette's voice clearly hissed at her husband, despite the fact she must have been standing near the window on the opposite end of the dining room. "I don't want you to say a word, except perhaps an echo of mine. Do you understand, Stanford? Not a word of your own."

DANE DESCENDED the steps from the Cranbury Inn, walking briskly away from the heart of town and out toward the main road that bypassed Cranbury. He hadn't bothered to find Checker; he was probably already taking a nap despite the early hour. Once again, the two of them had gone well into the night playing cards, in the privacy of Dane's room. But the scent of Mrs. Taylor's breakfast had called Checker downstairs with all the other guests, the same as it had for Dane. That was some time ago.

Yesterday had been an especially busy day, not counting the toll of leaving his family early and without a word. It wasn't the first time he'd done that, although when Dane suggested Checker should repack his bag, his friend had asked if he planned to let them know they were leaving. They were still eating on the verandah! But Dane hadn't said a word, just retrieved his belongings then walked out without a backward glance. Checker had followed.

Dane went straight to Cranbury to have a peek at the now vacant tea room his mother had mentioned. Then he'd hired Cranbury's Canary to take them to Williamsport. It hadn't taken long to look in the public telephone record to locate Claudette Norcross-Rice, née Claudette Donadieu, along with her husband Stanford Norcross-Rice, who now owned what had once been a tea room.

Dane had telephoned her immediately and to his delight he'd been invited to their home to discuss the sale, though they couldn't schedule a look inside until today.

A tea room! He was still shaking his head over that. Although it had sounded preposterous at first, its placement beside the road and just outside of Cranbury was, miraculously, ridiculously, well-suited for what Dane had in mind. He was chagrined over it being perfectly *ill*-suited for what it had once been. He knew tea rooms were growing in popularity; women seemed to have taken to the idea back in Philly, too, welcoming a public place just for them to frequent. But for pity's sake they belonged tucked inside a town or city, right next to a dress or hat shop, where women already frequented. Here, on the side of a road where no women traveled alone, it was ludicrous. A saloon couldn't have asked for a better location! Men didn't mind slinking out of town for a drink, whereas asking women to leave the safety of a busy main street was something altogether different.

Not that he had any intention of naming his establishment a saloon, even if his first impression of Claudette Donadieu Norcross-Rice had been that she wasn't limited by rules. Maybe she wouldn't mind her mother's legacy turned into a drinking establishment, or at least one where ardent spirits were served, albeit with a meal if he could find a cook willing to move to Cranbury. He doubted he'd find much talent in this little town.

So far, he'd only told the Norcross-Rice's that he hoped to open the place as an eating and refreshment establishment. His family's reaction had inspired caution. Neither Mr. nor Mrs. Norcross-Rice had asked him to specify what kind of refreshment he had in mind, so for the time being he'd left it at that. Mr. Norcross-Rice had seemed most interested in selling the place, and Dane had first directed his attention to him. But it soon became apparent that it was Claudette, not Stanford, who would make the decision.

He noticed someone raking the church yard as he came to the edge of town, someone who lifted his straw hat long enough for a casual wave. Dane waved back. No harm in being friendly to a potential new patron, church gardener or not. Although . . . was that a white collar on the man? Surely it wasn't the pastor himself doing such menial labor? This man wasn't Pastor McNichols, the bearded preacher Dane remembered from years ago—the man who had suggested to his mother that she might try glue on Dane's pants if she wanted him to sit still in church. Perhaps the parish had a new pastor. No matter. Dane had hosted plenty of clergymen in his old establishment; they might be men of God, but they were still men.

All irrelevant—and irreverent—thoughts were banished by the time Dane reached the door to what he hoped would become his newest business establishment. He was surprisingly enthused about this prospect, even while unsure how long this diversion from boredom would last. After all, he'd been surprised when Philly had bored him as fast as it had. For the moment, anyway, this was just the challenge he needed. This too-tranquil little town could use a bit of life.

Besides, the surrounding forest was a better playground for Ethel than brick, pavement and coal fumes. And if anything could keep boredom at bay, it was Ethel.

CHAPTER 5

*M*eli lifted the refuse pail quietly. It was filled to the brim, with more to be collected next to the icebox that she simply had no room for. Plus, the floor needed sweeping, the zinc countertops should be scoured, the water tray beneath the icebox still needed to be emptied. She could offer her services now that she knew whom to ask, but it might do well for her to go around and come in through the front door.

"Hey, who's this?"

Meli had her hand on the doorknob when Stanford's voice reached her. She had no hope that he referred to anyone but her, he sounded so near. She turned and there he was at the louvered doorway, holding it wide, staring at her with some surprise.

"I—I'm Meli—Melisande Atherton. I work here. Or . . . used to."

The blond haired man looked around the room, perhaps seeing evidence of her efforts. "Looks as though no one has worked here since Margaux passed."

"That's true, sir," she said, then would have left but he held out a hand to entreat her.

"Wait. My wife probably has some questions for you."

Meli shook her head, still heading to the door, but he was already calling Claudette's name.

"What is it, Stanford? He'll be walking through that door any —" She'd reached the threshold behind him, and spotted Meli. "Oh. Well. Who are you?"

She opened her mouth to answer, but Stanford spoke first, restating what she had just told him.

"And you're just now cleaning this kitchen?" Her nose wrinkled as she glanced at the pail Meli held.

"I . . ." Meli started, but once again Stanford spoke for her.

"It's not as if anyone told her to do it. You didn't," he quipped at Claudette.

Now Claudette lifted one brow at her, taking another look around. "How did you get in? I was assured this place was locked."

"Madame always hid a key for me outside, so I could let myself in before she came downstairs. I used to arrive early to start the ovens, lay out the ingredients for the day's baking and cooking."

In three long steps Claudette stood before Meli, palm outstretched. "Give it to me. The key."

"I—I returned it outside, to its spot. I can show you where it is."

"Oh, never mind. Just finish what you were doing and make it quick. Then put the key on the table before you leave. And hurry up about it. I'm expecting the new tenant as we speak."

Meli was once again tempted to flee. If any single one of the Wardmans was buying the place, he or she could take care of what would become *their* garbage.

DANE STEPPED inside the tea shop, hearing voices beyond the dining room. Rather than interrupt, he looked around. He'd noticed the lace curtains and small, flowering, though drooping, plants in the window on his way in. The room itself was pleasing, he supposed, in an overtly feminine sort of way. The floor was lightly varnished and polished. Presently there were less than a dozen small, round tables, each one shrouded in damask table-cloths the faint shade of a rose. Bud vases adorned the centers, every one of the roses wilted and browned. Perhaps no one, not even its new owner, had been inside since the previous owner's unexpected death. Vaguely, he wondered about the kitchen. The place had served food along with the tea; perhaps there might be a rodent problem if things had been ignored, no matter how long.

Three of the four walls were paneled and painted white in a sure effort to exude cleanliness. He supposed that had been more important to women patrons than it would be to men. He'd have the paint stripped from the paneling and stain the walls dark. Few men wanted bright white walls reflecting light to shine upon their drinking, invading their thoughts. He had no intention of staying open only during daylight hours, as one silly law or another suggested. Sunlight would only make the light problem worse. This place, like his previous one, would quietly mind its own busi-ness, even long after dark.

He eyed the wall that was free of any windows, opposite the road. Unlike the other three walls, this one was covered in flow-ered wallpaper. That must go first, though the wall itself was perfect for a long bar.

"Ah! Mr. Wardman, how lovely to see you again."

Dane turned to the sugary-sweet voice. Claudette Donadieu Norcross-Rice approached, both of her hands outstretched as if greeting a dear friend. Dane conjured a smile and squeezed both of her hands in a show of pleasure, though that pleasure was surface-deep at best. Before him stood the only means through which he could fulfill his newest interest. Once that was taken care of he would forget her as easily as he was already forgetting Squire Ridley—and Dane had almost liked him.

Stanford Norcross-Rice was nowhere to be seen, which Dane

found slightly alarming even if the man didn't have a vote about whether or not his wife should sell her inheritance.

But then the man emerged from behind a swinging door, from a kitchen, Dane assumed—the very place he wanted to inspect more closely. The building might be only a half-dozen years old, but it didn't take long for vermin to find food and warmth, or poor construction to let water, wind and weather take its toll. Dane had noted yesterday that the roof and exterior were in good condition, and the dining area adequately sized for a bar and a few tables, even allowing for a pool table. He'd have to add on if he wanted to provide a private gaming room. The kitchen, though, was the one place that might have suffered some wear since, unlike a barroom, everything the tea room had served was prepared in there.

Dane withdrew his hands from the grip of the man's wife. "Good-morning," Dane greeted them both. "It's nice to have a look at the inside."

"And?" prompted Mrs. Norcross-Rice. Her tone indicated enough hope to perk up his expectations. Maybe she really did want to be rid of the place.

He nodded once. "So far, so good. I'd like to see the kitchen. And upstairs? Are there living quarters, or just storage?"

"Let's see the kitchen first, shall we? We have someone in just now, making sure it's all nice and clean and ready for its next occupant. And upstairs . . . well, let's see." She looked around as if in search of a stairway.

"Through the kitchen," said her husband, who then led the way.

Briefly, Dane wondered if he should be bothered by her usage of the words "next occupant" in the place where "new owner" would better fit his plans. Then he followed them through the white louvered door.

CHAPTER 6

Try though she had, Meli couldn't follow her wish to leave the place in its current state. How often her own wishes departed from what God would have her do! Besides that, leaving would reflect badly on Madame. So, Meli had gone to the refuse wagon out in the yard—garbage had been picked up since last she was here—and the wagon echoed hollowly after she'd upturned the pail. Then she'd gone back inside to finish her job, albeit unpaid and unthanked, reminding herself God's smile was more than enough.

She'd just begun sweeping the floor when Claudette and Stanford returned to the kitchen, inevitably followed by the prospective new owner.

She blinked madly at Wardman's appearance—*that* Wardman —and clutched silently, desperately, to the broom's handle. It was the very same Wardman . . . the one responsible for . . . She could hardly breathe.

Meli had thought him gone forever—and good riddance. She'd only ever glimpsed the rest of his family, either in the tea room itself, or with the elder Mr. Wardman, when their carriage picked up or dropped off one Wardman wife or another in town.

This Wardman was the reason Meli hated all Wardmans. She had long ago decided it wasn't the other, older brother, who had killed her beloved Jax. He would have been too old at the time, judging by the speed with which both of the Wardman brothers seemed to grow.

Jax had been the loveliest of her little kestrels, the first one her mother had ever let Meli train on her own. He'd had a slate-blue head, light brown breast, rusty-red back and tail speckled in black. From the moment she'd seen him in the wild, when he was no more than a fuzzy little ball, Meli had loved him. Her family had made a holiday trip to hunt the baby kestrel in an early, cold spring. To this day, it remained one of Meli's favorite memories, even if the ending to the Jax's story was bitter.

On that fateful day, Jax had been doing what kestrels did: hunting for a mouse or grasshopper or smaller bird. Hovering made him a small but easy target. Wardman, only a few years older than she, had shot him down without mercy.

"Here it is." Claudette's voice invaded Meli's memory. "As you can see, the kitchen is amply sized for the dining room."

Meli barely heard the woman. Her eyes stayed fixed on Wardman even though she forced her memories to fade.

"The icebox is fairly large, and there are two stoves. Obviously, they're both Graf models, as you can tell from the bold plating on the front. Must be one of the best if they show off a name like that. Running water, of course, and—let's see, the same gas that runs the stoves must provide the best lighting. I don't see a telephone. But, you know, this place is pretty close to the road. I don't see why a telephone wire couldn't be brought in here sooner than the rest of Cranbury. Think of it, you could introduce civilization to this backward little town."

Claudette's voice droned on and Meli's lungs still barely worked. She stood in the shadow of one of the tall shelves, which remained laden with bowls, dishes and linens.

Then his gaze, which had been roughly following along the

kitchen features as Claudette named them, came to her. His brows lifted, as if pleased, and Meli's stomach turned sour.

"And who is this? Do you come with the place, too?"

His teasing tone might have been pleasant to someone else. She narrowed her eyes, realizing although she had harbored more emotion for him than any other human being save her father, for whom she felt the opposite, he did not even know who she was.

She threw down the broom and stalked out the back door. May God forgive her, she would no longer concern herself with the mess that remained, not even for Madame.

"WHAT—WHAT are you doing? Where are you going, girl? You come back here—"

Dane guessed the young woman, whoever she was, could hear the shocked outrage behind Claudette's call. He wasn't surprised when it went unheeded. Whoever she was, by the look on her face that girl wasn't about to do either him or Claudette any favors.

"I guess she's not planning to work under new management."

Although his statement made light of the action, it crossed Dane's mind that she had been looking at him when her lovely face changed from placid to downright volatile. In fact, it seemed as though she'd been staring at him before he'd even turned her way. He'd felt it. When his gaze met hers, it was as if no one else had been in the room. Not in a good way, unfortunately. He'd returned her stare, but only because he couldn't have looked away even if he'd tried. He wished he'd only been struck by the unusual shade of her light blue eyes, or the creaminess of her skin. But it wasn't any of that; it was the downright animosity exuding from her entire face.

It was also true that when he'd come into the tea shop, Claudette had already been in the kitchen. If she had anything to do with the young lady's sudden departure, why hadn't she fled before he'd arrived in the kitchen?

That clinched it. She'd fled because of him. Well, that was new. Women usually liked him. How had he gotten on her wrong side already? He didn't even know her—something he'd like to change. The stark emotion was one thing, but her pretty face had definitely factored in as to why he'd been unable to look elsewhere.

Dane shrugged. It was probably just as well she was so shy of him. Setting up a new business, especially his kind of business, would take all of his energy—at least for a little while. As Checker would surely remind him if he were here, Dane performed his best when focused on just one thing. Finding a new woman to charm wasn't on the agenda. For now.

"I'd like to see the upstairs, too," Dane said.

"Oh, of course," Claudette said. Her husband had been roaming the kitchen as if it was his first time seeing the place, too, but now he beckoned them with a wave of his hand.

"The stairs are this way." Then he added, "Storage room on the other side."

As Stanford stepped aside to let Claudette lead, her voice echoed along the narrow stairwell. "I haven't had the chance to send anyone over to clean out my mother's belongings, but rest assured it'll all be gone by the time you're ready to rent this place."

"Rent?" He repeated the word calmly, although inside he was growing impatient. First, the prettiest girl he'd seen in quite some time acted as though he were the devil himself—without even knowing he intended selling what some called the demon rum. And now this woman seemed unwilling to sell the place outright. Maybe it wouldn't be burdensome to avoid the local women, if they were all this much trouble.

Claudette waited at the top of the stairs, smiling. "Yes, after considering it overnight—and now seeing how much care and expense my mother took, I'm wondering if I want to sell it outright. Memories of my mother, you understand."

Dane eyed her, wondering if she was angling for more money to ensure she earned back the entire amount her mother had spent on what would, presumably, have been Claudette's inheritance. Surely she wasn't hesitant to sell something he'd guessed was an embarrassment to someone in Claudette's social circle? He'd heard of the Norcross-Rice family from the days he'd lived around here. Both the Norcross and Rice families were definitely higher echelon, hence the unwillingness to lose either surname on any children born to the union. Although Dane hadn't dwelt on the matter, he'd assumed Claudette had been lucky to marry into the family, considering her own mother had chosen to join the trade class by building—then running—a tea shop.

Even now, amid all the earthly possessions Claudette's mother had left behind, there was one important element missing that would have explained this woman's sudden hesitancy to sell: any hint of grief, despite this first reference to her mother's memory.

So, why the change from yesterday?

"A rental agreement isn't really what I'm interested in," Dane said slowly, not wanting to put an end to the discussion but hoping to convey the importance of a sale. He could get a liquor license; he could comply with the safety rules for the sale of food and spirits; he could pay all the taxes; he could even comply with county inspectors from time to time. But the rest of the laws, like closing after dark, prohibiting friendly games of cards, reporting certain kinds of women coming in hoping to make a bit of money —well, those kinds of things could be ignored if it was his own place. A landlord might not see it that way.

Claudette took a step closer, putting a hand on his arm. She was well inside the invisible, polite area of space surrounding him and Dane was once again relieved the woman's husband was in the room. Then he was embarrassed for the man because Dane would have been embarrassed if he had a wife who smiled at another man the way she'd just smiled at him.

"Let's finish looking around, shall we?" she asked. At least her tone was more friendly than intimate, saving Stanford a sliver of dignity. "We can discuss the possibilities afterward. Maybe an initial rental agreement, just until you're sure your business will thrive? I'd be doing you a favor, wouldn't I? Not to be stuck with a place you couldn't ultimately use."

She couldn't possibly guess there would be any doubt about the acceptance of his type of business among what he remembered to be the driest, most straight-laced dot on Pennsylvania's map. He might even concede her offer was something he *should* consider. But, confound it, what if she kicked him out at the first sign of resistance? If this place was his he could stick through a few hurdles. He expected them!

Ultimately, however, he had enough faith in the true ways of men, whether they resided in a city or a small town, to know opposition was worth fighting. He'd wage war for those who'd thank him someday for bringing a bit of entertainment to this little hamlet. Men deserved to be happy, didn't they? Even here in Cranbury?

CHAPTER 7

*M*eli stomped the ground, first with one foot then the other. She was in the forest between the church and the tea shop, going nowhere, pounding out circles. This was her forest, the one she'd crossed on her way home a thousand times. She wasn't ready yet to face a father who could read her moods as easily as he read the Word. She'd have to tame her anger or he'd caution against sin.

"He didn't even know me!"

She trampled God's earth again and a moan of pure frustration escaped. "He's . . . evil! A brute! This is righteous anger. God knows it!"

Thoughts of *that* Wardman running Madame's business drew another moan. "Ooh! And he will *live* there? In her rooms, in her home?"

Meli nearly screamed—but then the shadow of another woman's skirt caught her eye. She wasn't alone, after all. Meli ought to have gone deeper into her forest; she ought to have gone straight to her birds and orphans for comfort. But she would have hated to be near them while filled with so much anger—this anger that she preferred nursing rather than banishing or asking God's help to disperse, at least right now.

"Meli?"

She stiffened at the sound of her name, not expecting it. Her face might be vaguely known from working in the tea shop, but her name wasn't known by many. Then the woman approached, and Meli saw it was Mrs. Taylor, the preacher's wife.

Meli let out a sigh, knowing she couldn't show her anger in front of a woman as kind and gracious as this. She'd probably never wanted to soak in anger, let it permeate every fiber of her being. What kind of safe, protected life must she know, as a pastor's wife? What would such a lady have to say about the urge Meli had, to go up to Dane Wardman and slap him? Demand he remember that he'd slaughtered her favorite bird? Force him to acknowledge how wrong, how stupid, how evil he really must be?

No. A pastor's wife would probably remind Meli of the same Bible verses she already knew. The one from Proverbs about fools venting their rage. Or the one that said the wrath of man worketh not the righteousness of God. Or many others about how God demonstrated His forgiveness, so we ought to forgive others.

However, it was Mrs. Taylor's welcoming smile that did the most to calm Meli's mood—at least enough to notice the camera strapped around the other woman's neck. She'd seen her in the woods before, taking pictures of sunlight through the trees, or birds perched on a branch. Once, Meli thought she'd even taken a picture of one of Meli's gosses, mid-flight. But Meli never had the courage to ask about seeing such a photograph, if one existed.

"Hello, Meli," she greeted her warmly, but then her brows drew together. "I know God never leaves us alone out here in the forest, but I can't help thinking I've just interrupted you. I'm sorry if I did."

With some surprise, Meli wished she could talk to Mrs. Taylor. She might be a preacher's wife, but she wasn't much older than

Meli herself. It had been such a long time since Meli had a young friend, if she didn't count her animals.

"You probably did me a favor, Mrs. Taylor," Meli said, struggling to keep her voice calm. "My thoughts weren't the kind God was likely to smile upon."

"Anything you'd like to talk about? Other than to God, that is?"

Meli grinned, wondering why she always expected it to be so difficult to talk to near strangers. It wasn't so hard now. Still, this was a topic she wasn't going to admit. Hatred was nothing to boast about. "To be honest, I can't say I was talking to God, even if He was listening. I was grumbling. And if I talk about it, I'd likely go from one sin to another."

Mrs. Taylor's smile didn't go away, nor was there any sign of judgment. She reached beyond her camera to pat Meli's arm. "Well, I'd like to be your friend. It usually helps me to share things on my mind, so I want you to know I have a willing ear. But I won't press if you're not ready."

Then she took a few steps away, only to turn back and add, "Meli? Why don't you call me Essie? Anytime someone says 'Mrs. Taylor' I still look around for my mother-in-law, even after six years of marriage and two children."

Suddenly Meli was almost smiling, the first urge to do so all morning. Still, she let the woman carry on with her hike. Even if God had orchestrated their paths to cross, it had been so long since she'd had a friend Meli wasn't sure she knew how to be one. So she watched Mrs. Taylor—Essie—walk away. Meli would have to come to town, at the very least to church, to be a friend, and Meli didn't intend doing that very often.

Especially if Dane Wardman took over the tea room.

Dane found his way back to the Cranbury Inn, unable to rid himself of his annoyance. He had tried diligently and persuasively

54

to buy the tea room, but Claudette Norcross-Rice had refused to sell the place outright. She'd insisted on a six-month lease, and then, if he still wanted to go forward with an outright purchase, she would agree to sell at a fair price.

He could tell Stanford seemed as chagrined as Dane over his wife's decision, but his rather quick surrender convinced Dane the man was well acquainted with Claudette's stubbornness. And so Dane had agreed to the lease. The paperwork would be delivered to the inn this afternoon.

Dane found Checker on one of the white wicker chairs on the inn's porch.

"Well?" Checker's brows lifted expectantly.

Dane frowned as he nearly threw himself into the nearest chair.

"You didn't get it?" Surprise laced every word.

"Six months. A lease. Then, if we're still in business and I still want it, a sale."

"Huh." The single syllable conveyed surprise, but he didn't seem put out.

Checker mustn't have taken even a moment to realize the ramifications, so Dane enlightened him. "It means she can toss us out at the first sign of trouble."

That, at least, raised his brows again. "You told her your plans for the place, then?"

"I told her what I plan telling everybody, at least at first. We'll sell meals and spirits to go along with those meals."

"So—she likely assumes that means wine? Nothin' about the bar, the pool table, and the like?"

Dane rubbed the back of his neck. He hadn't liked her reaction to the little he had said. "She seemed more interested in me than in the business. Maybe too much. I had the feeling she might . . ." He stopped himself. He was old enough, and experienced enough, to know when a woman was interested in him. Claudette Norcross-Rice had shown all the signs, even in front of her husband when his attention might have appeared elsewhere. Anyway, why else would she have expressed a desire to "help" his business to succeed? "I don't know. That she might want to be a little more involved than as a landlord."

Checker grinned. "Well now, Boss, you do have that effect on women."

Not all of them. He still hadn't forgotten the abject dislike on the face of the girl in the kitchen.

Checker abandoned the wicker chair and it crackled as it eased from his weight. "Just be sure to use common sense around her," he added, "unless her husband's name is Potiphar, in which case I'd advise you to run, boy, run. Run like the devil's at yer feet."

"I think her husband's name is Stanford. Who's Potiphar?"

Checker shook his head as if an explanation shouldn't be necessary. "All right, then. I took a little walk through town—a stroll all of five minutes, don't ya know—and noticed there's a carpenter's shop right across the street. See there? *Levick and Sons.* If nothin' has altered your plans, it's time to see them about a job."

CHAPTER 8

*M*eli closed the back door to the mew, the wooden shelter her father had built to house her mother's birds. Before they'd married, he'd pledged to provide a good home, in the Biblical tradition of a prospective groom preparing a place for his bride, the way Jesus promised a place for His church in heaven. Dad already had the farmhouse from his own family, but knew no home would be complete for *his* bride without the mews.

He'd built something far more than a shed, less than a barn, at least in size. Along the back ran what anyone would have thought a tack room had they noticed the smell of leather, but it wasn't from bridles or saddles. Rather the familiar scent came from tethers and lures, jesses, hoods and gloves. Dried strips of meat hung from the rafters, other hooks held bells and whistles. It housed a wood-burning stove to keep it warm year round, and when the shutters were put in place on the mews themselves they, too were snug throughout the coldest weather.

The three enclosures in front were large enough to hold any hawk, each offering a stout metal tub for water and a perch on each side, edged with solid walls between while the outermost walls were a mix of sturdy planking and thick wire mesh. Strong enough to hold the mightiest raptor while the wire allowed plenty of fresh air and light. Each mew could be opened only from inside the tack room, a protection against any outsider who might think hawks needed to be free rather than caged—something Meli's heritage had taught otherwise.

Dad had taken so much care with the project that Mama used to say he'd wanted the birds more than he'd wanted her. Meli smiled in spite of her lingering sour mood, remembering how they'd laughed about that.

She had only two birds living there now. Hootie, the owl who had been fully grown even when Meli was a child, had died only a year ago—one more ache settled into place alongside Meli's others.

Guinevere, her mother's goshawk, lived on one end. She had been only five when Meli's mother had died. Well trained and hardy, Guinevere had helped Meli to mourn, because she knew the gos missed her mother, too.

An even older gos, Harriet, occupied the middle compartment. Meli had housed Harriet for almost a year, although she'd tried setting her free. She'd found her on the ground, thinking her dead, but when Meli lifted her for a proper burial the bird woke from its coma-like sleep. Someone must have trained her, because she showed little fear of Meli. Her red eyes watched closely, and she blinked once before flying off—only to return to Meli's gauntlet without a lure to entice her. She was an old raptor, her talons gnarled but still strong. She must have abandoned her owner, or been abandoned herself. She'd chosen Meli that day, who'd been grateful for her loyalty ever since.

Dad hadn't been home when Meli had returned earlier, but smoke from their stove's chimney said he must be back. He sometimes disappeared into the forest the same way Meli did with her birds, but today it was more likely he'd been out at the vegetable fields. Those were the crops he worked alone, unlike the winter rye that took up more than half their land. He planted that with the Packham's, who had an even bigger farm down the road. They'd been sharing seed and labor, at least for crops other than vegetables, for as long as Meli could remember. Somehow, though, the Packham's efforts had paid more dividends, more than just their stretch of land should yield. They had a gasoline powered tractor, an honest-to-goodness motorcar, and all three of them, Matthew—or Mattie as Meli called him—as well as Mr. and Mrs. Packham, wore fur coats in the winter. She knew they'd never set enough traps to have caught the pelts themselves, so they must have spent a fortune at a Williamsport store.

Despite the Packham's obvious success, the family was even less likely to go into town than Meli or her dad. They showed off their finery from time to time when they drove their motorcar, but locally they mixed only with Meli and her dad, and only with farm business. She was hardly the one to call preference for isolation an oddity. Come to think of it, the only odd thing was that their two families mixed at all. Meli hadn't seen either Mrs. Packham or Mattie for months now, and that was unusual only because it was spring. The two of them often went south—to family, they said—leaving Mr. Packham home alone. But the weather was warming and they were usually back by now.

Dad was at the stove, turning meat from one side to another in the same pan they used for eggs in the morning. They were having trouble consuming all the eggs she no longer brought to Madame, and had decided she would ask Mrs. Taylor—Essie—if her mother-in-law who ran the inn might be interested in purchasing some. If that didn't work, they'd sell them at the vegetable market, but that was seasonal.

Bread and cheese were already out on the table.

"Get that tea room all squared away, then? Didn't take you long."

She'd guessed he would ask, since she'd told him where she'd been headed. She just hadn't expected it to be the first question out of his mouth.

She grimaced as she took a seat, then tore off a hunk of bread and added a slice of cheese to her plate.

"Well?"

Meli knew he was more curious than concerned—curious at her hesitation. He hadn't objected to her working in town, even though it meant he had to take up some of the chores she'd no longer had time for. And he'd appreciated the leftovers Madame had sent home with Meli. But he was as disinterested in the tea shop and its goings on as he was in the rest of Cranbury.

Her lips tightened. "The new owner arrived before I finished, and I'd rather not do him any favors. So I left."

Dad looked over his shoulder. "I can think of only one reason you'd leave a mess for somebody. Did a Wardman buy the place, or what?"

Meli looked downward. "I guess so."

"Which one?"

Meli couldn't bring herself to speak his name.

"Oh."

Dad forked the two cuts of sizzling beef, one for each plate, added a spoonful of green beans from another pot, then set the plates on the table before taking a seat. Before either one of them reached for a utensil, he bowed his head and said the same, brief prayer he always prayed before any meal.

Afterward, he raised his gaze to her and said, "I was kind of hoping a new owner would keep you."

Meli eyed her father. "Why? Aren't you happy to have my help full time around here again?" She knew he often borrowed one of the Packham's hired hands, but she guessed he'd rather have her help than pay someone.

"Sure, sure," he said, cutting his meat now and not looking at her. He didn't often make eye contact, so this was nothing new.

"Then why hope I'd keep working there?"

He set down his fork and put his elbows on the table to tent his hands. Still without looking at her, he said, "Meli, I've been hoping you'd find a husband while you were working there. Oh, I know now that was a silly hope, since it was a shop for women. But, it brought you to town and I thought . . . maybe you'd meet somebody."

If Meli's mouth wasn't full, she might have let it drop open. "You never said anything like that before, Dad." Even as she spoke, she recalled her last conversation with Madame.

"Well, you're old enough now. Probably past the age when some get married. How old are you these days, anyway?"

She grinned. "Twenty-one. Just turned."

His eyes widened and met hers, obviously horrified. "Past the age, I'd say! Daughter, I'm sorry for that."

She laughed now. "I'm as old as all that, am I?"

Now he looked sorrowful, gently patting one of her shoulders. "No, no. As usual, I've bungled my words. If your mother were here—"

He cut himself off. Although Meli had never told him to stop, he seemed to have realized that the phrase was put to use far too often since her mother's death, even after all these years. Now Meli patted the hand that had just patted her.

"I know, Dad. I guess if Mom were here she'd have wanted me married, giving her grandkids. But it's not too late. Is it?"

He lifted his brows, a new forkful of meat suspended halfway to his mouth. "Do you have someone in mind?"

She shook her head. "No. But you know how I went to town for church yesterday?"

He nodded slowly, a look entering his eyes now that hinted sadness . . . or acceptance. As usual, he seemed to know what she was about to say.

"I guess if you want me to meet somebody, it'll have to be

there. Why don't you come with me next Sunday? The singing alone is worth the walk. Half the town sings better than I do."

He tended to his meal then, after a gentle shake of his head. "Maybe they sing better than me, but not you. I have a notion that angels passing by stop their own singing when they hear you, just to enjoy themselves. You go, though. I want you to."

She might have refused, except for two things. She knew folks in town could be friendly to each other; she'd seen that while working at the tea shop. She'd never expected any of them to be friendly to her, but Essie Taylor had been. Maybe all of Madame's advice about how to groom and dress and talk wouldn't be wasted, after all, if Meli mixed more.

She knew Madame was right about the other notion. Even Dad admitted he wanted her to find a husband. Meli had never dwelt on such a thing. She'd been good at being invisible at the tea shop, but knew if she attracted the attention of any young man that would be the end of her invisibility—maybe not entirely for the better. In so many ways, her parents had taught her that folks flocked together like birds of a feather and their family just weren't of that flock. She'd never asked why.

Maybe, for the first time in Meli's life, or at least since before Cari had died, she might find she could join a flock, after all.

DANE STEPPED into the carpentry shop, Checker behind him. Two things immediately impressed upon him: the smell of wood and something else. Glue? Varnish? He couldn't tell. The other impression was that the showcased pieces were fine, fine indeed. A round table and five chairs; a roll top desk; a rocking chair; hope chest; coat tree; bookshelf. The selection offered a variety of grains, stains and styles. Even toys were displayed on one of the shelving units, which brought back a vague memory of having been in this shop when he was a child. Back then, however, he hadn't been old enough to appreciate what he saw now: quality. Maybe he wouldn't have to go all the way to Williamsport to fill his needs, after all.

An older woman greeted him, immediately reminding him he was, after all, in a little town where things must never change if they still kept people working at her age. Her gray hair was swept up and back, and her voice as she called a greeting was high-pitched, followed by a wobbly laugh as she approached and looked up at Checker.

"Goodness, I heard a giant had taken a room across the street, but I thought they were exaggerating."

"This is Mr. Finnegan," Dane said. "And I'm Dane Wardman. We're here to see about some work we'd like done over at what used to be the tea shop."

Her eyebrows had popped up when he'd mentioned his name, but they went higher at mention of the tea shop.

"Well, now, you're little Dane Wardman? Goodness, not so little anymore, are you? Not as big as your friend here, but all grown up just the same."

Dane smiled, reminding himself to be patient. Unlike in Philly, people around here didn't tend to get to the point very quickly.

"You're planning to run the tea room?" she asked.

"No, ma'am. But I'll be opening for refreshments. Food and beverages. It's right near the road, so I thought it's a good spot for travelers to slow down and enjoy the view along with some . . . fortification." He smiled at his own word choice.

"I see," she said. "It was such a shame about Mrs. Donadieu. Did you know her?"

He shook his head. "Her daughter owns the place now, but she doesn't have much interest in reopening." He looked around, thinking even if the senior Mr. Levick wasn't in, or dead if his age was similar to this woman's, at least one of the sons might be available. The sign outside had said Levick *& Sons*, after all.

"Now that's another shame, that the town will lose the tea shop,"

Mrs. Levick was saying. "It was quite a popular spot. But I suppose Madame Donadieu's cooking had everything to do with that. That's a shame, too, that you mustn't have tasted anything from her menu. You missed something, there! But you say you'll be offering meals? Do you intend to cook, then? Or maybe you, large sir?"

Checker laughed, shaking his head. "No, ma'am. Mr. Wardman will be better off hiring someone for that rather than either of us giving it a try."

She looked about to speak again, and the friendly twinkle in her eye warned Dane he had to cut this short or they would be here until nightfall.

"I wonder if we could talk to you—or someone—about doing some work at the tea shop?"

"Oh? Work, there? But the building is barely a few years old! I'm sure you'll find it in good order. My husband and sons all helped on the building itself, and created every stick of furniture inside."

"Yes, I'm sure it's in good condition. But I wanted to make some changes, since it'll no longer be catering to tea drinkers."

She grinned again, and he welcomed that. It was better than a suspicious frown, which he'd prepared himself for. "I suppose it does offer a bit more femininity than most places. Madame Donadieu decorated it herself, and all of the women here in Cranbury took to it right away. I suppose if you want to draw families, well, fathers, you might want to tone down some of the flowers." Then she laughed, as if enjoying her own wit.

Dane joined in, knowing this woman hadn't a clue about what he had in mind for the place.

"What sort of remodeling did you plan, then?" she asked. "I can recommend a couple of young men in town who can peel that wallpaper, or paint."

"We'd like that, Mrs. Levick," he said. "And more. We wanted a new countertop installed along one wall. It would take a bit of craftsmanship, but seeing what you offer here, I'm sure whoever created this inventory is up to the job."

"Why, thank you," she said, eyes still happy. "It's always nice to hear our quality is appreciated, especially from a new perspective. Oh! But you're not really a newcomer, then, are you, Dane? Our family made your dining room table and—let's see—a dozen or so chairs to match, if I remember correctly. And a few other items, too, but I can't recall exactly."

He had no idea that long dining room table wasn't from Williamsport. He'd have been impressed if his annoyance wasn't growing over the length of this little visit.

"So, Mrs. Levick," he said gently, "should we arrange for someone to come to the shop for an idea of what I'd like? Measurements? Consult on a design?"

"Oh, sure," she said, but then grew more serious. "A counter, you say? To display something? Cakes, maybe?"

A subtle intake of breath behind him warned Dane that Checker was holding back a laugh. "I'm thinking more along the lines of a . . . a beverage bar. With stools, maybe a kickbar at the base." And spittoons, but he didn't add that detail; they would, after all, be made of brass, not wood.

If it were possible, Mrs. Levick's eyes went even brighter. "Oh, now won't the youngsters like that! A soda shop! And ice cream? Cranbury will have its very own ice cream parlor?"

That was all he needed, rumors starting about how he was going to offer ice cream. Dane held up a palm. "No, Mrs. Levick. No ice cream. We'll be catering mostly to adults. But I do want to offer counter service. Can your business take my order?"

Some of the sparkle left her blue eyes, but nonetheless she nodded. "My husband isn't taking on too many orders himself anymore, all our grandkids are keeping him busy. But my sons can handle any job made of wood, I guarantee that. Wait right here, and I'll see who's in the back."

She headed to a rear door, and Dane avoided looking at Checker for fear either one of them would burst into laughter.

CHAPTER 9

*M*eli woke well before sunrise, as usual. Groggy at first, she stretched and wiggled her fingers and toes, ending as she always did by feeling for the ring she so often wore. Suddenly she sat upright. It was gone. The ring her mother had worn all her married life was no longer on Meli's hand. She gasped, trying to recall the last time she was sure it was in place.

Then she remembered. She'd taken it off to scrub Madame's kitchen. If the new owner hadn't found it, it was likely still there. She must go back for it—before it was discovered either when the owner took possession, or Madame's daughter hired someone to finish what Meli had left undone. Even if they had no desire to keep it for themselves, how would anyone know it was hers?

The sun wasn't yet at the horizon, offering no more than a dim glow of its presence as Meli hiked through the forest. Night hunters were already bedding down for the day ahead, and only the earliest birds were starting to peep. She heard the high-pitched call of a pine warbler, the short chirp of a cardinal, the coo of a mourning dove. None seemed to mind her passage through their territory, though that was likely because she hadn't a hawk perched on her arm.

She hesitated at the edge of the forest, spying her target. No sign of occupancy; no windows had been left open to allow cool night air to flow inside. Quietly, she circled around to the front. The curtains upstairs in the two bedrooms weren't even pulled, suggesting no one had wanted to keep out the impending morning light.

Encouraged, Meli went around again, passing Madame's garden. Stepping closer to the back door, she eyed the loose brick on the nearby chimney that hid the key. Madame had instructed the builder to install the hiding place, and until yesterday only the builder himself, Irene and Meli remained to know about it. Meli conceded that although Claudette hadn't been shown where the key was hidden, if she'd searched hard enough in the area Meli had indicated, she likely would have removed it.

Meli wiggled the brick from its spot. There, left as securely as usual, was the key. Meli snatched it up, unlocked the door, returned the key to its hiding place, then let herself inside.

In the dim light of dawn, Meli could see—and smell—that very little had been done since she'd left yesterday. The broom had been picked up, and the second bucket filled with refuse had been emptied, but the icebox door was still open, the vinegar-soaked rag she'd used was left in a wad upon the counter. The last pile of now over-ripe vegetables waited to be taken away.

She walked past it all, going to the counter next to the icebox. Shadows darkened the area, so she ran her hand along the edge where she was sure she'd left her mother's ring.

Nothing.

Her heart began to pound, but Meli calmed herself by looking on the other side of the icebox. Finding nothing there, either, she went down on her knees and ran her palms over the floor. She wished she were bold enough to light the room, but knew she wasn't the only early riser in town. She had no real right to be here and wouldn't risk drawing attention.

Leaning back on her knees, Meli nearly cried. It *had* to be here!

This was where she'd taken it off, she was sure of it. She reached out again, along the bottom of the icebox, thinking perhaps the ring had rolled beyond her search.

A creak from the staircase halted her movement, though she'd barely made a sound. Then silence. She remained crouched, hidden between the icebox and work table. Perhaps she'd imagined whatever she'd heard.

But then she knew she hadn't, because it sounded again. Footsteps on the treads, nearing the bottom. Meli eyed the door; she'd closed it for fear of anyone from the road passing by and seeing it ajar. Could she make a run for it before . . .?

Meli darted. It was her only chance.

But strong arms caught her before she could make her escape.

DANE HELD FAST to the squirming intruder, thinking at first it was a boy looking for mischief, albeit at a very odd hour. But upon closer look he realized the dark hair—though pulled back in a tail, was too long—and the figure twisting beneath his hands far too soft in spite of its slightness. He let go with that realization, momentarily embarrassed for both of them. But he still beat her to the door after allowing her freedom, and barred her way.

"Who are—" Then the faint ray of morning light making its way through the single window shone on her face. "You! I didn't think I'd be seeing you again, the way you took off yesterday."

She was considerably shorter than he was and for the strangest moment he wondered how comical she would look standing beside Checker. Same species, but in vastly contrasting bodies. Just now she looked fairly irate, shifting her meager weight from one foot to the other, fists clenched, both signs of readiness to fight since fleeing hadn't worked. He might not be as big as Checker, but Dane figured he could wrest her flight in less than a couple of seconds—and this time, knowing whom he was touching, he'd enjoy it.

"Let me out." Her demand was softly spoken, without eye contact.

Curiosity made him ignore her request. "What are you doing here?"

No sooner had the question been asked than he already knew the answer. Checker had found a ring on the counter yesterday, and had offered it to Dane with the suggestion to return it to the building's owner. But even then, Dane had doubted it was Claudette's. It was small and dainty. Although it was gold with a tiny diamond imbedded in it, it seemed far too modest a piece compared to the gaudy ring, necklace and earrings Claudette had displayed on the two occasions he'd seen her.

He said nothing, because even now this beautiful young woman was nursing that same look in her eye he'd caught yesterday. More than mistrust of a stranger, deeper than simple dislike for men in general, even bolder than wariness of an intruder against an owner. No, what he saw in her eyes right now was pure hatred. Not even Ethel, in her wildest mood, had ever looked at him in such a coldhearted way. Did this girl hate everyone, or was he the only unfortunate one inspiring those lovely, pale blue eyes to cast such venom?

She hadn't answered his question, but since he no longer needed an answer, he decided to ask another. He'd find out why this woman had judged him so harshly, one way or another.

"What's your name?"

Again, no answer.

"Mine is Dane," he said. "Dane Wardman."

Now she glared at him harder. "I already know that."

The way she'd ground out the words hinted that he was, indeed, the sole recipient of her wrath. What he'd done to deserve this was as much an enigma as it was a challenge. But he'd tamed Ethel, hadn't he?

"If you know my name," he began, infusing all his charm into both words and smile, "isn't it only fair for me to know yours? Especially since we'll be neighbors now that I've moved in upstairs?"

She remained mute.

"I take it you must have worked here when it was a tea shop," he went on, ignoring her ire, ignoring his own bare feet and half-opened night shirt over the trousers he'd slipped on when he'd thought he'd heard, of all things, the sound of a brick rubbing against another brick. Then, more shocking than that, someone moving inside the kitchen. "I wanted to thank you for cleaning up, or starting to, before we frightened you off."

Her eyes grew colder. "I wasn't frightened."

"Oh, good!" He was pleased by that, even though he could tell she wasn't afraid of him now, either, despite their absolute privacy, the hour, and the dim light. Checker had stayed at the inn, because despite two bedrooms upstairs, there was only one bed. "That's one less thing to worry about, that you might be afraid of me. Tell me, would you like to work here? Finish what you started, then continue on when I reopen the place? I'm looking for cooks, servers, dishwashers. The works."

"No." The single word was swift and sure. "Now step aside."

"Well, can you answer a couple of questions first? You did work here, didn't you?"

She nodded, but that first concession to actual participation in their conversation was accompanied by folding her arms in a sure sign of self-protection.

"Someone was telling me at the inn that a few of the meals served here would be especially missed. I found a stack of recipes upstairs that I assume belonged to the previous owner. If you won't work here, maybe you'd have some advice for the cook I hire. About how the previous owner made certain dishes? Just so the town can still enjoy a favorite meal or two? You know, you could be a sort of . . ." He searched for a word. "Consultant?"

"Dane Wardman," she'd finally said his name, but the hiss behind it erased any enjoyment at hearing it from her lips. "I wouldn't help you succeed if you were the only business in town. Now let me out of here."

"Hmm," he said, leaning casually against the doorjamb now, still in her way. "I'm sensing you don't like me very much. Care to tell me why?"

"The fact that you don't know, that you don't remember, only —oooh! Let me out!"

She tried to lunge past him since he'd raised one of his arms, opening a pathway to the doorknob, but once again he was faster, and closer, to her target.

"Remember what?" he asked, more earnest now, because he truly wanted to know. He'd had a few dalliances with girls from Cranbury's church before going off to college, much to his mother's dismay. And of course there had been a couple of house maids he'd flirted with—besides Lollie, who really had had her way with him rather than the other way around. Surely he hadn't left this girl brokenhearted? He'd have remembered *that* face. And why would he even have stopped flirting with someone so pretty, anyway? A face like that could have inspired him to stay in the area, even propose to someone his mother would likely have thought totally unsuitable, even if she was local.

But she was so angry he doubted she'd ever held a soft spot for him, leaving him unsure how to pose his next question. Making unwanted advances, if that was what she thought, just wasn't something he would do—he always looked for interest first.

But sharp pain in his shin stopped his musing. She'd kicked him!

He bent over to rub at the offended limb but in doing so his chin met her knee. He'd been assaulted by drunkards and bad losers at cards, and once by a woman who'd been so inebriated she'd hit him instead of the man beside him who had the good sense to duck. But never once had someone so small and unintimidating risked the sort of chance she'd just taken. How could she know he wouldn't hit back?

She attempted to push him aside now that he was still bent over, but he righted himself and took her by the shoulders to hold her steady, more for his own protection than hers.

"Look," he said, breathing harder than he'd been a moment ago, "I don't know what you have against me, but listen to me right now. I won't touch you, and you won't touch me. From this moment on, forever and ever. A pact. Agreed?"

"Oh, it's a pact, all right. I wouldn't let you touch me if you—"

He nodded. "Let me guess: if I were the last man in Cranbury."

"If you'd have let me go from the start, I wouldn't have touched you at all."

He lifted his hands, holding out both palms. "All right. I was just trying to be neighborly. Go, then."

He stepped aside, and she was gone in an instant, disappearing into the woods before he'd even closed the door behind her.

CHAPTER 10

*T*he sound of sawing and hammering brightened Dane's spirits, despite his sleep having been cut short by his early morning visitor. He'd been downright glum since his near-dawn interchange with the girl. Even the return of her ring probably wouldn't have changed her mind about him—but how was he supposed to give it back now without knowing how to find her? He didn't even know her name. He decided he would keep an eye out for her rather than ask around. If her hostility for him was as deep and permanent as it appeared, he doubted she'd welcome hearing that he was asking about her.

The Levick brothers—Leo, Brom and Cade, the latter being the toymaker Dane had heard about—had agreed to start work on renovations right away, considering the bonus Dane was willing to pay. Leo had said something about looking forward to bringing one of his kids to the place once it was finished, giving away what they must believe from their mother about installing a soda bar. Dane was sure whatever disappointment Leo might feel on his young son's behalf probably wouldn't last long. Not in light of the fact that this town was finally going to offer some entertainment for its grown men.

Dane left the restaurant, planning to find Checker and the Cranbury Canary to take them to Williamsport. Today, he would start his search for cooks and a wait staff. For that, he would consult Jennie-On-The-Spot, Domestic Employment Services. Lollie had told him they had plenty of Johnny's, too, not just maids and female cooks. Dane figured he should probably hire more men than women, even if Checker did take the place of two or three men. A chef, he decided, instead of a female cook. Waiters rather than waitresses. Such a staff might tip off anyone paying attention as to the kind of customers Dane hoped to attract, but there was nothing to be done about impending rumors. They were bound to figure out what he was up to sooner or later.

Checker was already waiting for him just outside the Canary stable.

"The inn has a motorcar we might've hired," Checker said, adding with a shake of his head at Dane's instant look of interest, "but it's in need of repair."

Dane wasn't surprised. Most motorcars could be depended upon for one thing: the need for a good mechanic.

They were soon on their way, a man behind the reins Dane remembered as old even back when he was a kid. Dane didn't recall his name. Something that started with a T. Tummy? No, that was a name Dane would probably recall for the jokes he would've have used. Tumor? No, that was equally memorable, if only for slightly less humorous jesting.

"So I was asking around, like you suggested," Checker said, jumping into the last serious conversation they'd shared as if it had been minutes ago. "Turns out there is some kind of supply already around here, but mum's been the word so far when it comes to how to make a purchase."

"Hmm. No clue as to where to go?"

"At first they recommended Williamsport and any one of the pubs already established, don't ya know." Then he winked. "But another guest at the inn quietly suggested I might try a Mr. Packham, a farmer 'bout a mile up the road. Says he's got a way of supplying such things to those who want more than a cherry cordial."

"Packham, huh?" The name didn't sound familiar to Dane. "Which direction?"

"On our way."

Dane tapped on the front end of the Canary, speaking loud enough for Mr. Tumor-or-whatever-was-his-name to hear. "Do you know the Packham farm?"

Mr. Tummy nodded.

"Mind if we stop there on our way? If you can spare the time."

That garnered a look from the man. Dane wasn't sure what sparked the upturned brow, but guessed it wasn't because of a delay in getting to Williamsport. More likely he knew the kind of business Dane wished to investigate at the Packham place. Anyway, it was worth the scrutiny and potential rumors if Packham's inventory was whispered positively around town.

Far better to invite collaboration than to start a whiskey war.

Less than ten minutes later, Dane eyed the man who came out to the porch after inquiring if Dane was in the right place to purchase whiskey. Mr. Packham walked with a limp—a familiar one, judging by the relative ease with which he traversed the wooden-planked verandah. He had the gray hair to go along with the gait, but those were the only two things suggesting the man's age. Otherwise he was trim at the waist, well-muscled, evidenced by the width of his shoulders and brawny forearms extending past his rolled-up sleeves. Sleeves, Dane noted, that were made either by an extremely talented family seamstress or the man had sent away for the same kind of tailor-made shirts Dane and every Wardman had been wearing for decades.

After looking past Dane, first this way then that, he looked Dane up, then down. "I don't usually sell out of my house. The local folks'd come after my hide if I did."

Dane exchanged glances with Checker but Dane just winked at

Checker's frown. Perhaps Packham hadn't used any charm to sell his goods around here, or provided the right ambiance. This could work out splendidly for both of them, if Packham's product was any good. As long as it was legal.

Dane extended a hand, which Packham took after a moment or two. "My name's Wardman. Dane Wardman. Maybe you've heard the family name, we've been around for—"

One of Packham's brows had already lifted. "Oh, I've heard the name, all right. And if you're the young one, I already know you have a place in Philly." He folded his arms across his chest. "Tried selling my supply to you round 'bout two or three years ago. Had high hopes of expanding my trade, you having a city bar and all, and me coming from your own home town. I was told you didn't buy from moonshiners. I ain't one, by the way, but just the same I was sent off pretty quick. Surprised to see you now."

Dane tried to recall if he'd ever seen the man before, but nothing came to mind. Another glance to Checker said he didn't remember the man, either. It didn't matter; Dane had been careful about his liquor orders, particularly during that first year when a Philly distillery had helped Dane finance his costs if he'd sell only their whiskey.

Dane smiled broadly. "Well, then, the timing might not have been right back then, but today's a new day. I'm opening a place right here in Cranbury, and maybe we can take your supply now. If it's any good, that is? I'd like to sample the quality, of course."

He'd had to add that, despite the man's already sour impression of him. No sense letting the man think his age and experience outweighed Dane's youth and perceived snub at turning him down in the past.

"Oh, it's good, all right. The recipe's been handed down a hundred years, and only better for it." He still hadn't unfolded the barrier he'd made of his massive forearms. "The town know you're gonna sell whiskey 'round here?"

"Not exactly, not yet. I'm taking over the empty tea room."

Now those arms parted, but only to make way for the huge laugh that bubbled out of his chest. "Oh, that's a good one, young fella! Who are you, really? Somebody who's heard 'bout the Wardman family name and just stopped by for a nip or two? A sample, you said! Free, I suppose." He laughed again, then started to turn back to his door.

"No, sir. I *am* Dane Wardman, and I did have a bar in Philly. The *Peacock*, if you say you were there and recall the name. I've moved back here, and just signed a lease with the daughter who inherited the Cranbury tea room. I'm already making plans to renovate the place into something for men's company over real refreshment, not tea."

Although the man had halted his uneven steps back to the door, he was still frowning.

"Look," Dane went on, "I can just as cheaply order spirits from my old suppliers. I just thought I'd try the local brand first. As a courtesy."

That had Packham rub the back of his neck, as if he were considering something Dane hadn't thought of. What could be so hard about supplying a local place? Wouldn't it be easy to transport his goods just up the road instead of wherever he was taking it now?

"You come on in, young fella," he said. "I'll give you that nip and won't charge you, either. But darned if I know how you're gonna get that town to let you do what you're plannin' to do. I can save you some heartache by telling you to move on, 'cause they won't have it. They been trying to get ridda' me and my family for a hundred years." He led the way inside, talking all the while. "I ain't no moonshiner, though that's how they labeled me and my father before me. I have a license to sell, and a receipt for my paid-up-to-date excise taxes, too. I'm all set and legal according to the United States Government, though that government is about the same as a thief, the way they keep raisin' the taxes. But accordin' to those teetotalers in town, I'm a villain.

There's only two reasons I ain't been shut down by hook or crook."

He stopped and turned to Dane, extending a finger to start his count. "One: I agreed not to sell here in town. Well, not so as anybody knows about it. And two: they don't know where I make it." He shook his head, grumbling. "Why, if they knew my spot I think one of 'em would sneak in past my dogs and blow up the whole thing. They'd blame it on a faulty still and not a one of 'em would tell the truth, nor look for the truth neither. I had to show the excise man my operation, so's they could tax me fair, but I don't hand over a dime 'til he swears never to tell the location. I follow him out of town so I know he's not talkin'."

With that, Packham opened his front door and let all three of them inside. He was still murmuring, something about a third reason, but if he said it aloud Dane couldn't tell. Perhaps the man partook of his own product?

Already curious about the house, judging from the quality of Packham's clothing, Dane looked around the parlor. With every dropped 'g' or other assault Packham had waged against the grammar of their shared language, Dane had expected the fine clothing to be nothing more than an anomaly. Perhaps explained away by a persnickety wife who insisted they present themselves far above the station of a moonshiner or farmer living along the hills and trees that time hadn't quite caught up to yet.

But the parlor glistened, with furniture as fine as any Dane had grown up among. Surely there was a woman in the family, judging by the doilies on the sofa and chairs, the knick-knacks here and there, though there was no sign of anyone else at home.

Packham went to a sideboard where a crystal decanter and half-a-dozen glasses waited. He poured two drinks and handed one to Checker, one to Dane. Without ceremony nor any semblance of a toast, while Checker downed his, Dane sniffed what was in his glass. Vaguely cereal, like the grain it came from. A hint of pear from whatever process he used; wood smoke from the barrel it had been aged in, for however short or long this man allowed.

Dane looked at Checker, whose brows had already risen as if more shocked than surprised. His accompanying wide eyes hinted the shock was a pleasant one. Dane swallowed the contents in his glass all in one, just as Checker had. Smooth warmth, a touch of smoky sweetness. An aftertaste that blossomed, demanding more.

Now Dane raised his brows. "I can tell you this, Packham. If I'd have tasted your stock that time you visited me in Philly, I'd have found a way to carry your brand. This is good. Very good."

The man shrugged. "You ain't sayin' anything I didn't know already. Was your loss, not mine."

Dane wasn't quite convinced the man had so easily forgotten the snub, but if Dane's Cranbury saloon was the success Dane expected it to be, any hard feelings would soon be a distant memory. Especially if the man's wife liked the fine things currently filling their relatively modest home.

CHAPTER 11

$\mathcal{M}$eli breathed in deeply, the late afternoon air filled with sweet earth and pine needles after yesterday's rain. Guinevere was on Meli's gloved fist as she tramped through the woods, the hooded goshawk content to go along for the ride. The hawk was in its molting season, so Meli wouldn't fly her free. Instead, she kept her well fed so her weight was a little heavy, ensuring her replacement feathers would be strong while making it too difficult to comfortably fly. Rather than leave her in the mew day after day, Meli took her for regular jaunts through the woods. Inside Meli's fist, below Guinevere's talons, was a portion of chicken breast. She allowed Guinevere to peck at it during intervals when Meli stopped to take off the hawk's hood, encouraging the pleasure of eating with the removal and replacement of the item.

Stopping, in one smooth movement she pulled the leather covering from the raptor's eyes. Meli let Guinevere look at the meat below, take a swipe at it, before Meli replaced the hood again.

The hawk had been trained by Meli's mother some ten years ago, and was familiar with all the seasons they'd spent together.

Her underbelly was mottled, a blend of white and caramel stain. A slate gray cap stood above white eyebrows while red eyes stared at Meli. She always seemed to be saying: "You'll do. I prefer my first human, your mother, but you'll do."

Meli started walking again, a now-familiar hymn coming to mind. Guinevere liked her singing, Meli knew that from when she sang in the mews. The hawk's eyes would narrow and grow contented, so Meli knew that next to a full belly or flying free, music was practically all this hawk enjoyed.

> All the way my Savior leads me;
> what have I to ask beside?
> Can I doubt His tender mercy,
> who thro' life has been my guide?

This was all that was good about no longer working at the tea room, the time Meli now spent with her birds and the orphans she cared for. Perhaps she would hunt for another, younger bird or adopt one from a nest. Her mother had shown her how to trap young fledgings. When Meli was seven she'd followed along for the first time, but had cried when Mother had taken one of the young hawks away from its parents. Her mother told her the other young ones left behind would be better cared for, because she'd chosen a nest with a clutch of four—often too many for parents to care for well. Besides, eventually the siblings would spot weakness in one of them, and crowd one out until it starved. The young bird they spirited away would grow up healthy and well-trained, safe from hunters who were encouraged to shoot goshawks, Cooper's hawks and sharp-shins because they were prone to invading poultry farms.

> Heavenly peace, divinest comfort,
> here by faith in Him to dwell!
> For I know, whatever befall me,

Jesus doeth all things well.

She'd returned to church this past Sunday and sat beside Essie, who was as friendly as ever. Although Meli hadn't expected to linger, she had heard what everyone talked about the minute the service ended: the new restaurant that would take the place of the tea room. She'd stayed long enough to overhear myriad guesses about the type of food that would be served, how the bar that the Levick brothers were building would serve soda and maybe—not right away, since he'd denied it—ice cream, too. The fact that the new owner, or renter, it was rumored, didn't attend Sunday service was of some concern. But someone said it was too early to judge why he and his giant friend hadn't attended during this, the first full Sunday they'd been in town.

The most surprising news had come from Irene, who had singled out Meli to let her know she was keeping her Sunday afternoon job at the Wardman house but taking another job at the new restaurant as a dishwasher again.

"I figured he'd need a staff," she'd told Meli before she'd hurried off after the service, "so I went to the employment agency —I knew just the one he'd use, knowing which one is the Wardman's favorite. They told me they wanted men, not women, but I got the job anyway. I might only be doing dishes for now, but who cares, with the wages he'll pay? I shouldn't care about what kind of restaurant he plans to open, either, should I? It's none of my business. Gracious, he's planning to pay even more than what his folks pay my sister, and I'll only have to work a few hours in the evening. Besides all that, he's more than a little easy on the eyes!"

Meli had wanted to ask why Irene shouldn't care about the type of restaurant, but that last phrase had blotted out the rest. A handsome façade was nothing compared to a rotten core. He was a falcon killer! She was willing to concede that he might not have known her bird was something she'd bonded with, spent years training. And the irony did rankle about her kestrel's connection to hunting. But since Meli, like most others she knew, didn't limit herself to eating only vegetables, the idea of consuming meat was something to take up with God Himself.

But to kill anything for sport was harder to accept. There was no contest between a falcon and a rifle in the hands of a foolish boy. Visions of training Guinevere, who was a much larger hawk, for a revenge attack had brought a smile to Meli's face when she was younger, even if she had felt guilty afterward. Hawks were birds of prey, but God hadn't designed them to go after men—well, at least when they weren't trying to invade a nest.

She heard the rustle of underbrush and stopped. Guinevere, too, stiffened, either in reaction to the sound or to Meli. Even limited by the hood, the hawk cocked her head side to side, front to back, depending on her hearing alone to determine whether or not to become alarmed. Meli looked around. Maybe it was Essie again, taking pictures. She'd asked on Sunday if she might take snapshots of Meli and her hawks, but had agreed to schedule that in the fall when her two birds were finished molting.

Seeing no one and hearing no further noise, Meli kept walking. She hadn't wanted to be out long today. Dad had set off later than usual on another of his own forest jaunts, and she decided she would surprise him and have dinner waiting by the time he returned.

DANE KEPT STILL behind the massive trunk of an ancient oak tree. It was her—carrying a hawk. A goshawk! That little slip of a girl—well, woman—wasn't intimidated in the least by a bird that relished killing.

Dane had expected, or at least hoped, to come across a falconer on one of his daily hunts through the woods. There was a breeding ground not far away, so it was natural to assume there were a few falconers in the area. He'd told himself these daily hikes were to reacquaint himself with the forest, this wooded spot he'd known so well as a child.

But Dane couldn't ignore the other, underlying reason he'd wanted to come back. He wanted to know if the owner of the bird that had left an indelible memory was still here, after all these years. He'd even guessed that, whoever that falconer had been so long ago, would be a woman now. While he'd been chased on that awful day, he'd barely glanced back. He'd known by the dark hair flying behind her, the light step, the slight build, that it had been a girl. A girl who'd flown small birds of prey.

He hadn't expected it to be *her*.

Why did it have to be her? Why couldn't this one memory that had changed so many things in his life been attached to some withered old witch-like creature, the kind he'd designed in his mind who was ugly and cruel to anyone but the birds she'd bewitched? What other kind of woman—girl, at the time!—was brave enough, or mad enough, to work with birds of prey, a bird that could snap either one of her spindly arms?

He'd still have regretted killing a trained bird, even for the five-dollar bounty he'd been foolish enough to let inspire the act that day. But at least he wouldn't have cared much about being forgiven if the person really was mad as a hatter. Maybe it shouldn't make a difference now, but somehow knowing he'd killed the bird belonging to this particular girl made it that much worse.

There was only one thing to do. He followed her.

CHAPTER 12

*M*eli returned Guinevere to the mew, then went to the barn. Dad kept only a couple of horses, a cow, and several goats—the pigs and chickens had their own dwellings —but she passed all of those stalls. Dad had long ago sectioned off one generous corner for Meli's orphans.

Over the years she'd taken in abandoned ducklings, squirrels, bunnies, and songbirds. She'd needed a spot well out of sight and sound of her raptors; no sense igniting instincts from either side of the hunting spectrum. Besides, she never kept a rescued baby long. She didn't want them to forget their own kind—something she helped along with mirrors in the cages and a puppet or two from which to offer food, disguising her hand as the mother of one kind or another. There was something satisfying in saving small animals, even though she knew her hawks or others in the wild would devour any one of them given the chance.

She would let her two squirrels go soon. The siblings had fallen from a nest that must have blown down in one of the gustier spring wind storms. Even though she'd placed the pups in a padded box at the base of the tree and sat vigil for the mother to return—making sure nothing else found them instead—the mother had never come back. She'd either been killed in the storm or been the meal of a raptor or other creature roaming these woods.

The squirrels had been old enough to go outside for a few days now, getting used to what would soon be their natural surroundings. Their eyes were wide open, and they were fully furred without a trace of the fleas she'd found on them. Vinegar and water had aided her in removing the unwanted vermin. They'd already weaned themselves from the cow's milk she'd given them and were learning to forage vegetables from their garden.

Picking up their cage, Meli made her way back outside. She and Dad had planted a second, smaller garden, this one intended only for her orphans. It, too, was fenced, but not to keep animals out—this one was designed to keep her orphans in, at least until they were old enough to be released back to the wild. Between the widely placed knee-high white pickets and the chicken wire in between, it was secure for nearly all of her little critters—since she never left them inside long enough to dig, wiggle or chew their way out.

"I know who you are now."

The voice startled her. She stopped, still gripping the handle of the cage, and considered ignoring the words because she knew instantly to whom the voice belonged. How *dare* he come here? After what he did?

"And I know why you hate me."

Even that did not inspire her to turn to him. She guessed he was a dozen feet away, or less. Had he been waiting until she came out of the barn? Had he followed her from the woods? Had he watched her return Guinevere to the mew? Just how long *had* he been watching her? Maybe he'd been the noise in the forest she and Guinevere had heard.

She continued walking, without looking back.

Unfortunately, she heard his footsteps approaching, not receding. Beyond the two gardens was the back of the house, and next to it the lane leading to the road. There was neither horse nor buggy nor the town's Canary anywhere in sight, nor even one of those horseless carriages like the Packham's owned. Her unwanted visitor had come on foot. Surely he *had* been the noise she'd heard in the forest. He was following her!

And he'd figured out why she hated him. "Good for you," she said at last, without a trace of satisfaction. She wished the squirrel siblings weren't keeping her outside. She would prefer to keep walking, let herself inside her home—not without slamming the door behind her.

"I didn't know," he said, his voice quieter now. He was just a couple of feet away.

Finally she turned to him, rigid, allowing only a quick glance his way. "You didn't know what, Dane Wardman? That the falcon you shot wasn't just any old bird? That a boy with a gun isn't a fair match for a bird, even a predator?"

To her surprise, the look on his face went sorrowful. But she didn't recant her words, because the person she'd hated all these years was capable of acting in any way that served him. Not for one moment did she consider the word that ran throughout the Bible she read every day. Forgiveness—not that he'd asked for it.

"That's right." His words seemed hard to choke out. "I didn't know any of that. I was—I was shooting for a bounty."

"A bounty!" She huffed. "You're telling me you lived in the biggest house anywhere around, and you shot my bird for a few more dollars? As if you didn't have enough?"

He raised his hands, whether in supplication or frustration, she couldn't tell. "I know! But . . . my father had cut my allowance. I was trying to earn my own money."

She huffed again. With a roof over his head, the finest one within walking distance, and probably everything inside to match the outside, for what had he needed to earn money? She kept her back to him, bending over her caged squirrels.

"I wasn't a bad kid, the kid you remember," he said softly. "It was just hard for me to be good."

If he thought that explained anything, he had another think coming. How dare he try excusing what he'd done?

"Look," he said, and his face and voice were less gentle, more distant. "I have a hawk of my own now, a goshawk like yours. I plan to live at my business going forward, so I can't keep her with me, at least not at first. I'll have to get to know my customers, you know, and bring her in later if it works out. I want her to be well-cared for in the meantime, nearer to me than the city. Would you keep her here, take care of her when I can't?"

Hearing his words, she nearly dropped the cage. "You? *You* have a hawk?"

He nodded. "You might not believe me, but I am sorry about what happened. About what I did. I've been sorry ever since I did it. Once I figured out it must have been a trained bird, I learned about hawks, and eventually came to own one. She's barely a year old, healthy, well-trained for her age. Ethel, that's her name. I'll pay you to take care of her, of course."

"Where is she now?" The question came out before Meli could call it back. She didn't want to converse with this man, this killer who had taken her bird from her. And now he wanted her to take care of *his* bird? What if she did to it what he'd done to hers? That would serve him right.

But even as the horrid thought crossed her mind she knew it was ludicrous. She would never kill a hawk, not even in retaliation. Revenge was supposed to be left in God's hands anyway— although it also crossed her mind that He might forgive Dane Wardman more easily than she could.

"She's in the city," said Dane. "Well, technically just outside the city limit, in a barn with several other birds of her kind. That's partly why I think she'd be happier here than in the yard near me, even if I didn't have unpredictable customers and a busy schedule to work out first. She wouldn't be alone here."

Meli wished again she hadn't asked her question, hadn't prolonged this conversation. She wanted only to get away from him. Besides, the squirrels were restless in the confines of their protective cage while knowing freedom was at hand. Still, she couldn't help but say, "Raptors like being alone."

And so do I, she might have added, but instead turned her back on him to step inside her gated garden. She opened the cage and the squirrels scurried out, one after the other.

"But she's not used to being on her own," he said, now at the edge of the garden. Thankfully he didn't step over the gate to invade like some giant, unwanted pest. She moved closer to the center of the orphan garden to be farther from him.

"Why would you trust me with her?" Once again, she wondered at her own behavior. But she had to know the answer, even if she refused his request. Which she would certainly do.

"Why wouldn't I?" He sounded utterly baffled, then looked around, his gaze first to the squirrels then to the mews that housed the other two birds in her care. "Look at this place. It's a haven for animals. I don't think you *could* hurt a bird, even to get back at me."

She lifted one brow. "No." She held his gaze. "But I could set her free."

He returned her stare. He was at least curious, if not wary, so he must recognize what she'd intended for him to see: a warning, a dare. But then he smiled—the last expression she'd expected him to offer.

"I guess I'd just have to trust you."

DANE HOPED she couldn't tell his heart was beating faster than usual, or more importantly, that he wasn't at all sure he could follow through with his own words. *Could* he trust her? Was it worth losing Ethel if this girl wasn't worthy of that trust?

But then, almost immediately, he knew that was exactly what he needed to do. It might be the only way he could make up for what he'd done, even if she never forgave him. He had to trust her, though she had no reason to do likewise.

Still, the possibility of losing Ethel was a high price to pay. On the heel of that thought, acknowledging he'd been responsible for killing a falcon that likely had been as prized to her when she was a girl as Ethel was to him now, he still wasn't entirely sure he should take the risk.

Did he have a choice? Not if he was going to live in Cranbury with real peace. He was bound to see this girl again, and even if she didn't live in town she was bound to have friends. If others already knew what he'd done, he'd rather do what he could to erase any memory if the incident. What business owner wanted townsfolk holding a grudge against him?

Suddenly it was clear to him. The person standing in front of him had played a bigger role than he'd realized in deciding to come back; sure, he still believed all those points he'd made to Checker. Cranbury was a sleepy, boring, albeit pretty little town that could use some variety and more choice in their days—or at least for their evenings and nights. But, he could find that in any number of other little towns, ones not in such close proximity to his family with whom he was clearly not ready to reconcile. This young woman was the grownup person he'd wronged so long ago. It was one of those haunting kind of memories—one he could escape only if he made amends. Somehow.

"Well?" he prompted.

"And if I say no? What will you do then?"

"I wouldn't have much choice, would I? Tether her in my yard, since I want her nearby. She'd be alone while I work, without the forest to hide in. Come to think of it, she'd probably be easy prey. I guess I could leave her in Philly, at least until I could build a mew. I don't have time to build one yet, and I shouldn't divert my carpenters from the remodel—you know, to open my business as soon as possible." He knew he was offering the stupidest of excuses, but if he was going to get this girl to agree, he'd have to let her think she was his only option. It was true, of course, if he really did bring Ethel out here so soon, but he was also sure he would come up with some alternative if she continued to refuse him. One of the Levick brothers could probably build a mew in a day or two.

Leaving Ethel as far away as Philly was the one option he didn't want to take; even less so now that he knew of this place. Her place. "I can't leave her in Philly, even during her molt. She's still young. I don't want her to forget me."

He grinned then, the kind that usually drew a smile in return. He didn't expect one now, but he'd hoped for something other than the pinched gaze she cast his way. She was looking at him with something between pity and suspicion, he wasn't sure which. Either should rankle him, but it wouldn't be the first time he'd settle for less than he wanted in order to make a deal.

"I will take your hawk," she said firmly, "but only temporarily, until you have a place for her. You'll have to do what you said you don't have time for, and erect mews of your own. I'll take her for—"

"Six months," he finished before she could. She needn't know why he'd chosen that particular time frame.

"I was going to say a couple of weeks."

"A few weeks, a few months. What's the difference? I'll be pretty busy, opening a new business, getting it started. I don't think I can give her everything she'll need until then. Between the two of us, she should be fine until I can take her full time."

"But six months! She'll be finished molting in less than half that. You'll want to fly her often once she's in full form."

"Yes, of course. I can do that from here." He looked around at the canopy of forest surrounding this place. It had been cleared for the house, fields and outbuildings, but just beyond the trees were thick and mixed—exactly the kind Ethel preferred. "It's the perfect spot for a gos. You must think so, or you wouldn't have two of them yourself."

He could see she didn't want to agree. He decided to be even bolder. "I'd like you to think about another offer, too. A job at my new place. As a singer," he added when he saw the beginning of a head shake. "I heard you, out there." He motioned to the woods. "Do you ever sing for anybody other than your hawk?"

He grinned again because he could tell she was almost, but not quite, exasperated with him. He knew there was no chance, not even a sliver of one, for her to agree working for him. But maybe an additional request might make the one already on the table more harmless—and agreeable.

"I'll take your hawk," she said, turning her back to him again. "But I won't work for you. Not now. Not ever. Now I think it's time for you to go."

He didn't move. Instead, he watched the squirrels, one of them nibbling on a flower tip and the other at the base of a bean plant.

"Are you taming them, or going to set them free?"

"Good-bye, Mr. Wardman," she said over her shoulder.

"*Mr. Wardman?* I thought you knew my name? Dane. What's yours, by the way? I guess I could ask around, but I'd rather hear it from you."

She remained silent.

He wanted to stay; he had a thousand questions about her hawks, feeding schedule, training methods, which equipment she preferred. And how in the world had she gotten interested in falcons and hawks, anyway? Since such a young age, too? He had loved hawking only since his college years, but even then he'd known it was a desperate attempt to erase the one memory she, too, must recall too often for comfort.

Nonetheless, Dane doubted he should push his company on her any more today. He'd like to use his most tried-and-true charm on her, but that was sometimes more effective in smaller doses. With her, that was probably truer than ever.

Knowing he'd have more opportunities to thaw her toward him while she housed Ethel made him smile nearly all the way back to town. He hadn't planned to return to Philly so soon. But suddenly he couldn't collect her fast enough.

CHAPTER 13

$\mathcal{W}$ith a basket of eggs collected that morning and a roll of butter wrapped in cheesecloth tucked inside a wooden tub, Meli emerged from the woods in the same general area she always did when coming to town: not far from the tea shop.

Unlike before, she bypassed the building now. Even from the edge of the road she could hear sawing and hammering. She saw nothing of what went on inside because the once lace-curtained windows were shaded by darkly stained wooden blinds. She frowned, wondering to what extent Madame's lovely tea room would be erased.

When Meli reached the Cranbury Inn, where she planned to sell her butter and eggs, she noticed several people gathered on the porch, and a flock of children playing nearby. She hesitated, reluctant to approach the busy spot. Most were not guests at the inn, because she recognized several familiar faces as former patrons of the tea room. Arianne Prestwich and Phoebe Turner, Leta Phipps from Perkins Dress Shop, Raina Levick and the oldest Mrs. Levick, along with both Mrs. Wingate and Mrs. Taylor who ran the inn. Meli might have turned away—she could, after all,

bring her goods later when there weren't so many people around
—except Essie Taylor caught her eye, and she waved Meli closer.

"You might think we're just a bunch of gossips," Essie said,
meeting Meli at the base of the porch steps, "but we've heard
some rumors today about what kind of restaurant is opening at
the tea shop. You might want to know about it."

Meli searched the little group again, looking for Irene. Hadn't
she said something about ignoring rumors when she'd signed up
to work at the new business? But Irene was nowhere to be seen,
and all Meli could do now was wish she'd asked for more details.

Every eye had followed Essie, evidently as the leader of this
little party. Other gazes now fell on Meli, who swallowed an
uncomfortable lump, waiting for Essie to go on.

"You used to work with Irene Robinson at the tea room." It
wasn't a bid for confirmation; Essie just stated the fact and Meli
said nothing.

Essie continued. "Irene told her sister Nora that she heard—
from Dane Wardman's own mouth—he plans to sell spirits along
with those meals he's been talking about. Ardent spirits. Naturally, Nora told Leta Phipps about it when she came to town to
pick up a dress order for Mrs. Wardman. None of us here hold to
rumors, of course, so this morning Leta, Ari and I went straight to
Williamsport in search of Madame's daughter. We learned she
knows the new restaurant intends to sell wine with meals, but
didn't know about anything stronger than that. We aren't wrong
about ardent spirits, though. Just the other day, our own Mr.
Tummers said Dane Wardman stopped in for quite some time at
the Packham farm. And we all know what he makes from the
corn, barley and rye he grows."

Meli lifted her brows. Her own father raised each one of the
crops mentioned. What difference did it make?

The utter bewilderment coursing through Meli must have
shown. Judging by the surprise on their faces, she felt all the more
foolish for not knowing what they were talking about.

"He sells moonshine, Meli!" Essie said. "Well, I suppose technically it isn't moonshine because they say he doesn't shoo off the revenuers when they come around to collect the excise taxes. But his biggest source of income is whiskey, which we've all guessed is how he can afford to hire so much help to run that farm of his and buy all that fancy equipment. And a motorcar!"

"Not to mention the way Rita dresses," piped up the eldest Mrs. Taylor, and Mrs. Wingate next to her nodded and added, "Al John has a truck, besides that car Rita takes on those winter vacations. How does he afford all that, if not from whiskey?"

Meli almost volunteered that her father worked with the Packhams during both planting and harvest, and that he, too, afforded to bring in plenty of help during those two busy seasons. Dad had even mentioned buying a truck, though so far he'd not followed through. All it meant was that they were successful farmers, practicing prudence in some things to make way for extravagance in others.

But she said nothing, for the first time not wanting her father to be connected so closely to the Packhams—which wasn't hard to do, since neither family mixed with townsfolk. Who would know one way or the other? She shrugged off the shame of it; she'd never counted the Packham family as friends, yet their cooperative farming spelled some kind of connection.

"We're guessing the new owner of the tea room must plan to sell Mr. Packham's moonshine to customers," Essie finished. "What other reason could he have had to visit the Packham farm? They're not exactly the friendliest folk, so it wasn't likely a social call."

Mrs. Taylor stepped closer to the railing, overlooking where Meli and Essie stood. "We've tried for years to stop the Packhams from making such a thing altogether. But it never worked, so we've tried to look the other way since he sells his goods in Williamsport. But now he plans to sell it right here in Cranbury, and we won't have it."

"I thought my boys were building that bar to serve sodas!" cried old Mrs. Levick. "I suppose he did say he wouldn't be serving ice cream, but I thought soda was the aim. And maybe someday, if the soda bar worked, ice cream is a natural addition. Goodness, I have half a mind to tell them to rip it right out of there, no matter that I'm sure they're doing a good job."

Meli had never guessed Mr. Packham made and sold liquor. She wondered if Dad knew. At the same time, Meli had just discovered the answer to a mystery she'd grown up with. Little wonder the Packhams kept so isolated; evidently if they issued an invitation for supper to anyone from Cranbury, the answer would be a flat-out refusal. Because of moonshine!

She'd never really thought about such a thing before, why alcohol and anyone associated with it should be condemned. But vague recollections of ads in *Ladies Home Journal* Madame had once subscribed to about the evils of ardent spirits might explain why these women believed spirits to be dangerous. Meli had never pondered it.

But she had just discovered two more things. The first was an unexpected taste of community in having been taken into this circle of women. She'd never guessed it could be so complex, hiding her guilt about surely being the only one who'd seen the Packham's parlor, if only because her father was there discussing how best to share equipment.

The second fact wriggled through that residue of guilt: All these women were against the one man she hated. The man who planned to sell liquor, even if it was made here in Cranbury. Those two facts gave her all the courage she needed to speak up.

"What can be done about it?"

"For starters," Raina Levick said, "I'm going to ask my husband and brothers-in-law to stop working over there."

Mrs. Levick, behind her, nodded along. "We're waiting until this evening to talk to them, when we're all having dinner together."

"But in the meantime," said Arianne Prestwich, "Leta and I will visit the Temperance League in Williamsport, this very afternoon, to see what we can do. Mrs. Taylor told us about pledge sheets asking for signatures promising abstinence from any form of liquor."

"Someone tried starting a Temperance League here in town years ago, back when we all found out about Packham's still." Mrs. Taylor sighed. "The league petered out because the whole town stuck together against the idea of drunkenness. Everyone agreed he wasn't to peddle his poison around here, so the meetings just sort of went extinct."

"What's to stop us from proving this town hasn't changed?" Mrs. Prestwich asked. "I'm sure Mr. Pillifant will print pledge forms, and I'll supply the paper free of charge. If there aren't any customers for this so-called *restaurant*, seeing how we don't buy Packham's whiskey, that'll put an end to this whole thing before it even begins."

Meli nodded along, her support so thoroughly saturated in the desire to see the last of Dane Wardman that her courage didn't waver, not even under continued attention that came with speaking up again. "I'll help in any way I can," she said. "Madame may have cooked with a bit of wine now and then, she was from France, after all. But she would be horrified that her beloved tea room might turn into a—" She stopped, searching for how to name the kind of place these women were obviously trying to prevent from invading their little town. No word came to mind. "Such a place."

"We feel exactly the same," said Essie, looping one of her arms with Meli's. "Who knows what else will come with spirits? You all know my husband can tell you how criminals operated those kinds of places in New York. Once he finds out he'll be preaching the topic on Sunday, I can tell you that!"

Meli couldn't be more pleased. Maybe Dane Wardman would be run out of town! If so, it couldn't happen soon enough.

~

DANE DISEMBARKED from the train at the Williamsport station, carrying the crate he'd traveled with all the way from Philly. The goshawk had been calm the entire trip, aided as she was by a full belly and snug hood within the confines of a familiar holder. A few fellow travelers had asked to peer through the crate slats, which Dane didn't mind. He only discouraged unwary children attempting to stick their fingers inside.

As he left the station he welcomed the fresh air and sunshine, for the first time feeling as though he were coming home. Bringing Ethel helped make it seem so; she was, after all, the only possession he cared to transfer to this new version of his old life back in the country.

He scanned the road just outside the station, looking for a familiar yellow carriage. Tummers, he'd finally recalled the driver's name correctly, was indeed there, somewhat down the way. To Dane's surprise, he wasn't alone. On the other side of the Herdic carriage stood the figure few could ignore any easier than Dane's cage. Checker.

Shifting the satchel with Ethel's equipment more securely on his shoulder, still gripping the cage with his other hand, Dane stepped more lively toward the waiting pair.

"Well, I didn't expect you to greet me," Dane said to his gargantuan friend. He'd been about to make light of it, but the solemn look on Checker's face barred any jest. "Something wrong?"

"Only the first hint of a temperance riot," cut in Tummers, his voice high pitched and excited. "You've got trouble, mister, and you better do something about it. Now let's get."

Dane frowned, but spared only a glance to Tummers before looking again at Checker. Tummers was already moving toward the seat atop his coach. But he stopped, evidently hearing what Dane did just then: the flutter of Ethel's wing from inside the covered crate. "What in the name of all that's holy is in there?"

"A goshawk," Dane answered automatically. He'd normally want to show off the bird, especially since Tummers was a Cranburian and therefore would have to get used to having Ethel around. Dane still didn't know the name of Ethel's future caretaker, which continued to irritate him. Maybe Checker had found out.

But frustration replaced that thought, wanting to hear details of what the two were warning him about.

Tummers' scowl had deepened, if that were possible. "You know, those things aren't exactly welcome around farm country. Not to anybody with chickens, anyhow. What'd you bring that thing out here for?"

"She won't be the only goshawk in the area," Dane said, handing Checker the satchel but keeping Ethel's crate as they walked around to the back entrance of the carriage.

"Well, of course those pesky birds nest around here," Tummers called after him. "Which is why we don't need another one."

"She's trained, and I plan to keep her well cared for. Fed from birds I pay for."

Dane didn't respond to the older man's further grumblings. While Tummers boarded the driver's seat, Dane followed Checker into the carriage. He placed Ethel's crate on the seat next to his.

"So what's going on?" he asked Checker, already dismissing Tummers' cautions about his hawk.

Checker leaned forward from the opposite seat. "I was at the inn, mindin' me own business, as usual. But then I come down for a snack, and I spotted a gathering on the porch. Cool as can be, I neared the open window to hear what was awhisper." Dane ignored another jab of frustration. Checker did like to tell a tale from time to time, and evidently this was to be one of those times.

"Just tell me," Dane said. "Is my place still standing?"

"Of course it is," Checker said. "I'd have told you straight away if it weren't. And what would that have to do with the first *hint* of a temperance riot, I ask you? No, me boy. What I overheard on the porch of the inn was the rumblings of a Temperance League about to be birthed."

Dane groaned. "I leave for two days and return to this? Already? We haven't even opened. How did the town find out I was planning to serve anything more than the wine I mentioned to Claudette? Is that what they're objecting to? Just wine?"

"No, that's not all. But speaking of Claudette, you had a visit from her. I told her you were out of town. The tongues do wag in this little hamlet, and tales have already reached your landlady. She left a note, to be found upstairs in your quarters. Getting back to how everyone started the talk, that new dishwasher you hired, the one who already works for your family. She must have heard us talking at the table that Sunday at your folks' house. The little eavesdropper knows about the spirits you intend serving. She evidently told her sister, who evidently told a dressmaker, who evidently spread the news to anyone livin' in Cranbury or vicinity, albeit of the female gender, so far."

Dane groaned again. Gossip. He'd expected that, but not so soon.

"And that's not the only bit of evidence they're going on." Checker cocked his head once toward the front of the carriage, where Tummers was directing the horse away from the station. "Our Mr. Tummers added to it by telling one or all about a certain visit we made to the local supplier. They've been quietly trying to pressure the man's ways for years, but even ostracizing the entire family hasn't worked. They don't want you encouraging him with your business—local business, I stress."

Dane stared at Checker, not really seeing him for all of his size. Then he asked, "When did you hear about this? Yesterday?"

"Just this afternoon. It's why I tagged along with Tummers to fetch you."

"So it's early yet. Hmmm."

"Oh, no, Dane," Checker said cautiously, "you won't be able to talk them out of it. These aren't the kind of women you knew in the city. These kind go to church and have families, husbands. Most of them are mothers of young boys they don't want tested someday by the drink."

"All's not lost," he assured his friend. "All we need do is make our services clear."

But Checker was already shaking his head. "You won't be able to charm them, not a single one, is my guess."

"No, not them. I'm not and never have been after the patronage of Cranbury's women, anyway. But their husbands might be a different story altogether."

CHAPTER 14

*M*eli added the coins Mrs. Taylor had given her for the fresh butter and eggs to the money she stored in a small, old clay pot kept on top of their icebox. Despite its storage in one of the common rooms of their comfortable home, this money was Meli's alone. Though Dad did, on occasion, add to it when she wasn't looking, he'd never once taken a penny.

He wasn't home now, despite it being near noon. She set about toasting a few slices of yesterday's bread, opened a jar of pickled asparagus, put out a bowl of applesauce and a couple of hard boiled eggs and iced tea. All the while she wondered just how well Dad knew Mr. Packham. How well did she know the Packhams herself? How could she not have known they were selling spirits? But then, why would she know such a thing? Dad rarely talked about the Packham family, even less so about crops except in relation to the weather. If they were selling spirits, why should Dad talk about that? He didn't drink . . .

A sudden thought struck her. Mother used to quip about ladies and their homemade cordials, the kind that tended to add a flush to a woman's cheeks. But she only kidded about such a thing when Dad used to add his "little extra" to the cucumber- and lemon-water Mother enjoyed, especially on cool evenings. Meli's gaze flew to the cabinet above the icebox, the one that was still too high for her to reach despite having finished growing. Glancing out the window, seeing no sign of Dad, she dragged one of the kitchen chairs to the icebox, then hopped up to look inside the cabinet.

She knew it was a storage spot for pots or vessels too large for their simple use; Dad brought these out when they hired help at planting and harvest. He always hired a cook as well to provide meals for their seasonal staff. She saw familiar iron pots, a boiler pan inside the stack, a gallon pitcher, an extra rolling pin and Mother's porcelain tea pot, the one with a cracked lid that neither she nor Dad could toss because it had been Mother's favorite.

Moving aside each piece, Meli spotted her quarry: the slim, amber glass bottle tucked away in the farthest corner. She had to stand on her toes and stretch to her fullest to reach it.

"What are you after at this time of year, Mel?"

Startled, Meli plopped the bottle back to its hiding place, thankful she hadn't actually withdrawn it from the cabinet or surely her guilty fingers would have let it fall to the floor in a crash.

"I—nothing." Then she jumped down, pulling the chair back to the table. "Lunch is ready."

"So I see," he said, but was still eying her. "So you got up there to check on the pots and pans?"

Instead of looking at her father, Meli poured chilled tea into two glasses.

"You weren't by any chance going for a dash of my little extra, were you? I didn't know you had a taste for it."

"A taste for it!" She stared at him. "I didn't even know you had such a thing. That's alcohol, isn't it?"

He shrugged, taking a seat at the table. "White whiskey."

"Whiskey!" She could have shouted, but was barely breathing. How naïve she was! How blind! To listen to the women of Cranbury, no one in town would dare let such a liquid pass their lips. And her father had his own secret stash! It would be downright humiliating if anyone knew. The fact that she'd never before worried about what others might think was at once welcome and disheartening. Short-breathed, she managed to say, "Folks in town don't think alcohol is a good idea."

He speared several asparagus stalks from the jar, adding them to his plate. "And do we care about what folks in town think?" Without letting her answer, he sighed. "I suppose they might be right, for some people. Got to be mindful of what you put in your stomach."

"But not you?"

He'd been about to add a third egg to his plate when his gaze fell on hers, evidently noticing her fervor for the first time. "Of course, I'm mindful. When my bones ache now and then at the end of a busy day, taking a nip helps me get right to sleep. What's this all about, Meli? There's nothing wrong with a sip or two."

She wasn't sure how to argue with him. The women of Cranbury seemed to think no one could taste the stuff without trouble following. And those ads she remembered touted plenty of evidence on their side.

"If there's nothing wrong in it, why do you keep it hidden?"

He shook his head as if the question were silly. "Habit, I suppose. Wanted it out of your reach, when you were younger. Speaking of stomachs, it wouldn't be good for a child's. Besides, it's a glass bottle. We kept all the glass in upper shelves when you were littler."

She didn't mention this particular glass was still kept out of reach despite her age; she understood his point.

"Rumor has it the new restaurant that Wardman is planning to open will sell spirits. Not just wine, but ardent spirits like your 'little extra'. And they're saying Mr. Packham will provide it."

Dad's brows lifted. "Well, that's quite an order." Then he

frowned, almost as if he were as worried as the women about a local supplier.

"You knew, then? That Mr. Packham sells spirits?"

"Of course I knew. In fact—"

"But no one wants such a place here in Cranbury!" She really was shouting now. "Have you ever heard of something called the Temperance League?"

"Heard of it, sure. Can be a dangerous group, smashing perfectly legal beverages, leastways legal here in Pennsylvania." Then he eyed her again, this time sharply. "I don't want you in with a crowd like that. You'd end up in jail."

Now she really was confused. Her father must believe there wasn't anything wrong with imbibing now and then, making the women she herself had pledged to join wrong instead.

"But, Dad! The women talking about forming a Temperance League here in Cranbury are the best in town. They're only trying to protect their children, and the town itself, from a place that sells something no one should drink. And I've promised to help, do whatever it takes to stop anybody from selling it."

Although he was still eating while she had yet to take a first bite, the look in her father's eye grew suspicious. "Who says no one should drink spirits? It's all well and good to discourage anybody from getting drunk. The Good Book itself tells us drunkards are fools, and I hold to that. But there's nothing wrong with a nip, not as far as I read it." His gaze sharpened. "You'd better search your heart, girl. Do you want to stop such a business from opening because of the alcohol, or because it's that Wardman fellow who wants to open it?"

That was the one question Meli had been trying not to face since she'd heard what those women were talking about that morning.

DANE LOOKED out the Canary's window as they neared their destination. When he'd lived here as a youth the first sign of civilization used to be the church steeple reaching above the treetops. Now it was his soon-to-be restaurant. Or saloon, a label he probably couldn't hide much longer.

Nothing seemed amiss at its door. Checker went for Dane's bag while Dane reached for Ethel. He'd planned to go straight out to the woods to Ethel's new home, but knew that delivery would have to wait until he could gauge the extent of brewing trouble.

Not only did nothing appear out of the ordinary, the sounds of work came as a pleasant surprise. Added to that was the pungent scent of varnish; they had already started the long process of staining the recently stripped paneling and even the lower portion of the bar itself. Evidently the coming insurgence was in its earliest stages. Maybe Dane himself, thanks to Checker, knew more about it than the men of this town. He'd have to tell them something more than spirits was brewing.

He took Ethel inside, hesitant to leave her far off.

Cade Levick noticed him first, grinning at the sign of the crate.

"I hope you don't want us to build a cage for that thing in here. Not sure the moms and dads would like their kiddo's fingers at risk."

It was the perfect opening. Dane set the crate off to the side, but shook his head. "No, I'm planning to store her in the woods, where a couple other tamed birds already live."

"Oh, at the Atherton place?" Leo Levick said. "There's a couple hawks like that out there."

Ignoring what should have been the more urgent topic, Dane pounced on Leo's knowledge. "Atherton? Yeah, that must be it. A girl actually flies the birds. Do you know her?"

"Everybody knows the Atherton name, but nobody really knows *them*."

"They like to keep to themselves," Cade Levick added.

Frustrated that Dane's new knowledge seemed destined to be

limited to a surname, he decided there was nothing to lose by just asking. "What's the girl's name, the one who flies birds like this one?"

"Meli," Leo answered. "She used to work in here, when it was a tea room."

Meli Atherton! Now that Dane heard it, he even thought it sounded familiar. Household staff used to gossip about the reclusive family that had provided popular fodder for talk, though he couldn't recall details.

It should be the new set of rumors concerning Dane now, ones that had nothing to do with Meli's family. He motioned to Cade, Leo and Brom to approach. One by one, they set aside their tools, wiped a brow, brushed off sawdust, then came near.

"Well, men, I guess I need to talk to you. Tell you something I probably should've said before today, before you started working for me."

He looked past them, seeing the bar so nearly complete. The shelving behind it was finished, too, which had yet to be affixed to the wall. That task waited for the glass he'd ordered. The brass kick bar had yet to come, but tall stools were already in place. He'd splurged and ordered padded seats, topped with leather. No need to be too elaborate just for men in need of a drink, but on the other hand he wasn't averse to providing the best seating available. This was to be a refuge, after all. Why not make it comfortable?

"That's a beautiful piece of work," he said. "Probably the best bar I've ever seen."

The men looked at it, too, although their gaze on such familiar work lacked the admiration Dane knew filled his own. Checker, who had come in after him, looked at it too, and he nodded in agreement with Dane's assessment.

The moment of silent appreciation went on a second or two too long. Dane knew he'd have to say something, he just wasn't sure what. He ruffled his own hair, then took a fortifying breath.

The soon-to-be saloon smelled of wood, paint, varnish and work, all of which was every bit as pleasant as the fresh outdoors.

"Here's the thing," he said slowly, knowing he had their attention. "My friend Checker here heard some talk today. Some suppositions about what kind of bar I've hired you to build."

"A soda bar," Leo said. "Mother said so."

"Well, no, not exactly," Dane said slowly. "She assumed that, but it's not for soda." He might as well just say it, so he sucked in one more deep breath. "I plan for it to be a more traditional bar." He now pointed to where the shelving was to go. "And the bottles for those shelves won't be phosphate flavorings or ice cream toppings. They'll be for liquor. I mean to welcome mostly men into this place, a sort of club, you might call it. Where you could talk with like-minded men, maybe enjoy a relaxing beverage or two. Maybe play some pool, or a card game—well, that last bit of entertainment isn't exactly legal if money enters the picture, so just friendly games, if you know what I mean? Simple, pure entertainment men enjoy at the end of a tiring day."

He waited again, guessing all of them probably knew what he meant. Liquor. Friendly games. Right. The three men stared at him, then exchanged glances among themselves. Dane thought he could read faces pretty well, and if he wasn't mistaken he would say Leo was the only one truly surprised, Cade not so much—yet it was clear, too, that the announcement wasn't being immediately rebuffed. No Temperance League members here. And Brom, well, his face was the most promising. He looked downright interested.

"Like I said," Dane went on, "I probably should've said something already, but since I grew up around here I figured the less said, the better. New things take time to get used to. This place is in the perfect spot, right on the road for thirsty travelers. Let's be clear, we all know most travelers are men. Salesmen, laborers, delivery drivers. This place is far enough from Williamsport to attract the ones who don't want to stop in a city that size. Besides the travelers, doesn't a local man deserve a place to go after a day's work, a week's work? Farming is toilsome, everybody knows that. Why not offer a place of respite, where the proprietor—that would be me—doesn't care if somebody comes in covered in dust, just looking to quench a parched throat?"

He knew he was on the verge of babbling, trying to convince them with words that might not mean much. In Philly, he'd met two kinds of men who'd never frequented his place: ones that didn't judge others for taking a drink now and then because they might enjoy such a thing at home, and ones who never touched the stuff because they'd judged it sinful. He'd seen them on the sidewalk, in the shops trailing their wives or mothers. He knew there would be some of those kind here in Cranbury, but maybe, just maybe, some of those who looked like they belonged in either of these groups really didn't. Maybe they were prime patrons who hadn't taken the opportunity to become one—yet.

"I do plan to serve meals, that's still true," he went on, this time talking only to fill the silence. "Families can eat here, ones that don't mind sharing the room with travelers or seeing somebody enjoying a drink from Mr. Packham's best. I don't intend keeping out anybody who wants to come in. If wives or sisters want to come in, they'll be welcome if they won't mind being in the minority. I won't shut the door to anyone."

Cade Levick pulled out a chair and sat down. He folded his arms across his chest. "Saloons don't typically allow women, sure won't serve them if they do, and it's probably a crime to let in children."

Dane smiled. "I wouldn't serve children."

Cade shook his head as if he recognized Dane's evasion in the friendly answer. "But you will serve women the spirits? If one shows up, that is? Why don't you just name this place what it'll be? A saloon. If that's the case, you might be serving meals but it won't be to women and children."

Dane shrugged his shoulders, still smiling. The man was likely right.

"Any reason you chose today to make all this clear?" Cade asked. "Not *before* we started working?"

Dane tried to refresh his smile but swallowed instead. "Like I said, change doesn't always come easy, especially in little towns like Cranbury. But here's the thing. Checker heard the women in town talking, and I guess they don't think a place selling spirits is a good idea."

Brom let out something that might have been a one-breath laugh, or a snort. "My mother thinks it's inevitable that you'll be selling ice cream to the kiddies."

"I told her I wasn't planning on that," Dane said, though he also knew he hadn't made much of an effort to convince her otherwise.

"Well, I won't speak for my brothers here," Cade went on, "but I didn't figure you for the ice cream type. You know the folks around here. Everybody knows everybody and everybody's business. It's like a big family, mostly. Church attendance is as close to one hundred percent as you can get, at least for those who live in town."

"Why can't somebody who goes to church also go to a place like what this will be?" The question wasn't an empty one; Dane really wanted to know.

Cade threw up his hands, as if the answer was so obvious neither Cade nor his brothers needed to reply.

Brom spoke up again. "I like the idea of what you described, Mr. Wardman. Why shouldn't there be a place for men? Men could have come into this building when it was a tea shop, but didn't because it was . . . well, for women. Why not have the opposite for a change? A place for men? What's wrong with that?"

"Exactly!" cried Dane. "Nothing's wrong with it."

Now Cade really did laugh. "For one thing, when women congregate they usually go in for things that—well, are pretty harmless if you don't count a whispered rumor or two. Men left on their own can be pretty much idiots if there isn't a woman around to impress. We're perfect examples, Brom. We could get away with just about anything when Mom wasn't around." He looked at Dane. "All our mother had to do was step into the room and we shaped up. Not because she was so stern, but because we knew our Pops would box our ears if we misbehaved in front of her."

"Then it isn't that you don't approve, you just don't trust yourselves to a place like this?" Dane hadn't meant to challenge Cade, or anybody else, not personally. But that was exactly how his words sounded.

The three Levick brothers looked from him to each other, as if the assumption behind the question surprised them.

Bingo.

Dane had just scored his first point, if there was a battle in store.

CHAPTER 15

*T*he sun was setting when Meli came out of the barn, having just milked the cow. The heifer always seemed content after a day of grazing with the goats in the pasture. Dad was planning to sell Snowberry, their family cow, now that milk was easier to buy at the local markets. Something he'd called pasteurization or some such thing allowed milk—and, now that she was thinking of the topic, he'd mentioned beer, too—to be transported more easily. Besides, it lasted longer in ice boxes. Milking Snowberry would soon be one less task they'd have to do.

But until they sold her to a bigger farm that could handle pasteurization, Snowberry still had to be milked. They stored the milk cans on the floor of the ice house, where ice still remained from winter storage.

Lugging a bucket toward the mound of earth insulating their ice storage, she stopped at the sight of a man walking down their lane—the setting sun cast a very odd shadow. He carried a crate in one hand, which was fairly swinging alongside. On his shoulder, however, was the stately outline of a goshawk.

She'd have been thrilled if she hadn't instantly known to whom that shadow belonged.

He was still well down the lane, so she continued into the ice house, added the pail of milk to a large, empty can sitting amid the ice, then went back up and watched him approach. Dad was still away, having gone to see Mr. Packham shortly after Meli had brought him her news.

"Meli!" he called, a friendly smile on his face. "Hello!"

So, he knew her name. She was half-tempted to bark out an order for him to call her Miss Atherton, but she'd never been called that in her life and wasn't sure she could train herself to answer such an address.

Since she hadn't bothered to move away from the ice house, he approached her. The mews were well behind them. Taking her typical stance, feet somewhat parted, arms crossed, she was ready to stalk away the moment she found reason to do so. She even considered inciting an argument, equipped as she was with plenty of reason to dislike him. Any one of which was enough to refuse to store his hawk, after all.

He stopped in front of her, then without a word pulled away the goshawk's hood.

The moment she saw the hawk, any thought of refusing vanished. She simply could not think of doing so. She was lovely! Young and as plump as a molting gos ought to be, still brown above, light underneath, boldly streaked. Meli's two older goshawks were well into their grays, with whitish bellies. Beauties to behold, especially when soaring, but red-eyed rather than the golden of this one's youth. Meli could barely remember Guinevere with such eyes, and had never seen Harriet in her youth.

Still, Meli knew enough from her mother's tutelage that young goshawks needed to be watched more closely than her own, well-trained, mature ones. If this strong young hawk found a way out of her own end of the mew, she would eat anything she could sink her claws into—including Guinevere or Harriet. Which was why Meli already calculated doing two things: daily checks of the wooden slatting between this goshawk's mew and the others, and keeping her well fed.

Dane Wardman must have guessed Meli's reaction to the sight of his bird, the way he was smiling: as proud as if he'd fathered the creature himself. Meli tugged down the corners of her mouth and hid her eyes from revealing the pleasure she'd felt at seeing up close this prime specimen of a young gos.

"You do know that goshawks this immature require more attention than older ones?" she asked. "And I already have plenty of other responsibilities."

"Haggling for more money, when I haven't even told you what I'm willing to pay?"

"Just thought you ought to be prepared."

He stepped past her. "Let's introduce Ethel to her new home, shall we?"

She should have been affronted at his assumption she was still willing to take the hawk, but Meli walked around him to take the lead. In less than a minute they neared the wooden structure that housed her birds. The moment Wardman and his hawk approached, Guinevere bobbed on her perch. She was free inside the mew, untethered, since she'd long ago learned the limits of her surroundings. Yet she crouched just now as if to take flight. Instead of flying at the wooden slats that let in light and air, she let out a screech loud enough to echo through the forest around them.

Temper tantrum duly noted.

DANE FOLLOWED Meli through the door on the far side of the mews. Inside, opposite the set of three doors that must lead to each mew, was a veritable treasure of falconry equipment. She even had a balance scale with its cradle lined in cork. Dane had learned firsthand that scales were far more accurate than trying to weigh Ethel by eye, and this kind was more accurate than a kitchen scale. He supposed Ethel's size made weighing her less vital than a smaller variety of hawk, but was glad to see another sign of such care.

He already knew the mews were clean, and close up he'd found few signs of chalking or mutes. Even the excess feathers during this molting season weren't cluttering the floors or water bins. He eyed Ethel, who was clearly calmer than at least one of her prospective new neighbors. She would be happy here; safe. He couldn't ask for more.

"I can help with her feeding," he said as Meli opened the inside door. "I've been arranging food suppliers for my new business, so I'll have fresh chickens for Ethel, too, maybe a duck now and then."

She was frowning now, and he guessed it was because having him supply an extra portion of meat meant he would be in regular contact. What else did she expect? For him to just leave Ethel here, never to see her? Granted, he'd originally convinced himself to leave her in Philly during her molt, but now that she was close by, he had every intention to visit—whether or not he was bringing her meals.

Dane bent his head to enter the end mew which would become Ethel's new home. The perch was thick and sturdy, a natural branch rescued no doubt from the forest floor. Ethel went to it as if she were already home.

And the other bird, the goshawk they'd passed, had begun settling once Ethel was beyond her sightline. The goshawk in the far mew was evidently the calm kind, because Dane heard nothing from that end.

"Her weight is higher than usual because of the transportation from the city," he said. "I wanted her to be a little fat and lazy for the trip."

Still, the girl said nothing, just looked ahead with a face that hid what she thought of his travel technique. Meli. Meli. Meli. He gazed at her rather than at Ethel, her name repeating in his mind now that he knew it. He wondered if it was a shortened version of something, though he couldn't imagine what. A shortened version of any name suited her; she was small, fine boned. Definitely not what he thought of as a farm girl; she was too delicate for that. But he caught that thought. Delicate? A girl who flew goshawks? This girl who'd kicked his shin, kneed his face not so many days ago? It was hard to imagine she'd done anything like that, unless pure steel was beneath that fragile exterior. He wasn't sure he'd ever seen such light blue eyes, though the contrasting darkness of her hair and her smooth, somewhat sun kissed skin might have enhanced the pale shade.

"You sure are pretty," he said, though it was only after the words were out that he realized he'd uttered his thoughts.

Now she really was frowning. That was certainly a new reaction, even if he should have kept the observation to himself. She may not like the messenger, but surely she'd welcomed the message? What woman wouldn't?

She turned and reentered the connecting storage room. She'd made sure to close the outside door after they'd entered, and now that he stepped behind her again, closing off Ethel's perch, it was darker than the airy mews. She went quickly to the opposite end, pulling open the door, nearly faster than he could blink.

"Sorry about that," he said as he followed her outside. The words came as easily as the compliment had, yet he wondered what instinct prompted him to apologize. Yes, she'd stiffened, but still, it seemed more than a little odd to say he was sorry for blurting words more truthful than flattery. "The words just slipped out. Forget I said it."

She'd been walking away—stomping, really—but stopped to face him abruptly. "Already have. There's just one thing you need to know, Wardman. You better plan to *keep* that hawk fat and lazy, because I have a feeling you'll be moving her back to the city sooner than you think. Your business here is bound to fail. Folks around here don't want it."

"Are you sure about that?" Had she been one of the women in on that anti-saloon discussion this morning? Not that it mattered; that group of women, whoever they were, only represented half of this town. They could yip and yap aplenty, but it was the men who would see his business open. Or closed.

He pulled out the money he'd brought to pay her.

"Here," he said, holding out the greenback. "Payment in advance for keeping Ethel safe and happy."

She snatched it from him without even looking at it, then continued to walk away.

It was only after she was half way past the squirrel garden that she actually looked down at the thing. Satisfaction welled within him when she stopped, turned, stared at him a full second or two, then refolded the legal tender note and walked the rest of the way to her house.

Well, at least she kept it. That meant something. What, he wasn't quite sure.

MELI SANK into the kitchen chair, staring at the paper money. It might have been make-believe for all she knew. She'd never seen a note like this before.

One hundred dollars. Half a year's wages, if she went by what Madame had paid her—and even Dad thought that wage had been generous.

Meli continued to stare at it. If there had been other, smaller denominations, tucked in his billfold he hadn't touched them. Had he planned all along to give her so much? A high amount, for the care and housing of one healthy goshawk for six months. Less time, if he were run out of town. She'd probably have to give it back if his bird stayed less than the originally agreed upon time.

Not that she could spend it! Who could give her change for a one-hundred-dollar note? A bank, maybe, if she went all the way to Williamsport. She was tempted to find such an institution, open an account. The clay pot on the ice box was safe enough for the average twenty-five or so dollars she kept, but maybe not for this much money.

Wait until Dad sees it. He won't believe it!

Then she remembered, again, from whom it had come. Her scowl returned. She should have thrown it right back at him. It was obviously too much for a task she would, at least secretly, enjoy.

Was this the kind of profit he expected to come from selling alcohol? If so, then it was just one more reason she shouldn't have accepted it. She wanted no part in money earned from the ruin of others.

Standing, she looked out the window facing the lane. He was still in sight, but far off, obviously headed back to town. She could catch up to him if she ran, hand him back the money, tell him she'd watch the hawk for the hawk's sake. Not for his sake, and not for money.

But instead, she went to the ice box and grabbed the pot. As her father would say, his money would be legally earned, selling a legal beverage. And she would earn this, if only having to put up with him.

She threw the bill inside as if it would burn her fingertips, then slammed the lid in place so fast it was as if she feared it might fly out of its own accord.

CHAPTER 16

On Sunday, Pastor Alec Taylor gave what at least one parishioner whispered on the way out was part mercy and part brimstone. Despite his passion on the subject, it seemed to Meli he was more tactful than necessary. Besides, the real subject of condemnation, the one providing temptation to defile the bodily temples Pastor had referred to—namely, Dane Wardman—wasn't there to be offended, or at least to pretend his offense. Maybe if Pastor had shouted a little louder, Wardman himself might have heard if the windows on his lodgings above the new saloon were open.

Meli had taken what was becoming her regular seat, next to Essie. She'd noted curiously that Mr. Prestwich, a few rows in front of them, hadn't sat next to Mrs. Prestwich today. Their oldest child, too old for the nursery, usually sat on one side or the other, never in between. Meli had come to admire how the two parents held each other's hand, or one extended an arm on the back of the pew in some form of constant contact throughout the sermon. Such behavior would be downright scandalous if they hadn't been married so many years, and more than once Meli had thought if she ever did marry, she'd want to be as happy as they seemed to be. Today, though, their daughter had sat between them as if a buffer between two recalcitrant children. Not once had one looked at the other, or stolen a caress over the pew. After the service they made their way to the back, both staring ahead as if all they saw was the door.

"I have a number of temperance pledge sheets if you'd like to pass some along on your way home, Meli," said Essie as they emerged outside. "I can think of a few homes on the outskirts, can't you?"

Meli nodded. She opened the pouch she'd carried on the crook of her arm, but looked over her shoulder to see if her observation of the Prestwich parents had been mistaken. Though they, too, lingered in the warm sunshine, Mr. Prestwich joined a group of men farther off, while Mrs. Prestwich stopped to talk to Mrs. Phipps not far from Meli and Essie.

"I'll be happy to take them," said Meli, accepting a small handful. "But there is something I should share with you first, something I'd like to confess." She'd been pondering this talk for days now, still basking in this new acceptance, the possibility of friendship she hadn't experienced since Cari.

Essie's brows lifted. "Well, that sounds more serious than something we should talk about out here in the yard. Would you like to go back inside, once the church empties?"

Meli nodded.

Essie took Meli's hand and looped her arm with hers, a friendly gesture that was becoming familiar as she led her a few feet away to join Mrs. Prestwich and Mrs. Phipps. It was never so easy to join others as when Essie was at her side.

"Well, what could I say? I was just too—" Mrs. Arianne Prestwich stopped speaking abruptly as Meli and Essie joined the other two women. For one sinking moment Meli was sure the pretty lady had stopped due to Meli. Surely she *was* still an outsider and therefore not meant to hear whatever they'd been talking about.

But rather than glancing at Meli, Mrs. Prestwich's eyes had landed on Essie.

"Essie!" Mrs. Phipps' voice was nearly breathless, as if the last thing she'd expected was to run into the pastor's wife on church grounds just after the end of a service. "We—that is, *I*—was just saying we certainly have our work cut out for us to revive the temperance movement around here. More challenges than I ever imagined! We—that is, I—was speaking to old Doc Lancaster about it, and do you know what he called our effort to bring back the movement to Cranbury? Poppycock! He said he stands against making alcohol illegal, if not for the average person, then for its prescriptive value. He said it's medicine."

"Well, the book I was reading said if alcohol *is* medicine," Essie said quickly, "then there is no need for a healthy man or woman to ever consume such a thing. Besides, the majority of doctors have joined the cause because they see the damage alcohol does. We have to let folks know the national movement gets stronger all the time, because the fact is, alcohol's dangerous."

Meli thought of the reading she'd been doing, too, from old sermon collections and even Madame's magazines, of children starving because their father spent all his money on alcohol, or a woman pitched to the floor by the angry backhand of a drunken husband. She was sure her father would condemn any man doing such a thing, but would probably remind her that spirits had never turned him into such a monster. She couldn't argue with the truth, but it was hard not to want him to sign a pledge for the sake of the movement. He would hardly miss it, since he drank so rarely. Yet, she hadn't gathered enough courage to ask him.

After Mrs. Phipps stated she would support a national ban on alcohol, Mrs. Prestwich sighed. "I'm afraid Doc won't be the only one who won't sign our pledges. My own husband won't. It's what Leta and I were just discussing. Oh! I'm so embarrassed. I had no idea Jonas holds the opinions he has about this. I didn't even know he drank spirits! Well, other than an occasional glass of wine, and I've shared that with him myself, on New Year's Eve or some small celebration. Easily given up! But he told me when he meets with clients interested in purchasing our paper, or with other investors in the city, they often include spirits during meals. He said he wouldn't abstain altogether, that it would make clients and their business partners uncomfortable."

As Essie frowned, Meli saw her opportunity. She felt Mrs. Prestwich's frustration. "I have a confession, too." She looked at Essie. "There's no need to go inside for me to tell you. My own father likely won't sign a pledge, either, although I haven't asked him yet. He said I oughtn't get involved in the movement, because I'll end up in jail."

Essie put an arm about Meli's shoulders. "I don't counsel people to disobey their parents, but I can assure your father we don't intend doing anything to risk being arrested."

"Why do you think he won't sign?" Arianne Prestwich asked.

Meli held up the small bundle of pledges she would distribute on her way home. "I haven't put one of these in front of him, but when we talked about the bottle he keeps *in our kitchen*—hidden, mind you—he said there was nothing wrong with taking some now and then, so long as he doesn't consume too much. And he doesn't." She'd added that last line as a quick defense, but knew she wouldn't be a successful temperance worker without his signature on one of the pledges. After all, she'd searched the sermon books her mother had left behind for any wisdom on the subject. Meli was surprised at how long women had been working to keep alcohol out of their home. Every movement, one sermon said, started in one's own parlor. If the ultimate goal was to outlaw alcohol, it must start in each home, in each town or city, signing an oath of abstinence. If every home in Cranbury signed a pledge, that would put Dane Wardman out of business before he even opened his doors.

Which led to thoughts of another confession. Should she tell them of her split motivation, her confusion as to why she really wanted Dane Wardman to fail? Would it matter? This morning, during the service, she'd been convinced that if she were truly to be accepted among townsfolk, honesty must be a necessary ingredient. But maybe this second confession was only gossip, telling them Dane Wardman had not one but two marks against his character.

"Is there something else?" Mrs. Prestwich prodded. She stared so intently Meli wondered if the woman had somehow read her mind. Or maybe God Himself had whispered there was more to Meli's confession than she'd told.

"I—I'm not sure . . ." Even as she spoke she knew she must follow this nudge toward honesty. "It's just . . . I have some . . . animosity toward Mr. Wardman, other than against his wish to entirely ruin each and every memory of Madame's tea house."

"No need to feel guilty about that," said Mrs. Phipps. "I'd feel the same if someone tried blotting out the memory of my dress shop, should I sell for any reason."

Meli nodded her agreement, but frowned. "That's only part of it for me. When we were children, he—he—hurt me. I cannot forget what he did, much less forgive him for it."

She dared a peek at Essie's face then the others, alarmed to see sudden shock mirrored on all three women.

"He hurt you?" Essie's voice was aghast. "How?"

"He killed my favorite kestrel," Meli said. "Shot it right out of the sky."

Essie, along with the other two women, let out sighs. Sighs that sound like relief! When the man was very nearly a murderer?

"She was my pet," Meli added. "I'd spent more than a year training her, with my mother's help. It was a terrible time for me, when my best friend died of influenza—you remember Cari Elwood? Then my mother. Oh! I can barely think of it without hate refilling my heart."

If Essie had been close to issuing a relieved smile after Meli might have improperly built up his crime, she now frowned as she replaced her arm about Meli's shoulders. "We can talk about it, if you like. Hate is a powerful thing, and almost always harmful—but sometimes the ones we hate aren't the ones we're hurting."

"I just thought I ought to tell you," she whispered. "Because I may be hoping for him to be run out of town for more than just trying to poison us with alcohol."

Now Essie did smile, and Meli knew none of them were making light of her feelings. Each one met her gaze with what Meli was sure to be a mix of sympathy and understanding.

So this was what it felt like to have more than one friend at a time.

DANE LET himself into the storage door of the mew, where Meli kept the equipment required for her hawks. He saw the crate he'd used when walking Ethel here the other day, and deposited inside of it a pair of canvas bags, one filled with dried beef and chicken and the other filled with a variety of jesses and a second set of creances used to tether her. He'd purposely waited until well after the church bells had labeled this day a Sabbath, spotting Meli lingering outside after the service ended. Between his slow hike through the forest and frequent stops to gaze behind him in search of her, he'd expected her to catch up any moment.

After donning the glove he'd left when delivering Ethel, he let himself inside her mew. The compartment was large enough, and tall enough, for him not to feel crowded, so he took a seat near the corner. Moments after holding out his gloved arm, she hopped to the perch he provided. Good; at least she wasn't ignoring him. Perhaps she liked her new home.

Dane took out the paper he'd brought with him. Checker had swiped one from the inn's dining room table, a pledge sheet being circulated throughout the town. He hadn't meant to keep it, but having it now reminded him of a game he used to play with Ethel in the trainer's yard. He crumpled the paper—something he'd wanted to do anyway—and tossed it to the far side of the mew.

Barely moving her massive wings, Ethel floated after it. She pounced on it, shook it hard from the tip of her deadly beak, then returned to Dane's outstretched arm, dropping it at his feet. They did this for quite some time, and even though Dane enjoyed every minute with his hawk, he couldn't help wondering if he should have waited until after Meli had left the churchyard if he wanted to see her today. What was taking her so long to get home? He supposed he could have gone to the church service, where he'd have been assured of seeing her and having her see him. Perhaps he might have found a seat next to her. But the pledge sheet he used as a toy now seemed ample evidence that other church goers probably wouldn't have welcomed him any more than Meli would have.

So he would wait. He could see their lane from here, through the open slats; he'd spot her the minute she returned.

"Have to hand it to you," came a voice from the side of the mew, its owner out of sight until a moment later. A man appeared through the caged slats, one Dane couldn't recall ever seeing but whom he had no doubt was Meli's father. She had his eyes. "I don't know how you got her to keep that hawk for you, even if she does have her mother's fancy for them."

Dane stood, returning Ethel to her usual perch. Then he stepped into the store room, leaving his glove before emerging from the mews. The man was still on the other side of the slats, eying Ethel with his arms folded.

"She's a pretty one, that," he said. "Guess that's what convinced her in the end." The man glanced at Dane with unveiled wariness. "'Cause she sure isn't doing it as a favor to you."

Dane stiffened, though he'd already expected to tread cautiously. "I know. Do you know what she holds against me?"

He huffed. "If she didn't tell you, it's not my place."

"Oh, I know what I did. I just wondered if you did."

"She's my daughter. You don't think I noticed—or could forget —when she came home that day, even if it was ten years ago? She clutched one of those gloves as if it was all that was left of her little falcon. She'd buried her bird already, all by herself." Now he turned to Dane, his light eyes grim. "You were the first person to hurt my daughter, young man. I'm warning you: don't let it happen again."

Dane stood taller in an attempt to stop feeling like a boy in front of the school's principal. "I won't, sir. In fact, if you can think of any way I can make it up to her, I'd be happy to try. Just to be neighborly." He thought he'd better add that last part, so he wouldn't think Dane had any outrageously unrealistic designs on his daughter.

Meli's father raised one brow, though he didn't look surprised. Maybe curious; maybe amused. Maybe both. Maybe he wasn't convinced that Dane didn't have designs on his daughter. Maybe he wasn't so easily convinced because Dane himself wasn't convinced, either. He hadn't been able to forget she was the prettiest girl he'd seen in a very long time.

"You're the one who's opening that saloon, in place of the tea shop where she worked?"

Dane nodded.

"That's not earning you any favor with her."

Dane uncrumpled the piece of paper he'd used to play with Ethel and handed it to him. "I guess she's not the only one. Have you seen one of these yet?"

The man took the page, glanced at it, then handed it back. "I expected something like that, the way she was talking the other day."

Dane attempted to refold the paper but it was still too wrinkled to flatten properly. "This isn't the first saloon I've owned," he said. "And it's not the first temperance movement I've faced, either. I didn't think I'd find it out here, though."

Mr. Atherton snorted. "Out here where folks are set in their ways? Where churches are full on Sunday? I thought you grew up around here, boy. Don't remember much about the place, do you?"

Dane shook his head. "No, I guess I didn't." Then he looked at the other man squarely. "Do you think it's a bad idea, too?"

"Agh." He waved an impatient hand. "Isn't for me to say, one way or the other. Just because I'm not a member of that church in town doesn't mean I'm a heathen. But I'm no teetotaler. I happen to think a good man can drink in moderation if he doesn't let the demon part of the drink get hold of him."

"You do understand, then," Dane said, undeniably relieved. At least he wouldn't have to battle Meli and her father, too. "I just thought the men of this town deserve the equivalent of what that tea shop used to be. What's wrong with that?"

Meli's father cocked his head to one side. "You don't really think you're going to convince half the town—the female half—to accept your place with that kind of argument, do you?"

"Isn't half the town enough? The other half, I mean. The men. That's the only business I'm really after, besides the travelers, because it'll bring more profit than a tea shop, I guarantee you that."

"That may very well be true, if all you want is profit. Just don't expect to be invited to anybody's parlor—not this one, that's for sure, if Meli has anything to say about it."

The older man turned away, walked a few feet off, then turned back. "You see those mews, boy?"

Dane glanced back at them, confused. Of course he had!

"I built them, board by board, for Meli's mother, before we were married. Even when I did it, I was afraid of hawks. I was the son of a farmer on my way to the sea, because I wanted to get away from so-called polite society. But I gave up all that. The fear, the dream about the sea, because I wanted to please her. So I built the mews. Sometimes we have to change our plans."

He turned again, but once more stopped himself. "Oh, and I

have a little advice. Purely business. Don't get too attached to selling Packham's whiskey."

That came as such a surprise, Dane lifted his brows. "Why not? I've tasted it. It's the best I'm likely to get."

Mr. Atherton turned away again, this time walking off without another word.

CHAPTER 17

*M*eli had stopped walking with hope and purpose after the third unanswered door—despite evidence of people at home, either smoke from the kitchen stovepipe or hurriedly hushed noises.

The rejection demonstrated every fear she'd carried most of her life: that if she ever reached out to be neighborly no one would accept her. She didn't belong; she wasn't wanted.

In spite of that, she vowed never again to let a knock at her own door go unanswered, even if she knew it was some kind of broom peddler.

Perhaps she *looked* like a sales person, carrying her stack of pledges. Or someone asking for donations. They might even have heard rumors about their temperance movement. It could be any of that keeping those doors shut, and nothing personal at all.

No one expected their movement would be easy. Today hadn't been a complete failure. Two neighbors had answered, and they even signed pledges. Cari's mother, and Mr. Harting, who didn't often make it to church since his wife died.

Meli, who had been looking only as far as the ground in front of her, looked up after hearing someone calling her name. Someone was ahead, also on foot, and coming this way.

Meli's heart sank. It was him.

Forcing her chin a bit higher, her footfall a bit faster, she clutched the pledges to her chest and kept walking. She would have passed him without a word only doing that seemed the opposite of all she'd just vowed about not answering a knock at her own door.

"I was visiting Ethel," said Wardman as he approached, his smile so friendly she wondered if he might have some kind of deficiency. Surely he knew she detested not only him as a person, but his business.

"She's happy out here," he went on, "I can tell."

Meli nodded, then attempted to walk around him. She hadn't entirely ignored him; that was enough niceness.

"I'm hoping you'll be there during one of my visits," he went on. "So we can talk about falconry."

She let out the breath she hadn't known she was holding, eyed him with tightened eyes, then tried once again to go on her way.

So we can talk about falconry? Dane shook his head, watching her walking away. Oh, you're the charmer, Wardman. He couldn't follow her home, no matter how desperate he was at the moment to salvage some of his pride. Her father would think he was little better than a puppy dog, trailing her every chance he got.

He was about to call farewell when she turned to face him, a look in her eye that instantly intrigued him. For the first time, she looked at him with something other than the outright disdain she'd continued to show just a moment ago. She was almost smiling.

"I've been distributing abstinence pledges," she said airily. "Care to sign one of these yourself?"

She was teasing him! Well, that was probably better than loathing him. He glanced at the papers without taking one, even though she extended one his way. "As a matter of fact, I already have one of those. Not that I'll sign one, even though I rarely drink. I think each and every one of us ought to decide for ourselves whether or not we partake, and how much. We don't need someone else deciding for us."

"But it's poison! Why should anyone with sense put such a thing into their stomach?"

"Ah," he said. Even though he was about to counter her with an argument, at least they were talking. "Anyone with sense. As much sense as you, you mean?"

"If people knew what alcohol can do, then common sense follows."

"Funny how common sense might mean something different, depending on how you look at it. Because it may be poison for a few, but for the majority it's just a soothing tonic. There's nothing wrong with putting a tonic in our stomach."

She tucked the sheets back into the crook of her arm. "You know what I think, Mr. Wardman? Either Cranbury will have to change its ways, or you will. Which do you think more likely?"

He grinned, leveling his gaze at her. She might be glaring, but he couldn't help thinking he'd rather look into her eyes than anyone else's. "I'm not going anywhere, Meli. Just wait and see. Who knows? Someday you might realize how much we have in common, you and I."

He guessed the thought of them being friends horrified more than surprised her. So he shot her his most charming smile.

"The gosses, Meli," he whispered. "That's quite something to have in common, don't you think? Given how passionate we both are about them?"

Lifting her chin, she turned again to walk on her way.

"Besides, I'm really quite a nice fellow," he called. "Just ask anyone who knows me." Well, not family, and probably not many in Cranbury, yet. But back in Philly . . .

She ignored him, and he watched for quite some time. She never so much as threw a glance over her shoulder.

But somehow, he doubted he was so easily dismissed—or forgotten.

CHAPTER 18

"*A*nd so, my friends and consorts, now that you've heard what the *demon* whiskey has done to tear apart the lives of the families I'm here to represent, men whose *weakness* of mind and character allowed them to sink to the *deepest* depravity, I remind you of words from the great Mark Twain. He said, more than a quarter century ago: From that day Adam ate of the apple and blamed Eve, down to the present day, man, in a moral fight, has uniformly shown himself to be an errant *coward*.

"Friends, there is only one way for men to rise above that assumption. Let us exhort God Himself to show His power here on the outskirts of Williamsport, that He will answer prayers to prove the character of the menfolk in this town. Only He can strengthen the basest man against temptation, to resist the poisonous nectar of this world that will lead only to ruin."

Mrs. Delphine Smythe was nearly as short as Meli, though she carried a few extra pounds around the middle and was crowned with a thatch of thick, white hair. She continued her admonitory speech, but Meli looked instead at her neighbors. The church was nearly full on this early Sunday evening, mostly women but a few husbands, too. Even as Meli counted the meager number of men, she wished they hadn't been so obvious a target in the speech.

She wondered how the eldest Mr. Levick had received the scolding. To Meli, he'd always seemed the quiet but wise type, on those few occasions she'd seen him at the tea shop with his wife or one of his daughters-in-law. Though his toymaker son wasn't there, the toymaker's wife was. Mrs. Prestwich from the paper shop also sat alone. But Mr. Phipps the photographer was there with Mrs. Phipps the dressmaker, along with a neighbor or two whom Meli had gotten to sign pledges.

Even though Pastor Taylor was a popular speaker ever since Pastor McNichols took off for the wilds of the rain forest as a missionary, it wasn't often they hosted out-of-town lecturers. Curiosity alone probably accounted for a number of the seats taken, but Meli couldn't help wondering if it had been squandered by the speaker's general hostility toward men.

Dane Wardman, the man without whom this entire topic might never have been broached, was nowhere to be seen. He was the only one deserving of the speech coming from the pulpit tonight. Not a drop of honey, just gallons of gall. Surely the men of Cranbury, as of yet, could not be compared to those doomed to the insanity sure to befall any brain awash in such poison?

Mrs. Smythe had come from a well-established group in Philadelphia's Temperance League, one of the oldest groups in the country. The woman herself was probably near seventy, and Meli didn't doubt she'd witnessed or heard of a great number of lives ruined due to ardent spirits. But instead of finding inspiration in their first temperance meeting, Meli's spirit was too heavy to muster a fight.

Surely the speaker was nearing an end. Instead of listening, Meli prayed. God must indeed approve of their goal; all they needed was for Him to speak, without the filter of a woman who admitted being a victim of losing her husband to strong drink.

Applause, if mostly polite, came as Mrs. Smythe ended, but by then Meli was too lost in prayer to pay much attention to so mediocre a sound.

"Well, I'm glad that's over," whispered Essie, beside Meli. "I suppose we should have taken the time to listen to one of Mrs. Smythe's speeches before we invited her. And for our inaugural meeting, too!"

"Perhaps Pastor Taylor might take a moment to . . . to . . .?" Meli let her words drift away. By now the crowd was likely so eager to leave they'd hardly welcome anyone else at the lectern.

Essie was shaking her head. "Alec is fully on our side, but everyone in town has been calling this a woman's war. He said he didn't want his presence too visible. Other than on Sundays, of course."

"Then perhaps you might say something? A sort of bookend, to balance the introduction you made at the outset?"

"I—I wish I'd thought of that earlier! But I wouldn't know what to say."

"What about all of the things in the pamphlets? About how we mustn't stand by, voiceless and helpless in the face of an enemy. This is a real, tangible enemy—but the enemy is the drink, not the men! Wouldn't anyone bar poison from their dinner table? You're a mother, Essie! How can any woman allow such a thing inside the home?"

"Sounds like you would be a better speaker than—" Essie's words got lost in whatever thought was taking over her entire countenance. She stared at Meli. "You can do it. You can speak, if only those few words you just said to me. Oh!" She held up her palm because Meli was about to protest, and Essie must have guessed as much. "You've already refused to sing in front of the church, when you have the loveliest voice I've ever heard. You cannot refuse this. Think of what a blessing you'd be!"

Meli blinked. A blessing to others? Words Madame had spoken on the eve of her death flooded Meli's mind. Besides, she hadn't exactly asked God how she was to bless others, even if she had agreed with Madame that she had some catching up to do in this regard. In the most fervent moments of her prayer just now, a plethora of words kept filling her mind. Repetition, it was true, of speeches she had read in the last few days, but words of wisdom and persuasion. No anger or revenge but a simple, heartfelt plea for Cranbury to bar one heretofore unnecessary commodity. Hadn't the town gone well without alcohol since Cranbury's inception?

Could she be the blessing Madame had talked about, or just someone to increase the bile Mrs. Smythe had just stirred? Before Meli could ponder any answer, she found herself standing. Would she really do it? Why else were her feet carrying her forward? Part of her mind went nearly mad, while the other, the stronger part, would not be ignored.

Mrs. Smythe was just emerging from behind the podium, and because she was such a short and stout woman, Meli automatically offered a hand to assist the older woman down the two steps from the church's platform. Meli remained in front of the assembly. There was still time to change her mind, to return to the other empty seat on Essie's far side. But she could not budge. Meli didn't bother to climb behind the podium. Instead, she stayed level with her neighbors. She couldn't see all the faces, but thought any elevation might stir her stomach more than she could tolerate.

"Thank you, Mrs. Smythe, for sharing your experiences about the dangers of alcohol. Information about what liquor can do is why we're here. The real work of our temperance movement is for us to do, our Cranbury residents. Each of us must want protection and health for ourselves and our neighbors. Doesn't love for our fellow man start where we live? I'm only beginning to learn that, because I'm not known to many even though I've lived here all my life. There are others with better abilities than mine to speak, person to person, friend to friend. But shouldn't each of us want to keep our friends and neighbors from swallowing a poison that can change a person's behavior—not for the better, but to something less? Common sense tells me alcohol shouldn't control our actions instead of the healthy mind and will God gave us.

"We are a small group in this small town, but our message isn't small. It makes us strong. How can we let down our friends and neighbors by allowing in a business that could change our face, our nature, our reputation? All we ask is to keep the respect and goodwill Cranbury is known for. I am sure every rational mind will agree with those motives—because they're bigger than any one of us."

With that, she left the shadow of the podium and returned to her seat.

Maybe it was because of her words; maybe it was because she'd spoken with a purer passion to protect others, not from the retribution of old scars; maybe she'd spoken from something God Himself inspired—inside her, to bless others the way Madame once told her to do. Maybe God had prepared a spot in others to hear her, because she'd never properly "loved her neighbors as herself" and knew it wasn't too late to start now. Who would not be receptive to that kind of love?

Or maybe it was simply because her speech was brief in comparison to Mrs. Smythe's. Whatever the reason, the sound of the applause was loud enough to echo from the church's rafters.

DANE LEANED against the railing on the front stoop leading into his establishment. Even from here, he could hear the applause pouring from the open windows of the little white church just across the road leading into Cranbury.

He frowned. He probably should have attended the meeting, learned whatever arguments they would raise against opening a saloon. Not that it would have persuaded him; he knew his presence would've been as unsuccessful at changing their minds as they would have been at changing his.

His hope was that since this local temperance movement was new, they had no real power. Certainly they'd been too late to prevent him from gaining his liquor license, which a more coordinated and established local movement might have been able to achieve, or at least delay. There was no real obstacle before him.

Not even having the oldest of the Levick brothers quit would slow things. The toymaker had admitted his working on a saloon was bad for his real business, that of selling toys to the parents of young children. Dane saw Cade's point. The two other brothers had come back, though, and Dane had stepped in where he could, if only as a workhorse. They even promised that another brother, Giff, currently living in the city, would be coming to town for a few days and would lend a hand to finish the renovation. Dane was fairly certain he could open for business by the end of next week. He'd already received two crates of inventory and the local supplier, Mr. Packham, promised a case as well. Dane had hired a chef—an unexpected boon there, having had his old friend Lannigan accept the offer Dane had sent via telegram to Philly. All he needed now was a bartender, and he was working on that. Apart from someone like Checker, a good bartender was any saloon's most important asset.

Dane might have returned inside, found something to do without needing direction from his carpenters, if only to sweep up again. Unlike them, he didn't mind working on a sabbath. But a lone figure emerging from the back door of the church caught his eye, because she was coming this way. Daylight was dimming, being after six, and for a moment he wished that it might be Meli. But he knew it was not. This woman was too tall, and the style of her dress too formal. She wore a hat and light cloak, with feathers transforming the silhouette of her head into a strange combination of human and animal.

The moment he recognized her, Dane nearly hurried inside

like an errant tenant evading his landlord. Technically she might even view him that way, since he'd ignored the note she'd left behind from her visit some time ago while he'd been in Philly. She'd written that she continued to enjoy the idea of their partnership and wished he'd told her he would be coming through Williamsport to catch his train. Nonetheless, she hoped all was going well, ending with her hope that he would visit her soon. He hadn't, nor had he any intention of doing so. The lease was signed, legal and tight.

Dane had only a moment to act, but it was already too late. She waved his way. Too bad he'd spent that moment hoping the silhouette belonged to someone else.

"Good-afternoon, Mrs. Norcross-Rice," he greeted, the formality of the name nearly stumbling his tongue.

Her laugh was easy and instantaneous. "Please, call me Claudette. Isn't that what business partners do? Address each other on more friendly terms?"

He wanted to refuse, but if he was going to minimize the trouble that might come with his type of business, he ought not fight small points. "I wonder if you might think an outright sale a better option, to avoid involvement in what's going on in there." He cocked his head the church's way. "Is that why you're here?"

She'd reached the cement stoop now, which was barely big enough to hold both of them. "It is why I came, but I predict that little movement will die an uneventful death. Soon."

He hoped she was right. He glanced over her shoulder, looking for her husband but suspecting himself an idiot to think the man knew where his wife was, even if he had accompanied her to the meeting. "Waiting for Mr. Norcross-Rice?"

Another laugh, this one shorter, quieter. "He's just where I left him. At home. I came because any temperance fight is a woman's war, and he gladly excused himself from attending." Dane had continued looking past her despite her claim, but she called back his gaze by adding, "Shall we go inside? I'd like to see the renovations the town has been speculating about."

Knowing he couldn't keep her from her rightful property, he reached to open the door and let her in. He didn't close it behind them. Inside, he crossed the room to turn up the lighting. The gauges were just inside the kitchen, and controlled both that room as well as this one. He'd had new overhead lighting installed since the tea room had only used its lighting on dreary days—it had never been open beyond a late lunch crowd. Green-tinted glass shades suspended by gleaming copper holders hung in four symmetrical spots around the room. The effect wasn't much brighter than what still filtered in from the setting sun, but was as inviting as a warm light in a home's window. At least Dane thought so.

She looked around slowly, pivoting to fully face each direction. The paneled walls were dark and lustrous now. Wall art that had once heralded intricate details of various flowers, both wild and cultivated, had been replaced by replicas of men hunting, or working in a wheat field. Another, Dane's personal favorite, was of a hawk in the midst of a plummet, ready to do what hawks did to oblivious rabbits. At least Dane's choice of decor did not include a half-naked woman framed above the bar; even he had guessed that might not have gone well with Cranbury's still somewhat puritan population.

Despite his wish that this woman's husband was here, he had to admit he was interested in her opinion. She did, after all, own the place. She might not be representative of his clientele, but he guessed she was the kind of woman who not only formed opinions, she wasn't afraid to share them.

"Very . . ." She let the word linger, as if knowing he wanted to hear what she said and therefore deciding to let him wait. She turned to him, facing him fully, and the smile on her face—an appealing one, he acknowledged—made it clear she approved. "Masculine."

He pulled his gaze from hers. "Yes, well, since that's the kind of customer I intend hosting, we've succeeded."

"We? How nice that you consider me—"

"Checker," he supplied, "the man may not be a financial partner, but he knows the business and I find myself consulting him on most decisions."

"And what do you and this Mr. Checker intend to do about the rumblings going on in town? I admit I'm not so very concerned, particularly after the meeting I just left, but it will have to be dealt with, I suppose."

"I heard applause at the end. Sounded like they were enjoying themselves."

"Oh, some little mouse finally spoke up and we were all so relieved it wasn't the same cantankerous main speaker we gave her a hearty clap. Mostly it was boring, if you weren't squirming in your seat trying to miss the arrows of shame the speaker kept thrusting. Very little appeal overall."

He shrugged. "Then you said it yourself: it'll die a quick death. I don't want any trouble, and I doubt the men around here do, either. It won't take long to establish the fact that men can still be honorable even if they allow themselves a bit of recreation now and then."

She looked around again, her smile still in place. "Yes, this looks to be a very honorable place. Like a gentlemen's club in the city."

She obviously knew little of the men's clubs in New York or even Philly, since they were far larger than this little tavern would ever be. But he not only took it as a compliment, he encouraged the assumption. Men's clubs offering a variety of services from haircuts to lodgings were a far step up from any saloon. "As a matter of fact," he said, turning to the spot just inside the door, where three tables currently stood in front of the window that overlooked the road, "I plan to install a pool table right here. I'm hoping it'll arrive before I open."

"My, my," she said softly. "Pool tables sometimes come with gambling, don't they? Men betting against one another?"

It was true, but she sounded neither for nor against such a thing. Rather she spoke as if she were too feminine to know if she ought to be alarmed or impressed.

Then she smiled, and though she didn't step any closer, the look on her face closed the gap between them. "You don't mind flouting rules, do you, Dane?"

Though he held her gaze, he didn't return the smile. She wasn't talking about pool tables or gambling now. "Some rules can be broken. Some can't. Personal ones, for example, are harder to break. Or should be."

There was that laugh again. Confident; amused, but clearly convinced she was on her way to getting what she wanted. She was pretty enough to have him believing she was used to that. "All rule-breaking gets personal, eventually. Some rule-breaking can be very, very personal. And beneficial."

Dane knew, the sooner she was out the door, the better. The entire town probably wouldn't have any trouble labeling him a scoundrel, even the ones who fully intended frequenting a place that sold alcohol. He didn't need a mark against him with a married woman—especially one who could toss him out the minute she tired of him.

"I don't intend to keep anyone from entering," he said as he walked to the door, "Once the women see this as a place for men to gather, relax, enjoy a beverage not found at home—one to lift their spirits—there will be nothing to fear. They'll all see that soon."

He stood at the door as he spoke, hoping she took the meaning behind his action. Now that the rally was over she'd have to account for her whereabouts. Where was Checker, anyway? Even though the second bed for the empty guest room upstairs had yet to arrive, they'd agreed to another game of cards tonight.

Too early, Dane guessed, especially since he tended to arrive later than expected. Why, Dane couldn't imagine. Surely he wasn't keeping company with anyone at the inn, despite always dining there. He purchased meals for Dane, too, and frankly he was surprised they sold Checker food for either one of them. The two widows running the inn might not be entirely heartless, since they'd agreed Checker could stay until his bed arrived, but Dane wasn't sure how Checker withstood their self-righteous attitudes.

Slowly, gracefully, Mrs. Norcross-Rice followed Dane's path, all the while eyeing him with a smile. "Thank you for the advance peek, Dane. Maybe next time you can show me the rest of the place. The kitchen, when it's in full use." She paused, standing in the threshold with him. "And upstairs."

He'd have been shocked by her boldness if he hadn't fully expected it.

Then she raised a hand to one of his cheeks and stroked it gently, concerning him more than mere flirtation. "I think our partnership will be very beneficial, Dane. Don't you?"

He nodded politely, unable to slow his speeding pulse. It wasn't anticipation of her next visit that sent it racing. It was simple instinct, the kind that rabbit in the picture on his wall would have shown if he'd seen the hawk behind him. Like the rabbit, fighting was out of the question, but Dane would have made a run for it if he could.

CHAPTER 19

*M*eli wasn't used to being known by townsfolk, yet for the past week she could barely step onto Main Street without someone waving a greeting or calling her by name. She'd been surprised at first, unsure how to respond, but returning a smile came remarkably automatic. As of yesterday, she'd even begun initiating greetings, knowing Madame would have approved.

Mr. Phipps' account of the temperance rally, written up in the local newspaper with one of his photographs taken at the rally—of Meli, not their invited speaker—had brought her unexpected notoriety. He'd summarized her speech more sympathetically than he had Mrs. Smythes', making a point of naming Meli even though she hadn't introduced herself at the meeting. If anyone in town recalled that she was the great-granddaughter of the one they once whispered about, or the daughter of the woman who tamed wild birds, or the girl who seemed to have invisibly slipped in and out of the tea shop, all of that was forgotten. She was now the girl helping to lead Cranbury's temperance movement, and most residents approved. At least, she was approved by those who waved. She was accustomed to those who continued to ignore her.

She knew the title as leader belonged solely to Essie, but even Essie seemed determined to push Meli into the spotlight. At the close of their rally, she'd pressed Meli into announcing the day and time for their next meeting, as well as when they would gather for regular prayer circles. She'd even asked Meli to close the evening in prayer. That had immediately sent Meli's blood from pounding to whacking through her veins, but she'd been so caught up in the afternoon's events that nothing, not even her once-shy disposition, blocked the Holy Spirit's words fitting the occasion. She knew Madame would smile to see Meli taking her words to heart about being a blessing to others.

Tonight was another prayer circle, something Meli always prayed about in advance. They must rely on guidance and assistance from God Himself. She even planned to propose an idea or two, making her wonder if Essie might be right: perhaps God really had put her in a position to lead the temperance rallies. She didn't have a husband or family to divert her attention or demand so much of her time; she didn't even have a job anymore, other than caring for her animals and duties on the farm. Was she supposed to feel guilty that an underlying benefit might be to see the last of Dane Wardman?

She hadn't seen Wardman in over a week. To her surprise, he hadn't visited his hawk, not once, at least while Meli was home. Meli was content, even happy, about that; she was getting to know his hawk and couldn't resist planning a training routine. Ethel could fly, and fly well, even without her full plumage. But she was too slow to hunt. Without consulting her owner, Meli made plans to train Ethel for speed, once her molt was finished.

It would be easier with help, just as Meli had helped her mother when they'd taught Guinevere. She checked her old ropes and the lightweight box lid her father had made before Meli was born, the sight of which made her smile with memories of working beside her mother. Two ropes were better than one, but since she anticipated working alone she would manage. Once Ethel's plumage filled in a bit, Meli would place a chicken carcass in the open field, easily visible to any hawk, especially a gos like Ethel. Just as the bird would soar down to their quarry, Meli would pull the lid over the prey, quickly shielding it from view. All Meli needed was to be faster than Ethel, which was likely to be easy at first. Must swoop fast if you want to eat, goshawk! If she had help with a second rope on the chicken, to pull that out of reach beside just covering it, Ethel's training would go faster. But she would neither ask Wardman's help nor tell him what she planned. It was, after all, for the hawk's benefit, not his. At least when he left Cranbury he would take with him a predator better prepared for what predators do.

There were ten women gathered outside the church in the cool evening air, the ten most ardent devotees to their cause.

"I have another idea for the saloon's opening day," Meli said, after they went inside and Essie had led them in an opening prayer.

Essie winked at her. "We've liked the ones you've had so far. The white ribbons we're wearing to show our support, the article you'd like us to write for Mr. Phipps. The speeches you've copied for us to read. You chose the most inspiring ones. And the march, of course, on opening day. Right through the center of town. That's what we're all looking forward to, so folks intending to visit the place will know we're serious." She laughed, adding, "If they don't know already!"

"I can't claim any of those ideas as original," Meli confessed. "Only what we've all read from other groups. But this idea," she continued slowly, more carefully, "is a little . . . well, bold, I suppose you'd call it. The march is a good start, but I don't think it goes far enough. I'd like us to go into the place—the moment they open—and pray not a single customer darkens its door."

"Oh!" Meli wasn't sure if Essie was impressed or horrified. "Actually go inside? Or just block the door?"

Meli shook her head. "I don't think we could clog the door, not legally anyway. But why couldn't we go inside?"

"Is—is it legal for us to do that?"

"Why not?" The question came not from Meli but from Mrs. Prestwich who, despite her husband's apparent lack of support, hadn't yet missed a meeting. She had three young sons and was among the most vocal about protecting the next generation. "It's being advertised as a public place."

"But—" the elder Mrs. Taylor uttered the word quickly and loudly but haltingly. "Saloons don't normally let in women, or so I've read in the dime novels."

"It's called a grand opening," said Raina Levick. "Doesn't that mean to *everyone*?"

"We'll just have to show up and test that assumption," Meli said. "That giant of a man working for Mr. Wardman could stop us, I admit."

"Oh, he wouldn't hurt a fly, that one," said Mrs. Taylor, who, upon hearing her own words, blushed a bit. Then she added, "I mean to say, I don't approve of him at all, but he seems a gentle sort of . . . giant."

Meli took up where she'd left off. "I don't think anyone hoping to start a business would have us forcibly removed. Don't we have a right to see what's inside? Once we're in, we'll be living, breathing reminders of pious women. And a pious woman wants a man who doesn't drink spirits." She'd said that last part without even thinking. It was like pronouncing she herself was in the market for a husband. According to Madame and her own father, she should be. But thinking of her father brought another wave of confusion. He, after all, did drink spirits and he'd been an ideal husband, as far as she knew. Certainly he was an ideal father. Still, it was obvious any sensible woman would prefer a teetotaler to one who drank to excess. That, really, was the purest part of the temperance goal, wasn't it? To warn men of the dangers of drinking?

"But if we do get inside," Essie said, "what then? What do we do? Take turns praying?"

"Of course!" Meli said. "And sing a hymn, perhaps. Claim the room as a temporary sanctuary! Make sure God is felt. Surely there's no law against singing in a barroom."

Mrs. Taylor laughed. "According to the dime novels, singing is a regular event at pubs." She giggled like a far younger woman. "I cannot wait to see the faces of anyone inside as they hear what we think should be sung!"

Laughing assent followed, and they agreed to gather in front of the paper shop on one end of their Main Street, then march to the drinking establishment on the other. Four o'clock sharp, when the doors were supposed to welcome the first of their customers.

Meli's smile couldn't be stopped. Surely Wardman's grand opening would point to nothing more than its closing.

She wasn't sure who anticipated tomorrow's opening of Cranbury's newest business more: her, or Wardman.

DANE POLISHED the bar's smooth finish. The varnish was finally dry, though the clean scent of it remained. He'd thought it would've been ready days ago. Between that and waiting for deliveries that took longer than he was used to in the city, they were at long last ready.

Those Levick brothers had done a fine job, superb, even. The bar in his prior place had been old and marred even if it was sturdy and serviceable. This, on the other hand, was a work of art. The front edge was gently curved to prevent spills and welcome patrons to lean into its support. Carved images of hemlock boughs drew the eye to the panels below, the tree so prevalent around Cranbury, and the main source of material for this and many of the town's original homes. One of the few things Dane remembered from his schooldays was that some of the biggest hemlocks were hundreds of years old. There was something to be said for longevity, after all. Once the grumblings from town settled down, he envisioned this business to be around long after he was too old to run it. He'd probably be disappointed the first time the bar suffered a scratch or nick, but then something could be said about the patina of regular use. At least that was what he'd told himself at his last place.

If Dane had been a praying man, he might have credited something supernatural to the fact that his favorite bartender had agreed to come, if only on a trial basis. Marto Lutz was a veritable Jerry Thomas, a legend among barkeeps, with nearly countless recipes stored in his head. He knew everything from shooters to corpse revivers. His unbeatable memory, not only for beverage concoctions but for the names of his customers, made him absolute gold.

Besides Marto, both Dane and Checker had celebrated hiring Lannigan, who was already preparing a few things in advance of tomorrow's opening. Although Dane didn't expect many of his visitors to order dinners—especially since the rumors accurately described his place as a bar—he did want to offer some surprises everyone would welcome. Who could protest a well-cooked meal?

That might even soften the attitudes of a few of those pesky temperance women.

CHAPTER 20

"I just think you ought to stay home, that's all."

Hearing her father's words, Meli stopped at the door. She'd waited until the last moment before casually mentioning where she was headed. A prayer vigil; a march through town. She'd said nothing of her intention to go inside Wardman's brand new business.

"You know I can't miss this. Not everyone is comfortable praying out loud, and I am. You taught me that much, Dad."

He remained seated at their kitchen table. At least he wasn't worried enough to hop up and get in her way. Not that he'd ever done such a thing before. Not that she'd ever given reason. But it was a little late to try putting her under his thumb.

"Don't lay any of this on me, daughter. I know as well as you do why you're so set on ruining that boy's business. Let the town work it out for itself. Either they'll avoid the place and he'll move on, like you hope, or they'll keep him afloat. What happens, happens."

Her hands fisted at her sides. "If everyone thought that way nothing would get done. Nearly every woman in town worries about what spirits can do if a man gets a taste for it. I know—"

Now she raised one of her hands, palm out— "I know you're not one of the unfortunates who can't stop drinking once they start. But I've read the books and the speeches and the pamphlets. There are men out there who ought never let one little sip pass their lips. What right-minded wife and mother wants to find out if their husband is one of them? Or their son? We'd be better off if liquor is illegal; it's not exactly the milk of life."

"Perhaps so, but those cakes and puddings Madame taught you to bake aren't the milk of life, either. In moderation, both are perfectly fine."

"Perhaps our next consideration will be to form a sugar brigade." Meli pursed her lips, refusing to utter another heated word. "Are you not allowing me to go?"

Now her father did stand, but neither swiftly nor in anger. Instead, he came to put a finger under her chin so that she was compelled to look at him. He was fully himself, neither riled nor sad, just as steady as ever. "You're all grown, Meli. This roof is as much yours as mine now, so I won't be treating you like a child. That's how I expect you to treat our neighbors, letting them decide whether or not they choose to drink."

"But maybe they don't have all the facts about liquor."

"We can disagree about how they ought to hear those facts, or even how many of those stories might be true. I'm only worried there will be trouble. We've kept to ourselves all our lives, and now you're jumping into a fray? The only part that makes any sense is that you want to get back at the fellow. It's why I feared for his hawk, at first, even though I don't think there's enough room in your heart to hate anybody so much you'd harm an animal. But this . . . you're the one who could be hurt if you hope to run him out, and I don't want to see it happen."

She put a hand over his, and offered a smile. "Who's going to be hurt? All we're going to do is pray, Dad. And sing, maybe. Who would arrest anyone just for singing and praying?"

"Well, if even one of those bottles gets broken, by accident or otherwise, he'd have the right to see the whole lot of you arrested."

"We're not going to break bottles. We want them all to rot on the shelves, unopened."

He laughed. "Whiskey doesn't go bad, girl, not if it's stored right. And I'm thinking a man who sells the stuff knows how to keep it."

She smiled again. "Then we'll pray he breaks those bottles himself, without any one of us lifting a finger."

He shook his head. "You're asking for a miracle if you think he'll pour out an inventory he paid good money for. Either that, or if his character is as bad as you think he might just break a bottle or two and blame it on you just to see you arrested."

She gasped. "Thanks for the warning, Dad. I hadn't thought of that. I'll be sure to keep my eye on him."

Then she left the house, knowing that while she didn't exactly have her father's approval, he hadn't made much of an attempt to stop her. That was as near permission as she was likely to get.

DANE LINED up his new staff in front of the bar, from floor sweeper to Checker. They fairly glistened along with the place, from crisp white shirts he'd provided to their clean, dark shoes. Mirrors reflected the shrouded lamps hung overhead while the polished wood floor did its best to do the same. He hadn't allowed sawdust the way some barrooms used it to soak a spill, or the gastric effects of overindulgence, or blood from a raucous brawl. Insofar as Checker could stop such things, Dane would have none of that here. Claudette's assumptions were naïve, but even so, he wanted his place closer to a men's club than saloon.

"Men," Dane began, but then his gaze fell on Irene, the dishwasher, and nodded her way even as he wondered again if hiring her had been a mistake, "and lady. This establishment is the first of its kind here in Cranbury, which is why it's especially important to start with our best foot forward. That means we give the customer what he wants, and we do it with a smile. If a lady or two deems to join us, that's fine. We'll treat them with respect so their menfolk will know they won't find trouble here."

"But do we serve 'dem spirits?" asked Marto the bartender, his English every bit as accented as Dane recalled, his bushy brows gathered in concern. "I know in city we did, but here . . . what is rule?"

"Same as in Philly. We won't refuse anyone—well, except for kids, apart from the little ones just fetching a bucket of beer for their pappy. For actual consumption, let's say . . . twenty-one, to be on the safe side." That earned him a look from Marto as well as Checker, both of whom knew he'd served boys as young as nineteen back in Philly, or at least ones who claimed they were that age. The law didn't have an opinion on it, at least not in this state, but considering the local brouhaha surrounding his business, Dane was willing to be a bit more strict. Men that young didn't tend to have much cash to spend, anyway, so he wouldn't lose much by not serving such a clientele. "Somebody will have to vouch for their age on their first visit, either a parent or a neighbor—a fully grown neighbor, that is, not some young cohort wanting their first whiskey together."

Dane then addressed the lad he'd hired to keep the tables and floors clean. His name was Guyto, which Dane had originally thought a misspelling of Guido when the boy presented the employment card from the agency. The boy had quickly corrected him, and Dane was as impressed as cautious. His tone had suggested a certain cockiness that reminded Dane of himself around that age—thus the caution, especially since the terms of Guyto's employment included all meals and sleeping on a cot in the store room. Dane repeated what the boy surely knew already about the job, especially about keeping an eye on the floor. Guyto was more expensive than sawdust, but he'd be worth every penny if he kept the place clean.

He reminded Checker, unnecessarily, about watching the billiard table for misuse, although didn't mention their mutual understanding to turn a deaf ear on subtle bets players might offer each other. Better to ease into gambling at the pool table and once word spread about that, cards were bound to follow.

With one satisfied clap of his hands, he sent them off to their posts as he glanced at the watch from his pocket. Nearly four now. Still early for any sort of crowd, especially drinkers, but he was more than willing to let in those who were curious about what the old tea shop looked like now. It had grown up.

THE TEMPERANCE SISTERS had agreed to meet in front of the Casterton Stationery Shop, hoping to attract whatever attention they could along the street during their march. They intended their company to arrive at the saloon at precisely four o'clock, thus be among the first "patrons".

There were twelve of them, an appropriate number, observed by Essie: like the Apostles. What were they doing, if not God's work? What mission could be more noble than to protect their town, the future of their families? Just this morning, Meli had read a compilation of diary entries from a minister's wife recounting in detail her battle against spirits, and how devastating it was to the fabric of each and every society throughout history. Their Puritan ancestors had known from the start that spirits needed restriction, inspiring penalties from the scarlet *D* for drunkards to the land's first hope of banning alcohol altogether a hundred years ago. Generations, both past and present, were on prohibition's side—making Wardman completely and utterly wrong.

Essie must have noted the time because she took Meli's hand

along with her mother's-in-law on her other side. Everyone else followed the cue as they formed a circle: Mrs. Arianne Prestwich, the three Mrs. Levicks, Mrs. Leta Phipps and Mrs. Corrine Wingate, Miss Phoebe Turner, and two others Meli remembered as the most frequent customers at the tea shop: Mrs. Jenkins, and Mrs. Crane.

Essie led the first prayer, one Meli echoed in the depths of her soul. The Holy Spirit must indeed touch the hearts of everyone: the patrons, of course, but also the staff at what Wardman had decided to call the *Hawk*. The *Hawk*, indeed! Hawks weren't foolish enough to consume poison.

Then Essie prayed for Dane Wardman's heart to be changed, to be transformed by the power of the Holy Spirit. For the first time Meli considered something she'd never thought before: Wardman must have a heart, too. One in need of salvation.

The realization hit so hard a long moment of silence followed before Meli remembered she was to add her own prayers to Essie's, as planned earlier. She spoke up, a plea for herself and her companions, to sustain their strength and their courage, and for God to let the evening's impact remain peaceful. She owed that hope to her earthly father.

But Meli barely heard her own words. She was still stuck on Essie's petition. Meli had never prayed for Wardman, but suddenly more words echoed—without summons—inside Meli's head. *May God put Wardman into His beloved palm. Surely there, he'll think about what's truly best for the patrons he seeks to draw.* The sincerity of her words tumbled her heart and jostled her thoughts, and for a moment she could barely follow Essie's direction for them to be on their way.

Meli nearly wished she could recant that brief, silent prayer. While it was only right for Essie and all of them to pray for every aspect of this battle, she didn't want to pray for Wardman. But if succeeding meant Wardman's salvation, surely even the angels would rejoice. Meli would too. Wouldn't she, over a rescued soul? Of course she would . . .

How could the root of her goal be connected not to the business but to the heart of Dane Wardman? Surely God was mightier than one self-centered, heathen of a man! If God filled Wardman's heart enough to stop his business, it would benefit Wardman himself the most—something Meli should want if she truly loved God.

Something cracked inside of her. As they marched Meli prayed with awe as she begged God's forgiveness. God must love even someone like Wardman, and Meli mustn't stand in His way.

This first hint of something she'd never felt before confused yet amazed her. It wasn't forgiveness of Wardman, not exactly. But there was definitely a shift; God could change anyone, couldn't He? Even her. Look at her now, standing hand-in-hand with the townswomen when once she'd believed herself too shy to do so.

As for Wardman, all along she'd been so confident of her own righteousness. Why had her faith been so shallow to believe He'd made a mistake in creating Dane Wardman—such a mistake that he couldn't be touched by God? Was he not the same as any other human being? God was a God of miracles, not mistakes. Dane Wardman needed a miracle, but at the moment one had just happened inside Meli herself. She doubted anyone would stand before the throne of God boasting of a hard heart. God had just healed her of that.

Before this moment, who had been the bigger sinner? Her, for hoping a man made in the image of God, the same as her, would spend an eternity separate from his Creator, or a stupid little boy with a gun who had killed her hawk?

But there was no more time to dwell on it. Somehow the day's mission had changed, at least for her, yet the plan was still the same. Only now she had a better outcome in mind. She would look for ways God could reach the very soul of Dane Wardman.

DANE NEARED the blinds that had hidden the building's transformation from ladies' tea room to its new role as a men's refuge. The sun was already sinking to a sunset cut short by the mountains and trees, though a healthy afternoon glow remained. He hadn't expected any sort of lineup outside, and there wasn't, but he trusted newcomers would soon arrive.

Checker's softly uttered "Uh-oh" from the now open door warned him otherwise, and he peered through the window to see what was up. He looked not toward the road, but toward town, the direction Checker faced.

There, marching past the Inn that had been Checker's home up until yesterday's delivery of a new bed, was a small cluster of women—all headed this way, each face reflecting something between resolute and celebratory.

Two thoughts filled Dane's mind: he was glad there weren't too many of them and they weren't armed with clubs. He'd seen temperance marches in Philly of hundreds of white-ribboned women equipped with sticks, brooms, or even bats. He shouldn't be surprised, considering the size of the town, that this potential mob of petticoats hadn't resorted to armaments. Yet.

His final reaction was too quick and too familiar, and maddeningly beyond his control: the sight of one of the women in the forefront made his heart act like a boy's. Meli Atherton. Too bad her presence in that parade spelled that she'd just as soon run him out of town as talk to him.

"Looks like we'll be hosting some of Cranbury's ladies," Dane called over his shoulder in a voice more untroubled than he felt. "Just remember: don't give them any ammunition. Be cordial, even if you have to squash every single logical thought running through your head."

CHAPTER 21

"*M*eli," whispered Essie. She took Meli's hand again as they walked toward their target. "I think you should start the singing when we get there. You have the strongest voice among us. Sing first, then we'll join your song in the next verse or so. We'll pray after that. Will you do it?"

"I . . ." Her mind was still caught on the prayer Essie had inspired back at the inn. Wardman's face was planted so solidly in her head she could barely think of anything else, even the importance of their mission. But Essie's question helped dim the odd and unexpected fixation. "Wouldn't all of our voices together be best? United?"

Essie squeezed her hand. "And so we shall. But to start, just the first verse? Then we'll join you in the chorus."

"But which hymn?" She really must force herself to think straight; she'd been part of the plans they'd made and the hymns had already been decided.

"*God Help Thee Now to Conquer.* Remember?"

She'd practiced it with Essie at their last meeting, just to be sure she wouldn't forget the words. It was among the boldest of their temperance hymns, and if anything, would certainly make an impression.

She nodded.

The saloon was just ahead, and two men approached from down the road. She didn't recognize either, not that she knew everyone from town, especially the men. Customers? Or foot travelers who would pass right by? Then the sound of an approaching motorcar echoed from around the bend; its speed was slowing considerably, not just to accommodate the curve. As Meli and her companions neared, the motorcar pulled off the road not far from a signed emblazoned with *The Hawk*.

So. Their audience would consist of more than just Wardman and his staff. That was the point, wasn't it? To reach not only the provider of spirits, but the consumer as well. They'd discussed it in great detail, made plans based on the successes—and failures—of the decades-long temperance war.

But somehow there was suddenly a single person person Meli hoped to reach, despite those loftier goals. Direction from their group was one thing; direction from God another. One was noble enough all by itself, but the other was downright divine. Meli would sing with a new, more precise mission now. How could she not?

Now that she'd surrendered to the notion that Wardman had a heart, she would do whatever God directed her to do in order to change it.

"Come in, ladies," said Dane, adding a smile only because he'd learned long ago that facial gestures could be heard in the voice. "Come in and see your town's newest addition. I'm sure you'll see it's up to the fine standards expected around here. Hello," he added, looking directly at Meli. She was the second visitor to step foot into his place, but his simple observation paled when she turned her gaze to him.

It was so rare that she looked him eye-to-eye that he nearly gasped when she did so, even letting that gaze linger. She wasn't even issuing her normal frown. Rather she looked at him as if she'd never seen him before, studying him with something akin to curiosity. The look was so astonishingly unexpected that Dane knew a moment of uncertainty. He'd prepared himself well for today's grand opening: shaving, hair-combing, all the usual measures that went with meeting new people, new *customers*. What could she be staring at? He hadn't eaten anything since he'd checked his appearance, so there could be nothing stuck to his mouth or chin.

His mind refused to stop wondering, even as she walked inside and, once near the center where there was a bit of room between tables, she looked at him again. Concern soon emerged through his surprise. Did she have news of Ethel? Was that what made her finally let herself look at him? He dismissed that thought as quickly as it had come. She showed no trace of pity, or warning that his hawk was in distress. He conceded she might not have any concern for him if Ethel were in trouble, but even her well-established dislike wouldn't overrun pity for the hawk; that would surely spill onto him as her owner.

Besides, it was a question in her gaze, though on what subject he couldn't begin to guess.

Twelve new people now stood under his roof, all women, none a customer. He hadn't expected such a number from the fairer sex, certainly on any single night in this small town, let alone on his opening. While still at the doorway, Dane saw two men had emerged from one of Ford's Model T's. They didn't step forward, obviously having just watched the parade of women enter. Another pair of younger men approached from the road, but they, too, stopped near the others.

"Come in, gentlemen," invited Dane.

"This still isn't a tea house, is it?" one of the men on foot called.

"No," he answered, "the establishment is under my management now. It's unlike anything it used to be. Come in and see."

"What're all them women doing, then?"

"Everyone's welcome," he assured them. "Come in."

Then he heard the sound of a single voice singing behind him, a voice he recognized at first note. He'd once asked her to perform here. Surely she hadn't changed her mind, despite the fact that she'd looked him full in the face for longer than a twinkling a moment ago. She was here in protest, he wasn't foolish enough to hope otherwise. But why use her voice, one that anyone would want to enjoy longer, if she wanted him to shut his door?

Then he heard the words, and her reason took meaning.

> Nay, touch it not, 'tis poison!
> Touch not the madd'ning bowl,
> That robs thee of thy reason,
> And steals away thy soul;
> Thy best and purest feelings
> It turns to bitter hate;
> Then dash the poison from thee,
> Or sad will be thy fate.

The rest of the voices, gentle and charmingly female, joined in.

> God help thee, now, to conquer
> This great and dreadful sin;
> Oh, seek Him at the open door,
> And He will let thee in.

The four men behind Dane must have heard the singing as well, perhaps drawn to it as he himself had been. If they listened to the words, they made no impression, at least for the moment.

They even followed Dane all the way inside the barroom, an audience to the sound even if they wouldn't have chosen the verse.

One of the men folded his arms and leaned against the threshold. As soon as Meli's singing emerged again on its own, he cupped his mouth and called, "Hey, petticoat, how 'bout taking requests? Sing something we can all join in. Like *Little Brown Jug?*" Then he went into his own rendition, drowning Meli's singing:

> Me and my wife live all alone
> In a little log hut we're all our own:
> She loves gin and I love rum,
> And don't we have a lot of fun!
> Ha, ha, ha, Little Brown Jug,
> you and me, don't I love thee . . .

He might have started again, but Dane approached, waving at him to stop. "That's enough, young man," he said sternly. "I believe the ladies are here to make a point. We'll hear them out, then they'll be on their way."

The man clucked his tongue, "Well, somebody's gonna' be on their way."

Then he turned and walked back to his motorcar. It took a moment for his companion to follow, but once the motor was started he scrambled after, barely reaching the passenger door before the car sped off.

Dane's chagrin over turning away one of his very first true customers was tempered by the resumption of Meli's singing. In spite of the lyrics, he had no wish to stop her.

> Wand'ring in the paths of folly,
> Without peace, or joy, or rest,
> Jesus called me,
> Called me to him,
> That in him I might be blest.

Jesus loved me, oh, he loved me!
And he's still my loving Friend;
Jesus loves me, yes, he loves me,
And he'll love me to the end.

Something beneath Dane's collar pricked him like the tip of a knife, as if the war in his mind were tangible. He wanted to hear her sing, yet he wanted to show her the door. He wanted to keep her at his side, yet he wanted her away so his customers could be comfortable. These songs . . . those lyrics. This one wasn't among the temperance hymns he'd heard in Philly. Why couldn't she sing those songs, the ones he hated, so maybe he'd win this battle against the lure of her voice?

He said nothing, not even when Checker moved behind him to whisper there were a few more potential customers gathering outside. Dane looked over his shoulder, seeing familiar faces among new ones. Cranbury residents might be there only to watch, maybe even have followed the march to his place, but those first two patrons who had come on foot now stood in the threshold. They effectively barred the door from those who might follow.

Dane ought to go outside, explain the demonstration. The women had come to show their objections, and he had graciously let them. Surely it would be over soon? Then the rest of them could go about the business for which they'd come. Refreshment.

Dane's attention was once again drawn to Meli's singing, but this time not only to her voice. The words struck him, about Jesus loving him to the end. Where had he heard that before? It shouldn't sound familiar. God knew Dane had never willingly gone to church, and once there, had rarely listened.

Yet, there it was. The nagging sense that he'd heard those words before.

And had welcomed them.

CHAPTER 22

*A*fter Meli finished the last verse, she listened as Essie took up the prayer. Her friend's sweet voice carried well, so well that Meli was sure even those gathered outside could hear. She prayed for wisdom, expressing gratitude for how the Lord Himself set the example of goodness, grace and mercy. The inspired virtues of character and strength were surely mixed with self-discipline. She thanked God for the knowledge that temporal pleasures were of the selfish kind, and even if partaken did not excuse unwise choices threatening health and common sense, and how common sense was squashed by over-indulgence. She finished with an echo of earlier words, that man was made in the image of God, that his body was God's temple, so it ought not be abused.

Meli spoke up, too, adding to Essie's prayer. She hadn't planned to do so, but words came before she could hold them back. Surely Wardman could hear her; she hoped his soul could hear as well.

"We know your lovingkindness falls on everyone, even those who ignore you. We ask that your love be greater than the desire to indulge in what can so easily lead to ruin. Finally, we beseech you to touch the soul of the proprietor. Speak to him as only you can, as his Creator. Touch him within, at the depth of his soul that no one but you can reach. We ask you to redirect his efforts to something that will bring good, not ill, to our community, something that will bless those around him and do them good."

When the prayer ended, she turned to him. They had planned only to sing a few hymns and have Essie pray, and that mission had been accomplished. Theirs was to be a gentle and good protest, one to demonstrate which side was clearly right. Already Essie was leading the way back outside, but Meli's feet would not move. Instead, she looked again at Dane Wardman. Had she followed Essie to the door, she would have been closer to him. He'd stood aside to let the others leave, even thanked Essie for leading an orderly demonstration.

The two patrons who hadn't left before now went to the bar. Another half-dozen men—one of them none other than old Doc Lancaster—entered. Meli wanted to leave; the changes made to Madame's tearoom might be tasteful, elegant, even, to a man's eye. But like the walls themselves, this place was dark, and not only in its decor. The clear and amber liquors were as dark as they were poisonous.

Now Wardman approached and still Meli could not move. Instead, a thought occurred to her as she watched him walking nearer. Essie's prayer had reminded them all of the truth: this man, like her, was made in the image of God. Even the old hymn Meli herself had suddenly—unexpectedly—chosen to sing hadn't been on their agenda. Her mother had taught it to her as a child. The words of her very own prayer had reminded her that surely God loved Wardman as much as He loved her.

"Meli," Wardman greeted her, his tone as friendly as it had been to the others. He must believe she would be going, too. As she ought.

All the words she'd imagined she might say to him if given the chance flew through her mind. *You're serving venom! How can you provide a product that has the capacity to ruin the life of those who partake?* If he was so ignorant of the countless stories of neglect and violence and heartache, she would be happy to enlighten him.

And yet none of those accusations and remonstrations made it to her lips. "Will a business such as this help your customers? Truly make their life better?" Curiosity laced her words rather than the condemnation that so often went along with protests.

His brows rose, as if surprised. "Yes, why not? Our country has a long and friendly history of places just like this. Places meant to offer a bit cheer after a long day's work."

He'd started to smile as if his answer had been right, but she hadn't smiled in return. If her father were here, he might have agreed. After all, he used this same product to ease his rest. But somehow any supplier of demon rum, as detailed in the pamphlets she'd read that expressed so much family devastation, was far different from the little bottle Dad kept that needed such rare replacement.

"How will you know which customers need only a *bit* of cheer?"

"I . . . I won't. It's up to them. Let freedom ring, and all that. Freedom to choose for oneself."

She let a little smile touch her lips now. "Do you know how it feels when you watch Ethel soar in the sky? To watch her do what she was created to do?" She didn't wait for him to answer, didn't even wait for the hint of confusion on his face to clear. "Maybe that's what God feels when He watches us do what He created us to do. I'm fairly certain each of us possesses something that will give ourselves and our neighbors that sort of feeling. It won't have to come from drinking anything in those bottles. It might even be hindered by it, if it gives some kind of solace that's only false and temporary."

Meli knew her feet would obey her now, that she could follow her temperance sisters and know the day's mission had only been the start. A peaceful beginning to a noble mission. No need for her father to have worried about any trouble.

"There may be something else you're meant to do," she whispered with her first step forward, "other than this. Something better for you, and for those around you."

Then she offered another smile, this one as hopeful as she felt inside—impossibly so, yet somehow sincere. If this man truly was made in the image of God, then even he wasn't beyond redemption. And maybe God did have something better in store for him than feeding poison to men who didn't even know it was poison until it was too late.

DANE WATCHED MELI GO. The battle inside that had begun upon her arrival still waged. Foolishly, he wanted to follow her and hope she might treat him with more smiles and gentle words.

But the other part of him, the logical part, knew her words were silly, self-righteous and holier-than-thou. All temperance workers harbored such pomposity, thinking themselves better than the average man who, after all, just wanted a bit of relief from a harsh and often cruel world. He'd been a barkeep in Philly; he would be a barkeep here. He was good at hosting people, good at making them feel welcome. If he was meant for anything, it was certainly that.

And yet those eyes of hers, that smile . . . The way she'd asked him those questions about whether or not he was doing what was best. Not what was profitable or even pleasurable. It would take quite an effort to banish her smile and questions from his mind, but banish all that he must if he was going to bestow upon his customers the attention they deserved.

Soon the usual sounds of his business filled the room. He introduced himself to those he didn't know, which outnumbered those from the little town he'd already dealt with. The old doctor had shown up, along with the Levick brothers, two of them anyway. None stayed longer than to share a mug of beer. That was as good a start with the locals as he could hope. Several farmers and their laborers came, too, and a few people from neighboring towns.

As smoothly as this first evening was going, even considering the protest, Dane couldn't quite shake an odd feeling inside. Foreboding? Yes, that was it. He'd never been one to worry about the future, so why start now? Yet he had little hope that tonight's visit from the ladies in town would be the last.

CHAPTER 23

*M*eli left the mew, each of the three hawks comfortably fed, molted feathers swept clear from their compartments. Ethel, no longer shy since Meli spent what time she could with her, hadn't waited for Meli to leave before approaching the food. Meli grinned at her as she ate, surprised at how quickly the young hawk had learned to trust her. That would come in handy when she started her training.

That word clung to Meli as she walked back to the house: trust. Earlier that afternoon, before reading more of the material circulating among the temperance sisters, Meli had been reading from her Bible. She'd already underlined myriad passages clearly condemning the consumption of spirits: drinkers being fools, wine stinging like a serpent, drunkards not inheriting the Kingdom of heaven. Each one stood out as somehow more important than other verses.

How many verses referred to trust? Surely many. Even now, the word cast about in her mind as if looking for an anchor. Why was it repeating so often today, when she had plenty of other things to think about?

She'd known right off that Wardman had trusted her with his Ethel. She'd taken it for granted, easily accepting his trust because she knew in her heart she'd never harm a hawk, not even his. But how had he known that?

She shook her head. It was happening again: kind thoughts about Wardman. She wondered if she'd ever get used to that, after a decade of nurturing quite opposite opinions about him.

It was nearly time to go. The temperance sisters had decided to visit the barroom a bit later, when more customers were bound to be present. Not too late—surely before dark—but with the hope of impressing more people than mainly the staff.

Meli went inside to wash up after her day of farm chores, and change into one of the skirts and blouses Madame used to say looked best on her. Meli smiled to remember how Madame would talk of fashion while they kneaded bread together, how she missed the frills and flares of her youth. And fabrics! So many that Meli couldn't recall the name of a single one. But Madame had conceded the present, more sensible fashion was far more practical to suit her love of work. Straight skirts, no bustles, modest sleeves that wouldn't get in the way.

Meli tied up her hair as usual, but add Mama's comb to keep unruly tendrils in place. The only thing missing was Mama's ring. Meli sighed, feeling its loss. A day didn't go by without her thinking of it.

She hadn't said anything to Dad—either about the ring, or where she was going. He'd finished dinner some time ago and sat by the light of a lamp, reading one of the newspapers he'd brought back from Williamsport. He read every single article, sometimes more than once. When she emerged from her room all ready to go, he folded the paper in his lap.

"Where are you off to at this time of day?"

"I'm meeting the women in town."

The newspaper stayed folded. "Not for a sewing bee, I take it. The light's too far gone for it."

Sewing bee! She grinned at the ridiculous assumption. Dad himself did most of the mending, since she had little talent for it. "Have you read any of the literature I asked you to look at, Dad? About what a barroom can do to a sweet little town like Cranbury?"

The corners of his mouth went down, as if he'd bit into a lemon. "I'll say it again. That's for the town to decide. If it doesn't want something like that here, folks won't support it."

"But what about travelers? Or others coming to town just to drink? Shouldn't we have a say in wanting to prevent that? The women of town, I mean? It's not as if it's open to us anyway. Our only choice is to make our voices heard."

He lifted his paper, still scowling. "Guess I won't jabber on about it, since you're not listening anyway."

Meli smiled through her disappointment, guessing they probably would never see eye-to-eye. This was something new, not being on each other's side—not that their quiet lives had ever brought much reason to differ. She went to him, tilted aside the newspaper then planted a kiss on her father's forehead. "Thanks, Dad."

"Thanks!" he repeated. "For what?"

"For not being one of the men in that place."

He shook his head. "Don't be so quick to thank me for that. If I were the sociable kind, I'd probably have a favorite stool by now. It'd be a sad thing to see my own daughter using a public shaming to get me to change my behavior."

"Shame you! But we're trying to protect people, that's all."

He huffed. "That's the hardest kind of protection, the kind that's put onto a fella when he might not see the need. When maybe there is no need. Besides, you ought to know something about some of that liquor—"

She was so surprised by the turn of the conversation she couldn't let him finish. "That's why we're going! To point out the need."

Then she took her hat and gloves and the hymn book she'd borrowed from the church and went on her way, her mind more obedient now. Her temperance sisters awaited.

~

DANE LOOKED over the heads of the men gathered in his barroom —a good number for only the second day. Men had come from all over the area, including as far as Williamsport. He'd shaken every hand, welcoming each and every one who came through the door, learning names and whatever else he could to keep them straight in his mind.

He wanted not only to get to know them, but for them to know this could be their home-away-from-home. Even the parlor upstairs could be rented for an overnight guest or two. Not exactly private, but that likely wouldn't stop any customer too unsteady to get far. The lack of any real rooms for rent was helpful, in a way. If by any chance a woman on the opposite end of virtue came into his tavern, he wouldn't have an appropriate place to rent for her type of business. He'd looked the other way back in Philly, since nearby rooms were aplenty back there. He doubted, though, the women of Cranbury would be much impressed by his step up in morals.

But he must offer the upstairs parlor if he was going to stay comfortably within the law. Since he planned to stay open during most hours after dark, he'd have the ready explanation that "inns" couldn't really close, could they?

Tonight's crowd hadn't been forced to cross a line of Bible-toting, hymn-singing protestors. He didn't believe they'd given up already, but if they had he should be thoroughly relieved. However, the fact remained he would've liked to see Meli again, even if they were on opposite sides.

"Yeah, my wife all but tied my hands to try keeping me home," said one of the locals before taking a swig of Dane's bestselling brew: Packham's homemade whiskey. Dane thought the man to be Mr. Dewitt, the local postman.

Dane recognized the other one as being Jonas Prestwich, from the stationery shop. Most of those from Cranbury tended to stick together, as if in a bond of rebellion.

"So your wife is still talking to you?" Prestwich asked. It was hard to tell if he was joking.

Doc Lancaster sat on a third stool. "Cranbury women are sensible enough to realize there's no real danger here. They'll come 'round."

"From what I've seen of the ladies in this town," Dane said from the other side of the bar, "they're on the genteel side. Hopefully they won't come with your axes ready to smash the bottles on my shelves."

General assent and a few chuckles followed, as if trying to imagine their wives wielding an ax.

"You might be surprised, Mr. Wardman," said Dewitt. "The women around here might be genteel, but they're stubborn. I'd say the temperance group today has a better chance of lasting than the first one started a while back."

"But the first one *did* disperse?" Dane said hopefully. "All we have to do is figure out why, and repeat the cycle."

Doc was already shaking his head. "They didn't have a target, those women from the first group."

Dane's brows shot up. "Like me, you mean?"

"Precisely."

Just as Marto, from the other end of the bar, approached to see if anyone needed a refill, the room went unexpectedly silent.

Dane's heart skipped a beat, coinciding with his gaze falling on Meli Atherton. That same skipping heart squeezed a bit; even his sleepy lighting couldn't hide her prettiness. Her hair was neater than usual, and for a moment he missed the unruly tendrils that were wont to escape whatever combs or clips she used tonight. Her clothing was pleasingly form-fitting, a dark skirt and blue blouse that probably competed with the shade of her eyes, if he drew close enough to confirm such a guess.

It was later than the night before, near nine o'clock. The sun was already behind the mountains, still lingering in the glow, but he'd irrationally hoped they would come even as the later hour brought more risk.

Making his way around the bar, Dane greeted them with his friendliest smile. He noted a few of the men not only weren't smiling, but a few skeptical scowls appeared.

"Ladies!" he said, stopping in front of Meli, but addressing all of them. "Welcome to the *Hawk*, where no one is turned away."

"Then this ain't no home-away-from-home," called one man from a corner near the pool table. "I don't have to come here to see a woman readin' her Bible."

Dane held up a hand, now turning to the men in the room. "The women have come to voice their opinions, which they are welcome to do. They'll be on their way soon enough. Anyone who stays through their—ah, performance—earns a free drink tonight."

Among the gasps from the women, he heard:

"That goes against why we came!"

"We're here to stop men from taking that poison, not encourage it!"

"Free! A demon's bargain!"

"Ladies," said Dane above their protests, "let's keep this friendly, shall we?"

Then one of them started praying, something about imploring the Spirit of God to touch each and every heart present, a reminder to every ear about the dignity of man which the demon rum would rob, the false rest, empty confidence, traitorous promises of comfort. It was all lofty enough so Dane thought most of the men listening, even if their senses weren't dulled so early in the evening, probably didn't follow.

Meli started singing and the prayers some might have found insulting were forgotten—at least by Dane. Unfortunately, she chose that same song from the night before, about the drink being a poison to steal a man's soul, calling divine help to conquer the dreadful sin. Knowing she was easier to listen to than even an earnest prayer did stir him—but probably not the way the anti-saloon composer would have hoped.

Halfway through the chorus in which the rest of the women sang along, a chair toppled, causing most of the choir-like voices to falter.

"I didn't come here for a church service!" The tall man, unshaven for a day or two at least, had found enough boldness in whatever amount of alcohol he'd consumed to let his voice raise to the rafters. "Free drink or otherwise!"

Then he strode past the women, shoving one of them aside with such force it took two of the ladies nearby to keep her from falling.

"Hey, now!" called an irate, masculine voice from the bar. In a moment Jonas Prestwich stood a foot from the back of the man who had, intentionally or otherwise, propelled the woman out of his way. "Nobody pushes my wife and gets away with it."

The man, who'd been on his way toward the door, turned to the papermaker. Nearly nose-to-nose now, the two men stood at approximately the same height, though the papermaker was a good bit slimmer than the other.

"I didn't push her. She was in my way." If the man had acted like a bull trying to get past the women, he looked no less like one with his nostrils flaring, color heightened.

"An 'excuse me' would have worked."

"What are you going to do about it?"

Even as he wordlessly pushed back the first of his two sleeves, one gentle hand stalled him. Must have been his wife, the one who'd been shoved. "Jonas, don't be ridiculous. You can't actually fight—"

"No, ma'am, he cannot."

The words didn't come from the challenger, but rather from Checker whose shadow dwarfed the two men, the same as it did whenever Dane stood that close. He nearly grinned; the last thing Dane needed was a brawl to prove the unsavoriness of his place. Checker had stopped more than his share of fights back in Philly, there was no doubt he'd do so again.

"If either one of you desires fight, lads, you'll have to go through me." Checker looked at one, then the other, adding, "And do not play the idiot by saying you'll go outside. I can go out there, too, and follow each of you as long as it takes for a cooling off."

The men looked at him, then exchanged a glance with each other.

"There's no need for anyone to fight," the papermaker's wife said, obviously seeing that the men were still considering what to do. "I'm all right."

"Apologize."

The papermaker's demand was low but firm, his eyes fixed not on his wife but on the man standing on Checker's other side.

"I told you, I didn't do it on purpose."

"I don't care. It happened. That's what gentlemen do, they apologize, even for mistakes."

"I'd do it if I were you, son," said Checker. "Because I agree with him. If a fight is to happen I'll be on his side."

"Okay," the man spat. "Sorry. I'm sorry."

Then, although he'd directed the apology to the air and not to the woman for whom it was supposed to be intended, he plopped his hat on his head and turned to the door. As the man passed, Dane was close enough to hear him mumble something about

Irishmen and skirts, instantly glad no one else seemed to hear him or another altercation might have ensued.

"You're all right then, ma'am?" Dane asked the woman.

She squared her shoulders, obviously recovered from the incident far more quickly than he'd have expected from the refined— if somewhat sheltered—women in this haven of a town. "I am, no thanks to this place and the drinks you're serving. You don't belong here, sir."

"That's right!" said another at her side. "This is a God-fearing town, and we don't want a bunch of strangers stopping here for anything other than shopping our *legitimate* business or for proper rest."

He might have corrected her, since his business was fully legitimate and he had the liquor license to prove it. But voices erupted from both sides after that, men retaliating for him, shouting reasons they'd come—to a real business *and* for a proper rest— while the women condemned any form of respite that included not only poison, but attracted men eager for fisticuffs.

Every single one of the women, and quite a few of the men, erupted in some form of argument. Knuckles were soon raised against wagging fingers, thankfully without contact. But plenty of sensitive ears were likely assaulted over the language here and there. Even one of the women shouted the word "damnation" although Dane wondered if it could be counted against her. She likely used it in proper context, at least according to the church rules he remembered.

Meli, a few feet away now that Dane had moved, shouted at a man twice her size, spurring Dane to return. For a woman so petite, she displayed no fear.

"Look," Dane said, sticking his face between Meli and the burly man, "you both have your opinions, but let's leave it at that. Agree on one thing, that agreement might be pos—"

But the man only leaned around Dane and loomed over Meli,

continuing his shouts. She might not be afraid of him, but Dane was beginning to fear for her.

"People! People!" Dane bellowed, though the man didn't listen, nor anyone else nearby. Then he stuck two fingers between his lips and whistled so loud it pierced even his own ears. He did it again, and the room quieted.

Raising both arms, pumping palms downward in an invitation to stave off the noise, he offered a grin. "I'd invite everybody to sit down and have a drink so things can get friendly, but I guess that's the whole point, isn't it? Half would agree, the other half wouldn't. Ladies, we all listened to your songs and your prayers and so you've had your say. The gentlemen here just want to have a moment in the company of like-minded people. You wouldn't begrudge them that, would you?" He didn't dare pause long, refusing to spare a moment's silence as opportunity for either side to start the argument all over again. "So why don't we all go back to whatever it was we were doing earlier in the evening? Ladies? Have you given the men here enough to ponder?"

There was a gentle rumble throughout, but at least one of the women stepped forward—toward the door. It was the leader, the pastor's wife. "We did do what we came for," she said, "so we'll be our way." She sounded breathless but surprisingly strong. "Nothing has changed, at least not on our part. If you say those here are of like mind, so are we. This kind of place doesn't belong in Cranbury."

"Well," Dane said congenially, "it's new. We'll have to carve our niche like any new business must. There might come a day when you won't even remember us not being here."

"Not if we can help it," said another, and a few around her echoed the same.

Meli was, like last night, the last to leave. Dane watched her, hoping she might look at him the way she had before; granted, not affectionately, but with that curious curiosity he'd found so appealing the night before.

Try though he did, he couldn't read what was behind such eyes almost bright enough to see through. Or maybe he didn't want to see what was obvious: no welcome, there.

"I'm praying for you, Dane Wardman," she said, but if that was supposed to be a good thing, he couldn't tell it by her tone. Too much sadness there, perhaps even pity.

Then the door closed behind the gentle ladies of Cranbury.

CHAPTER 24

*M*eli rose late the next morning, coming downstairs to an empty kitchen. Dad was probably out in the field. The hired hands had long since moved on, those workers who helped with their biggest crops: harvesting spring barley and planting rye for fall. Still, Dad was diligent about plucking any weed apt to grow between the neatly planted rows. No sense letting anything so useless steal the good work of the ground.

She was relieved not to have to face Dad this morning. The night before, she'd returned far later than she'd expected, worrying all the way home he might have been waiting up. She'd been relieved to find he was in his room, and thought he'd been sleeping. But when she tiptoed past he'd called out, saying they'd talk in the morning. He'd sounded groggy and stern at the same time.

If she hurried this morning, she could escape whatever lecture he had in mind. And he didn't even know about last night's fracas! How could he? If he'd truly been keen on talking to her he would have let the weeds wait, even if she had taken her time this morning to come downstairs.

She went outside to see to her various critters, lingering now and then to offer a whispered word, a gentle coo. Mornings were her favorite time of the day, especially with animals so happy to see her.

She left the mews to last, but as she approached this edge of their farm closest to the forest, she was surprised to hear raised voices. Looking around, she saw no one but followed the sound echoing off the trees until she came up her father and Mr. Packham. She couldn't tell what they argued about with one voice drowning the other. All she could decipher was that her father seemed surprised by Mr. Packham's crop, which was more than odd since she passed his fields every day and he was growing what he always grew this time of year: rye.

"What's going on?" she called as she neared.

Both men stopped immediately. Mr. Packham turned his back on her, putting his hands on his hips, taking a deep breath as if he'd just participated in the same kind of fracas she'd seen last night at the *Hawk*. Dad turned to her, the lines on his face still deep—almost the same lines he had when he smiled, except his gaze was irate. Something she rarely, if ever, saw.

"Nothing, daughter," he said. "Go on about your business now."

"But you're upset, both of you. Is there anything wrong?"

"No." The single firm word came in unison.

Meli remained still for a moment, pondering whether or not to go, until her father raised a hand to shoo her away. She obeyed, walking slowly to see if the argument resumed. If it did, they kept their voices too quiet for her to hear.

She wondered what the disagreement could have entailed. They'd never been chums, her father wasn't that kind, but if he had any friend at all she'd have thought it was Mr. Packham. They had shared enough farm labor to assume that.

Surely it had something to do with Mr. Packham's white whiskey. After all, Mr. Packham had never sold his poison here in town before, so that was the only thing that had changed lately.

Was there no part of town that would remain untouched by this new venue?

She returned to her mews, keeping an eye out for her father. Perhaps he might tell her what was going on, without Mr. Packham present. But she didn't see him at all that morning.

As she walked to town later, her father's argument with Mr. Packham joined her thoughts about last night's confrontations at the *Hawk*. It added easy fodder to a flame too readily reignited against Wardman. She reminded herself of her newfound goal to see Wardman's salvation, but how could she not blame him for all of the strife? Even if she and her temperance sisters had taken a risk to enter the saloon so late, it only proved what they'd been saying all along: alcohol brought out the worst, even by those who hadn't consumed a drop!

Several of the ladies, including Meli herself, had hoped a later visit might be a good thing, even though their late arrival had been due to unforeseen delays: fussy children, husbands who needed more convincing that daily visits were a good idea. Arriving at such a time proved there would be more customers to impress upon. No one had anticipated the possibility of patrons having consumed enough liquor to become unruly. Surely it was that which had either emboldened or made unsteady that customer who nearly toppled Arianne Prestwich.

It would behoove them to regularly protest the barroom at its fullest—and not only to reach that many more hearts and souls. How long could Wardman stay in business if all he did was hand out free drinks to settle an argument? It wasn't exactly the way they wanted to run him out of town, but perhaps the right result would happen that much faster if his business proved unprofitable.

Essie had called a meeting to discuss how they might have better handled last night. With so many guests at the inn, they'd changed their plans and would meet at church. Unfortunately, it seemed more travelers had taken rooms in the last two nights—coinciding with the newness of the saloon.

Although not all the men of Cranbury had patronized the *Hawk*, it seemed clearer every day that few men were fully behind their movement. Those men who hadn't already visited the place didn't seem to think it wise to tell other men what to do, not even if it was for their own good.

Although Meli didn't arrive late, there was already plenty of chatter when she entered the sanctuary. Excited chatter.

"Who knew Freddy was such a prattler?" Mrs. Taylor's asked, her tone more high-pitched than usual. "He must've knocked on doors to spread the word about what happened."

"He had help," Mrs. Wingate added. "Don't forget, Tummers wasn't even there but I heard him telling one of our guests all about it at the inn—embellished, of course. He said Arianne was knocked down, Jonas nearly got his nose broken, and a brawl ensued!"

"Oh, no!" lamented Arianne Prestwich. "What's better advertising than notoriety? Now men might come just to see if there will be another incident."

Meli pursed her lips, joining right in. "I'll bet Wardman is having a good chuckle over the whole thing."

While the others nodded along, Meli caught Essie's gaze. She didn't have to say a word; Meli was already wondering why she'd spoken as harshly as she had. Even if Wardman was chuckling, there was no need to focus on him. She was supposed to be praying for him!

"Half the *Hawk's* staff is staying at my inn," Mrs. Taylor was saying. "I have a mind to turn them all out, except . . . well . . . Oh, I don't know what to do about that, since I'm open to the public and want to run my business in a Christian way. How can I put them on the street? I'm going to suggest they find other accommodations, though. And soon!"

"Let their employer find homes for them," said Phoebe Turner.

"I say you given them a date to leave, unless they find new employment."

"I suppose you could," mused Mrs. Wingate. "As you said, you're open to the public, but it's a private business, after all. Can't you run it as you please, make your own rules? Customers always have the choice to support you or not, depending on how you run things."

Meli couldn't help thinking the first person to agree with her might be Wardman himself, but she didn't voice that thought. The women chattered on about the right thing to do, in the end deciding Mrs. Taylor might at least remind the staff members staying at the inn that it wasn't a boarding house, after all. They couldn't stay indefinitely, or it would limit the inn's capacity to take in travelers and other out-of-towners who depended on the inn's availability.

At last Essie called everyone's attention. "We must agree on our plans," she said. "We've already decided to visit the saloon every single day it's open. Resolved?"

"Resolved!" came the unified response.

"Despite the challenge of last night, knowing we impressed upon more patrons than before, shall we also resolve to schedule our visits after, rather than before, dark?"

"Resolved!"

"Then, ladies, let's make sure we're wearing the full armor of God tonight, because we may need it!"

DANE STOOD behind his brass-encased cash register, replacing a portion of the money he'd taken to his upstairs safe the night before to make change for customers arriving this evening. From the kitchen came sounds of pans banging and a newly familiar whistle from Lannigan. Nearby, young Guyto swept the floor. Dane had already learned two things about the boy: he was more interested in taking dishes to Irene than cleaning tables or floors, and he was every bit a charmer. More reasons the boy reminded Dane of himself. Guyto had insisted on seeing Irene home after closing last night, naming the earlier commotion. By the time the boy had returned, Dane had been abed, only to awaken to a floor in the same state he'd left it the night before.

A bold knock drew him from the register. Peering through one of the window slats, he saw Al John Packham on the saloon's stoop. Dane had expected him sooner than this, considering the delivery of two whiskey crates Dane had purchased from him. Surely the man wanted to see the place where his goods were being sold?

Dane had good news for the man. Whoever tasted his liquor more often than not wanted more, making it a quick favorite among all the beverages served. A few patrons had admitted they'd come for that product alone, this location being closer than Williamsport where it was usually sold.

Dane unlocked the door. "Come in, come in," Dane greeted the man, stepping aside to let him enter. He was old enough to be Dane's grandfather, and he'd brought his cane. Dane noticed a faintly sugary fragrance, likely originating from the man's jacket from the fermenting grains he worked with.

"Come for a tour to see where your product is being sold?" Dane asked.

Packham was shaking his head before Dane had finished. "Came for two reasons," he said, not bothering to look around. Evidently the man was used to such surroundings, and nothing drew more than a passing gaze. Dane would have mulled his offense, but Packham was already talking. "Heard about a ruckus here last night. Any truth to it?"

"You do get to the point, don't you?" Then, even though he knew from Marto, who was living at the inn, that the town was buzzing, he asked, "Where did you hear about it?"

"Field workers helpin' out around here. A couple of 'em were here to see it. Said a lady got knocked down."

"It's good of you to show concern, Mr. Packham—"

"It's not concern, least not about any one of the women around here. They named me and mine pariahs a long time ago, so I wouldn't care if any of 'em suffered a bump or two. I just didn't expect my warnins' to come true so quick. They'll chase you outta here, mark my word."

Dane couldn't tell if the "told you so" equaled the man's eagerness to besmirch Cranbury townsfolk. "What happened wasn't serious," he said. "And there are a number of local men who seem to want to keep me in business."

"Ha! You think they'll keep their woman home, even if they do come? Who do you suppose really runs this town? Look here, I'll be happy if your place don't get burned to the ground, but I wouldn't put it past any one of them so-called do-gooders to do such a thing."

"There won't be any danger of that," Dane assured the man. "I keep a close eye on things, living upstairs. And I have a staff with sharp eyes, too. Once the women realize this place is nothing more than a club for their husbands, they'll be glad to have happier men around the house. And consequently, you and I will make a comfortable living."

Packham eyed him for a long, silent moment and Dane once again wondered what the man was thinking. That Dane was crazy, or just an idealist?

Packham retraced his few, limping steps back to the door. "Listen here, young fella, the men around here will do what their wives want. You better see those women don't muck things up."

Since it appeared Packham was on his way out, Dane called after him. "You said two reasons. What's the other one?"

The man frowned, as if frustrated by his own forgetfulness. "I have six crates if you want 'em. And one of my barrels that won't be ready for a few more months. If you pay now you can have it when it's ready."

Dane eyed him closely. Those were deals from a man strapped for cash. "Trouble with the business?"

"Which is none of your business. You want it, or should I sell it somewhere else?"

"Oh, I'll take whatever you want to sell. This wouldn't happen to be a closeout sale, would it?"

"Nobody said closeout." The words came a bit too harsh for what had been a weak attempt at either humor or a bargain, so Dane let it be. The whiskey had already proven its worth.

Dane watched Packham leave, wondering at the real reason for the visit. Maybe Packham just wanted to be sure Dane's whiskey orders would be consistent, a reliable source of income. Or maybe he really was worried about the impact of the women around here and wanted maximum money up front before Dane was forced to close.

If that was the case, Dane was ready to enact a plan he'd mulled overnight. It was time he made a real effort to win over the women of this town.

Upstairs, Checker's door was open. Dane tapped once then stepped inside—only to be taken aback. Checker was sitting on the side of his bed—reading a book. Not that Dane didn't believe the man capable; he'd just never seen him doing such a thing. Upon second glance, unexpected annoyance set in. It wasn't just any book. It was a Bible.

He held it up at Dane's surprised silence.

"This was left in the desk in the parlor. Did you happen to see it?" Then he went on without waiting for an answer. "It must've come with the place, don't ya' know. Take it, why don't you? It's yours." He extended it closer.

Dane did not move, and eventually Checker placed the Bible back on his bed.

"It's a funny thing, Bible readin'. Me own mother underlined some of these same places as underlined in this one." He stood, going to the bag he'd brought with him from the city. In a moment he pulled out a book similar to the one he'd left on the bed. "Care to see me prove myself right?"

"No," Dane said, a bit more curtly than intended. "I came to ask you a question. What if we bribe the women of this town into accepting us?"

Maddeningly, Checker returned to the bed and laid out the Bible from his bag to place it next to the one he'd been reading. In spite of his apparent lack of attention, he asked, "What sort of bribe?"

"A donation to some worthy cause—other than the Temperance League, of course. Though I'd wager they take it anyway, and call it money to offset my guilt."

"Hmm," Checker said, still not looking Dane's way. "Money can solve the problem, is that it?"

"It works in the city."

"True enough, at least for some." He looked up. "I suppose you might consider the church. They're usually happy to have more funds for one cause or another."

"I was thinking more in terms of a youth group, you know how they were popular in the city? The Boys Clubs?"

"Is there one here in town?" He sounded as surprised as Dane had been a moment ago.

"I don't know, but surely there are boys around here. That's who they say they're protecting. Men, and presumably their replacements."

"Well, you'll want the money to stay close if the bribe's to have any sway. The church is right next door, and they can start such a club if there isn't one already."

Dane might have explored the point, discussed it or other possibilities, but Checker had turned his attention back to the two books in front of him. Vexed, Dane nearly issued a scathing comment about Checker caring more about a couple of old books than the person standing in front of him.

Dane had successfully ignored God for years, and Checker knew it. On the rare occasion Checker went to church—at least on major holidays—Dane had consistently refused any invitation to tag along. Must Dane spell it out, how the church, at least as seen through his family, wasn't worth Dane's time—and especially not his money?

He shook off the growing tension in his shoulders. As perfect as this place was for a barroom, being so near the main road, that church was the one drawback. Working and living in the shadow of its steeple made it slightly more challenging to ignore God altogether—particularly when the women in town came in singing hymns every day.

And one of them kept telling him she was praying for him. It was downright disturbing.

CHAPTER 25

For the next few days, Meli rarely saw Dad. She had
decided it had been best to put off talking to him
since she rarely came home earlier than ten o'clock—a full hour
after he normally went to bed. That wouldn't change for the fore-
seeable future. How long their protests went on depended on
when Wardman closed his doors.

She couldn't delay the inevitable, though, so she ventured
outside to see if she might help with the stock. But Dad was
nowhere to be seen, and the animals had all been tended.

Meli went to the mews instead, visiting each hawk, freshening
water bins, inspecting and cleaning their feet, soles, and talons.
Afterward she looked over the equipment, noting which tethers,
jesses or hoods would soon need replacement.

Time always disappeared with such enjoyable work, so when
she went outside to see about their yard gardens—a chore exclusively hers—she had no idea how close lunch might be. The sun
was nearly straight overhead. Perhaps Dad was back, or perhaps
she could go out to the field and see if he wanted her to bring him
something.

Approaching the house, she was surprised to see Mr. Packham

emerge. So, Dad must be home. Ever since she'd witnessed their argument the other day, Meli had avoided Mr. Packham. She had enough contention in her life without trying to involve herself in theirs.

He walked off without even noticing her, back in the direction of his farm.

Inside the house, she expected to find Dad in the kitchen. But the room was empty. In fact, the entire house was much quieter than she expected.

"Dad?"

No answer.

It didn't take long to search. He wouldn't be in her room, but he wasn't in his, either, nor was he in the parlor. Even the cellar was vacant.

Perhaps Mr. Packham had been bold enough to go inside looking for Dad, if he thought her father might not willingly answer his knock. But he must have found what she had: her father wasn't there.

She was tempted to stay inside, to do what she'd planned to do that afternoon before going into town for their daily protest. Each one of her temperance sisters was devoted to gathering material to present at future rallies. She'd been scouring her father's book of sermons—something he read from every Sunday—for more references to the dangers of strong drink. Meli couldn't wait to see the fruits of all their research and study.

But she still had the gardens to tend for now, so she went back outside. It wasn't, however, the weeds she battled there. Thoughts of Wardman continued to confuse her. Her ill feelings toward him were as familiar as a habit, so she knew the desire to pray for him wasn't her own but from God Himself. She'd stubbornly tried limiting this urge to petition on his behalf, knowing she'd still be following the bare minimum of the original promise if she prayed once per day.

Dane Wardman had once symbolized for Meli a combination

of the greatest losses of her life; he'd been responsible for one of them. Yet she found herself praying for him longer and more often than she'd vowed to do—many more times than just once a day. What, other love than God's love, could explain such a change? Meli was convinced the unseen world—the one of angels both good and fallen—was surely busy around Dane Wardman.

~

DANE LINGERED NEAR THE DOOR. It was the most convenient spot to greet newcomers, but he didn't try fooling himself into ignoring another motive—to be the first to spot the *Hawk's* nightly visitors. One in particular.

He glanced again at his wrist watch. Despite his hope that they would go back to arriving earlier in the evening, it was already past nine. He had little hope they weren't coming, so in his estimation they were late.

Even though it was too delicate to be felt, Meli's ring fairly tingled in his pocket. After she arrived tonight, he would listen to their regular routine. The women would sing. They would pray. Someone would say a few words, not exactly a speech, just a few words on the evils of alcohol. Finally, they would sing their way out the door. Hopefully nothing would go awry, as it had some nights ago. Both he and Checker had been making sure of that by keeping a close eye on the mood of the men, cajoling, appeasing, quietly bargaining where necessary.

Tonight, Dane would ask to speak to Meli privately. He would take her away from the friction that came inevitably with why she was there. First, he would offer the church a donation. He'd begrudgingly concluded Checker was right about that. She needn't know the church wasn't his first choice. Surely Checker had been right in assuming there wasn't a boy's club already in place, and Dane had neither time to organize nor to recruit another leader to start one. Heaven forbid they'd expect Dane to do more than just hand over a wad of cash.

Wouldn't such a donation be worth tolerating his business? The church would reap a financial benefit, the women would feel as if they'd inspired it, and all would be well.

Once Meli warmed to that idea he would pull out her ring. Surely that would cinch her acceptance of him. She would celebrate the return of something she obviously cared about. He went so far as to imagine her entirely forgetting that silly pact he'd offered about not touching each other and throw her arms around him. She'd be that grateful to have the ring back. It wasn't such an impossible hope, was it? If the ring truly meant something to her, even if he didn't?

It was no longer rare that she met his gaze. Maybe after tonight she might even cast him a smile now and then.

ESSIE HAD INVITED Meli to come early again to the empty church, where they had spent more time in prayer than they had planning tonight's protest. They would soon join their temperance sisters at Leta's dress shop, where Meli and Essie would bring the power of their own prayers and add more to them there. How else could they face what might on any given night prove to be another show down with rowdy saloon-goers?

Meli stood.

"Wait, Meli," said Essie, taking one of Meli's hands. She sat again. "I wanted to talk to you before we go. About something that has nothing to do with any of us getting knocked down or shouted at."

Meli waited, though Essie's smile indicated that whatever she wanted to say couldn't be bad. There was a hint of sparkle in her eye.

"I wanted to tell you how wonderful it is to see God loving Mr.

Wardman through you. It's been very inspirational, a reminder that the man is only misguided, not irredeemable."

Her brows popped up. "Loving him? I'm sure it's not—"

"It's love, all right. The best kind, all the more wonderful considering your past with him. I've heard it in your prayers, even just now. You want him to know God's love. So you've forgiven him, then? For what he did all those years ago?"

Meli lifted one shoulder. She'd never actually faced that question, finding it easier to avoid even while uttering what felt like God-inspired prayers. If such prayers were answered, the town would be free of strife, at least the kind that most embroiled Cranbury these days—even between husbands and wives!

Even now, that single word stuck unexpectedly in her throat. Forgiveness. If she couldn't face it in her mind, how could she claim she'd done any such thing in her heart?

"If I have any love for him, it's God's, not mine."

Essie still held Meli's hand, and squeezed it. "Forgiveness and love are hard to separate."

"Then may God never leave me," Meli pleaded with a guilty grin, "otherwise all that's left might be that old hatred."

"God won't ever leave you. He promised that. But I'm not so sure He's left any room inside you for those old feelings anymore. He's made new ones. Better ones."

Meli wanted to deny it, push away something she knew to be true. Instead, she stayed quiet. She knew love, especially God's love, was better than hate or revenge, but that word—love—just wasn't one she was ready to talk about. She hadn't really lived up to what Essie seemed to see, not while she still hoped Wardman's business would be run out of town.

"If God can change your heart toward Mr. Wardman," Essie said as they rose and walked toward the church vestibule, "then he can surely change Mr. Wardman's heart, too. Maybe He's already working on it. Any night now, we may see this whole problem come to an end."

No sooner had Essie opened the door than Meli realized this was no typically quiet evening in their small town. Though the saloon was as brightly lit as ever, the hubbub wasn't coming from the edge of town. Instead, the sound of urgent voices came from the town's heart, the porch and lawn just outside the Inn.

Meli matched Essie's quick pace to see what was the matter. An argument was already in full swing, but without a single patron from the *Hawk* in sight. These were townspeople. Fighting!

"You've made your point." That came from Mr. Jonas Prestwich, standing with a small group of men on one side of the porch, opposite the women. "Now let it be, and see if the business stands on its own."

"Our point won't be made until that place shuts down!" Either Jonas or Arianne Prestwich had learned something from living with each other nearly a dozen years; her tone matched his exactly.

Another man, one Meli didn't recognize, stepped in front of Mr. Prestwich. He pointed a finger at the women. "Not a single one of you has the right to run anybody out of town."

"That's right," said another man. "This is a free country. And liquor isn't illegal. Hard as you're trying, it's not going to be, either, if you saw how it went at the polls last year."

"That'll change if we get the vote!" cried Raina Levick, and that started another upheaval.

"Look," rose the voice of another Levick, this one Meli knew to be Raina's husband, the toymaker. "You women have every right to voice your opinions. You've done that. But none of us want you going into a place you're not welcome."

"Cade's right," spoke up Jonas Prestwich again. "You want *us* to stay out of there, but can you blame us for wanting to make sure you're safe? We'll have to follow you inside every night. Is that what you want?"

"We don't want you to follow us in there," said Arianne, "we want you to go in *with* us to protest the place at our sides."

"We're not going to protest a place that has every right to exist." The papermaker's voice made it clear he wasn't persuadable, setting off a chorus of protest.

"Why won't you see reason?"

"It's a right we want taken away!"

"No one should have a right to poison people!"

Meli tightened her lips, wondering if she'd been better off living the reclusive life her parents had modeled. Every woman in their temperance group had to live with a man and their opinions. Even ones like the toymaker who'd so far stayed publicly neutral because of his own business reputation. Evidently that had changed.

"Let them all argue," Meli said to Essie, who still stood beside her. "You once said you never counseled someone to go against their parents. Well, I guess I wouldn't feel right counseling a woman to go against her husband. But *I* won't be going against anybody. I'm going in there without them."

"I'm not going against my husband," Essie said. "So I'm coming with you."

"Let's go."

"Yeah, all those hens are cluckin' away out there," said Mr. Tummers, taking a seat at the bar. "Too busy fightin' to come over here tonight. Can't fight on two fronts, I guess."

Doc Lancaster let out a chuckle but said nothing. It interested Dane that the doctor came every night, even though he drank so slowly one glass lasted him the entire evening. He was the model customer, like the kind who might come to a real men's club and not a saloon.

"The women are fighting among themselves?" Dane asked, confused. Surely they were too united for that. Nor would he believe they were fighting within their families, at least not in public. On the occasions he'd seen couples together around here, they'd always presented an indivisible front. One he'd have envied if he let himself.

"No, sir. The husbands are tryin' to keep 'em home. Says they don't want their wives gettin' shoved around. Don't blame 'em, I suppose." Mr. Tummers turned to look squarely at Dane, who had come up behind them. "Guess they don't trust you to keep it from happening again." He pointed his nose toward Checker, who lingered near a window. "Not even him."

"I have no intention of letting this establishment become a boxing ring between temperance women and the men who just want a place to relax."

Dane left the men at the bar and headed back to the door. Maybe his plan to bribe the women into compliance would be best offered to the whole town—and sooner than later.

"Hey," called Tummers, "you goin' over there?"

Dane didn't answer, but after he called Checker to follow, half of his patrons came along too.

Before he rounded the church, voices broke the quiet of the night. Dim light from a half-moon shone down on the inn, along with the dozen or so people brimming over from the porch. As he neared, he saw two figures already headed his way.

His heart did that familiar dance as he recognized Meli. Checker identified them with a whisper. "The two ring-leaders."

He nodded; he knew.

Dane waved. "We heard there was a discussion going on out here about the *Hawk*," Dane greeted them, hoping they didn't hear the hesitation behind his choice to call it a *discussion*. Another glance beyond the ladies' shoulders revealed no one else had noticed their departure. The rest of the town was still busy yelling from one end of the inn's porch to the other.

As if choreographed, both women folded their arms, a clear signal they had no intention of embracing whatever he had to say.

"You've already succeeded in splitting this town in two," said

Meli. "If you had any decency you would close that place and let us go back to the way things were."

Well, at least she wasn't demanding *he* leave town, as Packham suggested they would do. "Miss Atherton," Dane said, keeping his tone congenial but low, not wanting the others to know he was here just yet. "What the *Hawk* brings to this town is a bit of happy distraction from the burdens of life. I'm sure you'll see that your father—" he glanced at the other woman, "—or husband, will be much easier to live with if they have pleasant camaraderie to look forward to on occasion."

"They can have that without the poison you're serving," said Meli.

"Not even the Bible calls it poison, miss," said Checker, and Dane was immediately grateful he'd brought the man with him. He'd done so to convince the men that their wives would be safe with such a giant to maintain the peace, but this was even better. He'd just offered an argument Dane himself wouldn't have thought of. Maybe he'd have to borrow one of Checker's Bibles for more ammunition—the kind they were likely to listen to. "I remind you that Jesus himself turned water into wine," Checker was saying. "Was he attempting to poison the wedding goers, then?"

"Of course not!" That answer came in a unison.

"You know, of course, there is some question as to whether that wine was fermented or not," said the pastor's wife.

Even Checker drew a brow at that.

"Well, what about the fact that one of our most admired presidents sold liquor as a young man?" Dane asked. He'd thought of that argument the other day, little knowing he'd have the opportunity to use it so soon. "Abraham Lincoln—"

"Was killed by a man who plotted his murder in a saloon," Meli cut in, and so Dane changed his tack.

"Ladies," he said. "I don't want our discussion to look like that one." He pointed toward the porch. "To keep that from happening,

I have something to offer that might be worth your consideration."

Neither said anything, but with their arms still folded he knew he hadn't inspired much more than new suspicions. He looked at the pastor's wife, the exact person who needed to hear what he had to say.

"I'm willing to make regular donations to the church so you can improve the town or the lives of those who most need it. You could do things you wouldn't otherwise be able to do without the *Hawk*. A generous donation? Weekly?"

That warranted an exchange of surprised looks, but not for long. Neither one of them looked either impressed or particularly interested.

Meli did, however, loosen the hold she had on her folded arms as she leaned a trifle closer. Unfortunately, the movement reminded him of something a schoolmarm had once done when lecturing him about not pulling girls' braids, especially when she pointed a finger at his chest.

"Mr. Wardman. I'm sure I speak for everyone in the church when I tell you we wouldn't want a penny earned at the expense of a man's dignity."

Was it his imagination, or was she trying to calm a voice not much less angry than those coming from the inn?

Nonetheless, it was his turn to raise his brows. "You're refusing money that could fill real needs around here? Aren't you being a little hasty?"

"Ill-gotten gains, Mr. Wardman," the pastor's wife said, confirming that Meli had spoken for both of them. "Gains that come at the expense of others."

Dane was purely, completely, flummoxed. However, he had another argument. "If you and the others fearing some bad behavior might result from a place such as mine, I only ask that you give it some time. Say, a year? Six months? Long enough for the men around here to prove their own worth and self-discipline, which you so obviously doubt."

"You're saying we doubt their *worth*?" The pastor's wife had unfolded her arms, but apparently only in surprised rage. "How dare you twist our motives?"

"We *don't* doubt the good people of this town," added Meli. "But half the people you draw aren't from Cranbury. We don't want a place like yours around here, offering strangers a chance to sink to the lowest level such a beverage allows a man to do."

"He's right," came an unexpected, new voice not far from the porch—the men's side. Evidently the other argument had quieted long enough not only to notice but to hear recent words between Dane and the two women. "That's it in a nutshell. You women doubt us men can control ourselves if we have a saloon within walking distance."

Dane didn't recognize the man at first, but thought the voice familiar. When he came closer to the railing, Dane saw it was Leo Levick. He'd been in the *Hawk* on the night it opened, but hadn't returned. Maybe he'd planned to go tonight, if he hadn't been so busy stopping his wife from visiting.

That statement inspired another round of shouting, and Dane was nearly ready to throw up his hands and go back to the sane, welcoming world of his saloon. Let them argue it out; they didn't need his say in it—not that the one half would listen anyway. But he stayed. The outcome would have direct impact on whether he kept afloat.

Anyway, it was too hard to leave Meli's side. And besides, he hadn't forgotten her ring.

CHAPTER 26

*M*eli's growing unease tempted her to leave. She'd become accustomed to being around townsfolk as far back as working at the tea room. She'd even discovered she could fit in, just as Madame had once hinted. But this? She wasn't used to such strife; she'd never seen it at home. If there wasn't going to be a visit to the saloon tonight, she would just as soon go home, away from the arguing.

She would have, if her gaze hadn't fallen again to Wardman. How could he be older, richer, and obviously wider traveled than she and yet be so . . . unwise? He claimed to know how the men who visited his saloon would act, and yet surely he'd seen in person what the pamphlets, flyers and sermons said went on in such places. So many sources couldn't be telling fables. Did he just discount facts, when to save even one woman, one child, one family from the horrors of alcoholism was enough to demand he close?

"Have you never seen a person's life ruined by alcohol, then?" she asked curiously. "Is that why you have no qualms about selling what you sell?"

"Even if I agreed that drinking can be a problem for some, is that my fault? We're each responsible for ourselves."

"But why provide a product with the potential of such a disastrous by-product?" Meli asked.

"Yes," came a voice from the far end of the porch, Arianne Prestwich. "Why make it easier for someone to destroy themselves and possibly those they love?"

"If someone's capable of doing that," he said, "they don't need my help. They'd find a way."

"But you make it easy!" cried the innkeeper, Mrs. Taylor. "As if it's something men *should* do, stop in and drink."

Wardman's hands went up, but she didn't think he had any intention to surrender. "Look, I came out here to offer a compromise. I'm prepared to donate regularly to the church in order to improve the town. But it seems to me you're condemning any man who chooses to drink, not a gallon but a sip. That kind of thinking says you don't really want to discuss the topic—because you've already decided I'm wrong and you're right."

"Is your being wrong such an impossibility?" Meli asked, though she'd kept her voice lower than others. She was determined not to restart the previous noise.

He turned his gaze on her and for a moment she lost her breath, because he stared as if the tension around them didn't exist, pausing so long it was as if no one else was near. "No. We both know I've been wrong before. But not this time."

He was admitting, again, that he'd been wrong in the past. But there would be no changing the man about his business, she was sure of that, and that sent her heart on a downward spiral.

DANE SAW IMMEDIATELY that his answer had disappointed Meli— or worse, saddened her. Yet he'd just admitted, one more time, that he'd been wrong to have killed her bird. He'd thought he'd proven that by trusting her with Ethel.

He wished those around them would quiet down, go away, disappear, leave him alone with Meli. He didn't like having disappointed her, even if he couldn't have answered any other way. Of course he wasn't wrong about letting responsible men drink alcohol. If he thought that, he'd be out of business. No one could change his mind about that, not even the God she said she served.

He looked away, not wanting to see the evidence that she thought him wrong yet again. He didn't want to look at the others arguing anew, but had no choice since they were all around him now. Although the men on the porch hadn't jumped on Dane's briefly spoken idea about donations, the saloon patrons who had followed him had obviously heard and thought it more than generous if judging by the comments coming from behind him. They only added to the noise and tension.

It seemed obvious that everyone thought they knew what was best for the town, even the outsiders. But offering the best was his aim, too! Why couldn't they see that? After all, where one dispersed one's money was the real proof of a man's worth. He planned to have a healthy portion go to their church without even stepping inside the place.

But it was quickly apparent that while some supported his donation, others called it bribery.

Evidently there would be no coming together on this topic, either. But it did do one thing: increase his resolve to stay in business.

Dane would have slipped away, letting them finish the fight however they saw fit. But three new figures gave him pause, all coming from the house next to the church. Pastor Taylor, carrying one child while holding the hand of an older one.

"Quiet!" His voice roared over the rest, and the sleepy child in his arms was startled to awareness. Meli's co-leader came forward to take the now crying boy, while the pastor looked on with a scowl. "I thought I was back in the city in the middle of a gang for all I heard from my window. Is this the kind of example you want to set for my kids, for yours? Everybody fighting in the streets?"

He turned from those on the porch to the ones nearest Dane, the strangers who had followed him and Checker from the pub. "I don't expect any of you to have a say in what goes on in this town, so this isn't for you. But for the rest of you, listen. We've got to come to an agreement on this, or what's to be said of the faith we say we hold? Is it real, if we spend our evenings yelling at one another? I've known most of you all my life, and I've never once been embarrassed by any of you. Until tonight."

He took his child back from his wife, who was still crying. Patting the boy's back, he whispered something to him but then raised his voice again, this time more calmly.

"Go home. Whatever's to be done isn't going to be decided in the dark or on the street. Let's have a rational discussion about it. One week from Sunday, after the service, to give both sides ample time to present their case. Anybody who has something to say can come and voice an opinion. *Calmly.*" He looked at Dane then, who wasn't at all sure he welcomed the sudden attention. "That invitation goes for you, too, Mr. Wardman—whether or not you come to the service beforehand, although I hope and pray you do." He stepped closer to his wife, herding his family away, repeating over his shoulder, "Go home."

Dane wouldn't have believed such a simple command would have been obeyed just a few minutes ago. Surely it wouldn't have if he'd been the one to issue such a thing. But soon the street was empty again. Even his patrons had gone back to the saloon—those who hadn't gone home or to their vehicles. Tonight's business had definitely soured.

It wasn't until Dane undressed for bed that night that he realized Meli's ring was still in his pocket.

CHAPTER 27

"*D*idn't I tell you to stay out of it?"

Dad sat across the breakfast table. Though he was frowning, his tone was softly concerned.

"It was a spectacle, I suppose," she admitted, sipping coffee. "And even though both sides seemed like they couldn't be changed, one good thing did come of it. Everyone went home. Not one person from town went back to the saloon. That accomplished more than our hymns have done."

"You think a street brawl is better than a few men gathering in a place that sells perfectly legal alcohol?"

"It wasn't a brawl!"

"Closest thing to it, as far as I know about this town. The only thing I know to bring people out to the streets before this is that summer festival. What do they call it?"

"The Dash," she answered. "You're right, Dad. But isn't it proof that the barroom should close? It's not good for the town."

"So says a few of the women. Why not quiet yourselves down for a while, see if anything changes without your interference?"

"Dad! You've said it yourself: nearly everything in this fallen world goes to chaos if you don't interfere. What happens to the fields if you don't tame the land and plant seed? Weeds! What happens in this house if one of us doesn't clean? Dust! We're *supposed* to interfere if it's for our own good."

"Maybe there's something to what you say, Meli, or maybe there isn't. But if you can't stay away from those protests, then at least promise you'll stay away from Packham. He's not himself lately."

"Is that why you argued? Because he's not himself?"

"Partly."

She waited for him to explain, but they finished the meal in sad silence, sad, at least for Meli. As she cleared the table, her father stood but she turned to him, asking, "Dad, what do you think about the men going into the *Hawk* in the evenings?"

He tilted his head, frowning. "I don't know a single one of them."

"But imagine you did. What makes them go there? Just for the drinks?"

He shook his head. "Maybe for some. Probably fewer than you think."

"But why else go there?"

"If I were to go to a barroom, it wouldn't be because of the whiskey. Maybe for the company, if I liked such a thing."

The company. Wasn't that what Wardman had said he wanted to provide? A place for hardworking men to relax.

She sighed. Dad didn't need the fellowship of church, either, so at least he was consistent. Yet he partook of the things each building served, right here at home.

Instead of resuming his way toward the door, he looked across the kitchen at her. "Maybe you oughtn't think of the place as the fastest way to death and family destruction."

"It may be neither the fastest nor the only way, but *one* way. Why tolerate it, right here in a town that's done well without such a thing for so long?"

He studied her face. "Daughter, you cannot run a man out of town just for trying to run a legitimate business."

"I don't want him run out of town anymore," she said, words that left her mouth before she knew it. She instantly wished she could recall them, stamp them out so neither she nor her father had heard them. "I just want to close his business."

Her father lifted his shoulders. "There's no difference." He turned again but stopped with his hand on the doorknob, a look of surprise on his face. "Did you hear what you said, Mel?"

She tried to meet his gaze, but turned instead to transfer the dishes from table to sink.

She felt her father's stare. "Is there some possibility—just a little bit of one—that you don't want him to leave Cranbury, after all, Meli? If he was in a different line of work?"

Her face was too hot to convey much credence with what was supposed to be a casual shrug. So she concentrated on warming water at the stove, as if the tasks at hand needed all her attention.

DANE FILLED the last buttonhole on his white shirt as he made his way down the stairs. Guyto had burst into Dane's room five minutes ago, destroying Dane's pleasant state between half-awake, half-asleep. Destroying, with it, the thoughts of Meli Atheron's smile. An inviting one, not polite or pitying. Too bad it had been a dream.

Guyto had announced there was a lady downstairs claiming to be the owner, and she wanted to see Mr. Wardman right away. The boy hadn't bothered to ask the woman's name, but from the description of her gown, hat and jewels Dane guessed it to be the only woman he knew these days who matched such details: Claudette Norcross-Rice. And it sounded as if she'd once again arrived alone.

Dane passed Guyto, who was sitting alone in the kitchen, and found Claudette in the barroom. She stood near the pool table with the white ball in her gloved palm. Upon seeing him, she rolled it across the table, letting it hit the cluster of balls shaped but free of its triangle. None sunk.

"I would say good-morning," she greeted him, "except my pin watch says it's noon. It didn't occur to me how nocturnal you must be in this business. My apologies."

Her smile said she was anything but sorry to have awakened him. He hadn't even taken the time to shave. Nonetheless, he mustered his own simon-pure smile after the latest night he'd known thus far in town—a four-handed game of cards between himself, Checker, Marto and Lannigan. They'd had plenty of time to play. Last night's public argument had cut short the evening, even for out-of-towners, resulting in the leanest business since his opening.

Dane's only hope was that if word did spread about the continued controversy surrounding his place, it would keep drawing attention. There was nothing better than talk about a business, and sometimes curiosity worked wonders.

"Since I can see you're not equipped to offer lunch—or breakfast, or even a cup of coffee," she began, "I'll get right to the point of my visit. One of my husband's associates—a clerk in the lumber office—lives in this direction. He's been here twice since your doors opened, and I understand last night was something of a giant failure. You understand my concern, of course, if you won't be able to honor the rest of your lease?"

He raised his brows. "If you prefer an outright sale, I'm still happy to—"

She was already shaking her head. "No, of course not. I'm here only out of concern." She smiled again, this one slightly more sincere. Once again, he wished she'd let her husband carry on the business between owner and renter. She stepped closer, where he'd stopped at the opposite end of the pool table. "Is there anything I can do? To help, I mean?"

"I don't think . . ."

"Let's be creative, shall we? I could talk to the women in town," she said softly. "Perhaps join their little group and let you know their plans? An infiltration, of sorts? For the betterment of your business, which would obviously benefit us both. After all, if this place is a true success I could increase the rent." Now her smile turned impish.

Partnering further with Claudette was the last thing Dane wanted to consider. This called for a diplomatic refusal. "I've made no secret that I'm leasing this building from you, Mrs. Norcross-Rice—"

"Claudette, please."

"Wouldn't they question your real interest, since the ladies must know you have the ability to break my lease? You could evict me, which would solve their dilemma."

"I've already considered that. Technically, I did inherit this building from my mother. But as everyone knows, women have so little say in business matters. How could I, a mere woman, be involved in matters that my husband is no doubt generally believed to control? I'm sure I would be quite sympathetic if I expressed my lack of authority. They would be happy to have me on their side."

Would anyone who knew Claudette believe she didn't make the lion's share of decisions in that household? Yet as mad as the plan sounded to him, and as little as he wanted to conspire with Claudette, for one brief moment he considered the idea. But no. Claudette was one woman he needed to consistently rebuff. Clearly, but carefully.

"I couldn't ask you to be duplicitous for me, Mrs.—Claudette. It wouldn't say much for my gallantry, would it, to use you in such a way?"

She offered a slow, inviting smile. "Whatever the women in this town say, I'm sure they haven't considered your gallantry. But they may say you have strength in your convictions, which is very admirable."

"Not in the wrong convictions, to them."

"But strength. That's what they really see."

Dane broke the gaze she seemed intent on maintaining. He regathered nearby pool balls with one hand while reaching for the wooden triangle resting on the bank with his other. After placing them back in alignment, he rolled the loose white ball to the other end, then replaced the wooden frame to its spot on the bank.

"I appreciate your concern," he said, "and your generous offer, but there's to be a meeting of the minds a week from Sunday. I intend to be there. I'm sure we'll come to an understanding, since my place isn't without support from many of the locals. The locals who count, that is, who are willing to keep me in business." He faced her again with a polite smile. "Don't worry, Mrs. Norcross-Rice. Not only will I be here for the duration of my lease, I still intend to make an outright purchase. This business will flourish. You'll see."

"Of course you know I don't really care," she whispered.

"I beg your pardon?"

She leaned forward, and the cape she had casually draped over her shoulders fell open to reveal a generously low-cut bodice. "I've been waiting for you to visit me, to let this partnership develop into something of interest. And yet you continue to ignore me, even rebuff me when we're together. I do command the keys to this place, even if you hold them, and there's really only one way to insure you get to stay. It doesn't matter if you make a penny."

Then, evidently having made her threat clear, she turned away. She threw a grin over her shoulder as she paused, picking up the white ball then letting it roll, once again breaking the formation before making her way outside.

CHAPTER 28

*M*eli and her sobriety sisters went to the *Hawk* each evening, late enough to catch more patrons but early enough to avoid creating conniptions in various husbands waiting at home.

But it seemed only the night of the town's argument had fewer patrons visited the *Hawk*. Everyone could count heads; the barroom grew busier with each passing evening.

The ladies finished their last song. As had become habit, Meli avoided Dane Wardman. Yet he seemed forever moving into her line of vision, even after she shifted her attention to those filling the corners of the room. Why didn't he leave her alone? Did others notice this silly game of look and retreat, look and retreat?

It was Essie's turn to end the evening with a prayer, and Meli closed her eyes with relief. Silently, she begged God to end her confusion about Wardman. On the one hand she wanted his eternal salvation, but on the other she *must* want him run out of town, never mind the denial she'd so quickly admitted to Dad the other day.

Did Meli really want him to leave?

She pushed aside her tumultuous thoughts, concentrating instead on Essie's prayer.

Meli should have been the first out the door, since she was closest. And yet she stood as if the floor had somehow trapped her. At last, though, with only Essie and a few of the others left, she moved to exit.

"Hey," came a voice from one of the many shadows.

Meli looked in that direction, pausing along with Essie.

"Hey," repeated the faceless voice. "Thanks for the entertainment. Wouldn't miss it!"

Laughter burst from shadow, along with echoes from others. More comments emerged about how they should take their "floor show" on the road, followed by other suggestions for different songs and, worst of all, an adjustment to their wardrobe.

It was then Dane Wardman stepped once again within Meli's range of vision. He already had a smile on his face, though perhaps it had faded somewhat with the last comment. He'd let her see that smile, though, and it added to her shame. He was laughing at them, too!

Then he raised a call to the bar, advertising a reduction in the cost of drinks for the next half hour. Meli left the barroom without looking back.

None of her fellow reformers spoke once they joined the others already outside in the cool night air. They had agreed to meet again to discuss their presentation at Pastor Taylor's invitation for next Sunday, but no one mentioned it now. It was dark, and Meli had a long walk home. Oftentimes one of the ladies' husbands drove her home in a carriage, but tonight Meli refused any offers. She wanted to be alone.

Her father, as usual, was already abed by the time she slipped into their home. After readying herself for the night, she went to her knees as usual. But she knew, even then, her night would be long.

To make it worse, Wardman invaded the measly hours of her

sleep. She awakened gasping for breath as if her life had been endangered. The dream had begun with his smile, the kind she thought she'd seen tonight. But somehow that smile transformed into something else, something sweet and inviting. So inviting that, in her dream, she'd walked right up to him and there, in front of all of his patrons and all of her temperance partners, she announced she would end their pact not to touch each other. Then she'd kissed him! A kiss that might have been initiated by Meli but was positively usurped by Wardman. And she'd enjoyed it! Her traitorous sleeping mind hadn't done a thing to either end the kiss or stop her heart from fluttering in pure pleasure. At least the more sensible part of her mind had awakened her, albeit out of breath.

Meli tossed and turned, praying, confused that she'd remembered that promise not to touch one another, that the dream labeled her as being the one wanting to break it.

In an attempt to purify her mood, she lit her lamp to read pamphlets, mulling ideas on how to ruin Wardman's business while reminding herself how vital was his salvation. Sunday would be another opportunity to spread their message, and she must clarify it, hone the speech she'd been planning to give at their next rally.

But when she closed her eyes in another effort to capture rest, the image of Wardman's kiss came back just as vividly as when her mind had created it to begin with. She woke in the morning with nothing on her mind but a headache.

Meli headed to town by early afternoon, hours before she was expected. Perhaps Essie or one of the others had succeeded where Meli had failed, and come up with how to proceed on Sunday.

An early escape from home also ensured she would be nowhere near her mews if Wardman arrived to see Ethel. He had come several times before and she'd avoided him at the expense of her pride by hiding in her bedroom—from which she could clearly see him sitting in the mew with Ethel, tossing some sort of crumpled paper he'd brought, letting Ethel retrieve it.

If he came to the mews today, at least she would avoid cowering. This man had brought nothing but trouble to her, forever and always.

Cranbury was quiet as Meli left the cover of the forest and stepped onto Main Street. The luncheon hour had passed, but she remembered from working at the tea room that many businesses saw their most lucrative time while children were still in the one room school nearby, leaving their mothers free for commerce. Yet today it seemed residents had chosen to stay at home, like a holiday when all the stores were closed—except there wasn't a hint of festivity.

Was she imagining that the town seemed like a kettle waiting to boil? Did they fear, as she did, as Sunday afternoon neared, that venting would lead to a repeat of last week's argument? If both sides hoped for a favorable decision, one side was certain to be disappointed.

As Meli passed the Cranbury Inn, she stopped. A small circle of young children was on the porch, including two belonging to Essie. Voices came through the open window and Meli went inside, finding not only Essie but every one of their movement's most faithful followers. Unfortunately, not a single smile could be seen among them.

"Ah!" said Essie, as if relieved. "There, you see, ladies! God's spirit really is moving. He's brought all of us together, hasn't he? It took Meli longer to get here because she lives so far."

"Either that," quipped Raina Levick, "or our misery is wanting some company."

"You're right about misery," said Meli, taking a seat near Essie. Tea was already set, and Meli accepted a cup from the elder Mrs. Taylor. "Nightly entertainment! It still sets my blood to boiling."

"Every movement takes time to make a difference," Essie said. "Perhaps we just haven't been at it long enough. We're all together now. What we need to do is double our prayers, and prepare for Sunday."

"Doubling our efforts at the *Hawk* would only give them *more* entertainment!" said Arianne. "They're laughing at us, you heard it yourself."

"I know we don't want to repeat the speech from our first rally," Meli said, "because the Smythe message wasn't appealing. But wasn't it true, the shame part? My own father hasn't signed a pledge, and isn't likely too, either. What confuses me is that even though he still takes a drink now and then, he continues to keep that bottle hidden. I'm not even forbidden from it, so he's not hiding it from me. So does he keep it tucked away because he's ashamed to have such a thing? What else can it be, really? Some of our neighbors, even a couple of husbands, if they do go to the *Hawk*, go when they don't have to see us there. Is shame keeping them away? The shame of having to face us, knowing we represent the truth of what alcohol can do to bring a person down? Drunkenness is nothing to be proud of, after all."

"Exactly!" said Arianne. "My husband may think it's fine to share drinks with businessmen in a communal way, but it's something altogether different when a man goes into a saloon all alone just to get a drink."

"But our hymns already target the shame of drinking," Essie said. "They remind everyone it's a sin."

Meli almost spoke but checked her thought. Was drinking a sin? Or was the sin drunkenness? Her father would say they were different, after all. She couldn't possibly raise such a thought, even if it did confuse her. Still, there might be something to this way of thinking. Surely shame was alcohol's companion.

"I for one would rather inspire a bit of shame instead of entertaining them," she said.

Suddenly Raina laughed. "We might try not to sing so pleasantly." She winked at Meli, who warmed at such a friendly gesture. "Can you sing off key so they won't enjoy it so much?"

In spite of the glum mood, the room filled with giggles and laughter, especially when Raina offered an attempt at something closer to a cackle than the voice she employed on Sunday mornings.

"Ladies," said the eldest Mrs. Levick, "it's all well and good to bolster each other's mood today. But I think we ought to do the opposite of what the esteemed Mrs. Smythe suggested about shaming. We'll catch more flies with honey, you know."

Meli's weren't the only eyes to widen at that.

"Now, girls," hastened Mrs. Levick to say, "I'm only suggesting we present the gospel, but not with shame—with the good news that it is! And, of course, follow the instructions we've been given about turning the other cheek. If they insult us, we just smile and keep on singing."

"That's very wise, Mrs. Levick," said Essie slowly. "Shaming is altogether different from a healthy reminder that civilization is supposed to improve, each generation learning from the last. Alcohol doesn't do learning any favors."

Meli nodded, but frowned. "Trouble is, most of the men don't think we're trying to teach anything valuable."

DANE WALKED SLOWLY AWAY from the Atherton land, back toward town. He'd visited with Ethel longer than ever today, finally giving up on his meager hope to see Meli. Today he'd even tapped on their door. One, twice, three times. No answer.

He considered all the places she could be. She wasn't flying either of her goshawks; they were still in their mews. She rarely went to town this early. It was a long walk and even if she did arrive early for her nightly protests at his establishment, he doubted she would have left right after lunch. Was she out in the forest, searching for more orphans or wounded critters? He knew she'd already released the pair of squirrels she'd been caring for.

If she was looking to re-fill that cage, she could be anywhere. It would be foolish to go in search of a moving target. Still, he zig-zagged home, going in the general direction of town but taking his time and stopping often in the hope of spotting her along the way.

He told himself he was doing this only because he wanted to return her ring. He'd been slipping it into his pocket every morning, fully intending to return it to her. But between her absences near the mews and her avoidance of him at night, he'd kept it. When he did give it back, he wanted to draw her away from the others, speak to her. He couldn't give it to her in front of everyone —especially if she reacted the way he dreamed. A dream that reminded him of that silly pact he'd proposed about not touching each other. How fun that would be to end!

This was probably his most stubborn hope; something as innocent as a hug filled his mind every time he imagined the exchange.

But she was nowhere to be seen, all the way back to town.

CHAPTER 29

*M*eli knew she would have to leave soon; she hadn't planned to be here through dinner. But as they were moving collectively toward the door, a whisper from Essie detained her.

"Do you need to talk about anything?" Essie whispered. "I mean—anyone?"

Meli knew immediately to whom she referred, but shook her head even as Essie patted her hand.

"When you do want to talk about him, I'm here."

That small contact was enough to break Meli's fragile resolve. Instead of letting Essie leave on with the others, she stayed her with a light touch to her forearm. "I—I know I should be focused on his salvation." No need to say his name. "If he submitted to God's direction, he'd probably sign one of our pledges and the town's problem would disappear."

Essie smiled at Meli's idea of Wardman signing a pledge, but must have observed what Meli had: many of the faithful men in town hadn't signed pledges, either.

"I think you should ask him," Essie said, "and the sooner, the better. You wouldn't be the first woman to wear away a man's resistance to something that's for his own good. Besides, it'll give you a chance to show him that God loves him, even now, when he's the biggest troublemaker in town."

"I already did! Once. He refused. Surprised?" Perhaps she should explain she'd asked him as a dare, fully knowing he'd refuse.

"Then ask him again, and again, and again."

Meli had half expected to hear God's word through Essie, her being a pastor's wife and all. Instead of telling Meli to steer clear of Wardman, here she was pushing her toward him! Anyone could see Wardman was an attractive young man; didn't Essie see the possibility of Meli confusing some ridiculously unrealistic infatuation with doing the Lord's work?

"Go now, Meli," Essie whispered. "While you're here in town and he's not expecting you with the rest of us."

Meli's heart twirled, something that only added to her confusion. "But—"

"Go, Meli," Essie urged. "To show him you're thinking of his own good."

Barely three minutes later, and despite all of her self-inflicted reservations, Meli knocked on the tea room's rear door. With all the changes to the place, this back door looked exactly as it had that awful morning she'd arrived to find Madame. A fresh stab of grief stung her, somehow easing the confused anticipation she felt just then.

But all she heard in response from inside was an echo of her own tap.

"Hello?" she called, knocking again to see if whoever had sounded would do it again.

This time the door opened, and a boy stood there. She had seen him before at the *Hawk*, and despite his youth he stood several inches taller than Meli. Upon sight of her, a grin replaced the frown he'd answered with.

"You're one of the temperance gals," he said. "And with a mighty fine voice, too. I always look forward to your visits, miss."

She knew she should scold him; the comment reminded her of last night. No one was supposed to look forward to a protest, particularly those associated with the target of their protest. She kept her face placid so he wouldn't mistakenly believe she was flattered. "Is Mr. Wardman available?"

"No, miss. He's out with his hawk this afternoon."

Now she did frown; if she'd hurried home immediately after praying with her temperance sisters, she might have found him there. Maybe Essie's advice had been wrong; maybe God Himself was keeping her away from Wardman, knowing her confusion was leading to bad decisions.

Immediately she scoffed at that. God wasn't in the habit of standing in the way of the gospel being shared—although, she conceded, if her motives were wrong might He do that very thing? Confusion engulfed her yet again. She couldn't make sense of what to do!

She almost turned away, suddenly convinced she'd be wasting her time even if Wardman had been here. How could it be God's leading to ask something as far-fetched as Wardman signing a pledge, seriously this time? Of course he would refuse! Worse, he'd laugh at her the way everyone had last night.

Still, she should offer another try, one that was more heartfelt. If she went home now, wasn't it possible she might catch him in passing? But the boy had already turned from the door, heading to the large ice box. She saw the panel that held the ice tray was askew, evidently the source of tapping from a moment ago.

"It's temperamental," she said. "Are you opening the panel, or closing it?"

"Closing. Just emptied the tray, but I can't get it back right."

Meli approached, another idea coming to her as she stepped farther into the room. She hadn't been back in this kitchen since that futile search for her mother's ring. Could it still be here?

Surely it must be. It was the last place she knew she'd been wearing it. She looked around, fearing this might be as hopeless as her other idea, yet undeterred. Perhaps it had rolled under the very panel this boy needed help with.

She went to the drawer of mixing spoons, grabbed one, then knelt beside him. She tilted inward the side that always stuck with the end of the spoon. "The problem is here," she said. "Bend it inward, just so." As she did, the panel sprung free from where he'd shoved it to fit. She pulled out the empty water tray even if the boy did find it odd to start over after she'd righted it. But she found nothing. If the ring had been there when he'd dumped the water, it would have gone by way of the water. How many times must this very tray been emptied since that day? Before replacing it on the wooden track, she reached underneath as if to make sure nothing stood in the way.

No ring.

She replaced the panel, showing him how to start with the end that never gave any trouble. "Always start here, and push the temperamental edge last."

It snapped easily into place.

"Gee, thanks! Won't take me half the time now." He grinned. "But I guess the last thing you want to do is help this place or anybody in it."

She sighed, sinking back, still on the floor next to him. "I've nothing against you. And I do want to help. I want to help those who think they need to drink to find a better way through life." She looked at him, then added, "I want to prevent young men like yourself from ever getting into trouble with strong drink."

"Aw, there's no need to worry about me." He still knelt at her side, his hands on his knees. "I guess I could tell you something nobody else knows. I swiped a glass of that white whiskey everybody around here says is so good."

"Oh! That's exactly what we're trying to prevent—"

The boy was already shaking his head. "Like I said. Nothing to worry about. I can't figure out why everybody talks so high about that stuff."

"But that's just the sort of thing that could've gotten you into trouble. Do you know there are people out there—both men and women—who take their first sip and then can't help but take another and another? As if they've discovered a craving they didn't know they had! You must stay away from it."

If he'd had a defense, it quieted under rounding eyes as he looked past her. Something—or someone—had stolen his words. In a moment, Wardman strode closer and reached out his hand as if to aid her to her feet, but no sooner had she reached up to accept than he suddenly withdrew, as if the action had been a mistake.

Despite the rude withdrawal, he bowed. "I recall a promise made that precludes me from offering even a hand of help—a promise made in this very room, in fact." Then, before Meli could respond, Wardman looked at the boy. "Guyto, help the lady to her feet, please."

The boy had just stood, and so he bent over her, hand extended. Meli did not accept, easily hopping back to her feet on her own. The day she needed help to rise was the day she was too old to let herself kneel in the first place. "Thanks anyway, Guyto," she said, glad to know his name.

The promise Wardman referred to rushed back into her mind —along with her dream. Wondering if the sudden warmth in her cheeks came with an obvious blush, she realized it couldn't be helped. It was foolish to hope he hadn't noticed her embarrassment, the way he stared at her. The same way he always did, as if she were some kind of bug under a glass. A curiosity.

"Have you come to convince my staff to leave this unworthy profession?" The serious accusation in no way matched his tone. He might not be laughing, but he didn't look at all worried that she would succeed if that was her quest.

Meli pulled the pledge sheet from her pocket.

"I came to ask you to sign one of these," she explained. There was no persuasion in her request, something she should have contemplated had she been given the time. Blunt and artless, even she would have refused if the roles had been reversed. Surely she must exhibit God's love if she were to stay out of the way for God to change him, not blurt the purpose of her visit with less grace than one of the hatchet-wielding protestor's she'd heard destroyed city saloon's.

He looked at the paper but did not reach for it. Instead, he smiled. "You already know that goes against my own interests."

"Not at all," she said, stepping closer since he'd stepped a few feet back after withdrawing his hand. "It's in your personal interests to refrain from consuming something that could harm you."

Instead of answering, he looked at Guyto who stood by with a look of some interest. "Guyto, did you empty that water pan already?"

"Yes, sir."

"Empty the trash bin?"

"Yes, sir."

"Swept the barroom?"

"Done, sir."

Wardman laughed. "The one time I hope you've been lax, you disappoint me again."

"Sir?"

"Leave, Guyto. Shut the door behind you and don't come back until I open it." He stepped aside, inviting Guyto to use the back door.

The moment they were alone, the clear memory of Meli's dream filled her mind again. Why couldn't she forget, the way she almost had forgotten the promise not to touch one another? Why had the dream seemed so real, as if she'd actually been the one to break that pact—one *he* had instigated? And why, oh why, had that kiss invaded her sleep in the first place? She may no longer hate this man, thanks entirely to God, but Wardman was the last person she wanted to think of in such a way.

For a scant moment she was afraid her thoughts were as obvious as the blush warming her face a moment ago. Nonsense! No one could read minds, least of all this man whom she'd purposefully avoided since he came back. He didn't know her, so how could he possibly guess at a thought she herself didn't want to entertain?

But there he was, studying her yet again in that way of his. It was downright disconcerting, and likely the reason for her dream. His way of staring was every bit as invasive as an uninvited kiss. Of course, the kiss in her dream hadn't been invasive at all, at least not the way her mind had pictured it. She'd not only initiated it, she'd more than willingly participated in its lingering nature.

"I think I've already made it clear that I don't think alcohol will hurt me," he said easily, as if the extended moment of his uncomfortable scrutiny hadn't just happened. She shoved away her thoughts to concentrate on his words, but to do that she needed to look at his mouth to help listen, and the vision renewed itself.

Shaking her head, she turned away. She ought to leave, she was ready to give up on why she'd come. She'd been ready for that defeat before she'd arrived. But another thought stopped her, giving her the courage to look at him again.

"Do you stop serving someone who takes too much?"

"A man can decide these things for himself, I'm not a nursemaid."

"But you do employ a boy here. Surely you want to protect him from spirits?"

"I can't watch everything he does."

"So . . . you're not your brother's keeper?"

"Right," he said, as if failing his fellow man—even if he was little more than a child—was nothing to be ashamed of. If he knew she'd been quoting the Bible, he didn't say so.

Now that she'd refused to dwell on her memory of the dream,

it was her turn to scrutinize him. She wondered if she imagined him bristle when she stared at him now, just as she must have when he'd been looking at her. She wanted to feel a bit of triumph, but something altogether different filled her. A spirit of love that had little to do with victory of the moment. Her constant confusion regarding this man was gone. This truly was God's love, not hers.

She took yet another step closer. "But aren't we? Our brother's keeper, that is?"

He met her gaze, and she thought she still detected his discomfort. He raised a brow. "You're my keeper? Then why are you trying to close my business?"

"Not close it," she countered. "Change it."

He shook his head. "Oh, no. You want me to stop selling what I sell. That's the same as shutting it down."

"Not the meals. Or the companionship. That's really the most important part of your business, isn't it?"

"Men don't want to gather over a cup of tea."

"If not tea, then a meal." But he was already shaking his head. She pushed a little harder. "The scents from this very kitchen are still wonderful, I know that. New, different, but inviting."

He not only continued to shake his head, he turned away.

"Mr. Wardman," she said, circling around so he had to face her. "You may not think of yourself as your brother's keeper, but if you really want to offer comfort to men, then you're setting yourself up as their keeper. In any case, you ought to be aware of what your youngest employee is doing, if you care about his future."

"Do you want me to fire him? All right, I'll boot him right out of here and who knows where he'll end up. He needs a job, Meli. His family can't support him."

"I don't want you to fire him! I want you to protect him from the evils of liquor.'"

"This job is protection for him."

"But if you set an example by signing this pledge, you might even inspire some of your customers not to over indulge. Unless you couldn't give up alcohol, despite the impression you've given others that you don't need to drink?"

"How have I given that impression?"

"Because you rarely do drink! I've never seen you—" She stopped herself, afraid she'd just given away how she'd been watching him as much as he'd been watching her during her visits with the brigade. She began again. "More than one husband has remarked on it. You sell a product while you yourself don't even imbibe."

"But I do. On occasion."

She held up the paper again. "Then perhaps you should offer only the same amount you imbibe. Let's say, a limit? To one drink?"

He laughed. "A barroom limiting each customer to one drink? I wouldn't make any money."

"Money, then? That's your goal? Not to offer men a place to relax?"

"It's both!"

Nonetheless, she dangled the pledge between her fingertips, her gaze fixed on his.

The moment started so promisingly, a remnant of the purest kind of love still coursing through her. But suddenly she remembered that dream again, her gaze captive to his. His eyes were dark brown, so unlike hers, yet more striking for the mix of gold found within. Why had she never noticed? She should have broken that look, held the pledge sheet higher, but her gaze only slid downward to his mouth again, that same mouth she *had* noticed, because she'd felt it upon her own as real as if it had happened.

If she'd been thinking clearly she might have condemned the change in the moment, called it yet another instance of the battle going on in Cranbury. This was every bit a spiritual battle. All of a sudden he was looking at her lips, too, and she thought he surely knew she'd been thinking of a kiss that hadn't really happened. There were little more than two steps between them, and he closed that gap silently but surely just as she dropped the pledge sheet altogether. He even leaned closer, so that while she told herself he couldn't possibly read her mind, she believed he could. He knew, surely he did, that she wanted him to kiss her.

And then, as unexpectedly as the moment had begun, he cleared his throat and shattered the impossible notions she'd imagined.

"The promise," he whispered, in a voice that seemed as strained as the look on his face. "I won't be the one to break it."

Yet he did not move away.

She wanted to groan. She, who had harbored hate for this man far longer than the softening God had cultivated in her, had not only let go of that hate, but seemed to be experiencing something more than God's love. How could she have hoped for a kiss? That certainly was her own desire, not God's. There was nothing holy in those kinds of thoughts.

He stood there now as if he expected *her* to kiss *him*! For her to end the pact when he'd initiated it! Why else had his words protested while his proximity invited her even closer? He was even, ever so slightly, still bent toward her.

In a prayer she couldn't put to words, Meli pleaded for God's love to fill her in the place of whatever imitation she might have felt a moment ago.

"Nor I," she said, not as stiffly as pride, if she had any left, might have demanded. She took a step backward. There was no pride in winning her resistance, only the stark reminder that God was still loving this man, even through herself as an imperfect vessel. "You show self-control and strength in more than one area. It's the weaker men whom I and my temperance sisters want to help. Because we love them more than they deserve. We want to spare them—and their families—from the destruction spirits can bring. That's all we want. Not to harm your business, but to help the ones who need it."

She took hold of his gaze again, this time from two feet away. She was no longer shy about her thoughts, even if he could read them.

SELF-CONTROL? Strength? He almost laughed at the idea. A moment ago he'd been convinced she wanted him to break that pact he'd so foolishly started, take her into his arms, and kiss her. He probably should have, since it might be the one and only chance he'd get to claim he'd simply misread her actions. Because right now she looked at him differently, a look that made him want to believe in the God she was always talking and singing about. A moment ago there was something more than what he read on her face just now. This new look was a sort of love, but the sympathy kind, like she knew God was sorry for the man He'd created.

That cooled his desire to kiss her—somewhat—but it ignited something else. Dane had stolen more than one kiss in his life, and had been the recipient of countless more—some of them after that first one he stole. But seeing Meli's face transform from whatever he'd read or misread to looking at him now with something pure and honest, he realized this was likely the only kind of love he'd ever have from her. Not the kind other women had offered him, not the kind he'd offered them in return, either. This was altogether new, this pity-love.

Such thoughts sent a sharp thrust at his chest. She may have just said she loved others; she may even love weak men like himself. This woman who'd once looked at him with hatred in her eyes could now look at him squarely and openly. He wasn't foolish or vain enough to think it was his charm that had changed her. No, it had nothing at all to do with him—well, except that now, instead of that hate, he was the beneficiary of this new "love" of hers.

Another jab. He wanted whatever love she had to be *hers*, not ignited by the hope of a greater good. He wanted her to love him on her own, not because a cause or her God told her she should love him. And, even more surprisingly, he wanted to love her in return.

This new love—this *benevolent* love—wasn't the kind of love he wanted from anybody, not even from God. Love like that surely couldn't be trusted, and would never go both ways.

He turned away, walked back to the door leading to the yard, and yanked it open. Outside, Guyto was leaning against the chimney. And he wasn't alone. Lannigan, the Irish cook, loitered beside him, obviously waiting to begin cooking. If they'd been any nearer to the door they might have been trying to hear what was being said.

"Come in," he said curtly, but before they could, Meli left without a backward glance.

CHAPTER 30

On Saturday afternoon—just one day before the expected face-off at church tomorrow afternoon—Meli stood back from the poster she'd just painted, assessing it with more than satisfaction. With Arianne's sturdiest paper and Raina's artistic talent outlining each of their chosen messages, all Meli and the others had had to do was color in the lettering. They'd each come up with a slogan.

Meli had kept hers short. *Take a walk! Avoid the Hawk!*

Essie's, also finished, read: *You know it's a sin. Let your family win!*

Mrs. Taylor's sign read: *Don't let your family sink. Destroy the drink*, while Raina's sign was: *Love your wife, Save your life.*

The opposite side of each sign read: *Sign the pledge.*

Like the others, Arianne's sign was two sided. One read: *Blood is thicker than liquor.* While the other revealed a hint of her British heritage: *Stay free of rum. Or you'll land on your bum.*

Leta had already finished hers but had started another one, evidently a spare in case someone showed up without one in hand, but Meli couldn't see what it said.

They planned to march from one end of town to the other, their signs held high, hoping their words of condemnation would reach their mark. This might be just what their protest needed: visuals. Besides that, henceforth they would sing songs aimed only at temperance. No more lyrics of a loving God; rather they would limit their tunes to those which reminded anyone in the vicinity that alcohol resulted in degradation, humiliation—and ultimately death, if not of a person, then all too commonly, of a family.

Meli was more quiet than usual as they waited for the paint to dry. Ever since yesterday's disastrous attempt to get Wardman to sign a pledge, she'd thought of little else. Somehow the reality of their near-kiss had blended with the one from her dream, until that was all she thought of. It did no good to condemn such useless musings, so each time the image came to mind, she reminded herself that the Bible was clear on what sort of thoughts she should keep. True and honorable thoughts, just and pure. Virtuous! Praiseworthy! The visions invading her mind about Wardman hardly fit such counsel.

Her struggles never allowed her peace, not even earlier that morning while working with Wardman's goshawk. She'd spent hours in the woods, preparing the young hawk's training, wishing she could ask Wardman for help. It was always easier with two. But even that idea raised questions. Didn't taking care of his hawk, taking good and excellent and praiseworthy care, reflect what God would have her do? Yet was it really innocent, even sensible, to ask for his help? When it felt as though she *desired* his company? Worse, had her motives ever been pure? At first she'd wanted to drive him away, punish him for what he'd done. Now she wanted nothing other than to see him!

It was enough to make her wonder if she should go back to the safety and seclusion of home, give up the cause because her motives were obviously mixed. But always, always at the base of her battle lay the reality that a man's eternity was surely more important than whatever Meli truly wanted, even if he didn't return her admittedly uneven feelings. She could never give up on her truest mission. Even now, as the owner and dispenser of something that could harm others, Dane Wardman was still loved by the God who wanted what was best for him and the entire town.

Leta soon pronounced the signs to be dry, and took it upon herself to hand each woman their sign as they prepared to sing and march down the street. Still distracted, Meli fell into line, singing along without her usual gusto. Half way along, she stopped singing altogether to offer up prayer instead, knowing she would need all the strength God dispensed.

DANE HEARD the parade before Checker called him to the window for a look. If half the town's women were part of the anti-saloon group, the other half stood cheering them on from the sidewalks —along with a good portion of men and an even larger portion of children. Along with the appearance of protest signs, none of which he'd be able to read until they drew nearer—they were handing out little white flags. In spite of the white color, he doubted they were flags of surrender.

The dinner hour had passed, a time of day this sleepy little town usually reserved for winding down from whatever work had occupied them during the day. Porch sitting; sipping a cool lemonade; he'd even seen spontaneous choirs spring up on the Inn's porch, serenading the town as it prepared to end another productive day.

Who knew there was so much energy left at the end of this particular day, one to inspire a parade and cheering onlookers? Dane should probably be worried. Rather than the temperance women's group waning while his business grew, they were obviously gaining as well. As he looked back at his crowded barroom, he knew some men from the surrounding towns had first been drawn by the protest itself; curiosity remained a good marketing tool alongside word-of-mouth recommendations. Yet he did wonder how long this could continue before one side or the other realized they were at a stalemate. Such a crossroad of war had only one answer: one side must attack—something that was bound to happen as soon as tomorrow. Sunday's meeting would be a skirmish.

Dane shook his head at the idea. If he was to lead the charge on his side, he doubted he was up to it. Not if the enemy put Meli at the forefront. How could he fight someone with whom he only wished to break a ridiculous pact not to touch?

The parade drew closer, and Dane scanned their signs, each one capitalizing on flowery lettering, appealing colors, and best of all, a rhyme. If he hadn't been the target of a message he would never agree with, he'd have enjoyed the artwork as much as he enjoyed the quality of their singing.

But he didn't see Meli. She wasn't at her usual spot front and center with the pastor's wife. The signs had momentarily caught his attention, but there she was, having lagged to the center of the two dozen or so marchers.

His gaze, as usual, was difficult to pull from her once it landed. But when he looked at last at her sign, he had to act fast not to frown, gasp, or outright cave in to the demands on her particular poster.

Lips that touch wine will never touch mine.

Was that an admission to the entire town that he'd nearly kissed her yesterday? Or was it aimed more privately at him, if he hadn't already gotten the message?

Dane wasn't sure about anything just then, except that message was, so far, the most persuasive argument he'd faced toward putting his name to one of those blasted pledge sheets.

He wondered if they would bring their parade inside this time, placards and all. Such an accessory would take up more room than usual, and he feared for a few of his light fixtures suspended from the ceiling.

But even as he wondered such a thing, from the corner of his eye he saw two men emerging from vehicles already parked on the grassy area where his customers left their autos or buggies. He saw immediately the one from a Model T was no ordinary customer. The tall hat, shiny buckles and telltale star affixed to the man's jacket identified him as the county sheriff.

Dane had enjoyed the support of Philly's police force for years, so he felt no alarm. But was it coincidence that a scowling Al John Packham had arrived at exactly the same time?

To Dane's surprise, they walked as a duo, but not toward the *Hawk*. They stopped in the path of the parade, the sheriff's arms crossed, Al John's hands fisted.

The object of their attention was nearing—the temperance women.

Dane's pulse raced when he glimpsed something not quite hidden in the crook of the sheriff's arm. A billy club similar to the kind he'd seen more than once in the city: the kind temperance women used to smash liquor bottles.

THEY SANG STRONG AND TUNEFULLY, any notions of yesterday's jest to sound less appealing forgotten. Meli was sure she wasn't the only one to spot Mr. Packham and the sheriff. Why were they here? Mr. Packham hardly looked as though he'd arrived to see others enjoying his product.

Surely Wardman hadn't sent for the authorities to stop their protests! Or had he?

> . . . We may call every gin shop a mantrap.
> For you just drop in for a glass of stout . . .

The two men stood rock still, evidently not intending to move out of their way. Surely they *were* waiting for the ladies! But why? Meli and the others had done nothing but voice their objections in this free country of theirs.

> We have God's own approbation;
> And the pow'rs of hell shall one day fail,
> We will leave not a trap in the nation.
> O the mantrap!

Their temperance tune faded as the women were forced to either step around the two-man barrier or stop altogether. Meli moved forward to stand beside Essie, exchanging worried glances. They stopped.

"Sheriff," said Essie, nearly but not quite in greeting. She eyed Mr. Packham but did not address him.

The sheriff said nothing, but from under his arm he produced at stout club. Mrs. Taylor, directly behind Meli, gasped.

"This belong to one of you?" The sheriff's voice was quiet, but threatening all the same.

Meli shook her head, then looked at the ladies behind her. They all did the same.

"Mr. Packham here thinks otherwise. His still was destroyed today and he thinks one of you might have had a hand in it."

"That's ridiculous!" Raina Levick was the first to protest.

"Nobody in town even knows where he keeps that devil's contraption!" claimed the eldest Mrs. Levick.

"As you can see," Essie pointed out above the shouts, "our protests are peaceful."

"Besides," called Arianne Prestwich, "if we were going to destroy something, don't you think it would be the place we've been protesting all these days?"

"Destroying my still is the same thing," cried Mr. Packham. "It's what brings in the customers! Oh, you've all been waitin' for the day to ruin my business, and now here you've done it. Couldn't go directly to that saloon or they'd know for sure it was you. So you tried to do away with its biggest draw, my own white whiskey."

"More nonsense," said Raina Levick.

Meli agreed, adding, "By that line of thinking we'd have to go after every supplier who comes to this saloon. It's ridiculous. Besides, as Mrs. Levick said, no one knows the location of the still. I live out near your place, and even I don't know where it is."

Al John Packham glared at her. "Oh, don't you, missy? You sure about that?"

Her heart tumbled at the way he aimed his words at her, as if an accusation. "I just said I didn't. Why would I lie?"

"Because you done it, that's why! You know where the still is, just ask your Pa if he never took you out there. And you got more against me than just what I sell here, haven't ya?"

Meli tilted her head. "I haven't any idea what you're talking about. I've always thought of you as a friend of my father's."

"Friend! That's not what I call it." He turned to the sheriff. "You arrest her! She done it, I know it."

The sheriff reached for Meli's arm, and before words could gather through her shock, protests echoed around her. Meli felt herself being pulled along, even though she'd told herself to stay put.

Essie rushed behind her, and Meli handed her the sign she still managed to carry. She really was in a dream, because the words she glimpsed on the heavy cardstock had nothing to do with the ones she'd painted earlier. Something about lips! Had she gone mad?

Her head went light as she turned to Essie.

"Could you—let my father know? He'll clear this up, I'm sure of it. He knows Mr. Packham. I—I can't think what's come over him!"

The sheriff clamped something around her wrist as he led her to his Model T. Somewhere at the periphery of her vision she saw Mr. Packham going to his own car to follow.

The last thing she saw was Dane Wardman standing outside the *Hawk*, watching her go.

CHAPTER 31

$\mathcal{D}$ane shot back inside the *Hawk*, but only long enough to call orders to Checker to watch the place and close early if there was any sign of trouble or if Dane didn't return by midnight. Then he rushed back outside after Essie Taylor, who was already leaving the scene. He was certain she would be the one most concerned about Meli.

Before she could speak, he said, "I'm hiring the Canary to take me out to the Atherton place and let Meli's father know what happened. Then I'm taking him after her."

"But—she asked me—"

"If you want to help, ask your husband—he's the pastor, right? —to meet us at the Williamsport jail. It's on the corner of West Third and William."

Essie Taylor's eyes were already wide, so wide he was surprised when they went wider still.

"They—they won't put her in jail!" she cried. "Not a woman!"

"It's what—" he stopped himself, knowing this county didn't have any alternatives to jail when it came to the women they arrested. In with the men they went, drunk or sober. "That's why I'm going, to make sure that doesn't happen."

All he had to do was convince Packham and the authorities she couldn't have done what she'd been accused of doing. Wasn't it obvious? Even if she did have the strength to swing that club, she was such a little slip of a woman she couldn't possibly do much damage to a full size still.

The crowd of parade goers and participants still mingled in the street, though the parade had ended the moment Meli had been taken away. If anyone thought it odd that Dane was springing into action on Meli's behalf, no one tried stopping him. Even Essie must have been in shock because she didn't think to question him; he saw her hurrying in the direction of the house next to the church, evidently in search of her husband.

Tummers was easy to find outside the livery, easier than that to hire for the job Dane described. Dane soon sat atop the Canary beside Tummers, wishing he was the one driving if only to spend some of his anxious energy. But as a driver, Tummers didn't need any help; he commanded the pair of horses as fast as Dane could hope.

The Atherton house was dark. It wasn't late, just past nine, but Dane felt no compunction about jumping from the Canary, running to the door and laying his fist to it. Finally! Something he could pound on.

To his surprise the door flew open but surprise turned to horror: the man stood there with a shotgun pointed straight at him.

Instinctively Dane raised both hands. "It's me, Mr. Atherton. Dane Wardman."

Mr. Atherton looked at Dane then over Dane's shoulder at Tummers still atop the Canary. He lowered the gun—a bit too slowly for Dane's taste. "You alone?"

He nodded.

"What're you doing here?"

"Because of Meli," Dane said, annoyingly aware that he was as out of breath as if he'd run instead of ridden all the way from town. "She's been arrested."

"Arrested! My Meli?" Then he raised the shotgun again. "You come here to tell me that, when you're the one who must've had her carted off? I've heard you saloon keepers don't like the temperance gals, but this isn't any way to draw her attention, let me tell you."

"I had nothing to do with it!"

"It's true," Tummers called. "The Williamsburg sheriff came for her with Al John Packham. He said she took a club to that still of his out in the woods."

Mr. Atherton not only lowered the gun, he let it crash to the floor. He stood as still as a statue until Dane put a hand to his shoulder, which made him jump.

Then he made a beeline to the Canary. "You take me there, Tummers," he called. "Especially if that's where Packham is, too."

"Oh, he's there, all right," Dane assured him. "The look on his face said he wanted to see her locked up."

Mr. Atherton had one foot on the ramp and two hands on the seat rail near Tummers when, instead of boarding, he hurled himself back to the ground. "Wait!"

Then he ran back into his house. For a moment Dane feared he was going back for his gun—something that could only get them into more trouble if the man tried using it—but he scurried past it and disappeared into the shadows. He was gone long enough for Dane to go inside, too, finding the man in the parlor where he had lit an oil lamp. He was bent over a sea chest with the light balanced on top. He rattled, without success, the lock dangling from the front enclosure.

"Get that gun, fella. This lock's so rusted the key won't open it anymore. I'm going to shoot it open."

Dane couldn't imagine what the man needed from inside a sea chest just now, but he also guessed one swift kick placed just so would likely have the compromised lock in shambles. Dane reached down for a closer look, seeing immediately someone had stuffed putty into the key chamber. It oozed from around the tarnished key.

"This lock has more than rust keeping it locked." But that was the extent of Dane's delay. He kicked the lock once, but it took a second blow for it to tumble to the floor.

Mr. Atherton grabbed the lamp and opened the chest so quickly the top hit the wall behind it. At first if bounced back, threatening to fall on the arm of the old man reaching inside, but Dane caught it in time. Pulling the lamp from the man, Dane held it nearby, shedding light on contents that appeared to be a mix of innocuous items like blankets, books, old catalogs and clothing. At least it wasn't an armory of more weapons.

"Here it is," Mr. Atherton said, almost as if he was surprised to have found the small, leather-bound book. "Now let's go."

SHERIFF HEAGAN WAS able to shift gears and rotate the Ford's steering wheel while still holding the free end of what he called the "Darby"—a bracelet of sorts that he'd clipped around one of Meli's wrists. He'd claimed to have brought with him the smallest restraints his department owned, but she knew if she really wanted to she could slip out of the manacle without much trouble.

However, resisting the law, innocent though she knew herself to be, didn't sound like the best idea. She would cooperate with the sheriff, endure whatever baseless accusations Mr. Packham threw at her, and then convince them of her innocence. At least she must convince those who mattered, like the sheriff, even if she might not be able to convince her neighbor himself. Mr. Packham was assuredly not himself; he must be suffering some kind of health ailment, some attack of apoplexy or even a stroke. What else could explain his extraordinary behavior? Surely if a physician was brought in to help him regain his senses, Meli would be allowed to go home.

The sky was fully dark when the sheriff parked his Model T in front of the stone Lycoming prison. Mr. Packham pulled up behind them in his motorcar, emerging to hurry to their side. Meli had passed this two-storied building more than once on visits with her father to the farmer's market, some blocks from here. It had always seemed an imposing, somewhat frightening building. But now, actually headed inside, it terrified her.

She walked so slowly up the few stairs that the sheriff pulled on the tether.

"Mr. Packham!" Meli didn't care that her fear showed so blatantly in her voice. "Tell him I couldn't have done what you said. You know I wouldn't do such a thing."

"I know no such thing, little lady. My still's broke. Nobody but me, the taxman, you and your pap know where it is. If you didn't do it, then your pap did, and having you hauled off to jail is the quickest way I can think to get him here and confess it."

"Why do you think my father would do such a thing? You're his neighbor! You've shared crops, and crop workers. You've been like partners all these years."

"Partners!" He huffed the word, as if the idea was ridiculous.

Meli started to speak but the sheriff tugged on her wrist again. "Better stop arguing out here, miss, or I'll have to add incorrigibility to the list of charges. We'll figure it out in the office, or else get you processed. One or the other."

Meli followed along, heart in her throat, stomach in the pit of her being. She stumbled, and the sheriff paused long enough to catch her at the elbow, but he never stopped.

He led her inside toward a long, dark corridor.

DANE WAS the first to hop from the Canary as it pulled up behind the Model T that had taken Meli away. Mr. Atherton followed close behind. Tummers stayed put and Dane didn't care. The man glanced about as if concerned over his rig, as if criminals were likely to hang around outside a penitentiary.

Dane half expected the door to be locked at this time of the evening, but it opened so easily he nearly lost hold as it swung forth. The halls were empty and dimly lit, and Dane had no idea where to go. He did what came naturally. He yelled.

"Meli Atherton! Sheriff! Mr. Packham!"

Mr. Atherton soon joined in.

A door opening and slamming shut echoed from one direction, followed quickly by an unfamiliar voice calling out for them to shut their traps. Quick footsteps brought a guard of some kind, uniformed, tall, a stick dangling from his belt. Dane cut the distance between them by hurrying forward.

"We're looking for Meli Atherton. She was brought in by Sheriff Heagan within the last half hour."

His brows rose. "She, huh?"

"That's right," Dane said. "It's all a mistake—"

"One big mistake," Mr. Atherton cut in. "And I've got the proof right here. Now you tell us where she is so we can get her home."

"I'm just getting off duty from the coop," the man said, looking them over and evidently finding them no threat. "Somebody should've been up here, though. Probably back with the sheriff. He's thataway." The guard pointed down the opposite hallway using his club. "First door you see."

Dane had conjured a thousand questions all the way here, but from the moment he walked into this place housing the dregs of society—more likely associates of his than hers—those questions had been scattered by a deep sense of doom. What was she thinking, right now? Was she afraid? She was mighty enough to train no less than predator goshawks, but she was still only a little slip of a woman. Any man alive could snap her delicate bones if they wanted to.

But he knew women were thrown in jail right alongside the men, maybe some of them as innocent as he knew Meli to be. How was he going to get her out of here?

He reached the first door just before Mr. Atherton did. Hand on the knob, he spared a quick second to look at the older man.

"I hope your proof is convincing," Dane said, glancing at the book in Mr. Atherton's hand. "Because one way or another, we're getting her out of here, that's for sure."

CHAPTER 32

*M*eli sat on the hard wooden chair that hadn't seemed so uncomfortable twenty minutes ago. Before that, she'd been too nervous to sit, even though the wrist shackle had been removed and all the sheriff had done so far was fill out paperwork. He seemed in no apparent hurry to "process" her, as he'd said he was doing.

She'd tried multiple times to implore Mr. Packham to reconsider his ridiculous charges, but he hadn't said a single word to her since they'd entered the room. He'd answered the sheriff's questions, confirming such things as trespassing, vandalism, and destruction of property, but had ignored each one of her appeals.

The sheriff soon set aside his fountain pen but did not look up. Instead, he appeared to be re-reading what he'd written.

"You've got your paperwork, now lock her up," demanded Mr. Packham.

Meli looked again at the man. It would be a waste of breath to implore him another time, and so she stared. What sort of demon had gotten into the man, making him so eager to see her behind bars?

"Just want to make sure it's all here," the sheriff said, not bothering to take his eyes from the forms. She should be glad he was taking his time, since it appeared the next step was to grant Mr. Packham's wish. "Don't want the judge to throw out the case on a technicality, do you?"

"A what?" For the first time this evening, he looked curious instead of angry.

"Technicality. An appeal on account of a mistake. Details matter, Mr. Packham. Especially in the law." He glanced up then down the page. "You know, I can't get the judge to look at this until tomorrow?"

If Mr. Packham had a reply, he didn't have the chance to voice it. A noise at the door caught even his attention. Voices—familiar ones—were followed swiftly by not only a firm thud but by the knob rattling and the door swooshing open.

Standing so close behind the sheriff, she heard a single word muttered almost under his breath. But it couldn't be. Had he just said *"Finally,"* as if he'd been expecting the new arrivals?

She had no time to contemplate the odd notion. Before her stood not only her father but, astoundingly, Dane Wardman. What was he doing here?

Her father did little more than look her way, offer a nod of assurance, before he planted himself before Mr. Packham. Mr. Packham was a much larger man—Meli had always known that, but seeing them standing off made the contrast all the more stark. Not quite a David and Goliath, but echoes of them nonetheless.

"You stop all this trouble, Al John," Dad insisted. "You know as well as I do she didn't do anything against that still. She didn't even know you had such a thing, let alone know where it was."

"That's a lie! You took her there yourself."

Dad snorted. "You're crazy! She was no more'n three years old back then. You think she knew what she was looking at, let alone how to get there or back?"

"Then who did it? You?"

"Wasn't me, but if you want to accuse somebody you might as well charge me instead of her. Before you do, though, I'll just let the sheriff see this so he can make up his own mind about who to arrest."

He waved a book in his hand, something Meli had never seen before. It looked like an old journal of some kind, leather bound, the cover carved with images of birds—*hawks*, she realized with a start. A bronze clasp bound front cover to back, but her father easily unhinged it. The book was larger than his hands, but as he opened it on one palm the pages opened naturally to what must have been a familiar spot.

Absorbed as she had been by the cover, she almost missed her father's face transform from a look of triumph to one of astonished distress as he flipped first back then forward, page to page. A moment later he didn't even try protecting the book when Mr. Packham snatched it away.

"What's this, except some worthless diary?" he scoffed. He threw it back to Dad before facing the sheriff. "He's so eager to take her spot in one of your cells, why don't you lock him up instead? Better yet, since you have your precious paperwork, lock them both up!"

"Now just a minute, Mr. Packham—"

Mr. Packham turned on Dane before he'd even finished his protest. "You've got no business here, Wardman. Even the big and mighty Wardman nose isn't welcome in other people's affairs."

"It's my business if you're trying to have an innocent woman arrested. That's everybody's business. What right did you have to make the sheriff bring Meli here this way? To have her arrested in front of the whole town as if she were some kind of criminal?"

Just then more havoc erupted as Essie and her husband Reverend Taylor rushed into the room.

"I second that," said Pastor Taylor.

"And I third it!" claimed Essie, as she hurried to Meli's side.

Meli nearly burst into tears of relief as she fell into Essie's embrace.

~

DANE WISHED he'd had the courage to take Meli into his arms the moment he'd busted into the room—hang their silly no-touching-pact—but was relieved nonetheless to see her comforted by Essie in such a way. She'd looked so fearful and confused, even her father's presence hadn't seemed to help.

Nor had the book Mr. Atherton brought, the one that was supposed to claim her innocence. Obviously Packham hadn't thought much of anything Mr. Atherton had said so far.

"Quiet down, all of you," commanded the sheriff, who had come around to the front of his desk. "Who are you, and what's that book you say I should look at?"

But Mr. Atherton didn't look capable of speaking, so Dane spoke even though he should probably have let Meli do the introduction. Dane wasn't part of their family, and wasn't likely to be one unless Ethel somehow connected them.

"This is Thomas Atherton, Meli's father. He said there was something in that book that would exonerate Meli."

"Mind if I have a look?" the sheriff asked.

The question seemed to penetrate whatever had suddenly bedeviled Mr. Atherton. But instead of complying, he gripped the book and stepped closer to the desk, placing it in the circle of light from the lamp on the corner. He flipped through the pages, one at a time.

"What is this, Mr. Atherton?" asked Dane. "Anything I can help with?"

"It's got to be here," he muttered as he studied the pages. "It's been in here for a hundred years."

"What has?"

"The recipe. And the contract."

"Contract?" That perked up the sheriff. "What kind of contract?"

"For the white whiskey."

Dane lifted his brows. "The Packham whiskey? You're connected to that?"

"It's de Brus whiskey." Mr. Atherton never looked up, not even as he offered his answer. He kept turning the pages, searching for what he thought should be there.

"He's lying!" cried Packham. "Spun out of whole cloth."

"Let me get this straight," the sheriff said. "You own the still, Mr. Packham, but you've been using a recipe that Mr. Atherton has—or had? Where does this de Brus come into it?"

"That's my great-grandmother's maiden name," said Meli. "Isn't that right, Dad? Is that journal hers, then?"

"It is. Partly."

"So it's her recipe?" asked the sheriff. "The de Brus grandmother's?"

"Yes," Mr. Atherton answered. "It was her father's concoction originally, but she made it better. Story goes, whatever she touched she made better. Even whiskey, though there aren't any tales saying she had a taste for it. She just had a way with recipes."

"Eleanor de Brus?" Meli was fairly breathless, something that could mean nothing based on the events of the evening. But Dane didn't think so; the coloring in her cheeks was redder than ever. "She made *whiskey*? Isn't she the one everybody hated and called a witch? I thought it was because of the crops? It was because of whiskey?"

"Hold on now." The sheriff held up his hand. "Let's stick to the subject at hand. First of all, what did you mean about a contract?"

"It was in the book," Mr. Atherton said, holding it up again. "Along with the recipe. The contract is between the de Brus and the Packham families. Binding for a hundred years."

"Don't listen to this!" erupted Packham. "Witches, crops, contracts, a hundred years. Both of them are babbling! No wonder the town's shunned them all these years. See here, Sheriff, I want him arrested along with the girl. He's as much as admitted he did it, and she's hiding what she knows with some cockamamie story. Arrest them both!"

But the sheriff shook his head. "I think I'd like to hear this cockamamie story. Mr. Atherton, if you don't mind explaining yourself, it might get both you and your daughter out of this mess."

At last he stood as tall as his five and a half feet allowed, his attention to the book diverted. "You can ask anyone from Cranbury," he said, glancing between Pastor Taylor and Dane himself. "Well, the older folks, anyway. Memories are finally fading about my wife's family, thanks to Meli. She's the first one in a couple generations to be welcomed in town, even if she did have to jump right into another fracas. You ever heard the name du Brus, either of you young fellas?"

Dane shook his head, as much as he wished otherwise. He'd have been happy to back up whatever claims Meli and her father offered, not only to save Meli from jail. He'd caught the look on her face when her father had said she'd been the first of her family to "be welcomed". Hang that! She was too good, too pure, too much a servant of God's green earth not to be accepted *everywhere*.

To his surprise, the pastor, standing beside his wife who was still holding onto Meli, nodded and spoke.

"I guess my mother knows all the stories from town," Pastor Taylor said. "And I heard every one of them, because she used to entertain the guests when I was little." He paused, aiming an apologetic smile Meli's way—who looked as though she'd rather be anywhere but there. "She hasn't done it in years, though. Probably most of my generation doesn't know about it."

"If you could get to the point," the sheriff prodded. "Whatever information you have might help, given your profession, if it corroborates whatever the Athertons say. As long as it's pertinent, of course."

"I only know there used to be a tale about Eleanor du Brus being a witch." He shook his head. "Nobody nowadays would believe such a thing, but a hundred years ago there were still enough stories going around about the first witch hunt. Eleanor du Brus was what we'd call today a veterinarian. Stories went that she could heal any animal, including wild ones."

Dane glanced at Meli, thinking of the menagerie at her farm. She must have sensed his attention, because she returned the look at last. He couldn't tell if she was still afraid, because at the moment she looked, of all things, embarrassed. Surely she knew he was on her side, witch or no witch in her family history?

"And she practiced falconry," came the next predictable words, even before Meli's gaze broke away from his. "Women aren't known for such things, so she was looked upon by others as . . . eccentric."

Dane silently applauded the pastor's choice of words.

"Anyway, one year her family's crop flourished, but the farm next door—the Packhams—failed. No one could explain it, and the Packhams were none too happy about it. They complained, not about the weather or the seed or pests or whatever else could explain it naturally, but about the de Brus family. At first they said it was the deer that ate away their crop while leaving the de Brus crop alone because Eleanor healed injured deer. Evidently they didn't stop talking, and one story led to another until witchcraft started being bandied about again."

Mr. Packham huffed. "Why are you listening to this bedtime story, Sheriff? He's wasting all of our time."

"Proceed, Pastor," said the sheriff.

"All I know is that one day the stories were on everybody's lips, and then the two families mended their ways. My mother embellishes, but it's a story about how Cranbury folks always get along, that feuds are short-lived, even incredible ones. I wish my mother was here. She told it much better than I did."

The sheriff looked at Mr. Atherton. "Do you have anything to add?"

"I can tell you why the feud ended. It was in the contract!"

"We're back to that, are we?" Mr. Packham lifted his hands, obviously disgusted.

Mr. Atherton held up the book again. "You can see for yourself that pages have been ripped from this book. For all I know you broke into my house and stole those pages yourself, Al John!"

Then as if to prove pages were missing, the sheets riffled and settled once again at the gap in the binding. Dane could see it from where he stood.

"You're accusing *me* of something?" Mr. Packham declared. "When you're the one ruining my business!"

Meli reached up to take the book from her father, and as he handed it over words on the spine caught by the light drew Dane's attention.

Several names, the last of which read: *Meli*.

"Did you say you haven't seen this book before, Meli?" Dane asked, before caution had a chance to stop him. If she hadn't, the inscription wouldn't support her claim.

"No, I haven't."

"May I take a look at it?"

Meli looked at her father who unaccountably blushed so furiously even Dane felt for the man. "Her great-grandmother Eleanor started the journal . . . about marriage things . . . to her daughters and their daughters. There weren't any more blank pages left, so my wife carved Meli's name because she'd be the last daughter to receive this one. The plan was for her to start another, if she wants the tradition to continue. It'll be Meli's on the day before her wedding, not before, and it's for her to read, nobody else. Not even the man she marries, unless she wants to share it with him someday. It's filled with—well, things of a personal nature that women understand."

"It's just," Dane began, despite knowing he was asking something far too intimate, "somebody should read it right now. If neither of you knew about the missing pages, then Meli's mother must have been the one who tore them out. Who else?"

Mr. Atherton clapped his hands once. "Holy smokes! You could be right. I knew she never liked Al John, maybe because she figured he'd be the generation to hand back the rights to the recipe. He knew it, too." Mr. Atherton looked at Mr. Packham. "That's why he's saying I'm ruining his business, because I refuse to extend it."

He now looked at his daughter. "Maybe, just maybe, she thought ahead of all of us and went and hid the original, along with the contract." He smiled proudly. "Isn't that just like your mom? Although I have to say she likely thought you'd have been married a few years before the contract ran out, given your age. We'd probably have found it before the hundred years was up if we knew it was missing."

But Meli wasn't looking at all proud, or pleased. "I didn't inherit Mother's foresight." She looked from her father to Mr. Packham. "I saw you leaving our house, Mr. Packham. I thought you'd been visiting Dad the other day, maybe make right whatever argument you had a while back. Only when I came inside Dad wasn't even home."

Mr. Atherton stroked his stubbled chin. "Al John was inside our house, and neither of us home?"

She nodded.

He waved the book. "Lookin' for the contract! He probably doesn't want us to have so much as a copy of our family's very own recipe, he said so when he offered some money to extend the contract. But I refused. That's what we argued about."

"Did you take the pages, Mr. Packham?" asked Meli.

"Course not! Now listen, you're the one in trouble, not me."

But her father was shaking his head, any outrage at Mr. Packham now gone. "The recipe by itself isn't worth much to him, since he's always had a copy. That's the only thing written on the missing pages. The contract was folded up inside this book. If he had that, he wouldn't have started this trouble tonight. He likely would've altered it somehow to prove he's in the right."

"Or destroyed it," Dane said quietly, and he saw not only Mr. Atherton's horror, but Meli's.

The sheriff folded his arms, as if not quite convinced by the whole story but definitely interested. "Why did you refuse Packham's offer to buy out the contract, Mr. Atheron? Didn't he offer you enough of a cut?"

Mr. Atherton shook his head. "Wasn't the money." Then he glanced between Meli and, to Dane's surprise, Dane himself. "I didn't want this man selling the whiskey anymore. As I see it, this fella here is the closest my daughter has ever come to having a beau, and she's not going to so much as smile his way if he's still selling white whiskey. Even if it is a family recipe. I figured I'd let them work it out if they want to let Al John keep selling it."

Dane glanced at Meli, who proved her father's words correct by not even looking his way, let alone offer him a smile. Nonetheless, this was the first hint that her father might think Dane actually had a chance with Meli. At the very least, he was on Dane's side, and Dane welcomed one less obstacle.

Then the sheriff caught his attention. "You're the barkeep, aren't you? And she's one of the temperance gals. You don't see a problem here?"

He ignored that question, but was still pleased it wasn't only himself thinking in terms of working something out with Meli. "Is she free to go, then? Now that there's some doubt about Mr. Packham's accusation?"

The sheriff went back around his desk. "The still remains demolished, and we don't know who did it."

"You don't really think a woman Miss Atherton's size could wield the club Packham claims was used?"

Pastor and Essie Taylor backed up Dane's words with protests of their own.

But the sheriff shook his head. "I've been on the receiving end of one or two punches from female inmates, and I can tell you not all women are as weak as they want us to believe."

"Then you can arrest me for it," said Mr. Atherton, thrusting his wrists forward as if awaiting the shackles on the desk. "Just let her go."

"Did you do it?" the sheriff asked.

"Course not, but neither did she. My Meli wouldn't do such a thing, and besides, until now she didn't know we had any connection at all to that still. She doesn't even know where it is!"

"Mr. Packham says otherwise." He leaned forward, directing an intense gaze at Meli. "For all I know you did it because you're a temperance gal. Might have had nothing at all to do with any family history."

Meli shrank under the accusation, or perhaps Dane only imagined that because Essie, beside her, seemed to puff up. Essie mimicked Mr. Atherton, holding up her wrists.

"Then you might as well arrest me, Sheriff, though I assure you no one in our group played any part in such destruction. Our *peaceful* protests are to protect our young. But if you think Meli did it because of her association with me, then I as her temperance sister must be a suspect as well. In fact, you'll have to arrest every one of us if you arrest Meli."

The sheriff held up a hand even as Pastor Taylor covered his wife's hands with his own, gently pulling them out of reach from anyone but himself.

"I'm not arresting you, Mrs. Taylor, and I'm not keeping Miss Atherton here, either. There are enough questions about the case so we'll have to bring it to the judge, since I have little to no hope Packham can be convinced to drop the charges. Although Miss

Atherton is a suspect, I can't arrest her without evidence. I'm not going to pester the judge at this hour, so I'll release her. But," he turned to Meli, "you can't leave the county. Understood?"

She nodded quickly, still wide-eyed.

"I'll trust you on that, so don't disappoint me."

"Start reading, Meli," said Essie. "Maybe there's a note inside, about why your mother took out the pages. Maybe it'll say where they are."

Without another word, Meli opened the book.

CHAPTER 33

*M*eli's hands shook as she flipped the pages to those last written, those penned by her mother. She wanted both to laugh and to cry. This book was to have been a happy surprise, as if her mother wasn't really gone from the wedding Meli should probably have already had by this age.

She wanted to be alone to read each word, savor them, imagine her mother speaking each one. But not here, not now. So she tried to keep her breathing even, tried slowing the beat of her heart. Just make it through one more moment, and then the next, and the next after that—but Mr. Packham's renewed objections made any sense of calm impossible.

Nor would his ire let her forget what she'd felt during every word of the "tale" Pastor Taylor told. How recently her family had been the subject of talk and speculation! All these months she believed she'd been a part of something, a member of the community at last. Embraced far more easily than she'd ever expected. But even as she was helping the cause she'd been what she'd always feared: an oddity. An outcast. Someone others whispered about. Mrs. Taylor! Who else, beside her, used to tell tales? All the older women must know the story, obviously better than Meli herself. Did the others, too? Did Essie?

She stole a glance from the journal toward Dane Wardman, wishing she didn't care what he thought. Somehow she'd been relieved to see him, eager to accept his unexpected help. Now she wished he'd never come; all his presence had done was allow him knowledge about her family's ostracized history. Arsenal to use against her, knowing her family had somehow aided him to attract more whiskey drinkers to his establishment because it was, after all, her family's white whiskey that people hankered after.

As she skimmed each page, looking for specific words like contract or whiskey, she tried not to feel all she was feeling.

"I'm afraid you'll need some proof of this contract, Mr. Atherton," the sheriff said, after telling Mr. Packham to hush. "That is, if it has anything to do with a feud between your family and the Packhams. It might explain Mr. Packham's eagerness to have you and your daughter arrested."

"It has everything to do with it!" Dad said. "The contract ended the talk around town a hundred years ago, because Eleanor de Brus gave the Packhams the use of the recipe if they'd stop spreading rumors about how their crop failed. Now that the usage contract has come to an end, Packham's starting the feud again by wanting to keep the recipe to himself. He's built such a business he makes more money from that whiskey than all the crops he's ever sold!"

"Yes, all of that may be true, but the fact remains without a contract, this is just a nice tale to tell."

"That's all Al John's accusations are, a tale!" Dad exclaimed.

"But if they *can* find the contract," Dane Wardman said slowly, "this can all be cleared up? You don't have any evidence that Meli vandalized the still, but with a contract that returns the rights of the whiskey to Mr. Atherton, there's reason to believe Mr. Packham himself could have destroyed the still. He wouldn't have much use of it without the recipe he's known for. Or maybe he wanted them too busy defending themselves to bother with regaining the rights to the whiskey."

"True enough," said the sheriff.

"But even if they don't find the contract," said Essie, "you can't arrest Meli just because Mr. Packham *thinks* she had something to do with whatever happened to his still."

"That's right," said Dane. "In fact, why don't you leave, Mr. Packham? I assume the paperwork the sheriff needed from you has all been signed, so there's no reason for you to stay."

"Why are you on her side?" demanded Mr. Packham. "If it weren't for my white whiskey—yes, *my* white whiskey—that barroom of yours would be half empty every night."

"Let's just say," said Dane, "they may not want me on their side, but I'm definitely not on yours."

Despite his protests, Mr. Packham smashed his hat on his head then left the room.

Dane's words were was so far from a proclamation of friendship, loyalty or—more ridiculously—love, that Meli should have been reluctant to accept such a lukewarm show of support.

But she didn't have time to dwell on it. She'd found the words she'd been looking for.

THE MOMENT PACKHAM LEFT, Dane returned his focus on Meli—only what he saw now prompted him to take a step nearer. "You found something?"

She nodded, and whatever nervousness he'd seen in her before seemed to disappear. She looked at her father with a smile.

"She said the contract is where I can find it."

"That's it?" asked Dane, but it seemed to be enough for Mr. Atherton.

"All right, then," said her father, "let's go."

"Will you be going back to your place?" asked the sheriff.

Both Meli and her father nodded.

"Go then. I'll wrap up the paperwork here and visit in the morning, if you think you know where this contract is. Nothing will happen here tonight."

"Oh, we know where it is, all right," said Mr. Atherton.

The sheriff, along with Dane himself, took that as good enough. He followed Meli and Mr. Atherton from the room.

CHAPTER 34

*M*eli was never so glad to see Mr. Tummers and the Canary as she was when they stepped outside the jail. He was there, ready to take her back to Cranbury.

She wanted to hug each and every one of her rescuers—including Dane Wardman. As unlikely as it seemed, there was no doubt he'd come to help rescue her from this catastrophe.

But hugging him? She simply couldn't. The repugnance she might once have felt had nothing to do with it. Somehow, of all her rescuers, wanting most to hug him made the idea far more dangerous than a simple act of gratitude.

Besides, *she* wouldn't be the one to break their pact. He was the one who initiated it; he'd have to be the one to end it.

She grabbed Essie's hand instead, and they approached the Canary.

"Saying thank you isn't enough," she said, loud enough for all to hear. "But I'll start with that, anyway."

She was just beginning to think better of her words, wondering how Dane might extract her gratitude. That she stop protesting his barroom? Start being present when he visited Ethel? Worse, for her to actually take the job he'd once offered in what had been Madame's lovely tea room? But he mustn't have heard her open-ended wish to repay each of them. He still stood at the top of the stairs, looking from one direction to the other.

"What're you looking for?" Dad called.

Dane trotted down the steps. "Packham's motorcar. Don't you think it's a bit odd that he left, even if he wasn't wanted? Why didn't he wait if he was so sure the sheriff should keep Meli?"

Everyone seemed to agree with that, and Meli did, too. Where was Mr. Packham?

"It sure won't be the last we see of him," claimed Dad. "Not until we find that contract, anyway."

"Yeah, about that," said Dane as Pastor Taylor assisted Essie aboard the back of the Canary. To Meli's relief, she'd insisted on staying with Meli, so the pastor was destined to take the Cranbury Inn's motorcar back alone. "You know where the contract is, then?"

Meli had been thinking about that since she'd seen the words in the journal. Surely Dad had the same idea, so she wasn't surprised when Dad's gaze met hers.

"Wait'll we're on our way," was all Dad said.

Maybe it was silly to worry Mr. Packham might somehow still overhear them, but Meli glanced around anyway, thinking even now she didn't want him nearby.

With Essie aboard, Meli was next. Dane had stepped between her and her father as he'd asked about the clue, and now seemed to shoulder his way in front of the pastor, too, until he stood in front of her. She couldn't hold back a smile, though she knew it was a tremulous one. She was still so nervous over the evening's events!

Such a thought was ridiculous. The truth was that he seemed as eager to assist her aboard as she was to have him do so.

She reached a hand upward just as he extended one—and then, as if some invisible shield lowered between them, he stopped at the same time she did.

No touching.

Surely he must remember the pact, too, this thing that was suddenly so huge between them that any form of polite and simple contact seemed wasted on its obliteration. As awkwardly as he'd stepped forward, he suddenly stepped back.

From the periphery of her vision, Meli saw her father and the pastor exchange a confused glance. And from inside the carriage, Essie's attention had been arrested, too.

Rather than admitting the moment had been anything but ordinary, Meli grabbed the handle at the frame of the doorway, planted one foot on the stair, and easily hopped in the back beside Essie. Staring straight ahead, Meli was glad it was too dark for anyone to see what she was sure were very red cheeks.

"What was that all about?" whispered Essie.

"What?" Meli whispered back, desperate for the embarrassment to pass. Better to just pretend it hadn't happened than try to explain, at least right now.

Once everyone was inside and Mr. Tummers had the rig in motion, Dad leaned forward, elbows to knees. He sat opposite Meli and Essie, with Dane at his side to even the balance. "Meli knows as well as I do what the words meant."

She should have been the one to speak first, since the clue had been directed to her, but she feared her voice might not be quite as steady as it would have been had she been breathing more evenly.

But then, inhaling to steady an altogether different form of excitement, Meli matched what she knew her father was about to pronounce. "The mews."

DANE SHOULD HAVE KNOWN what the clue meant from the first glance at the words. Of course Meli's domain was the mews! Anyone who knew Meli—

His heart shot between his stomach and his throat. Obviously Packham hadn't been the one to tear the pages from the journal. But he might still have looked at it. He'd called the book a diary almost right away. Did that mean he'd seen it, read it? Maybe, just maybe, he was headed to whatever he thought might be Mellie's domain.

There were only three choices for that: her bedroom, the barn where he kept her rescues. And the mews.

"Tummers!" he cried, banging on the passenger ceiling. "Get this rig going! Faster! We need to get to the Atherton's right away."

He leaned around Mr. Atherton to see the pastor driving the inn's car. What model was it? A touring car served the needs of any inn, this one designed to carry as many people as the Canary, plus baggage. It looked to Dane like a Moyer, though he wasn't entirely sure. Was its currently slow speed only because the pastor kept a steady trail after the Canary, or because it couldn't go much faster? If it was a Moyer, the frame was wood! Dane didn't doubt most horses could travel faster than one of those models, including the horses Tummers treated like his children.

Besides, it would take time to stop and transfer from the Canary to the motorcar, moments they did not have.

Already, the Canary had widened the distance between it and the car lagging behind.

"What's this about?" demanded Mr. Atherton. "What's the hurry?"

"Packham," Dane said, wishing he was better at hiding his emotions. He'd never realized he possessed no talent at all for such a thing, not when it really mattered. He'd always believed himself such a great poker player! Heck, the entire town probably knew he'd do Meli Atherton's bidding if she only asked him. "If Packham did sneak into your house and read that book, he might have figured out the hiding place was Meli's spot on the farm."

"But . . ." Meli's voice was hard to hear over the sudden rattling at the rig's greater speed, but Dane didn't mind leaning closer. "He would've done something before tonight."

"Yeah," Dane said, "he did. He tried having you arrested so you'd never see that diary. But it didn't work. Right now, neither one of you are home—the other thing he might've been waiting for. No one to stop him."

"What else explains why he wasn't out here waiting to for the satisfaction of seeing either you or your father arrested?" asked Essie. "He must know it's there, hidden on your farm somewhere."

"He won't go near the hawks," Meli said.

Her father nodded. "He's afraid of them."

Dane's gaze met Meli's and without a single word spoken he once again spilled every thought he would have disguised if only he could. If Packham's goal was to destroy the contract, he wouldn't need to touch a single hawk to do it.

All he need do was pull away a few boards and scare them away.

CHAPTER 35

*M*eli grabbed hold of the seat beneath her and didn't count the bounces, wishing the horses could go even faster.

When Essie grabbed her arm and started praying, Meli leaned into her, never as grateful to have such a friend. Maybe Meli was still a curiosity to some in town, maybe her family was still gossiped about, but Essie had been a true friend from the moment they'd talked. Meli wouldn't doubt that now.

At a lapse in Essie's prayer, she glanced across at the opposite seat.

Her father elbowed Dane, saying, "We're *all* prayin', young man. If you want to be of any use between here and home, if you want to save Meli's hawks and yours, too, you'd be wise to do the same."

He looked at Meli, and she at him. She stared, willing him to agree, to nod, to show some hint that he might pray even if he didn't believe it would do any good. Simple obedience, after all, could be a first step to real faith. She breathed one tiny bit better when he nodded and then closed his eyes. Even if he was pretending, she didn't care. God could reach even the greatest of pretenders.

Meli begged God as they seemed to inch their way back to Cranbury. She begged Him as they put Williamsport behind them, passed the Wardman house she could never look at as the same again, passed the *Hawk* that already looked closed for the night, passed the section of forest she knew so well. Breaths came in spatters—then stopped altogether when she saw the light in the starless sky. A dance of light that could be seen for miles.

Fire.

Was it theirs? Of course it was. Each moment drawing them closer made that all too clear. Smoke rose through the trees, higher than the flames.

The house.

The barn.

The mews.

At last Mr. Tummers' horses slowed and Meli had meant to be the first out, but Dane beat her to it. He ran past the house, past the barn, and straight to the mews. She followed, while Dad raced to the barn.

The flames were tall and bold in all three, but at the mews they were the smallest, as if it had either been the last to have been ignited or somehow the sparks were slow to take hold—until now. Like Meli, Dane's first instinct must have been to pull at the open end, where the slats of wood were strengthened by the firm wire netting that let the birds feel as though they were outside.

But the wood and thick wire held fast.

Meli heard the frantic flaps of wings and short, sharp kek-kek-kek, not the joyous shrieks reserved for freedom of flight, or the higher pitched sounds of wild males alerting other predators while announcing its territory. No, the only sounds coming from the hawks were short and high-pitched, full of fear, afraid of the very air around them.

She threw herself at the planking just as Dane had done, but like everything her father created, it was sturdy and strong, able to endure nearly any assault. She saw Dane kick at it then, but even that seemed to have little effect.

Then he was gone.

The fire had surely been set at the back, in the storeroom part of the building where solid walls would provide the most fodder. She ran to the edge in time to see Dane peel off his coat and use it as the worthless shield it surely would be.

Then he went inside.

She started to follow, only to be caught back by Essie.

"Not both of you!" her friend cried. "He'll save you instead of the hawks if you're in danger, too. You might all be lost—give him a chance!"

Meli's prayer, from that moment, contained no words—just a single, incoherent plea for God to save them all.

DESPITE HAVING PREPARED himself with a deep gulp of the less smoky air outside, Dane knew he must take another breath. Shallow, short breaths, his jacket draped over his head as an ineffective filter, his shirtsleeve offering next to nothing. Even the flames left little light through the smoke and darkness, but he knew his way to each of the three mews.

They'd been designed to enter only from inside, with shutters outside that had been left open on a night like this. Dane went to the first door, though he'd never been so close to the one Meli called Harriet. A jess hung just outside each mew, and he grabbed the one belonging to Harriet. She was much larger than his Ethel and he had no time for protection from the birds' frantic instincts. His only hope was to reach the inside latch on the outer door and hope—yes, pray—the bird flew toward the unexpected direction of freedom and not at him.

And that was what happened. In a moment, Harriet was flapping, limping, toward the fresher air and into the night. Or, perhaps, toward the sound of Meli's cry. Her anklets dangled inches below her feet, and he threw the jess out after her.

Flames spat closer to the second and third doors and through tearing eyes Dane caught sight of the table scale Meli used to keep track of her hawks' weight. He grabbed it, using his coat to protect his hand against the heat of the metal. The cradle, too, was hot even through the cork lining, but if he was burned he didn't feel it. Instead, he held the scale aloft, protecting his face and arms as he slipped too close to the fire to hope for much safety.

And he made it, at least as far as the mew belonging to Meli's hawk. She was smaller, more familiar to him than the older one had been and so he had less fear. Nonetheless, the moment he entered Guinevere flew at him, tearing through the shirtsleeve that even the flame hadn't licked. He felt the slash but gave it no thought, rushing to the latches and setting the hawk free, trailed by the second set of jesses he'd snagged a moment ago.

Before leaving the middle mew, he thrust off the makeshift scale-shield that had proven so heavy and too quickly hot, and instead bent over the larger, lighter round metal trough in the center of Guinevere's mew. He should have thought of this in Harriet's! First he dunked his jacket in what was left of the water, then lifted the circular tankard before he rushed back into the flames. The last mew, his own Ethel's, was next.

The ceiling of the mew was already aflame, including the top of the door frame. The door fell away the moment Dane yanked at it, and there was his Ethel, as if so frantic for escape she was willing to go through the flames.

Dane waved his arms, fearful and relieved all at once. She was alive!

He grabbed her in a way he never would have done had it been any other day, and with her in his arms he unlatched the last of the three mews and ran out to the night.

CHAPTER 36

ummers had given Meli his coat, which was now
wrapped around Meli's arm as a makeshift gauntlet to
protect her skin against Guinevere's talons. Meli had already torn
the side of her skirt, draping it over Guinevere's head like a hood.
Harriet, obviously traumatized, looked to have no interest in
either flying away or being tethered, even away from the imme-
diate flames. She half-hopped, half-waddled off into the shadows,
her red eyes catching a glint from the fires whenever she looked
back Meli's way.

Meli wanted to get as far from the smoke as she could, for
Guinevere's sake, but couldn't—wouldn't—budge until Dane
emerged.

And there he was!

She didn't know she was crying until sobs wracked her body.
Dane Wardman, the man she'd hated all these years, had saved all
three of the hawks in her care. He was covered in glistening
sweat, bits of dirty ash clinging here and there. And never such a
welcome sight.

Just as he stepped close enough to look him directly in the eye
she noticed what Ethel obviously just had.

Dane was bleeding from his arm.

"We need a place to put her until you can stop confusing her with your blood," Meli said, and to her surprise Dane grinned.

"*Confusing* her?" he repeated. "Can I ask if you care why my blood is there in the first place?"

"Of course I care!" Meli issued the words before she could caution herself about what, exactly, she meant. "But she's a raptor! *She* doesn't care, only that it's there."

"Bring her here," called Tummers, who was already opening the back door to the enclosed cabin of the Canary. "My rig's been named for this night since I purchased her fifteen years ago. The Canary eats the hawks!"

His humor was too soon for Meli, and maybe for Dane, too, because he didn't offer more than the leftovers of his previous grin.

They went to the Canary, and Meli took away the makeshift hood from Guinevere just long enough for her to flutter inside, looking for a place to perch. She landed on an iron arm rest, where Meli used one of the rescued jesses to tether her.

Dane deposited Ethel inside the Canary, too, tethering her as far from Guinevere as possible. If either gos attempted to bate or made much of a fuss, there simply would be no room to do much harm. Meli knew Guinevere, at least, had never shared such close quarters.

They were safe, but where was Dad? Had he tried to save the horses, the cow they'd meant to sell but hadn't, their few goats? Since she'd set the squirrels free, at least there were no wild ones in her corner of the barn.

She sucked in a deep breath of air that still reeked of smoke but was refreshing all the same. There he was, on the far side watching the barn burn. There was nothing anyone could do to save it.

Their pair of horses were behind him, as was the cow. The goats, now that she was thinking more clearly, had been kept in the paddock across the way during tonight's fair weather, surrounded by a fence tall and secure enough to keep wild dogs and coyotes at bay.

The barn crackled from all corners so the roof was sure to cave in. He stood far enough back with Essie and Pastor Taylor, watching the power of fire as it ate anything in its reach.

Meli turned to see with one glance that the house was entirely engulfed, on its way to melting into a pile of embers. Everything she owned in this world would be no more than a memory.

Whatever tears Meli had shed were now gone. She felt nothing. Would she, tomorrow? Her father, the goshawks, their animals, all were safe. She would mourn, she was sure, the loss of her home and everything in it. Her mother's books; her mother's clothes; her money pot. They had nothing now, except the land, the crop, and each other.

Inevitably, her gaze went back to Dane, who seemed to watch the flames with the same fascination as everyone else now that the goshawks were safe. Harriet was still off to the side, as far from the flames and smoke as she wished. Meli longed for their sturdy leather hoods, knowing she couldn't even improvise with remnants of her skirt. The only thing keeping the two gos's in the Canary safe, who could likely see the fire and still smell the smoke, were the jesses tethering them to opposite armrests. She wished none of them could see the flames that had tried taking them all.

They must get them away, and soon. Just then, Meli turned her attention back to Dane. There was a flame in her breast now as she looked at him, one that burned brighter than the only home she'd ever known.

"You saved them," she marveled. "All of them. Yours, and mine."

His brows rose, as if surprised either by her words or perhaps in the way she'd spoken them. She knew her tone was tender; she'd meant it that way. It wasn't awe, which might have been read as disbelief that someone of his perceived lack of character could have done something noble. It wasn't that, anyway. It was gratitude and respect and admiration for his bravery.

And forgiveness, if she'd still needed to offer any. Perhaps she'd already forgiven him, well before tonight.

FLAMES fascinating the others offered little allure compared to what Dane saw on Meli's face. She looked at him as if she'd done so a thousand times, even though she'd never once gazed at him this way. And her voice! Pure kindness, the way he'd heard her speak to others, or in the songs she sang or the prayers she'd prayed under his very own roof.

He wanted to speak, but it wasn't just his sore and scratched throat that stopped him. He was afraid he would say the wrong thing. Not for the first time tonight, he was desperate enough to seek some power outside himself, certainly greater than himself. God, he supposed. He should ask for wisdom, because the last thing he wanted to do was have her go back to hating him.

Now she was stepping closer, and even though he wished she would still look him in the eye, he wasn't disappointed when she turned concerned attention to the cut on his arm that he had entirely forgotten.

She reached for it, but held back before touching him. The pact again. Blast! How did one break a pact?

However, the care on her face compensated—somewhat—for the loss of her touch. Still, he said nothing.

"How did that happen?" she asked gently.

More than ever, he didn't want to speak; maybe the fact that her gos had attacked him would remind her that she, too, had reason to hold something against him. Maybe somehow Guinevere knew he ought never get off scot-free.

"It's nothing more than a scratch." He settled for that because he decided right then and there he would never lie, not to her. She deserved the truth, among the other things he owed her.

"I would clean it for you," she said, adding with what he was amazed to see was a teasing smile, "except for two things. One, my kit is—was—in the barn."

"And two?"

"You know reason two.'"

They were just a couple feet apart, yet the pact might as well have had them on opposite ends of the earth. "Yes, about that." He was whispering now, which was easier on his throat and safer from the others, in case anyone noticed they were the only two not watching the flames with them. "How does one go about ending a pact?"

She frowned and shook her head. "I'm obviously not the one to ask, if a pact is anything like a neighbor's feud." She pointed her chin at the destruction around her. "Look at how that ended."

"But you can't take the blame for that," he assured her. "You didn't know anything about it until tonight."

"That's true," she said, and to his delight she spoke quietly too, as if she wanted the conversation to be as private as he did. She turned back to the mews, and he was sorry because she was no longer looking at him. "The mews are destroyed, like everything else. But," she looked at him again, her smile back in place, "I'm pretty sure the contract is still intact."

"What? How?"

"It's buried in a metal box underneath Harriet's mew. Under the water trench."

"*Under* . . ." Dane couldn't help but shiver. Divine guidance? Somehow, he'd let that water trough remain in place, marking the spot that added protection for what Meli and her father needed to be kept safe.

Dane shook his head at the implication; there might indeed be a God, Dane was beginning to see that now. But surely He hadn't taken the time to tell Dane what to do, or even notice what Dane did.

And yet . . . God was obviously speaking to Meli and her father. Why not direct Dane for their benefit? That thought made him shiver again. He wasn't used to being touched by no less than the Creator of the universe.

THE MOIST FOREST around Meli's home was in no danger of damage from what Mr. Packham had done, with so much land cleared generations ago for crops. Still, they waited for the fire to consume what it would, taking the precaution of a bucket brigade to encircle the burned out buildings with as much more moisture as their energy allowed.

Eventually, Pastor Taylor and Essie took his mother's motor-car, not back to town but back to Williamsport, to summon the sheriff. Mr. Tummers took Meli and Dane, with all three goshawks, back to Cranbury. Meli would have stayed behind with her father, who refused to leave, but she'd wanted to see her goshawks settled. There was no safe place left here, with their home and barn and mews all ash and rubble. Dad said he would bunk in with the goats once he was sure all the fires were out.

Essie had insisted Meli ask her mother-in-law, Mrs. Taylor, for a room at the Inn. She would find her waiting at Essie's home next to the church, since she'd agreed to stay with their children when they'd left so abruptly. She could take something from Essie's drawer for Meli to sleep in and Essie would bring more fresh clothes in the morning.

Dane had offered the lining of his jacket for Meli to fashion an aba for Harriet who perched on the rail in front of them on Tummers's top seat. Meli had wrapped it around Harriet's wings to immobilize her. It wasn't a long ride into town but crowding a third unmasked gos into the back of the Canary would have added more stress for them all.

Meli had been the first to board the Canary, with Mr. Tummers's assistance. To her vague surprise Dane went around the other side, but without even looking at him she knew he'd chosen correctly. It was right for Mr. Tummers to sit between them, wrong to have broken their pact for something so mundane as a carriage seat shared with Mr. Tummers.

If this pact was to be ended, it appeared Dane was as determined as she that the moment be intentional, pre-planned, and private.

CHAPTER 37

N o one spoke all the way back to town, and that was fine with Dane. He suspected even Mr. Tummers felt some measure of shock over having watched nearly the entire Atherton homestead burn to the ground. Dane's own horror over that no doubt paled in comparison to Meli's.

Obviously his living quarters above the *Hawk* was the only safe place for the gosses, at least for now. Their tethers would surely hold firm until he could go into Williamsport to buy longer leads, leather hoods and proper perches. Until he could procure water bowls, he could bring large copper pots from the kitchen. And although her ledgers were gone, Dane was confident Meli would remember the feeding schedule for each one of the goshawks.

The temporary accommodations would be far inferior to what the gosses were used to, but he would make sure they had new mews as soon as possible. A new thought attacked the heaviness of his heart, dispersing a portion of it. *He* would build the mews. Never mind he hadn't built anything in his life, at least not by himself. He could learn, couldn't he? For the gosses?

No. For Meli.

Something else came to mind just then, another thought to lift his spirits. He moved a hand to his pocket, a habit he'd had for weeks now. Every morning he placed Meli's ring there, and many times each day he patted the spot just to feel its presence. It connected him to her. As much as he enjoyed having such a reminder, he knew tonight would be the night he would restore it to her. Surely the ache from the loss of her home would never be stronger than tonight, but maybe, just a little, this ring would help.

He only hoped she wouldn't be disappointed over the amount of time it had taken him to return it to her.

Mr. Tummers pulled the Canary to a halt at the back door of the *Hawk*. Grabbing the tether, Meli transferred Harriet to her protected forearm, then, using her free hand on to the seat railing, she let herself down to the ground. Harriet might have bated when Meli jumped, but couldn't with the aba still in place.

Dane was already at the back of the Canary, holding one of the two long jesses they would use to secure the birds once they were inside his home. As Dane opened the door, Meli could see the Canary would need a thorough cleaning after the tumultuous evening. Unlike falcons, gosses muted in any direction. Chalky mutes dusted the bench seats, and several feathers swirled here and there.

But the gosses were relatively calm despite the trip and lack of hoods. Meli would have to leave Guinevere a few minutes longer, while she took Harriet inside.

Dane's jacket sleeve was surely thinner than any gauntlet, but he didn't flinch as he extended his uninjured arm long enough for Ethel to spot and hop aboard. He pulled her outside the Canary, where she tested her wings but didn't bate as Dane held fast to the anklet secured at her foot.

Dane approached the kitchen door, unlocking it then holding

it wide for Meli and Harriet to enter first. As he did so, he called quietly. Guyto was likely sleeping despite Dane's voice warning him of his entrance at such an hour, because there was no response.

Meli already knew the way, so she hurried up the sparse stairwell with Dane close behind. In the upper living room, Dane went straight to the dining set Madam had left. He pulled forth one of the wooden chairs, its high back railing suitable for tethering.

"Here," he said, looking at Harriet. "You can place her here. Let me get something to weight the seat so it'll stay steady even if she fusses. I'll wrap a towel to make the top rail more comfortable for her talons, too."

Meli watched, undeniably impressed, as Dane served the goshawks as if they were children. But to her dismay the counterweight for the chairs he brought forth looked like a crate of Mr. Packham's whiskey.

"Sorry," he said, obviously seeing her face even in the milky light of the moon from the nearby window. "But it'll serve the purpose, and I'm thinking Harriet is on your side when it comes to an opinion of alcohol."

Meli tried to smile, but feared she failed. After transferring Harriet, she left the aba in place until she secured the jess to the chair.

"I'll get Guinevere while you make Ethel this comfortable," she said, then sprinted from the room.

Outside, Mr. Tummers offered a tired salute after she emptied his Canary, then he called for his horse to move on home. Meli returned inside, tiptoeing past the cot on the other side of the stairs even though it appeared the boy was the soundest of sleepers.

Another chair awaited Guinevere. Dane had illuminated the room, but only dimly from the gaslight hanging above. Each of the gosses had been assigned a corner, as far from one another as allowable, all at the same height. Dane was bent over the table, a knife in hand as he sliced a long strip of leather. Drawing closer, she saw the end held a buckle to what had once been a belt.

"This'll work for Ethel," he said, holding up a long, slender strip. "I couldn't grab her jess. There wasn't time."

"But you saved them," she said softly, knowing her tone once again held the near adoration she felt.

He turned to her, only a few feet away, studying her face as he had in the past. She neither turned away nor averted her gaze.

It was Dane himself who broke the hold. He cleared his throat, then stepped around her on his way to Ethel. He'd cut off the belt's buckle in case she bated, using the leather as a jess. A widened belt hole allowed the clasp on her anklets to slip in place. All three of the gosses were secure now, and evidently relieved to be safe and well away from smoke or fire.

Meli ought to leave, having accomplished what she came for. Mrs. Taylor wasn't exactly waiting for her, but she was surely waiting up for Essie and her son to return to their children.

"Perhaps you might sing to them for a few minutes," Dane suggested. "Just to calm them?"

"They appear relieved to be here," she said.

"To calm me, then," he said, the slightest of grins on his face.

"We should cover the furniture if you want to protect it from them. The jesses are long enough for them to make quite a mess if they choose to."

"I'll get some sheets," he said, but made no move to leave the room. "Tomorrow we can go into Williamsport and bring back everything we need to make them more comfortable until I build the new mews. No, Monday, I suppose. Nothing will be open on Sunday."

"Ah, I'd forgotten tomorrow is Sunday," she said. How was that possible, considering it was practically all she'd thought about since the night of the street hubbub?

"Yes, Sunday," he said, confirming the importance of the day.

He'd said it sadly, though, as if it wasn't anything to look forward to.

So she went back to what he'd just said, though it would be Monday, not tomorrow. "I know of a shop. I've only purchased a few items there—" She stopped herself. Had he just said *he* would build the new mews?

He was facing her again, nodding as if she'd finished her reference to the store. "They don't have much of a selection, but I'm sure we can find what we need. There's a much bigger supplier in Philadelphia. I can send for whatever we can't find here."

She shook her head, although her thoughts weren't entirely following the conversation. "I can make what's needed. I need a bit of leather, and some wood. Levick Brothers' has what we need."

He took another step closer. "Why am I not surprised you make your own equipment? Patterns handed down from generation to generation?"

She nodded. They were so close all she needed to do was extend a hand—no farther than that—to touch him.

"Meli."

He spoke her name so softly she'd barely heard him. Was he still asking her to sing? Perhaps she ought to, or she might do something foolish.

"Shall I sing one of the anti-saloon songs?"

His grin was wider this time. "I was thinking a church song might be a better choice. There's something you ought to know, Meli. I think, if that contract really is still safe beneath Harriet's water bowl, God Himself told me not to grab what marked the spot. What do you think?"

"I think God's voice is always there, and if we listen we can hear it."

"Would you think it odd that He'd speak to a sinner like me?"

"We're all sinners, Dane."

"Ah! You said my name. I like hearing you say it."

A sudden wave of shyness enveloped her, his voice was so soft and inviting. She didn't want to turn away, to give in to the shyness, but she did. She looked beyond him to the gosses, and did as he'd asked a few moments ago. She sang, choosing one of her favorite hymns.

While she sang, she saw him smile as if doing so for the gosses, the way he looked at them, then at her. When she finished, he put one of his hands to his pocket and withdrew something.

"Meli," he whispered, "I have something that belongs to you. I'm sorry it's taken me so long to return it. I meant to, several times in fact, and have been carrying it with me every day. But perhaps tonight is the right time, after all. I suppose if you wore this all of the time it wouldn't have been lost in the fire, but if you didn't, then perhaps it was meant for me to keep it safe so it could be returned to you right now."

To her astonishment, the dim gaslight sparkled on a tiny diamond set in gold. Her mother's ring!

"May I break the pact?" he whispered. "To touch you, to put this into your hand?"

She nodded. "I—I've wanted you to break it. You had to be the one."

He stepped closer, mere inches away now. "And I'd have welcomed *you* breaking it for quite some time."

She raised her hand, and she trembled—though from his nearness or for accepting a treasure once lost, she couldn't tell. Slowly, he lifted both of his hands. One rose to come beneath hers while the other slowly, gently, placed the ring in her palm. He covered her hand, top and bottom, caressing her skin as if he didn't want to let go even after the ring was delivered.

Then he pulled her closer, his face just above hers. "I'm going to miss carrying it, Meli. It was like having you close to me, even though you didn't even know. But maybe, if you'll let me, I can follow you around like the lovesick idiot that I am."

"Dane—"

"Don't talk just yet," he said. "I know we have a few things to talk about, important things. And I know I must deliver you to Mrs. Taylor before her son and Essie get there. But right now I want to well and truly shatter that stupid pact. Kissing you will do it. May I?"

Her heart beat so fast Meli thought the pounding could be heard beyond her insides. Truer words had never been spoken that they needed to talk. But at the moment, words didn't seem to have much importance. She nodded, raising her lips to be accessible to his, rendering impossible any talk whatsoever.

His kiss was softly tentative, as if he couldn't believe she was allowing it, or afraid she might stop him. But she didn't. She pressed herself closer and the kiss deepened—this first kiss of her life, if she didn't count the one she'd shared with him in her dream.

"Meli," he whispered. "Earlier tonight your father said something about your family not being welcomed in town."

She stiffened, when only a moment ago she'd felt pliant, nearly weightless.

He held her more tightly. "I know you're wanted now, I've seen your friendship with Essie, and the others. But, Meli, *I* want you. You belong anywhere you choose to be—hopefully with me, especially with me—because of who you are. You wouldn't be who you are without your family, and I'm only glad of one thing: you didn't stay isolated. Because I aim to make sure you feel wanted wherever you go."

And then he kissed her again.

MRS. TAYLOR ANSWERED Meli's gentle tap, and Meli wasn't sure what surprised the older woman more: that Dane was at her side, or their disheveled appearance.

"What in the world!"

"There's been a fire at the Atherton place," Dane said. "We're pretty sure Al John Packham set it. Meli needs a safe place for tonight. Can you help?"

"Of course! Essie and Alec aren't back yet. I thought they were with you."

"They went to report the fire to the sheriff," Meli said. "They should be back soon."

"Well, you stay here with me. I'm watching the kids, but you can have a room at the Inn and we'll go there together just as soon as they're back." Mrs. Taylor eyed Dane. "She won't be alone, if you're thinking Mr. Packham means her some harm."

"I'd like to stay until your son gets home. If you don't mind."

Mrs. Taylor looked between the two of them, perhaps coupling her impression with assumptions she might have had when Dane ran to Meli's rescue earlier that evening. She widened the door for both of them to enter.

"Are you hungry?"

Meli shook her head, though she glanced at Dane, who seemed to be letting her answer for them both. She probably should have been famished, but the thought of food held no appeal.

She was grateful to him anew, realizing she wasn't ready to be alone with Mrs. Taylor. Meli wasn't yet sure how she felt about the stories Pastor Taylor grew up on, stories his mother had told to countless guests at her inn. She remembered what Dane had said about knowing she was accepted now, that Essie's friendship proved it. That, and his pledge for her always to feel wanted, calmed whatever uncertainties lurked.

Such thoughts made her speechless, even when Mrs. Taylor asked for details of the night. Maybe they both thought Meli was simply tired, which was true. Nonetheless, she was glad Dane recounted the events—until he added the part about Pastor Taylor knowing stories of Meli's family.

Mrs. Taylor raised a slow hand to her mouth, as if aware the tales she'd told, no matter how long ago, might have come in handy tonight but likely weren't so wise during the original telling.

"Oh," she whispered, touching one of Meli's hands that rested in her lap. "I completely forgot about all those stories. I—I'm glad it helped tonight, but until knowing you, Meli, I never had any real faces attached to that history. I'm sorry I resurrected all that nonsense just for local color. Will you forgive an old woman?"

Meli was unaccountably close to tears. After all that had happened tonight, this was what would break her? She let Mrs. Taylor pull her into a swift embrace, even as she looked at Dane. He smiled as if he approved of both apology and forgiveness.

"Let this be another lesson," Mrs. Taylor said. "Try not to give yourself so much to regret when you're my age. We'll likely all do better if we have plenty of memories building each other up instead of the other way around."

CHAPTER 38

Dane washed his hair twice the next morning, scrubbing vigorously but he still smelled of smoke. Well, it would have to do.

He was tempted to rush to the Cranbury Inn to find Meli, visions of last night's kisses spurring him on. But as much as he needed to see her, she must need rest. They also needed to see the sheriff, and Meli probably planned to go to church this morning. Even with so much going on, he didn't doubt she would attend this afternoon's meeting. He should attend both that and church as well—a thought that seemed so expected that he didn't ponder why going to church appealed to him for the first time in his life.

He guessed Checker was already downstairs, though Dane was surprised he hadn't tapped on Dane's door to ask about their new roommates. Instead of going directly to the kitchen for breakfast, Dane lingered in the living room.

He would have to consult Meli about when to feed them next. A pang of regret reminded him that all of her journals were lost, those keeping track of weight, molting, food intake, training progress and so on. A sudden wish for revenge against Packham erupted at the very same time visions of God came to mind. Odd, this sudden certitude that it wasn't his place to see Packham punished, though he wouldn't hesitate to do what he could to make sure justice was done.

Dane hoped the contract was intact where Meli's mother had buried it, but that, too, didn't seem anything to worry about. Hadn't God made sure Meli's mother had put it in such a safe spot?

Checker was at the kitchen table when Dane went downstairs. Glancing at the clock, thinking it still too early for a call of any kind, he forced himself to recount for Checker the previous evening, every incredible moment of it except the kiss, which Dane vowed to keep between him and Meli. Although he did little more than mention how the goshawks came to reside upstairs, he couldn't help noticing Checker's scrutiny after that.

"I'll take you up to see them before I go," he said to Guyto, who'd expressed dismay that he'd slept through any portion of the excitement.

"If I just peek at the door, can I go up now?"

"All right," Dane said. "Just don't cross the threshold. If one of 'em mistakes your scrawny arm for a chicken leg, I'm not responsible."

Guyto looked momentarily fearful, but nonetheless he scrambled to the stairs, his footsteps slowing the higher he went.

"Something's changed," Checker said. "Either you finally got through to her, or she did to you. And all it took was rushing into burning mews to get her hawks."

Would Dane never be able to hide his emotions? He grimaced. "Since I'm apparently as transparent as a woman, I'll admit I'm full of opposites this morning. Meli lost everything last night. Her home is gone, along with every material thing she ever owned. But I can't help wanting to rush over to the inn and let her know I'll provide her a new home. If she lets me."

Checker nodded along with each of Dane's words, slowly, not meeting his eye until he'd spoken the last thought. "A home here?" The words were incredulous on their own, eliminating the need to snort, but he did anyway. "Above a barroom? Maybe you should wait until after today's meeting to offer something like that."

Dane had neither defense nor alternative, but that assessment sounded about right.

MELI STEPPED out from behind the changing panel, tucking in the white shirtwaist at the back. It was early yet, only seven-thirty, plenty of time before the eleven o'clock service. Both Dane and Pastor Taylor had shown Meli and Mrs. Taylor back to the inn last night, and despite Meli's restlessness over all that had happened, she'd slept deeply.

Essie was considerably taller than Meli so she'd folded up the borrowed skirt's waistline, as well as the sleeves of the blouse. It looked well enough, provided the folds stayed in place. But what about standing before the entire town at this afternoon's meeting? She didn't want what she wore to be a distraction.

Essie frowned. "We can ask Leta to alter them, but perhaps she'll have something readymade that you can wear while she fixes these." Her frown went lopsided. "Unfortunately anything already sewn in your size will likely have been made for a juvenescent. Perhaps altering these really is the best option."

"I've never much cared about clothes," Meli admitted, staring at her reflection. She'd enjoyed a bath, grateful for the rose drops Mrs. Taylor had supplied. Her skin was pink, her hair glistened, and she no longer smelled of smoke. "Madame used to scold me for not caring. But now I wish . . . well, if clothes can improve what I look like, then I ought to care, I suppose. Because of today's meeting." She turned from the mirror to face Essie. "Oh! I'm so silly. Just now I missed Madame at the same moment I'm finding myself inexplicably thrilled to be alive—and not in jail for something I didn't do."

Essie tilted her head to one side. "I suppose you do have more than one reason to be thrilled. You might have lost everything, but everything you love is safe: you, your father, all the animals. I'm sure by now your father has even recovered the contract. Is that all you're grateful for, do you think?"

Wide-eyed, Meli nodded, knowing that didn't quite cover every reason to feel so light on the heels of such loss.

Essie burst into laughter.

"You really are silly if you think you can hide the truth from me, Meli Atherton! I know very well why you're thrilled to be alive, and even why you're thinking of clothing for the first time in your life. It has more to do with Dane Wardman than anything else. You're in love with your nemesis, and as of last night even he knows it. What's more, he feels the same way!"

Meli covered her face when a smile tugged at her lips while tears filled her eyes. "I've lost my battle against him, I know that now. He saved them! All of the gosses. How could every barrier I've held against him all these years not tumble away knowing that?"

Essie approached, rubbing her palms against Meli's arms. "Those barriers had cracks in them long before last night. I've seen it for weeks now." She glanced at the clock on the mantel. "It's early yet, but I'm sure we can knock on Leta's door. She'll be happy to make your clothes match the rest of your beauty."

"Beauty!" Meli scoffed. "I'm no such thing."

Essie had been in the process of grabbing Meli's hand to pull her from the inn's room, but now she stopped abruptly. "Meli, I'm going to say something that might sound harsh, and I don't mean it that way. All I can guess about your father, bless his heart, is that he's been missing your mother so hard he likely didn't pay enough attention to you. He should have mentioned how pretty you are, so you'd know. I wouldn't hold it against him, though, men often don't know what's best for the women around them. But believe me, there's a reason Dane Wardman fell in love with you when you wouldn't give him the time of day. That's another thing about men. At first, all they see is . . . what they see. He obviously liked what he saw in you, or he would have given up long ago when all you wanted to do was cause trouble for him."

Essie hadn't let go of Meli's hand and now attempted to pull her along again—but Meli wouldn't budge. She frowned. "I did cause trouble for him." She pulled her hand free to slap both of her own suddenly hot cheeks. "And that hasn't changed! He still runs a pub and I'm still against alcohol even if my own great-grandmother did have a recipe for such poison. Can we just forget that?" She turned, pacing back then forth. "Maybe I shouldn't see him at all. In the long run, that might be easier for both of us."

Essie took up Meli's hands again. "Oh, no, you don't. You're not giving up before you've even talked to him. Besides, today's meeting might provide some kind of solution. Maybe?"

Meli neither agreed nor disagreed, but did allow Essie to tug her along to the dress shop.

LETA PERKINS PHIPPS appeared more excited to provide Meli with an attractive ensemble than Meli was to receive such a thing. She hadn't had a dress sewn for her since her mother had done so before Meli was big enough to wear altered hand-me-downs. Leta and Essie conferred as if Meli had no say, both of them circling, staring, assessing, muttering.

While that was disconcerting enough, wondering if they saw what she did in that huge mirror on the wall—her frame was so small that, from the back at least, she resembled a girl, not a woman fully grown—new fears attacking Meli had nothing to do with clothing. How could Leta not view her differently, once she knew her very own kin had been responsible for creating one of the bestselling liquors served at the *Hawk*? Not to mention that Meli was here, now, not just because she'd lost all of her belongings in the fire but that she hoped somehow to enhance her appearance because she was drawn to the owner of the very place they'd been trying to shut down?

"Leta," Meli said tentatively, because it was obvious by now that Essie wasn't going to say anything more than she had about Mr. Packham starting the fire, "you should know that my great-grandmother was the one who concocted—or at least improved upon—the whiskey recipe Mr. Packham used to make the whiskey to begin with."

"You don't say!" She'd taken up a measuring tape and was already using it on Meli's shoulders. "I guessed if Mr. Packham started the fire, there was some connection to your family. Now, what's your favorite color? I'd like to start with that, but of course we'll hold up some swatches to see if your favorites warrant your actual choice."

"But, Leta! My family is as good as one of them! And maybe you didn't notice the way Essie did, that I—well, I—may have to stop protesting at the *Hawk* because I'm . . . that is, Mr. Wardman isn't quite the monster I always thought him to be and I—"

"Oh, for heaven's sake, Meli, first of all, stop fidgeting. Did you think none of us noticed the way he looks at you?" She laughed. "Why do you suppose I tricked you into carrying that sign yesterday? I figured a warning he wouldn't be able to kiss you would get his at attention! I must say, you've held out longer than most of us would if we were in your shoes. He's quite handsome! Charming, too."

She let go her surprise about the sign, relieved it hadn't been part of the nightmare. "But he's selling everything we're opposed to!"

Leta held up one of Meli's wrists, indicating she should hold out her arm. "Who better to influence a man than the right woman at his side? You, my dear, are in the best position possible to accomplish everything we've set out to do."

Such potential power only horrified her. "And if I can't? I admit I do think he's interested in getting to know me better, I learned that last night, but that doesn't mean I have true influence over him. He's a businessman in a business I detest. I'm not even sure whatever is between us is strong enough to overcome that."

Essie took up Meli's free hand and patted it. "You wait and see, Meli. Love conquers all, as the saying goes. That, and don't forget prayer."

After that pronouncement, the two of them returned to the topic of fashion. They decided almost immediately to skip morning garb, the sensible sort of clothing Meli was accustomed to. For Meli, they proclaimed she needed something light, airy, and surely pastel. A day dress, of course. Leta had just the thing, one that was already nearly finished. She'd planned to display it in the window as the epitome of summer fashion. It was, of course, too large for Meli, but Leta assured her she could do the alterations quickly.

"I—I can't pay you," Meli said, adding hastily, "at least not right away. My money jar might have survived the fire, it was clay, after all. If it's not melted, I'll be able to pay right away. But if—"

Leta stared down her nose at Meli. "My dear girl. I know you don't mean to insult me, but what in the world would this town say if I charged someone who'd just lost their home and fortune to a fire? Why, I couldn't hold up my head if anyone heard such a thing!"

The moment Leta finished Meli's measurements, Essie grabbed her hand again and pulled her to a chair in front of yet another large mirror in the room.

"While Leta works on your dress," she announced, "I'm going to do your hair. Leta? Curling irons?"

"Over there," Leta pointed, the two words muffled by pins protruding from between her lips.

Meli was compelled to sit while her shame melted away. She marveled at the entirely new sensation of being pampered by friends—good friends, indeed.

CHAPTER 39

*E*ver since Checker had moved from the inn to the quarters above the *Hawk*, Dane hadn't any reason to visit the Cranbury Inn. Nonetheless, he approached the attractive guest house confidently, imagining his destination to be Meli's side, not the inn itself. But the moment he put a foot to the porch's lowest porch step, he stopped.

Here was where nearly every rally, every march, every protest against his place had been hatched. Every one of his employees—well, at least those who needed a place to live closer to the *Hawk*—had been turned away. The owner had no reason to allow Dane into her establishment today, either, even if he didn't intend staying long.

Crazy ideas crossed his mind, everything from wishing he knew Meli's room so he could toss pebbles at her window to simply standing at the base of the porch shouting her name. The innkeeper herself might call him inside, if only to shut him up.

However, as wildly impetuous as he'd allow himself to be if he thought it would bring results, he ought to reserve such acts for when, or if, he truly became desperate. For now, he could simply take a seat on one of those wicker chairs and wait until she emerged. If he was quiet enough, no one would notice him until he saw Meli.

His inconspicuous spot remained so for less than five minutes, with no sign of Meli.

Mrs. Taylor herself came outside, and from the deliberately unhurried manner in which she opened the screened door he knew she'd already spotted him—perhaps from the moment he'd stepped on the porch.

Or was he mistaken? While she did step to his side of the porch, she kept her gaze averted. She stopped within three feet of where he sat, but faced the railing as if looking at the flowers planted beneath the huge tree.

Just when he was beginning to believe she was somehow unaware of his presence, she turned to face him.

"Mr. Wardman," she said, nodding her head once in a formal, if not stiff, greeting.

He stood, tipping his straw hat now that she'd acknowledged him. "Ma'am." He could think of nothing else to say that didn't include begging to let him remain long enough to see Meli.

"Last night proved something's going on between you and Meli."

He chose to remain silent, especially since she had a firm look of disapproval on her face.

She folded her arms. "On the one hand you must realize if you'd never set up a den for alcoholics Meli wouldn't have lost her home."

He might have countered that, since it was entirely plausible Meli's father could have declined an extension on the one-hundred year contract anyway. But Dane thought it wiser to say nothing.

"However," went on Mrs. Taylor, her arms loosening, her face softening, "on the other, it's clear you're in love with Meli."

"I am." Dane didn't just say the words, he declared them. Even he was surprised by his lack of hesitation, but more than that, he'd admitted the fact with confident boldness, as if he believed the sentiment might be returned. Was he an idiot, or just too hopeful for his own good? One thing was clear, he didn't care about his pride. If Meli rejected him, everyone in town would know.

"Well, then, you know what to do next, don't you?" She asked the question as if the answer would have been obvious to a ten-year-old. "Sell that barroom. You really have no choice if you want a chance with Meli."

"Mrs. Taylor, the *Hawk* isn't mine to keep or sell. I'm only rent-ing. But I don't intend breaking the lease." He wasn't sure what that meant, exactly, since he hoped his establishment would provide an income not only for himself but for Meli. How, remained to be figured out.

She shook her head. "Do you discount Meli's feelings so easily?"

He stared at the woman's earnest face. Evidently *both* sides thought their feelings were being discounted. "No," he said. "Maybe today's meeting will help resolve all this."

"I hope that's possible, though I don't know how." She started to turn away, then stopped to look him in the eye. "But I am glad you're considering Meli's side, Mr. Wardman."

He hardly had time to ponder if she might share even a sliver of hope for resolution. At that moment he caught sight of three women approaching the inn's porch. He guessed immediately the middle one to be Meli, by virtue of her petite size. Yet he still needed to look twice because never, in the time he'd known her—years, if he included their awful encounter as children—had she looked the way she did now. Her hair was swept up in a way that might have made him miss the way she normally let it loose, subtly inviting him to touch to see if it was as soft as it looked. Nonetheless this style was appealingly feminine and modern, fit to enter any respectable establishment in the world. Her clothing, too, emitted an aura of comfortable wealth and elegance, the kind of garment worn by a woman in his family's class. She was, without an iota of doubt, a woman any man would be proud to have at his side.

So drawn was he to her that he stepped around Mrs. Taylor, belatedly calling "Pardon me," over his shoulder, as he descended the porch and walked up to Meli as if she were the only one on the sidewalk.

A jumble of words came to mind, all inadequate. About how she'd not only survived last night's ordeal but had emerged like a Phoenix, reborn and renewed. About how lovely she looked, except he'd always thought that of her so it seemed somehow wrong to say aloud that she looked any different to him now.

And so he just said, "Good-morning."

Vaguely, he heard one of the two women at Meli's side give a little giggle. Could he blame her? He must look as lovesick as he felt, but there wasn't a thing he could do about it.

"How are the gosses this morning?" Meli asked.

He blinked. "Fine, fine. You can visit them if you like."

This time he knew which of her friends uttered a noise. It was Essie, clearing her throat. "I'm sure your birds—"

"Goshawks," corrected Meli and Dane simultaneously, prompting another giggle from the woman on Meli's other side.

"Goshawks," Essie corrected herself, "will be happier out of doors? Can you keep them outside, or somewhere . . . well, frankly more appropriate for them and for Meli to visit if you plan to keep joint custody for any length of time?"

The slimmest of frowns clouded Meli's face, probably because she was missing the mews her father had built as a gift to Meli's mother.

"I intend to build new mews," he announced.

Meli's brows rose. "Yes, you mentioned something about that last night. You're not going to hire the Levick sons to build something for Ethel?"

He grinned. "I may need the Levick material. Their tools. Their know-how. I suppose that adds up to a lot of help. But I intend to build the new mews for your gosses and mine, Meli, just as your father built the ones that didn't survive the fire."

Her cheeks tinted pink, and he knew she'd taken the offer as the prelude it was meant to be. He wondered if the others guessed, but it didn't matter. Boldly, he took Meli's hand, relieved again that their pact had been broken.

"If there's time before we go to church this morning, I'd like to take you out to your place, see how your father fares."

"Th-thank you."

"You make it sound like you might join us for our regular morning service, Mr. Wardman," said Essie.

"I do. This morning, and this afternoon for the meeting about the *Hawk*."

His gaze was still on Meli, but he still saw the other two women exchange surprised glances over her head.

Then he tucked Meli's arm under his and they headed to find the Canary.

"You tell your father the town will do all it can," called Essie as they walked on, "until you're on your feet again. Just to be neighborly, that's all."

As EAGER AS Meli was to see her father, to mourn with him the loss of their home and barn and especially the mews, she wasn't disappointed when Mr. Tummers and his Canary could not be found. Likely he'd cleaned out the cabin from last night's unusual occupants and was already in Williamsport, meeting the early train or picking up someone for this morning's service.

So they walked the path Meli had walked many times between home and town. The forest, as always, welcomed her, welcomed them. It was still early, so the sun only peeked through the lower branches and trees. Birds and yipping chipmunks greeted them, in between the sound of leaves rustled by animals too quick to be spotted. The only thing missing, Meli thought, was a gos soaring above.

"Even if the contract is somehow gone," Dane said as they walked, "those fires were set intentionally. Only Packham could have done such a thing, or had any reason. He's going to jail, Meli, if they haven't already picked him up."

Her heart, which had already been through so many calisthenics even since she woke that morning, once again fell. "I can hardly believe him capable, but after last night I don't know what else to think."

They walked a little farther and Dane, who had released Meli's hand while still on the sidewalk in town now took her hand again. She kept breathing, but quicker, more shallow.

"You knew what I meant when I said I wanted to build the new mews myself, didn't you, Meli?"

She couldn't look up from the ground in front of them, afraid she'd misinterpreted his words even if inside she knew she hadn't. "I—I think so."

He stopped, pulling her to stop as well. "It's a good tradition." He whispered, like the leaves around them. "If we have a daughter, I'd expect whoever she picks to marry to do the same for her. Because she'll love the gosses, too. How could she not, with us as her parents?"

Meli's heart twirled and her head went light. She wanted to let him pull her into an embrace, but something stronger than she expected held her back. She put her palms to his chest.

"But what about the *Hawk*? You must know I couldn't live in town, especially not above a barroom. And even if you did move out to whatever we build back on my family's land, I couldn't live off of money earned that way. Not at the expense of others."

He put his hands on her arms. "I wish you could consider the way I see the *Hawk*. It's not a place for men to get lost in. It's there for them to find rest and welcome and relaxation. Spirits help them to relax, to forget for a little while all the pressures and responsibilities of life."

"But the pamphlets say men can forget too long, and too often! They need women to remind them to take the better path."

"Do you know how that sounds, Meli? Like we're animals without women around. Maybe all those pamphlets make the problem sound not only worse, but more common than it is."

"I know you have self-discipline but the natural man must fight against temptation to forget responsibility. All of us, men and women alike, have to fight what sometimes feels natural."

"Now you sound just like one of those pamphlets."

His tone was neither curt nor exasperated, but rather amused, which she didn't welcome any better. "You've read them?" she asked.

He shrugged. "Only one or two left behind in my place by the crusaders in Philly."

"I know life is hard," she said softly. "But that's when we should think of God, and eternity, and others, to help us through. Because shouldn't we try to add to the world, not take something away? Doesn't alcohol take, not give? It takes away common sense, dignity, energy to work, and replaces it with foolishness and embarrassment and lethargy. How can more than a sip of such poison add anything good to the world?"

He looked away, letting his hands fall to his side. "I guess I should have expected you to bring up your faith." Then he looked at her again, so intently she wasn't sure if she should be cautious or glad. "It's the one thing I'm not sure how to fight any more."

"Why would you fight faith? When all God wants is your good, and the good of others? He does love you, you know."

"Well, I believe He loves you, anyway. Last night didn't end well, but it could have been worse. You could have been kept in jail, or worse, been in the fire." He lifted a hand to swipe the back of his neck, looking as if whatever more he wanted to say came reluctantly. "I have to admit, I've never really given God much thought —until recently." He grinned again. "Maybe it's those blasted songs you keep singing at the *Hawk*. They've been haunting me."

"Haunting might be just the word for it," she said. "God is a Spirit, after all, and He's after you."

He lifted his hands again, this time to her shoulders. "For my own good, you say?"

She nodded, but even as she did he began to frown.

"Is it God who made it possible for you to forgive me?"

"Dane," she said slowly, wondering if she could put words to thoughts she barely understood herself, "I know now that you see how hard it was for me to lose my little kestrel. And I know you didn't have malice in your heart when it happened. I know something else, too. If the price for you to understand God's love was the life of my Jax, then he didn't die in vain. If you can find a way to listen to God, then the future—yours, mine—"

"Ours," he interjected.

"Ours," she repeated, "will be clearer if we're both listening to God. Don't you think?"

He nodded, and her heart twirled anew as he bent closer, pulling her to him, kissing her deeply. She'd never been kissed in such a way, even counting last night. That first kiss had been thrilling in its own way, but careful somehow. Gently tentative. This was bolder, longer, revealing one thing: this wish to be close. It sent her entire being into a spin. Thankfully his arms were strong enough to hold her steady, but the thrill lasted all the way home.

MELI SPOTTED Dad beside the corral watching the horses munch on carrots harvested from the house gardens. The goats and pigs remained oblivious to the hardships of the now-destroyed barn occupants, and even the cow, whose sale was likely closer than ever, seemed happy enough to graze far beyond the lingering ashes.

Dad watched Meli and Dane approach, her hand in Dane's. Through the grime of last night still darkening her father's face, the teeth behind his smile seemed all the whiter.

"You're a sight, Meli!" he said. "Look at you, a prettier girl never lived."

Meli blushed, remembering what Essie had said about her father. Not that he might not believe her pretty, just that he'd never thought to say so. She couldn't hold that against him anymore.

"I certainly agree with that," said Dane, and his words only deepened Meli's blush, especially when he lifted her hand to give it a kiss. She was glad when he spoke again, diverting the attention from her. "How did you fare through the night, sir?"

"Wasn't the first time the goats kept me company. Though seeing you two, I guess I better get to the creek for a good cleaning."

Meli laughed, remembering the night he'd spent outside with a shotgun, ready to defend their goats from a coyote that had caused a ruckus the night before.

"Did you find the contract?" Meli asked.

He patted the breast pocket of his shirt. "I did."

"Mr. Packham will have no choice but to withdraw his charges," Meli said. "Maybe even admit what he did here."

"Oh, he's done that already," Dad said, to her surprise. "When the sheriff saw this place he asked how to get to Packham's. I took him, and we found him, all right. Passed out with an empty bottle of the white whiskey in his grip. When the sheriff woke him he confessed it all, even to smashing his own still. Then he showed me a letter from his wife, saying how she wasn't coming home. He liked the whiskey and she didn't. But she did like the money that came with it, and with that going away all he had left was a taste for the stuff. Guess blaming me for all that was enough for the sheriff to think it was our family's recipe, even without the contract." He sighed. "It was all just too much for him, losing everything all at once like that. I almost feel sorry for him."

"Dad! Not after what he did."

All three of them looked around, as if Dad wasn't the only one who needed a reminder of the devastation.

"Yeah, not much left, is there?" he said softly, sadly. "Not even that old money pot of yours, Meli. It cracked. Left a few coins, but that's it. I'm sorry."

"I suppose I'll be sorry, too, once I can sort through all the rest of this loss. But," she added, holding up her free hand, "I still have this."

She'd never told him her ring had been missing, so she didn't elaborate now. "And I have the journal. I'll always be glad that wasn't lost. It's such a gift."

Dad eyed the grip they still shared with each other's hands. "It's a little early. Not supposed to have it until right before your wedding."

"Which will be just as soon as I rebuild the mews," Dane announced. "I plan to use your design, as near as I can recall it."

Dad offered another pleased smile.

"And we'd better see about rebuilding the rest," Dane added, looking in the direction of the other lost buildings.

"Guess all this means you two worked out your differences."

"We've been talking about that all the way here, Dad. We plan to present our thoughts at church this afternoon, to the whole town."

"With the two of you coming to an agreement, maybe the rest of the town will, too."

"There's one thing I wanted to ask you, sir," said Dane. "Last night, before Meli and I had even talked to each other, you seemed to think I had a fighting chance to win her. What made you think so?"

Dad grinned. "I've thought that some time now, ever since she said she didn't want you run out of town. Wasn't much of an admission, but considering where you started, boy, that was when I knew you'd gotten to her."

"Not exactly a confession of love," Dane laughed, releasing her hand but only to draw her nearer with an arm around her shoulders, "but I'll take it."

"I do love you," she said, without hesitation or embarrassment, even in front of her father. "I guess there's no hiding it now, if my dad's figured it out."

Dane pulled her into a full embrace now. "Even better," he whispered. "Because I love you, too."

CHAPTER 40

*T*hat afternoon, every seat in the church was filled. Meli and Dane arrived together, but no one seemed to notice two members from opposite sides of the day's issue looking for room to sit together. Meli glanced around, seeing an open spot near the middle of the sanctuary. It wasn't until she'd tugged on Dane's arm that she noticed the sparsely occupied pew was taken up by the rest of the Wardman family: Dane's parents, brother and sister-in-law.

His arm beneath her fingertips stiffened and he stopped briefly before continuing. There were, after all, no other seats available. His parents looked up at their approach, but neither offered any sign of welcome other than scooting closer to allow more room on the center aisle. Dane's mother, however, sent Meli a second glance, one that slid down to her elbow connecting to Dane's.

Pastor Taylor was already at the podium, but nearly the moment Meli and Dane were seated, he called for everyone's attention.

"Much as I'd like to start with a sermon," he began with a grin, "especially with such a full house, I won't. Everyone knows why we're here, so I'll get right to the point. This town—my town, your town—this town we all love, has never been so divided. Wouldn't it be easy if we could find a way to talk it out—you know, explain where one side is right and the other wrong—and somehow end up agreeing? Problem is, both sides think they're right about everything and in the meantime nobody is listening. That's why we're here today, in hopes a word or two gets through, on both sides.

"Because," he continued, "I have a feeling what we all really want is the same thing: a good, decent town we can be proud of. We've always been known for our friendliness, haven't we? Can't we live up to that reputation with each other?

"All right, that's enough from me for today. You all know my wife Essie has been one of the spearheads in the temperance movement here in town. But she already told me she wants to give her time to Meli Atherton, who's been another strong leader in the cause. Meli, would you like to speak? Then perhaps you, Mr. Wardman—Dane Wardman, that is—would care to follow?"

Meli looked at Dane, who looked right back. On their return from her farm, they'd already decided how they would present their sides. Meli only hoped she wouldn't let hers down. Not entirely, anyway.

Dane stood first, offering Meli a hand as she rose. They approached the podium together, hand-in-hand.

She had no opening to soften the half of the audience set on disagreeing with her, so instead she went straight to the confession she needed to make. One that might push some from one side onto the other, or at least want her to make the switch. "Everybody here likely knows how I feel about alcohol. What you may not know—what I myself didn't know until recently—is that Mr. Packham's white whiskey came from a recipe that originated from my family." She allowed a moment for a few gasps and whispers, but went on before the room was entirely quiet. "That doesn't change how I feel, however. And my father has rescinded the contract Mr. Packham used to produce the whiskey, so insofar as that particular brand is concerned, our movement is successful. Mr. Packham's whiskey will no longer be available anywhere—neither in the city, nor here in Cranbury."

"Easy enough to stop now that he's in jail!" came one voice from the pews.

"I see you've heard at least something about last night's trouble," Meli said, unable to pinpoint to whom she should direct her response. "And it's true. Mr. Packham is in jail, on suspicion of arson. He was easy to find for arrest. Do you know why?"

Silence.

"My father led the authorities to Mr. Packham's home, where Al John Packham was found, ladies and gentlemen, unconscious. Alone, in his empty home, a bottle of white whiskey in one hand and a letter from his wife in another. She left him because in recent years he'd been consuming too much of his own product. He is a perfect example of what can happen with over-indulgence."

There were murmurs after that, until one voice rose above the others. Jonas Prestwich stood.

"Miss Atherton," he said, "since this meeting is for all of us to speak our mind, I hope you'll permit me to interject. There may be a number of unfortunate men out there who end up like Packham. And it's sad, I'll give you that. But there are also a number of men just like me, who don't believe letting an occasional drink pass our lips is the one unforgivable sin, or any sin at all."

"Yes, I know that, Mr. Prestwich. And if my father, were here—"

"I'm right here, Meli."

She turned large eyes to the back of the room where, sure enough, there stood her father. Here, in town! They'd left him back at the farm, when he'd been headed to the creek for a bath. Unfortunately, he'd had to re-don the clothes he'd worn last night, which she didn't doubt still smelled of smoke.

"Dad! I'm glad you're here. Maybe you can speak for yourself then, about what Mr. Prestwich just said."

He nodded, clutching his hat so hard she thought he must be a little nervous to be speaking in front of everyone at the same time. "I agree with him. And so did your grandmother, Meli. The good Lord gave us a lot of gifts we ought not use too much or too often. I'd put spirits in that category, not that I've been able to teach my daughter that kind of wisdom."

There was a chuckle here and there, and even Meli smiled. "The fact remains," she said, resuming control of the discussion, "that my temperance sisters and I wanted to completely close down the *Hawk*."

Sounds erupted this time, shouts for and against. Meli tried to speak again, but the room didn't entirely quiet until Dane, at her side, yelled louder than she ever could, "Let her speak!"

"Thank you," she murmured. "A very wise woman told me just last night that when we get older, we'll want to remember what we did to build up our neighbors, and vice versa. I'm not sure we have to like our neighbors to love them the way the Bible tells us, but loving thy neighbor means wanting what's best for them. Today we've to come together to decide what's best. As Pastor Taylor mentioned, both sides feel they're right. I know I did. But it might surprise you to learn that up until today *both* sides have also felt disrespected. Misunderstood. Even assigned motives that aren't true.

"On the part of the temperance sisters, we've always said we want to protect people, men in particular, from the lure of alcohol. But we've been told men don't appreciate such protection, that men can decide for themselves whether or not, or how much, to consume. In short, the men think we don't trust them to make the right choice, while the women want to make it easier by removing opportunity and temptation, especially to those who might not know there could be a problem."

Murmurs started again, grumbling about women telling men

what they could or couldn't do, women calling such reactions nothing more than pride and not seeing what was best. Meli had hoped they could avoid the kind of argument the town had already had on the street, but saw it happening again before her eyes.

"If you could just listen, I think we can negotiate," she said, in as loud a voice as she could muster. She prepared to repeat what she and Dane has discussed on their way back from her farm, details she thought sounded like a true compromise.

But Dane's sharp whistle stopped not only the congregational noise, it stopped Meli as well.

"I'm closing the *Hawk*."

Meli turned to him, wide-eyed. That hadn't been an option when they'd spoken privately.

"But, Dane—"

Shouts and jeers erupted from all corners, some in triumph, others in anger. Meli couldn't catch a single coherent argument flung from one side of the sanctuary to the other, because all of her attention was on Dane.

DANE WINKED at Meli before turning to the townspeople.

"Temporarily," he added, then his eyes searched the room and stopped on a face at the edge of one pew.

There sat Claudette—Mrs. Norcross-Rice, as he was determined to call her forevermore. Judging by the look on her face, probably having already guessed his budding relationship with Meli, she probably would demand he do so.

"As you may or may not know, I don't actually own the building. But when my lease is up, I'd like very much to buy the building outright."

A few protested, though they couldn't know what they were protesting yet.

"Ladies and gentlemen," Dane said, now sharing the podium with Meli, "well, at least gentlemen, to whom I'm now speaking."

He took Meli's hand, raising it above her head.

"Gentlemen, I know there isn't a man among you who hasn't been influenced by the woman they love. Now tell me, those of you who love a woman, would you rather live your life alone, or compromise and live side-by-side?"

A few voices rang out with answers, some in jest, some in question. As more questions rose in volume, Dane lowered Meli's hand but kept it wrapped in his. He wanted her attention but she was focused on the pew in front. Following her gaze, he saw her looking at Jonas Prestwich and his wife—now face-to-face as if they were just discovering one another after some time apart—and then taking each other's hands, too.

Dane squeezed Meli's hand, knowing they weren't the only ones looking for the same path. He smiled, catching Meli's eye and letting her take up the message again.

"Before Dane—" Meli stopped herself—"Mr. Wardman, that is, defines the compromise, I must ask my temperance sisters to consider the same. Total abstinence may indeed be the healthiest choice, although Doc might disagree since he's been at the *Hawk* during several of our visits—and not on our side, I can tell you that. Total abstinence is certainly required for the young, the most vulnerable. But, as my own father just reminded me, God has given us many things we ought not consume too much. I recall Madame's cakes, which surely were as tempting to some as alcohol is to others. Maybe we, too, need to compromise. Just a bit."

She looked at Dane, who nodded and took up the presentation.

"Neighbors," Dane began, then he turned his gaze in his family's direction, landing on one member in particular. "Mother." He looked over the crowd again. "When I first came to Cranbury, some people were under the impression that I was opening an ice cream parlor, that the bar the Levick brothers built would be perfect for treats and sodas and phosphates. Well, maybe it is. Maybe that's just what Cranbury needs."

Not everyone sounded happy about the prospective new business, so Dane raised his voice again. "Listen, those who are disappointed. I promise you one thing, that I know you deserve a place where you're welcome, away from home. That much won't change. Because if I do one thing well it's making someone feel at home. I hope you'll still give me a chance to do that, whether you come on your own for a good meal and a treat or if you bring your families."

"Where's the compromise in that?" called one voice, then echoed by others.

Dane looked at Meli, who spoke. "Alcohol will continue to be served in the evenings. But the *Hawk* will be a true 'wet-your-whistle' stop. Dane will still offer the hospitality everyone knows he's good at, and the town will have a business to be proud of, because no one will be served more than two drinks in any given evening, and not on empty stomachs. Absolutely no youths will be served. We'll give our young men a chance to mature a bit before they test their willpower, so they have a fighting chance if they gain a lick of wisdom first."

"That's right," Dane said. "Besides those precautions, you'll have a few new reasons to visit the *Hawk*. My chef will be recreating some of the recipes left behind from the tea room. We'll serve real meals, with more variety than ever. And if anyone twenty-one or older wants to imbibe in something a bit stronger, and if I do say tastier, than water or coffee to go with those dinners, they'll be able to do so."

Some voices rose again, some in approval, others disappointment, but Dane spoke again above them all.

"Meli and her sisters-in-cause have made me realize that drinking just for the sake of drinking probably isn't good for any of us. I guess the Good Lord let liquor be set before us like any other test of our free will. Maybe a taste is good for community spirit, but more than that probably isn't what He had in mind. It makes most of us sick if we overdo it, and that seems easy to do if you don't eat anything while you're drinking. So let's be friends about it, shall we? The *Hawk* will be open to everyone, men and women, young and old. Soda, phosphates, wine and some spirits will be available to the adults with a meal. We might even find a way for men to gather exclusively, or women, too, the way the tea room used to be, on occasion. Alternating community events? We'll work on that. But for now, can this town get back to what it was before I brought so much trouble?"

Rumblings turned to conversation, scowls softened even from those who would have to go farther away if they wanted to sit and drink and drink and drink. A bubble of laughter even rose here and there.

Dane's attention fell on his family as they left their pew. Rather than head to the door now that the meeting had ended, they came to him—with no less than handshakes from his father, hugs from his mother and sister-in-law. And curious gazes toward Meli from each one of them.

"Mother," said Dane, then glanced at his father and nodded. "I'd like you to meet Melisande Atherton. Soon to be one of the Wardman family, as my wife."

With that, Dane smiled at Meli and drew her close. To his delight she threw her arms around his neck, just the way he'd envisioned so long ago.

EPILOGUE

Two Months Later

The forest was preparing itself for a long winter's rest, covering its feet with layers of leaves, drinking in fall rains to nourish sturdy roots while limbs and branches shed the last of their burdens. Its animals gathered a bounty of seeds and acorns, nuts and berries, burrowing to familiar spots deep below ground. It was almost time for slumber and undetectable growth, secure against the months ahead.

So it was for Dane. He knew he was changing, growing in ways he'd never expected. From the outside, others might have been surprised to see him attend church every week—until perhaps seeing Meli at side. Anyone like his father might have attributed that to her. Other changes in Dane weren't so obvious, like his generosity to the church, or visits to his family which someone who didn't know him might have expected as the normal thing to do. Checker knew, and approved.

Besides, those visits were unexpectedly enjoyable, because of Meli. She had found a connection with his mother and sister-in-law in fond memories of the *Hawk's* first owner as the tea room. And his father had welcomed Meli as heartily as he had Susanna, making Dane wonder if patriarchal approval increased after his brother's marriage, too. Perhaps all their father had been waiting for was for his sons to go from unknowable children to grown up sons. It had taken marriage to accomplish such a thing.

Changes at the Atherton farm were more obvious. It was no secret Dane was responsible for most of that. Dane immediately began construction on the mews, following the design Meli's father had used. He sought advice almost daily, and there was always one Levick or another handy to ask. Dane worked steadily, not as quickly as he would have liked, but carefully because he knew Meli's gosses and his own would be housed there and it had to be right.

While he forced himself to attend to details, he fought what Meli would have called his natural man, knowing the sooner the project was completed, the sooner he could marry her. Excellence, however, was better than haste, and in this case that went against his natural man.

Meli's father seemed to understand that, who came to lend a hand when he wasn't working on rebuilding the rest of the farm. He let Dane hire a designer and workers from Williamsport who constructed a house fit for a family, not just two anymore. It wouldn't be as large as what a Wardman might expect, Meli's father had discouraged anything too large, but nonetheless it would be far more luxurious than what it replaced—and have room enough for their family to grow.

Change on the inside of the *Hawk* portended the most change. He sold the pool table to Jonas Prestwich, whose home in the city could accommodate it. That left room in the *Hawk* for more tables, an absolute necessity for diners. After cutting back orders from his liquor suppliers, Dane shared some of the Packham whiskey with Meli. She would use it, pint by pint, to make cooking flavorings like almond and vanilla, mint and lemon. Whatever aged ambrosian she didn't use for Madame's cake recipes she would put in little bottles to sell on the end of the bar suppling soda and ice cream. Like the spirits, her cakes and flavorings would be sold in moderation.

Lanigan, the chef, was happy to try some of Madame's old recipes, and judging by the number of men who now tasted such meals, they were as popular with them as they had been with the women.

Even the travelers proved faithful customers, especially on hot days when a cup of ice cream was even more satisfying than Packham's whiskey.

Checker, surprisingly enough, proved to be an excellent soda jerk. His ice cream sodas brought as many customers, albeit pint-sized, as Packham's white whiskey had once attracted. What surprised Dane most wasn't that Checker attended church each and every week, but that he never failed to find an open spot next to Mrs. Taylor.

Only Marto, the bartender, wasn't satisfied with the changes. He'd stayed for a while, but his last straw came with a literal one: the delivery of bright red and white ice cream soda straws. He announced he was going back to Philly to work for Squire Ridley.

Ultimately, the best argument against a barroom had been Meli's, that Dane should want to provide something that added to the little corner of the world called Cranbury. He still provided a place of community and relaxation, where men and women could comfortably forget their labors. He was, after all, a host at heart, whether hosting a barroom, restaurant or ice cream parlor—or all three.

Funny thing was, that had become exactly what Dane wanted.

And that, he knew, was a miracle all its own.

Thank you for reading *The Cranbury Troublemaker*! I hope you enjoyed the story. If so, please consider leaving a rating or review on Amazon, where my books are sold exclusively. Thank you!

THE CRANBURY CHRONICLES

Dear Reader,

Cranbury is an imaginary little town set along the non-imaginary Susquehanna River in Pennsylvania. I've enjoyed researching not only the area and historical era, but also the crafts and interests presented in each Cranbury character. If this series has taught me anything, it's a reminder that the work we're passionate about isn't really work at all—it's the niche we're designed to fill. A little taste of heaven!

The Cranbury Papermaker

The Cranbury Toymaker

The Cranbury Picturemaker

The Cranbury Troublemaker

If you liked this book or any of my other titles, please consider leaving a rating or review on Amazon. Ratings are simply choosing the number of stars you'd like to give. For a review, nothing elaborate is required, just a phrase or two mentioning what you liked about the story, setting, or characters. As a reader myself, I value the opinion of other readers and often purchase books based on reviews.

I love hearing from readers! Contact me at:

maureen@maureenlang.com
Or via snail mail:
591 Press
P.O. Box 23
Belvidere, IL 61008 USA

ALSO BY MAUREEN LANG

The Cranbury Chronicles

The Cranbury Papermaker

The Cranbury Toymaker

The Cranbury Picturemaker

The Cranbury Troublemaker

First World War Novels

American Settings

Pieces of Silver

Remember Me

European Settings

Look To The East

Whisper on the Wind

Springtime of the Spirit

Split Timeline

The Oak Leaves

On Sparrow Hill

Contemporary Novel

My Sister Dilly

Gilded Age Novels

Bees In The Butterfly Garden

All In Good Time

The Matchmaker's Match

Engaging the mind. Renewing the soul.

www.maureenlang.com

ABOUT THE AUTHOR

MAUREEN LANG has always had a passion for writing, particularly stories with romance and history. She wrote her first novel longhand around the age of ten, put the pages into a notebook covered with soft deerskin (nothing but the best!), then passed it around the neighborhood for friends to read. It was so much fun she's been writing ever since.

Her debut inspirational novel, *Pieces of Silver,* was a 2007 Christy Award finalist. She has won the Romance Writers of America Golden Heart award, the Inspirational Reader's Choice Contest, the American Christian Fiction Writers Noble Theme award, and a HOLT Medallion, and has been a finalist for Romance Writers of America's RITA, the American Christian Fiction Writers Carol Award, and the Gayle Wilson Award of Excellence.

Visit her website at www.maureenlang.com.